PRAISE FOR THE PATH TO MISERY
Book I in the Hallowed Treasures Saga

"A sheltered princess's desire to travel before her arranged marriage places her at the center of a legendary quest in this YA novel....A page-turning fantasy set in a richly textured world, made all the more delightful by a thoughtful yet spirited heroine and her wonderfully oddball companions."
-*Kirkus Review*

PRAISE FOR IN LONELY EXILE
Book II in the Hallowed Treasures Saga

"The series continues to stand out for its foregrounding of friendship, diplomacy, and exploration over gory sword fights. A delightful reunion with old friends, sure to leave fans of strong female heroines craving the final installment."
-*Kirkus Review*

DEATH'S DARK SHADOWS
Book III in the Hallowed Treasures Saga

DEATH'S DARK SHADOWS

Book III in the Hallowed Treasures Saga

VICTORIA STEELE LOGUE

DEDICATION

This final book in the Saga is dedicated to
the *legendary* designer David Hayworth
whose graphic design brought the
Thirteen Kingdoms to life.

Western Kingdoms

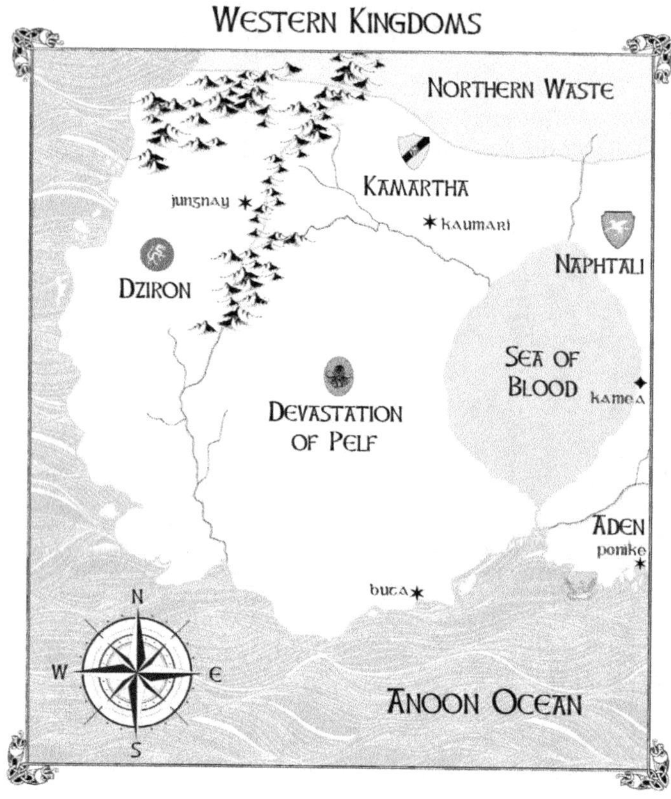

Eastern Kingdoms

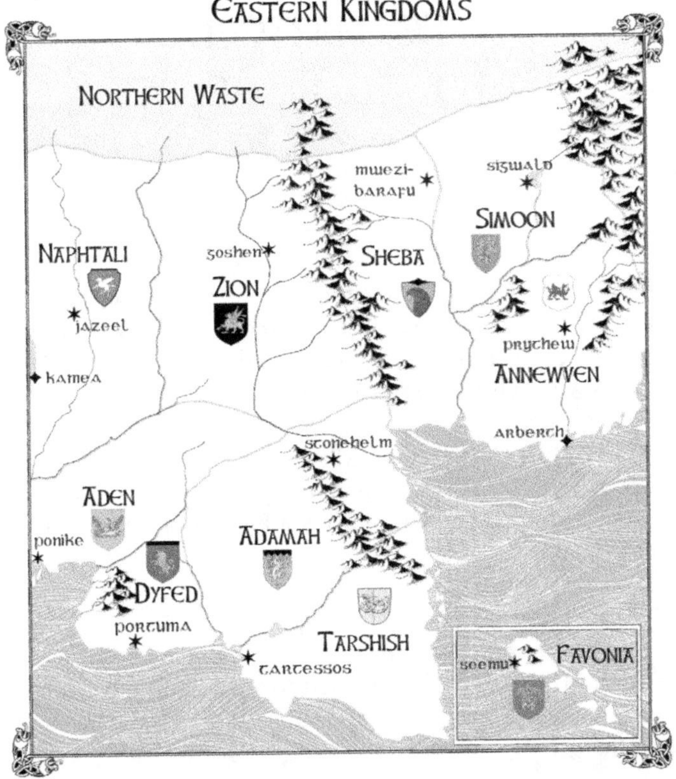

The Thirteen Hallowed Treasures

The quest central to this saga centers on recovering the Thirteen Treasures of the Thirteen Kingdoms. These hallowed treasures come from a Welsh tradition dating to the 15th-16th century, which lists these treasures as:

I. White Hilt: The Sword of Rhydderch the Generous
or *Dyrnwyn: Gleddyf Rhydderch Hael*
If a wellborn man drew it himself, it burst into flame from its hilt to its tip.

II. The Hamper of Gwyddno Long-Shank
or *Mwys Gwyddno Garanir*
It is said that one could put food for one man into the basket and when it opened, for one hundred men could be found within.

III. The Horn of Bran
or *Corn Bran Galed O'R Gogledd*
It was said that whatever drink one might wish for could found in this horn. It is also rumored that Merlin obtained the horn, which had been cut from the head of a satyr.

IV. The Chariot of Morgan the Wealthy
or *Car Morgan Mwynfawr*
Once in the chariot, a man could wish to be a certain place and thus get there quickly.

V. The Halter of Clydno Eiddyn
or *Cebyster Clydno Eiddyn*
When attached to the foot of the bed, this halter would be filled with whichever horse one wished for.

VI. The Knife of Llawfrodded the Horseman
or *Cyllel Llawfrodded Farchog*
This one knife would carve enough food to allow twenty-four men to eat at table.

VII. The Cauldron of Dyrnwch the Giant
or *Pair Dyrnwch Gawr*
The cauldron would boil food for brave men only; never boiling for cowards.

VIII. The Whetstone of Tudwal Tudglyd
or *Hogalen Tudwal Tudglydd*
If this stone was used by a brave man to sharpen his sword, and he drew blood with it, that person would die. No harm would come to the opponent from a coward's sharpened with it.

IX. The Coat of Padarn Red-Coat
or *Pais Padarn Beisrydd*
If worn by a well-born man, it would fit; if not, it would not go in him.

X. The Crock and Dish of Rhyngenydd the Cleric
or *Gren A Desgyll Rhyngenydd Ysgolhaig*
Whatever food might be wished for would appear in the crock and dish.

XI. Mantle of Arthur
or *Len Arthyr Yng Nghernyw*
The cloak has the ability to make the wearer invisible.

XII. The Chessboard of Gwenddolau, son of Ceidio
or *Gwyddbwyll Gwendolau ap Ceidio*
Made of silver and gold, the chessboard was said to possess mystical powers and would continue to play by itself once set up.

XIII. The Ring of Eluned
or *Eluned's Ring and Stone*
When it is placed on one's finger, with the stone inside the hand and closed upon the stone, the wearer is invisible.

Following the book, you will find information on each of the Thirteen Kingdoms, a pronunciation guide, as well as lists of the days of the week and months of the year.

DEATH'S DARK SHADOWS
Book III in the Hallowed Treasures Saga

"Peace cannot be kept by force;
it can only be achieved by understanding."

-Albert Einstein

Part Five

"Honey, you ain't never gonna find peace in this world
lookin' down the barrel of a gun."
-Delevan Aden
The Gunslinger's Troth

"If there is to be any peace it will come
through being, not having."
-Henry Miller

18ᴛʜ Luees

Eluned's heart was beating wildly in her chest as she hurried down the hallway toward the staircase that would take her downstairs to confront King Uriel. She barely noticed the portraits of former kings and queens of Zion that lined the walls of the corridor. The Princess had seen them nearly every day for eighteen years, had studied them numerous times over the years, but now her eyes were fixed on the marble floor as she rehearsed what she was going to say to the King.

Descending the main stairway to the castle's entrance hall, she tried to swallow the lump in her throat. It felt as if her heart had broken the bounds of her ribcage and lodged itself there.

Shortly after she'd returned to her tower bedroom from her daily sword practice, she had received word of King Uriel's arrival. She had been floored—his unannounced appearance had been both sooner than she'd calculated and completely unexpected. Why the surprise? Why hadn't they been warned of his approach?

When the page had delivered the message, the Princess had stared at him in horror for a full ten seconds as the shock ricocheted around her brain. She finally pulled herself together enough to dismiss him. And that was odd too. Why hadn't it been her mother, or at the very least, Jabberwock, to have brought the message? The Bandersnatch had asked her every day for the past seven weeks or so if she still loved Gwrhyr. And everyday she had replied in the affirmative. Eluned missed him desperately—his touch, his kisses, but most importantly, she missed his companionship. She hadn't realized how much she'd come to depend on his being there whether it was just to make a silly observation or to have a serious discussion or even sit in amicable silence.

Now if she wanted to talk to someone she had to seek out Jabberwock or her former tutor, Brother Columcille. It just wasn't the same.

Once the shock of Uriel's arrival began to subside, she hurried to her armoire to change into something a little more appropriate. She was still in the leather breeches and wool sweater she'd been wearing that morning during practice. Gwrhyr liked her in pants, but she assumed that the King would not. Not that she actually cared what he thought, but she didn't want to outrage her parents. They would see her manner of dress as an insult to the King of Aden if she wore pants.

Eluned decided to go for modest and pulled from the armoire a dove grey tulle skirt and lavender sweater knitted from soft rabbit's fur. After she had changed, Eluned braided her hair in a long ponytail although it took her several tries before her hands stopped trembling enough to do so. The Princess frowned. It was occurring to her that perhaps the imminent arrival had been purposefully withheld from her. Perhaps not a bad idea considering her shaking hands and the butterflies in her stomach, she thought, but it still irritated her.

Walking over to her window seat, she sat down and spent the next ten minutes with eyes closed deliberately trying to calm herself in the way in which Brother Columcille had taught her. Long breath in, "Omni Within," long exhalation, "Omni Without," she repeated. She'd been dreading this day for months, and now it was finally time to face it, and she needed to be in control when she did so.

Eventually she felt her strength and resolve return, and with determination she walked to the door and began her walk down the long hallway to the top of the staircase. It only took a couple of steps before her heart was once again hammering against her ribs.

She reached the stairs, took a few deep breaths, and began the descent. As the staircase curved to the right, she risked a peek over the marble bannister. His back was turned toward her, but she'd know that stance anywhere. She stopped, confused. He wore a simple gold crown, and it glinted in the winter sunlight that poured through one of the tall and narrow windows in the entry hall. The dark brown hair that fell in waves to just above his shoulders was as familiar to her as her own ebony curls.

What was Gwrhyr doing here, she thought, mind racing to fit the pieces of this puzzle into something that made sense. Why was he wearing a crown and dressed in the finery of a king? He was supposed to wait until . . . and then the realization struck her like a blow to her gut, and she grunted audibly. The blood drained from her face and black dots swam before her eyes, and she felt herself sway dangerously forward. Her hand reached blindly for the stair rail to steady herself.

The shock was quickly replaced by anger and the blood rushed to her head as tears filled her eyes. What a fool she had been! At her gasp Gwrhyr, or, more appropriately, King Uriel, had turned toward the staircase taking a step in that direction as she reeled forward. By the time he reached the bottom step, she had recovered her balance and was running headlong back up the stairs toward her tower room. Her only consolation was the deeply pained expression on his face, the gleam of tears in his blue-green eyes.

Slamming the door and locking it behind her, she threw herself across the rose pink counterpane that topped her bed, sobbing. She was so embarrassed. How could she have been so blind? Had anyone else figured it out? Had they been laughing behind her back all this time?

There was a knock on the door.

"Go away!" she cried. "Leave me alone!"

"Darling?" It was her mother's voice.

Eluned slipped off the bed and padded to the door. "Did you know?" she asked from behind the closed door.

"Sweetheart." Her mother's voice was placating.

"Mother! How could you?" Eluned began weeping again.

"Please open the door, Eluned."

"No!" She turned her back on the door and walked over to her window seat and stared bleakly out the leaded glass. The Mountains of Misericord to the east were blanketed in snow, and under the overcast sky looked as cold and desolate as her heart felt.

Is this why Jabberwock insisted that I remind myself each day how much I love him, she wondered? It was impossible that he wasn't a part of this. Could she still love Gwrhyr knowing that he had purposefully deceived her from the moment they first met? The joke's on me, she thought, another sob hiccoughing from her. I fell in love with the man I'm supposed to marry. How could she still love him and feel so betrayed at the same time?

She walked over to her bed and retrieved Eira, her stuffed unicorn, before returning to the padded window seat and curling up on it. She hugged Eira to her chest before burying her face in its soft to the touch rainbow-dyed mane. Nyx's mane had been white but opalescent so perhaps Eira's mane was not far off.

"You're avoiding the obvious," she murmured to herself, sitting up straight and taking a deep breath. It was true. It was much easier to muse on the meaningless than to try to decide what to do about Gwrhyr.

There was another knock at her door—this one loud enough to cause her to jump.

"Eluned!" This time it was her father.

"I'm sure you were in on this too!" Her voice was petulant.

"Jabberwock convinced us it was for the best," he explained.

Jabberwock. She should have known. The conniving little beast. She remembered the smirk on his face when she'd been asking Gwrhyr for help that night at the inn in Mjijangwa. "Arghh," she shouted. "I'm going to kill him!"

She propelled herself from the window seat and stomped over to her armoire where she'd placed Dyrnwyn. There was a rasping sound as she pulled the sword from its scabbard.

She flung open the door. "I'm going to kill them both," she told her father, the blue light racing up and down her left arm.

Her father frowned and placed a conciliatory hand on her shoulder. "Don't you think that's a little extreme?"

"Not for Jabberwock," she glared at her father, who chuckled.

"I have to admit that there are times I might agree with that, as would have my father."

"Hmpf," she snorted. Jabberwock had been part of the reason his father, King Simeon has grown up without a mother. The Bandersnatch had helped her run away from the castle and back to the Kingdom of Kamartha.

"And yet," King Seraphim said.

"And yet he claims that everything he does is because he has been led to do so by Omni," the Princess concluded for him.

She lowered her sword. "Then why do I feel so betrayed Papa?"

The king pulled his daughter close, and she placed her head against his chest just as she had when she was a little girl crying over some imagined injustice. He let her tears flow silently for a moment, stroking her black hair just as he had when she was a child, before saying, "Do you think you'll be able to join us for dinner."

She looked up at him, eyes still red and swollen, dabbing at her nose with a handkerchief that was clenched in her right hand. "Absolutely not."

The king nodded, grimly. "I'll have something sent up."

"Don't bother," she sighed, stepping back into her room. "I'm not hungry anyway."

"Regardless," he looked at her sternly. "I will have something sent up. I take it you have no wish to see Uriel?"

"Gwrhyr, you mean?" She shook her head. "No, I have to face Jabberwock first. He needs to convince me that this was absolutely necessary." She sighed again. "I'll let you know when I'm ready to face him."

"I love you, Eluned." His eyes were a shade greener than hers, the green of the fjord to her tropic sea, but it was clear whom she'd inherited them from.

"I love you too, Papa," she gave him a tentative smile before closing her door. But this time she didn't lock it.

The Princess returned to her window seat, removed the cushion and then opened it and peered into the compartment. Some of her favorite books and treasures lay within, but she wanted one of her extra special books, one of the novels that had belonged to Queen Fuchsia. She removed the board that revealed the secret compartment and withdrew a small stack of paperbacks, well worn and pages yellowed with age. She inhaled the distinctive musty scent. I wish I could create an incense that smells like old books, she thought as she perused the stack before selecting *The Gunslinger's Troth*. She had discussed this book with her friends while they were at Castle Indalo. Maybe by the time she finished it, she might be ready to speak to Jabberwock. Eluned had to do something to distract herself—her mind kept flitting back to all the times she embarrassed herself in front of her future husband early in their relationship and her cheeks would flame again and the tears would well in her eyes. There seemed to be a never-ending supply of them.

THE PRINCESS WAS DEEP IN THE HIGH DESERT world of the gunslinger, Ivanhoe, and his beloved Rowena, when there was a knock at the door. She reluctantly put down the book, and walked over to the door to open it to the servant carrying a tray containing a bowl of soup, a slice of bread and butter. Simple fare. Her father was a wise man.

The young woman holding the tray was unfamiliar to her—a sweet-faced young woman with hair the color of corn silk and eyes the pale blue of a cloudless summer sky. "I haven't seen you before, have I?"

"No, yer highness," it was clear the girl wanted to curtsey but was prevented from doing so because she might upset the tray. "Me mum jus' hed a bebby, and I'm fillin' in fer her."

"Please call me Eluned." The Princess indicated that the girl could place the tray on her desk. Any distraction was a good one at this point. She wasn't sure she could look King Uriel in the eyes ever again, and the thought of facing Jabberwock filled her with rage. "And you are?"

"Eleanor, yer highness, tho mos' folks call me Ellie."

"Eluned, Ellie."

"Eluned," Ellie repeated, eyes lowered and the color rising to her cheeks.

The Princess glanced at the window seat where The Gunslinger's Troth lay spread-eagled on the cushion, and had a sudden thought. "Can you read, Ellie?"

Eleanor's eyes widened in surprise. "O'course not, yer highness, er, Eluned."

"Would you like to be able to read and write?"

"That's not fer the likes of us," Ellie stared at her feet, clearly uncomfortable.

"Malarkey!" Eluned snapped, and then apologized. "I'm sorry, but I never want to hear you say anything like that again. Now answer in truth. Would you like to be able to read and write?" She'd had a lot of time to think about the idea of teaching reading and writing to those who wished to learn while travelling back to the Kingdom of Zion from Naphtali, and in the ensuing weeks once back at Castle Mykerinos.

The girl stared into the Eluned's eyes for a moment trying to determine if she really meant what she was saying.

"Yes, I am serious," the Princess assured her.

Ellie's eyes widened as the truth of what the Princess was saying began to sink in, and Eluned smiled. "I will take that as a yes. I intend to talk to Brother Columcille to see if we can arrange classes for those who are interested. I will let you know as soon as something is settled. Does that sound good?"

The girl nodded, and curtsied, but a grin split her face and joy lit her eyes. Eluned dismissed her, and Ellie drifted from the room in a trance-like daze. The theory had been that to teach the servant classes to read and write might lead to an overthrow of the current system. Whether or not that was true remained to be seen. It just seemed so wrong to Eluned. As far as she was concerned denying education to those who sought it was the greater injustice, and she had the power to change it. She would speak to Brother Columcille in the morning. Meanwhile, she had soup to eat and a book to finish, and that would hold off a meeting with Jabberwock a while longer.

She retrieved her book and sat down at her desk. She was lifting a spoonful of warm broth to her mouth when she realized that it was Gwrhyr who had encouraged her to educate the people. She wondered if he had similar programs available in Aden. Her heart was still aching, but she just couldn't find it within herself to be angry with him. She knew how manipulative Jabberwock could be, and she blamed the Bandersnatch completely for the ruse Uriel had been forced into.

When she was finished with her dinner, Eluned placed her tray outside her door so that she wouldn't be bothered again. She was halfway through the book now, and intended to finish it before she fell asleep, but first she'd get ready for bed. She'd kept a fire roaring in the fireplace all evening, but as the hours crept closer and closer to midnight, the winter's chill began to make itself felt. She wanted to don her flannel nightgown and snuggle up in her down comforter for the remainder of the book.

It was well after midnight when she finally closed the book, tears streaming down her cheeks. Sometimes it seemed like she cried earlier and harder each time she read it although the current situation no doubt added to the flow of tears. The strangeness of the world portrayed, and the passionate romance between Ivanhoe and Rowena despite the fact their love ended tragically, made the book a compelling read to the Princess. It had, she reflected, probably been the reason she had left the castle a year ago searching for love and adventure.

Eluned was about to extinguish the candle on her bedside table when she realized she'd left another burning on her desk. Cursing silently to herself, she slid out of bed and into her slippers, as the floor was cold, and walked over to her desk. She was just leaning over to blow out the guttering flame when there was a light knock at her door.

Who could be rapping on her door this late at night? She felt an ancient poem rise unbidden to her conscious, one she'd learned as a child and adored for its macabre flavor. "Suddenly there came a tapping, as of someone gently rapping—rapping at my chamber door." Should she ignore it? The tap came again, this time slightly louder, and curiosity got the better of her as it had the protagonist in the poem. She opened the door to find Gwrhyr standing there, his six feet of height nearly blocking the doorway.

"How did you know I was awake?" she glared at him.

"I saw light flickering beneath your door," he explained.

"And you just happened to be passing by?" Her brow wrinkled in perplexity.

"I couldn't sleep, and I just wanted to be near you." He looked at her more closely, and his hand rose to brush away a stray tear. "Are you still crying?"

"What?" She raised her hand to remove his as he was still cupping her cheek. She took another step backwards releasing his hand. "Oh. No! No. I just finished reading The Gunslinger's Troth. It always makes me cry."

Despite the fact she seemed wary and her voice was emotionless, Gwrhyr attempted a smile. Wasn't that just like her—to get so caught up in a book? "I love you, Fy Drysor," he said using his pet name for her meaning "My Treasure" in the tongue of the Hallowed Treasures. Then he touched his chest over his heart using his forefinger before touching hers in the gesture the two of them shared.

"I know that Gwrhyr does." She took yet another step backward into the room, breaking the contact with his finger. "I don't know if King Uriel does." She paused, and frowned. "You might as well come in. We're letting all the warm air out."

The Princess walked over to the window seat and sat down, and he joined her there.

"Gwrhyr and Uriel are one and the same," he said.

"Are they? Is there anything you would have done in the past year as King Uriel that you wouldn't have done as Gwrhyr?"

"I would have killed King Arawn, I can promise you that," Gwrhyr frowned, remembering. "But the real answer is no. The person you fell in love with is the same person you see in front of you now."

Eluned bit her lip, wanting to trust him, wanting to believe him. Could she? She had forgotten what it felt like to be near him. What she once had identified as annoyance had turned out to be desire.

"I wanted to tell you so many times." His voice was choked with emotion. "If you had ever acted like you even suspected . . ."

"I can see it now in hindsight. I think I just wanted something more exciting than being married off to a man I didn't know. So I deluded myself into believing that you were someone you weren't when clearly all the signs were there." She tilted her head and stared off into the distance, remembering. It had irritated her to no end that he had known so much about everything, that he wouldn't give her an inch in the beginning. Always harassing her while expecting the best of her.

"I tried to give you clues," Gwrhyr murmured, taking her hand in his. She tried to remove it and he gripped it tighter.

"The pocket watch should have been a dead giveaway," she admitted. "Did Jabberwock know that you were trying to clue me in?"

The King laughed. "Are you kidding? Why do you think he insisted on being our chaperone?"

The Princess couldn't help but smile though it didn't quite reach her eyes. "Ah, it now makes more sense. He was more afraid of what you might say than what we might do."

"I'm sure the thought of us being alone up on the plateau unnerved him completely."

Eluned giggled before clapping a hand over her mouth in horror. How did he make it so easy to be with him? "We were very good though," she admitted, "or restrained should I say? Even after the time we went swimming. And to your credit, as far as Jabb is concerned, you never said anything to make me suspect that you were anyone other than the son of one of King Uriel's lords."

Gwrhyr chuckled. "None of my lords have sons my age, actually. It would have been nice to have a peer to grow up with."

"I know what you mean," Eluned mused. "Njima said she had the same problem. I wonder if that's unusual or just the plight of the only child?"

"I hadn't considered that," he said. "As far as I know, Faolan is the only one in our group who has a sibling."

"Chokhmah did grow up with someone she believed to be her brother."

"We'll have to ask Bonpo whether he had any siblings." Gwrhyr was thoughtful. "Despite the fact we've spent so much time together, there is a lot we don't know about the others on our Quest."

"Or each other," Eluned reminded him, her voice dry. "You know more about me than I know about you."

"Well now you can ask me anything, and I will answer truthfully," he promised.

Eluned was silent for a moment as a thought occurred to her. She took Gwrhyr's other hand in hers, and looked into his eyes. "I am deeply sorry about Irirangi, Gwrhyr. I can't even begin to imagine how much that must have hurt you."

He looked down at their joined hands then back into her eyes. "It hurt," he admitted, "but as I said at the time, it was a wound that could heal."

"There's significantly more meaning to that now."

"What's most important at this moment is that I've missed this—just being together. I've missed you." Gwrhyr cupped her chin in his hand and gazed into her eyes. "Please tell me you feel the same way."

"Every single moment of every single day," she whispered. Damn it, why couldn't she stay angry with him, she thought as he leaned in to kiss her.

"We should go ahead and get married," she whispered into his ear a few minutes later. She desired him as much as she had that last night in Jazeel.

He sat back so he could look at her more fully. "Are you serious? Why?"

"A number of reasons," she explained, "but the most important reason right now is that I don't want to have to wait any longer. Do you?"

He kissed her again. "Of course I don't." He chuckled. "Are you sure you're ready to give up unicorns?"

Eluned paused, clearly considering.

"What?"

"I'm thinking. This is a difficult decision."

Gwrhyr stood. "Well, if you need me to come back tomorrow and ask again . . ." He feinted toward the door.

"It's already tomorrow. I think I have a better idea."

She stood, and indicated he should come closer. He leaned forward and she whispered something in his ear.

He laughed and pulled her into his arms, kissing her gently on the lips. "I'd be honored to be your unicorn." Lifting her into his arms, he carried her to her bed.

19ᴛʜ Luees

A repetitive knocking on her bedroom door finally nudged Eluned from a dream in which she was tapping a wall looking for any hollow spots that might indicate a hidden room.

As her senses swam back into awareness, she sensed the presence of something heavy across her chest and nearly panicked before she realized it was Gwrhyr's arm. His chin was pressed firmly into the top of her head. She began to stir and he awakened as well. Sunlight filtered through the leaded glass windows making it clear that the sun was already high in the sky.

When she was sure Gwrhyr was awake enough that it wouldn't startle him, she sat up and called out. "Who is it?"

"Eluned?" It was her father. "Are you all right?"

She looked at Gwrhyr, who had pushed himself up against the headboard, and smiled.

He returned her smile. "Good morning Fy Drysor," he murmured, pressing one of her wayward curls back into place. She scooted back so she could sit next to him before answering her father.

"I'm fine," she answered, voice raised. "I just stayed up late."

"That's an understatement," Gwrhyr noted quietly.

She smothered a giggle with her hand.

"Can you come to the door?" King Seraphim asked.

"Just a minute, I'm not decent."

"Oh, I'd say you're more than decent," Gwrhyr murmured.

Eluned punched him softly on the bicep, and shushed him. Retrieving her nightgown from the floor next to the bed, she pulled it over her head. She found her robe on the floor at the end of the bed where it had fallen during the night, and she drew it on before tossing Gwrhyr his clothes. She'd never actually had the chance to put on the robe the previous night because she thought she was only going to blow out a candle.

The Princess smiled to herself. How quickly things can change, she thought, and then glanced at Gwrhyr to make sure he was dressed. He was fastening his pants, and she bit her lip in appreciation. He really was an attractive man—tall and lean with defined muscles. But she loved his face the most— the straight nose over full lips, and the way his eyes could look green or blue or grey depending on the light. And the dimples at the corner of his mouth, mostly hidden by his facial hair but she knew they were there. He looked up to see her studying him, and pointed to his heart and then to her.

He was also really sappy. Faolan had mocked him when he'd seen him make that gesture, but she returned it before heading to the door. She could ask Gwrhyr to hide in the bathroom, but it seemed pointless. They were betrothed after all, and she hoped the fact they had just consummated their relationship might make her father more willing to allow them to move up the marriage.

The King took one look at the rumpled bed and at Gwrhyr standing beside it pulling his sweater over his head and his eyes flashed in anger. "Shall I take this to mean that the two of you have come to terms?" His jaw was clenched in an effort to remain civil. He'd spent the past month or so worrying that Eluned might be so angry she'd break the betrothal anyway.

And where would that leave Zion? He was certain there wasn't another suitable match available other than Prince Irirangi and he already knew how his daughter felt about him. Possibly Paul, the second prince in line for the Kingdom of Sheba, but he wasn't certain about it. Mostly, he just wasn't sure about how he felt about his daughter losing her virginity not only under his roof, but before she was married to King Uriel.

That King walked over to the door and stood behind the Princess, placing his right hand on her shoulder.

"We have, Papa," she said, covering Gwrhyr's hand with hers. "And we want to go ahead and get married as soon as possible."

"And that won't be detrimental to your quest?" King Seraphim queried the couple.

"Actually, Sir," Gwrhyr responded. "I think it will help. When everyone gathers here at the vernal equinox, we intend to split up in pairs to gather the last four Treasures, as I'm sure you're well aware. I was going to insist on travelling with Eluned, and it would be much better to do so as a married couple."

"Then we could travel either as King Uriel and Queen Eluned or as Gwrhyr and, hmmm, whatever name I choose," The Princess added. "It will really depend on where Jabberwock chooses to send us although I am guessing that it will either have to be Kamartha or Dziron."

"Or the Devastation of Pelf," Gwrhyr added.

"I hope not," Eluned shuddered. "Those Aberrations were horrible."

"I thought we handled that situation easily," Gwrhyr said.

"Only because it was an ambush of sorts," Eluned noted. "Regardless. King Hamartia and Queen Foehn know me, and probably aren't particularly happy with me."

"That's one way of putting it," Gwrhyr agreed.

About that time the pitter-patter of claws on marble was

heard approaching their room. Gwrhyr squeezed Eluned's shoulder, but whether it was to warn her or reassure her she couldn't be sure.

"I'm not happy with you," she said when the Bandersnatch arrived at her bedroom door.

"I understand that," he said, taking in the situation, and trying not to let the relief he was feeling show in his eyes. "But I had to do what I did. Omni required it."

"They want to be married immediately," King Seraphim told Jabberwock who pondered that bit of information for a moment or two before saying:

"That's probably a wise decision, but I hate to state the obvious."

They stared at him blankly.

He shook his head in disbelief. "Apparently, it's not that obvious."

"What?" Eluned snapped. "Just tell us."

"It's just that it would be very inconvenient for you to have a child before you finished this quest," Jabberwock explained, thinking of how Queen Fuchsia was found to be with child less than a month into her marriage.

"Maybe you should of considered that before all of your little machinations," she replied in an attempt to needle him. Her voice was icy.

"I honestly thought it would take longer for you to fall in love with him," he admitted, "that is, when you didn't fall in love with him at first sight."

"What? Seriously? You expected me to fall in love with him that night in Mjijangwa? By Omni, Jabberwock, I was exhausted and frozen and despite the fact he was attractive, he was a complete ass." She paused. "I'm sorry, that's unkind to the memory of Hayduke and Derry, and even Tikvah, for that matter. Only humans act like that. It's unfair that we compare ourselves to animals. They're better than us."

"Focus," Gwrhyr whispered.

"Besides," she continued, "Mother taught me how to prevent that from happening when she was teaching me everything I needed to know before I became a woman when I was twelve. I really am not the idiot you seem to think I am."

Gwrhyr chuckled.

Jabberwock closed his eyes and sighed. "I don't think you're an idiot Eluned, and I should have known that you wouldn't do anything deleterious to the Quest."

"Exactly," she frowned at him. Jabberwock started to say something else but Eluned interrupted him. "My feet are freezing and I am absolutely starving. Can we do this later?"

King Seraphim took a step backwards after glancing down at his daughter's feet. Her toes were curled against the marble floor in an effort to allow the tiles as little contact as possible with her bare soles. Gwrhyr was also barefoot. He was desperately trying to take the turn of events in stride, but anger warred with relief. He was not looking forward to telling Ceridwen. She would be even more appalled at the impropriety of the situation. "I apologize. Why don't we let them get ready for the day, Jabberwock? Shall we meet in my sitting room at three o'clock?"

"Thank you, Papa," Eluned smiled up at him. "We will be there at three."

After she closed the door, Gwrhyr lifted her, bride-over-the-threshold style.

"What are you doing?"

"I'm going to warm our feet," he answered, heading back toward the bed.

"More than our feet, I'd wager."

"You'd win that bet," he replied, tossing her gently on the bed.

"Will this involve the removal of clothes?"

"Preferably." He was already pulling his sweater off.

"I never got to ask," she began later, as she lay snug and warm in Gwrhyr's arms, "who else besides Jabberwock knew your true identity?"

"Other than your parents, Brother Columcille, and Bonpo," he replied, "I'm not sure anyone else knew."

"Bonpo knew?" She tried to think back, but he had never given any indication that Gwrhyr was anyone but who he said he was.

"Jabberwock had to tell him before you three arrived in Mjijangwa. He couldn't risk him accidentally bungling our first meeting."

She nodded, remembering. She had been impressed when she first saw him, but he had immediately gone and ruined it all by embarrassing her. "Were you trying to humiliate me that night?"

"Humiliate? No! But trying to see you as three strangers walking into an inn, I was suddenly struck by just how bizarre your little entourage was. I was just trying to get you to see it from another point of view. Who knew I would be so adept at pissing you off?"

"And I hadn't realized just how much I'd been spoiled," Eluned said.

"Anyway," he continued, "we'll have to ask Jabberwock about the others. If they knew or even suspected, they didn't make me aware of it."

The Princess looked at the clock on her bedside table. It was already past one o'clock. If they wanted to grab something to eat before they met her father and the Bandersnatch, they had better get moving.

A bowlful of steaming and velvety rich tomato soup and a grilled extra sharp cheddar cheese sandwich later, Eluned felt fortified enough to face her father and Jabberwock. It also didn't hurt to have Gwrhyr by her side. She now realized that not only did she feel more comfortable with him than any other person in her life, but that she also knew with every fiber of her being that he would do everything in his power to protect her. And that was a nice feeling even if she felt competent enough to defend herself.

Not that she expected any real push back from her father about moving their marriage date up, but she liked his being there to help persuade King Seraphim and Jabberwock, if necessary. Her mother and Brother Columcille would no doubt be there as well.

In order to give herself every advantage, she'd chosen to wear one of the dresses the Queen had insisted on having made for her daughter once she realized the bizarre state of Eluned's wardrobe. She'd nearly fainted the first time she'd seen her daughter in her leather breeches, and it had taken a lot of persuading to be granted an allowance to wear them when she was practicing her weaponry. That, too, had been a major sticking point until the Princess had explained that more than once Dyrnwyn had saved her life.

Of course, her mother didn't want to hear about that either. When she reached the part of her story in which she described being tied to the altar in Prythew, her mother had actually fainted. Once Queen Ceridwen had recovered, Eluned had recommended she leave the room.

"Papa will tell you the horror-free version later, Mother," she had promised. "I don't think you want to hear any more."

"I'm sorry, darling," her mother had risen from the sofa, still visibly shaken. "I just can't bare to hear about your being in danger. I know you're alive and well, but my head immediately fills with 'what-ifs'. I can trust your father to give me a version I can handle later. Are you sure that you're okay with this?"

"Absolutely, Mother," she had assured her. "I love you."

"I love you too, sweetheart," she had said, departing from her husband's sitting room.

But there would be no scary story today unless, of course, the thought of her daughter marrying her betrothed a couple of years early was a problem for her.

She chose a simple but striking gown of emerald green silk with a sweetheart neckline, long close-fitting sleeves, a fitted bodice and full skirt to wear to the meeting with her parents.

After she'd donned the gown, Gwrhyr buttoned up the back of the dress for her. She turned to thank him, and he pulled her into another embrace.

"Stunning," he told her after he'd kissed her. "It makes your eyes shine like opals." The mention of jewels reminded her. What more perfect to wear with this dress than Cuhvetena's necklace! The emeralds and opals would set it off quite nicely, but she would have to remove her suede pouch. While Gwrhyr fastened the necklace for her, she had pulled his betrothal ring from the pouch.

"I wasn't allowed to wear this until I was eighteen," she had explained, sliding it onto the ring finger of her left hand. The band of rose gold was an intricate design of knot-work with hands embracing a diamond heart. "And then I couldn't wear it because it didn't seem appropriate. I thought it would draw too much attention."

"And you weren't quite sure you wanted to be betrothed to the man who gave it to you," Gwrhyr had noted.

That had made Eluned wince. "You know me too well, dear heart."

"You want to wear it now though," he'd replied, "and that means the world to me."

The Princess had held up her hand to survey the way the ring glimmered on her finger and a ray of sunlight passing through one of the tower's windows caught it and caused it to dance and sparkle. "Very much so," she'd agreed. It looked quite lovely on her hand. Difficult to believe she had once despised the thing.

And now they approached her father's sitting room with varying degrees of trepidation—Eluned terrified that they would make her wait the additional two years, and Uriel relatively confident that he could convince King Seraphim and Queen Ceridwen of the necessity of marrying their only child sooner than anticipated. What Jabberwock would think, on the other hand, was a complete unknown.

As they entered the room, the Queen rushed to her daughter and wrapped her in a particularly fervent embrace.

"I am so relieved to see you looking so happy," she said, wiping away a tear. "And that dress is so becoming." She inspected the necklace. "Is this?"

"Cuhvetena's necklace," Eluned confirmed. "Yes, it is. Nearly lost Gwrhyr to her."

"That's debatable," he replied.

Eluned wrinkled her nose and shook her head, and mouthed, "no it's not," to her mother.

Linking arms with her daughter, Ceridwen led Eluned over to a small sofa where they sat down together. Gwrhyr seated himself in an armchair next to the king, and nodded to Jabberwock and Brother Columcille, who occupied another sofa.

It was the Queen who spoke first. "I think I am the only one who has a problem with your getting married sooner than anticipated," she said, taking her daughter's left hand in her right and raising it so she could see the betrothal ring more clearly. "It's been a long time since I've seen this," she murmured.

"I don't understand why." Eluned's brow wrinkled in confusion. "I thought that the plan was for me to fall in love with Gwr, uh, Uriel."

"It's just that the wedding is too important to be arranged that quickly," Ceridwen said.

Eluned and Gwrhyr looked nonplussed for a moment. It

was true that the marriage of a king and a princess probably required a little more than the usual pomp and pageantry, but Eluned couldn't bear the thought of taking a step backwards in their relationship.

"Perhaps, I can offer a solution," Brother Columcille proposed.

"Yes?" Eluned asked eagerly.

"I could perform a private ceremony before you return to the Quest," he offered, "and then when the Treasures have been gathered and war averted, we could plan something more fitting?"

"That could work," Jabberwock agreed. "We could tell the others in our group, but otherwise they'll remain King Uriel and Princess Eluned."

"Or Gwrhyr and Rowena." Eluned eyes lit up as she imagined playing the part of a non-royal couple travelling together.

"Rowena?" Gwrhyr asked.

"She's a character in one of my favorite books," she explained. "What do you think, Mother? Is that possible?"

"How soon did you want to be married?" Queen Ceridwen still appeared doubtful. "Even if the ceremony is private, I would still like it to be special. Just in case."

"Just in case?" King Seraphim asked.

"Well, darling," the Queen replied, "we all know how dangerous this quest has been. What if," she paused, unsure if she wanted to voice her fears.

"What if one of us dies?" Gwrhyr supplied the answer.

The Queen nodded.

"We cannot deny the possibility of something bad happening," Jabberwock agreed. "Although I feel strongly that it won't be to either the Princess or Uriel," he added hastily when he saw the Queen blanche.

A servant interrupted the conversation when she entered the room with a tray of tea. They waited in silence as she poured.

"Thank you, Ellie," the Princess smiled at the young woman. "I still intend to talk to Brother Columcille, here, about instruction in reading."

"Thank you, yer highness, um, Eluned," she blushed and scurried from the room.

Gwrhyr smiled and nodded at Eluned, and gave her a thumbs-up.

"What's this?" King Seraphim was frowning.

"I told Eleanor that I would look into a way to provide instruction in learning how to read and write to those servants who are interested," Eluned explained.

"Without asking me?" Her father didn't seem pleased.

"Can we discuss this later?" Queen Ceridwen interrupted. "We have a more pressing matter at hand, and Eluned still hasn't answered my question."

"Well, I haven't had a chance to discuss this with Gwrhyr," the Princess began.

"Do you not intend to call him by his proper name?" the King asked. He was still frowning at his daughter. Clearly she had annoyed him by taking the initiative to offer to teach his servants to read, but this was an issue on which she intended to stick to her guns, as Rowena might say.

"He'll always be Gwrhyr to me," she explained. "I've been calling him that for nearly a year. But," she looked at her betrothed, "if he prefers that I call him Uriel, I will try to do so."

"You can call me Gwrhyr for the rest of our lives," Uriel smiled. "I trust you to know when it's proper to use my given name."

Eluned pointed to her heart and then to him, and he returned the gesture, and Jabberwock chortled. It was difficult to miss how much in love they were. They were practically giddy with it.

"Anyway," Eluned continued, frowning her displeasure at her father for taking her to task about Uriel's name, before turning to her mother, "I was thinking about three weeks from now on my nineteenth birthday. Is that enough time, Mother?"

"I think I can work with that," her mother squeezed her hand. "Uriel will never forget your anniversary."

"That wasn't likely to happen, anyway," Gwrhyr added. "But, yes, Eluned, that date is fine with me." As long as we can remain together until then, he thought. He had been dreaming about the previous evening ever since that night in Mjijangwa. There was no going back now. Besides, the Queen was correct. The Quest was dangerous. Who knew what might happen. Even if they grew old together, he still intended to relish every moment he was allowed to share with Eluned.

"I'm glad that's settled," Eluned replied. She turned to look at the Bandersnatch, eyebrows raised. "I have some questions for Jabberwock."

"No doubt I owe you some answers," the Bandersnatch admitted.

"Then let's start at the beginning," the Princess continued. "Tell me how this magnificent ruse came about and how it proceeded," she paused. "And don't start with 'it was long ago and far away.'"

Jabberwock snorted. "No faery tales, I promise, but it did begin with Queen Fuchsia."

"Just one more thing," Eluned interrupted him. "I promise not to interrupt."

The Bandersnatch shook his head. Only the Princess. Rolling his eyes, he continued, "When Fuchsia and I became aware that you had been betrothed to the Prince of Aden at such a tender age, Fuchsia grew worried that you might end up like her.

"We discussed it at great length and finally decided that the only way to avert what might be a future tragedy was to arrange for you to meet Uriel when he wasn't Uriel."

"I will concede that it worked," Gwrhyr said when Jabberwock paused, "but I want you to know, Eluned, that I wasn't thrilled about Jabberwock's plan. There just didn't seem to be any other option."

The Princess nodded to Gwrhyr in understanding, and then turned once again to Jabberwock. "And so?"

"And so I set off for the Kingdom of Aden to discuss the plan with King Gavreel and Queen Angharad."

"You went to them first?" Eluned was surprised into interrupting.

"I knew that I needed to make them understand what might be at stake. I arrived there shortly after Uriel's tenth birthday," he smiled, remembering. "His parents were easy to convince, but the ten-year-old boy who didn't give a fig about girls . . ."

"Not so much!" Gwrhyr laughed. "I honestly could not have cared less for some girl I was supposed to marry years in the future. I understood that that was what grown ups did. I just couldn't imagine ever being one."

"I didn't care, either," Eluned smiled, "but it really ticked me off that you refused to meet me."

"It was supposed to," Jabberwock explained. "We wanted to cloak him in a little mystery. Not to mention the fact that it was important that you didn't know what he looked like."

"I never even got the traditional portrait in a locket," Eluned remembered. "But, by that point, I was already opposed to being forced to marry someone against my will."

"Just as Queen Fuchsia predicted," her father chimed in. "And, it's my turn to confess. My grandmother started writing me shortly after my father died. I was still young and your mother and I had been married less than a year. She was deeply stricken by the fact that her son died and she had never reconciled with him. She didn't want that to be true of her grandson."

"So you were writing her about me, and she realized that

I was a lot like her?" Eluned asked, but it sounded more like a statement. "Why didn't she come here herself?"

"That had been the plan," Jabberwock admitted. "Once I was assured that she would be well received, she was to travel here."

"But she died before that could happen," Eluned said sadly. And so the castle had continued to maintain its silence about the Queen who had abandoned them, she thought. Poor Fuchsia.

"I remained for several months at Castle Bennu," Jabberwock continued his story, "getting to know Uriel better and impressing upon him the importance of what I was undertaking to accomplish. Then I travelled to Zion and met with your father."

"And you never saw Uriel again?" Eluned asked.

"I saw him every year, actually," Jabberwock told her.

"What?" She closed her eyes, remembering. Of course. It all made sense. No wonder they had sounded so chummy that day in Mjijangwa. They had hit it off right away because they had known each other for eleven years. How could she have been so blind? Blind and deaf?

"Confirmation bias," Jabberwock said, reading her thoughts.

Eluned nodded, horrified at herself. She had only seen what she wanted to see, and when they first met she had seen a vainglorious commoner who had slowly morphed into a spy for King Uriel before finally becoming the son of one of his Lords. But never Uriel, himself, because that wasn't a possibility her mind was willing to accept. And now, looking back, it was all she could see. Would she have fallen in love with him had he been introduced as King Uriel that night in Mjijangwa? She would never know, but she thought the chances were roughly less than zero.

20ᵀᴴ Luees

"I thought it would be bigger."

"That's what I said," Eluned replied in a monotone before sliding a wicked glance Gwrhyr's way and bursting into laughter.

"Why you little," he grabbed her and silenced her with kisses.

Eluned snickered a final time, and Gwrhyr punched her playfully on her upper arm. "I meant the famous boulder," he rolled his eyes, indicating the granite rock where Eluned had met the Bandersnatch. "The way you described it, it seemed like a miniature mountain."

"I knew what you meant, but I just couldn't resist," she chuckled, grinning. "Besides, you have to remember that I was seven when I met Jabberwock so it seemed pretty impressive to me at the time."

"Do I seem impressive to you?" He pulled her into his arms again.

"I have no one to compare you to," she traced his lips with her finger, "and by Omni, I hope it stays that way."

"Good answer."

"I'm probably the one that should be asking that question, anyway."

Gwrhyr's cheeks colored, and to give himself time he vaulted onto the boulder. Extending a hand to the Princess, he pulled her up onto the rock with him. Sitting in silence for a moment, they studied the clearing. The grass was brown and little patches of snow glimmered from the edges of the glade where they were protected by the shadows cast by the trunks of the trees. The air smelled of pine and the day was cold enough to turn their noses red.

"It was just sex," he finally admitted.

"Was it 'just sex' for her, or should I say them?"

The King cleared his throat. "I really don't want to talk about this."

"I'm sorry Gwrhyr, but I think there are some things I am entitled to know before I make a vow to spend the remainder of my life with you. I just need to know that you haven't left broken-hearted lovers scattered across the Thirteen Kingdoms who will demand to know why I stole their man from them."

Gwrhyr laughed. "I love you, Fy Drysor, but don't you think that's a little overly dramatic?"

"I'll admit to a little hyperbole, but . . ."

"Don't worry," he assured her. "Let's just leave it at this: the few women involved were well compensated for their favors."

"One of the perks of being a king?"

"Not exactly flattering," he admitted, cheeks coloring again, "but nonetheless true."

"Do princesses and queens get similar favors? Should I be taking advantage of this perk before my birthday?" Eluned nudged him in the ribs.

"Have you made me feel sufficiently guilty yet?"

"Yes, that's probably enough. Just promise that from now on, it's only me."

"Eluned, it has been only you since you walked into the Trade Route Inn."

"What about Chokhmah?"

He looked at her in surprise. "Nothing happened with Chokhmah."

"But she wanted it to."

"I won't deny that, and I will even admit that I was intoxicated enough to almost let it happen. But I didn't." Drunk as well as angry with the Princess, not that he'd admit to that. But thanks to Jabberwock, he thought, he'd been rescued from doing something that he would have regretted for the remainder of his life. But, what was even scarier, and what Chokhmah hadn't noticed, was that Jabberwock had nearly blurted out his real name that night. Fortunately, he had caught himself, but it was a close call.

"Don't worry," Eluned said, "I believe you."

"Besides," Gwrhyr said. "I think we all know how she feels about Faolan so it's no longer an issue."

The Princess shivered and Gwrhyr put his arm around her and pulled her closer.

"Getting chilled? Should we walk back?"

"Not yet." She scooted onto his lap and leaned into his chest as he wrapped both his arms around her. "Much warmer," she murmured. "Do you know what I'd like to do?"

"I'm open to suggestions," he said as he buried his face in her neck.

Eluned giggled. "You'll be disappointed. I was going to say that I'd like to go visit Bonpo at his inn, and invite him to our wedding. He's only a little over a day's ride away. We could stay there a day or two before coming back here."

"Actually, that's not a bad idea," he admitted. It would be nice to have some time alone with Bonpo, and perhaps even Jabberwock, he thought. "We should invite Jabb to go with us, as well," he added.

"Good, I'd love for you to see Bonpo's place, and it would be fun for it to be just the four of us again." She paused. "But I'm skipping the part where I climb over the Mountains of Misericord. If you want to experience hiking in a snowstorm, you can do it on your own."

"I am more than willing to leave that adventure to you," Gwrhyr assured her. "Besides, we don't know where we'll be heading come spring, and we haven't been able to escape the extremes yet."

"That's true," Eluned sighed. "And it's something I want to discuss with Jabb and Bonpo. Let's go back and talk to Jabberwock. I think we can camp the first night, and make it to the Crossroads Inn before lunch the next day."

WHILE KING URIEL WAITED with King Seraphim and Queen Ceridwen in the latter king's sitting room, the Princess ran off to seek the Bandersnatch.

Gwrhyr settled himself on the smaller of the two sofas, a solid burgundy affair which wasn't quite as comfortable, but it would force Eluned to sit closer to him.

Old habits die hard, he thought as they waited. It was no longer necessary to manipulate ways to be near her.

"I still haven't come to terms with how much our daughter has changed," Seraphim startled him out of his musings.

"Sometimes, neither can I," Uriel admitted. "There were several times in our first week together that I was sorely tempted to let you know that I wished to break the betrothal. She tested my patience, that's for sure, and I didn't always respond well."

"But despite that," Ceridwen said, "she seems to love you deeply."

"I still can't believe it," Gwrhyr mused. "Even as she was driving me insane, I was falling more and more in love with her, and when we were in Favonia, I despaired of her ever feeling the same towards me."

"She said that both Chokhmah and Jabberwock assured you that she would come to her senses," Seraphim said.

"They did, and she did, and I guess in the grand scheme of

things it didn't take that long." He paused. "And from there on out it was all downhill in a positive way. She came to trust me more, and then like me more, and finally love me. I cannot tell you how relieved I am to be uniting our kingdoms. Nor how much it means that she shares my feelings."

Seraphim nodded as Gwrhyr spoke. "And it's no little thing that both Naphtali and Pelf have allied themselves to us as well."

"True," Gwrhyr spoke as a king. "It's actually my hope that we can turn Tarshish and perhaps either Dziron or Kamartha, or both. It would be to our advantage if we gathered all the Treasures, which I feel is ordained to happen, and there are nine or ten of us to stand against that malefic triumvirate."

"Indeed it would," Seraphim nodded. "I hear things are getting really bad in Simoon."

Gwrhyr was about to reply when the telltale clatter of Jabberwock's claws could be heard on the marble floor.

The two kings stood as the Princess entered the room, completely disregarding the page standing there to announce her. Jabberwock trotted in behind her rolling his glassy eyes as if to say, 'some things never change.'

Seeing her father and Gwrhyr stand as she entered, it was Eluned's turn to roll her eyes. "Sit," she ordered. "Seriously, we're family. You don't have to stand for me. If it's someone we don't know or someone we're required to be formal with then standing is appropriate, of course. Otherwise we don't need to be, as King Uriel once said, all uppity about manners around each other."

Gwrhyr couldn't help but laugh. Patting the seat on the couch next to him, he said, "You're right Princess, I did once say that. Apparently, you took that lesson to heart."

She sat down beside him and grinned up at him. "And you thought I wasn't listening."

"Touché."

"I assume there's a reason you've gathered us here," her

father interrupted their flirtation despite the fact he actually enjoyed seeing his daughter head-over-heels in love with the man she was betrothed to marry. He would always be thankful that she hadn't run off like his own grandmother. He had been leery when Jabberwock had proposed the plan, but the Bandersnatch had been right.

"It's not really anything," she sighed, thinking, "that important."

They all remained fixed on her, watching her expectantly.

She took Gwrhyr's hand in hers. "It's just that we'd like your permission to go visit Bonpo and invite him to the wedding." She looked over at Jabberwock. "And we'd love for you to come with us if you want to Jabb."

"How long would you stay?" the Queen asked.

"We'd probably have to camp one night on the way there," the Princess began.

"You wouldn't stay at the inn in Roodspire?" her father asked.

Eluned looked at Jabberwock.

"Camp," he stated.

"It might be warmer," Eluned said, "but I'm accustomed to camping, and I think our staying at the inn would cause more of a commotion than necessary."

"Commotion? Why?" her mother asked.

"How do I put this?" Eluned closed her eyes briefly to think.

"Let's just say," the Bandersnatch admitted, "that a certain someone said something he shouldn't have the previous time we were there."

Seraphim and Gwrhyr were already chuckling, but Ceridwen was still confused.

"I don't understand," she confessed.

"What Jabberwock is trying to say, Mother, is that he said something to the innkeeper's wife when we left there last year. It's highly unlikely that she's forgotten in the past year that a dog spoke to her." Eluned turned to Jabberwock, "Sorry, Jabb, but she thought you were a dog."

Jabberwock nodded and Eluned turned back to her mother, "And, I am absolutely certain that she didn't keep it a secret. She reminded me of a little bird, and I am sure she twittered all about it to everyone she met."

"I've learned," Gwrhyr said, "that a little gold buys a lot of silence, but in this case, it's probably too late."

"You bribed the innkeeper and his staff in Mjijangwa, didn't you?" Eluned turned to him, yet another mystery solved.

Gwrhyr shook his head, apologetically. "A part of the plan."

"Where else? Ruisidho? Thírnagall? Ponike? The mind boggles." She was shaking her head in wonder.

"I couldn't risk being apprehended as a warlock," Jabberwock explained. "When it was safe to do so, I admitted that I was a Janawar. Otherwise, we paid people off. Silence is golden, but gold is . . ."

"Even more golden," the Princess was smiling, but it was clear it was in self-deprecation. She had freely allowed herself to be fooled into thinking Gwrhyr was the son of a lord.

"Exactly," Gwrhyr squeezed her hand.

"Scratch Ponike," Eluned said, removing her hand as casually as possible from his grip. The thought of the months-long, years-in-the-making ruse still irked her. "The king could have ordered his people to accept Jabb."

Gwrhyr nodded. "I won't deny it."

"By Omni, everything is making sense now," Eluned said, raising an eyebrow at Jabberwock and frowning.

Gwrhyr wanted nothing more than to pull her off the sofa and carry her to her room where he could apologize to her once again in private. And despite her apparent displeasure, he sensed she wanted that as well, but he was nothing if not self-disciplined. "So, I assume that means you intend to travel with us, Jabb?"

"Honestly," Jabberwock admitted, "I miss the oaf. I'd love to see him again."

"So, Papa? Mother? Is it okay? I was thinking two nights travel time, and two nights at the Crossroads Inn. Less than a week. My dress should be ready for fitting when I return," Eluned turned to her mother knowing that she was more worried about the wedding, as casual as it might be, than anything else. "Oh!"

"What is it?" her mother asked, brow creased in worry.

"Can Bonpo cater the reception? I know there won't be a lot of us, but his cooking is to die for."

Jabberwock and Gwrhyr nodded in agreement.

"The man is a master," Gwrhyr said.

Man, Eluned mused. It was difficult to think of Bonpo as a man. Because, if he was a man then what had he left behind in Dziron? A girlfriend or, she couldn't rule it out, a boyfriend? A family? By Omni, she had promised herself when she first met Bonpo that she would look more deeply at everything, but the truth was—what did she really know about her fellow Questers?

Gwrhyr, Eluned and Jabberwock got a later start that Deethyeen morning than they had hoped. They sent off a courier just before the weekend as soon as they'd been given permission to travel, and had spent an anxious two days waiting for the man to return with word that they were expected. The messenger hadn't arrived back at Castle Mykerinos until late on Deethseel, and Gwrhyr and Eluned had already been asleep for a couple of hours by that time.

While they had already packed what they would need for the trip prior to turning in for the night, it took them awhile to get breakfasted, the horses and Tikvah saddled, and their gear attached to the donkey.

By nine o'clock, they were on their way, and were passing

the Golden Gryphon Inn in Roodspire about an hour before sunset.

"Oh look, Jabberwock," Eluned remarked as they skirted their former lodging, "they've refurbished the sign." The lettering now glittered in the late afternoon sun, and someone had made a real effort with the drawing of the gryphon. She was impressed. The Princess found herself wondering if she would see the faces inside differently now. She had met so many people of so many different types in the past year that it was difficult to think that she wouldn't.

Gwrhyr noticed her looking back at the inn. "Having second thoughts?"

"No, I still want to camp," she assured him. "Just thinking about how much has changed in the past year."

They rode for another half hour before stopping to set up camp in an empty field adjacent to a small strip of oak and hickory forest. Within a couple of miles the road would begin to wind through the hills with their barrows and standing stones.

"And I don't want to be anywhere near them come nightfall," Eluned had told them when they'd started out that morning. She'd rather arrive on the late side for lunch at the Crossroads Inn than risk the nightmares that might accompany being too close to those haunted hills.

The following day they passed through the gently rolling hills without incidence, and arrived at the Crossroads Inn shortly after midday. Bonpo was ecstatic to see them, enveloping Eluned in a bear hug before slapping Gwrhyr soundly on the back, and causing him to stagger a few steps before he regained his balance.

"A rittle bird terr me dat you two gettin' marry," Bonpo said.

"What!" Eluned cried, "I wanted to tell you that." She glared at Jabberwock who shook his head.

"Not me, Princess," Jabberwock said. "Trust me, news travels fast around here."

"Don' berieve it 'cause you plegnant, eida," Bonpo assured her.

"Faster than the speed of accuracy, I should have said," Jabberwock chuckled as the Princess exclaimed again.

"Was I supposed to have arrived home that way? Gwrhyr has only been in Zion a week!"

Gwrhyr was shaking his head. "Unbelievable. People can believe what they like. They'll know soon enough that it's not true."

"Tikvah!" Bonpo changed the subject, hugging the big donkey. Scowling, Eluned started to remove their gear from Tikvah's packsaddle. Bonpo nodded to the porch, and the Princess handed a load to Gwrhyr to deposit there.

Once everything was removed, they gathered what they would need for the next couple of days, leaving their camping equipment on the porch. Eluned deposited their baggage in the main room while Bonpo and Gwrhyr led Ruari, Ronan, and Tikvah to the stable and got them situated for the night.

WHEN BONPO AND GWRHYR RETURNED to the inn, they found Eluned and Jabberwock situated in front of the fireplace. The Princess was trying not to be outraged by the fact that her father's subjects assumed she was with child. She guessed it was an obvious conclusion to jump to if they knew the marriage was being moved up by two years, but it still smarted.

The Bandersnatch was reaching the painful decision that he would have to return to the Devastation of Pelf in order to look for the knife. Bonpo would be his travelling partner. There was no other way around it. They stood out too much to head to any of the other kingdoms. He would discuss it with Bonpo that evening, but he really didn't see any other way.

"You rike me show you to you looms?" Bonpo asked. "Ol you leady to eat?"

"I am hungry," Eluned admitted.

"Good," Bonpo smiled, "'cause I plepale lear Yeti mear fol you. Even make barrey beel. Be right back." He hustled from the room.

"I love that dzu-tch." The Princess smiled and stood. She had really missed the giant's cheerful presence, but neither had she forgotten that she wanted to broach the serious subject of who and what he might have left behind in the Peaks of Vulpecula.

She sat down at one of the tables and was soon joined by Gwrhyr and Jabberwock. Bonpo appeared a minute later with mugs and a pitcher of beer, before disappearing into the kitchen again.

Gwrhyr poured the beer, and Eluned was just taking a tentative sip, when Bonpo reappeared with a large platter and a stack of plates. The giant joined them at the table and explained the appetizers—beef dumplings seasoned with garlic, onion, ginger and soy sauce, and small balls of roasted barley flour, salty butter tea and dried cheese.

"Save loom fah da soup," he told Eluned as she placed some appetizers on her plate. "I arso make weddin' desselt."

"You've outdone yourself, Bonpo," Gwrhyr said, after consuming one of the dumplings. "These are really good."

Eluned and Jabberwock nodded their agreement.

"Very good," the Princess said. "And the beer is the perfect thing to wash them down."

Bonpo filled a plate and mug, and then returned to the kitchen to finish preparing the soup.

"It feels both really odd and very right to be here again," Eluned noted after he'd gone. "I'd forgotten how completely in his element he is here."

"He definitely seems right at home," Gwrhyr agreed. "It's difficult to believe that he's willing to give it up again to finish the Quest."

"Perhaps it is more than a quest to him," Jabberwock suggested.

"A way of atoning for the poacher?" Eluned mused, thinking of the man whose death Bonpo had caused.

"Something like that," Jabberwock agreed.

While they were pondering this, Bonpo returned with another tray laden with bowls and a pot of soup. They were soon all enjoying the spicy noodle soup packed full of strips of mutton, tomato, carrots, cabbage and onion.

They lingered at the table for about an hour before finally moving to the seating area closer to the fire. Bonpo and Gwrhyr carried the trays laden with dirty dishes to the kitchen.

"We wash ratel," Bonpo said when Eluned offered to help. "You go sit file."

The men returned a few minutes later with butter tea and deep fried cookies sprinkled with powdered sugar.

"I make dis weddin' desselt speciar fah you, 'Leened," Bonpo told her as he set the tray down. "Rittre donkey ear fah speciar 'casion."

"Donkey ears!" Eluned laughed. "How perfect."

"Suppose make big fah decolation," he explained, "but I make rittre to eat. You can dip in tea."

The Princess tried it, and nodded in approval. "Excellent, Bonpo, which reminds me. I was wondering two things—first, would you please come to our wedding; and, secondly, if you will, could you please cater the reception afterwards?"

"It's going to be a small wedding," Gwrhyr explained, "but it's also Eluned's birthday so we'd like for it to be even more special."

"Absorutery!" Bonpo grinned. "Dat two week flom now?"

Eluned nodded, and Bonpo pondered for a moment.

"And den tree mol week tir we reave Quest?"

"Yes," Jabberwock said. "The plan is for everybody to be at Castle Mykerinos by the vernal equinox, which is the fourth of Feharn this year."

"P'raps den I be leady reave by day afta 'morrah," Bonpo said.

"Seriously?" Gwrhyr asked. "You mean to stay at Castle Mykerinos until it's time to set out?"

"Rots to pran," he explained.

"That's true," Jabberwock agreed. "We will be setting out as four different groups, and while some of us may be able to travel together, briefly, whoever goes to Simoon will be completely on their own."

"And that's going to have to be Chokhmah and Faolan," Eluned said. "All the rest of us would be recognized. Well, maybe all of us but Njima."

"And Njima can't go because her skin is the wrong color," Gwrhyr added.

They all nodded glumly. It was true that King Hamartia did not allow persons of color into his kingdom—yet another reason to prevent his coming into more power.

"I assume you've given this a lot of thought, Jabberwock," Eluned finally broke the silence.

"I have," he agreed. "I think what will work for the best is if you and Uriel or Yona and Njima travel to Dziron as neither I nor Bonpo are welcome there. And because we stand out so much, our only choice is to go to the Devastation of Pelf."

"No!" Eluned cried. "You don't want to go back there."

"Of course I don't," the Bandersnatch said, "but perhaps it's time for me to come to terms with the past."

"I ploteck you," Bonpo said.

Jabberwock chuckled. "I have no doubt about that."

"Which reminds me," Eluned said.

"What reminds you?" Jabberwock asked.

"Coming to terms with the past."

"Yes?" He thought she knew most everything about his past.

"Actually, I'm thinking of Bonpo." The Princess turned toward the giant. "Because of recent events, I was thinking back to when we were discussing or rather, pointedly not discussing our virginity. As I recall, no one, other than myself, said anything, leading me to assume that I was, indeed, the only virgin present."

Bonpo's cheeks were turning a healthy shade of pink.

"So?" Eluned prompted, "either you're a virgin, Bonpo, or you left behind a girlfriend, or . . ."

"It tlue," the dzu-tch admitted, swallowing hard. "When I banish, mus' reave behine wife and chirdlen."

"Your family," Eluned's eyes stung with impending tears. "They made you leave behind your family?"

Bonpo swiped away a tear of his own. "I haf no choice. Karlha's fadder make me reave dem behine."

"Your father-in-law?" Gwrhyr was horrified. He hoped he never did anything to force Eluned's father into a similar position.

"I bling danger to Yeti. Plice I mus' pay," Bonpo said.

The Princess experienced a moment of epiphany. "Bonpo's not your real name, is it?'

Bonpo shook his head. "I change. It joke among Yeti. We plactice ancient lerigion of B'on. Folbidden now in Dziron. We call oulserves 'bonpos' 'cause we walk 'lound playel stones 'long way."

"I don't understand." Eluned's brow creased in confusion.

Jabberwock chuckled. "What he means is that they walk counter-clockwise around the prayer stones, which would be against the universe. Is that right?"

Bonpo nodded.

"I thought it was an unusual name," Jabberwock said, "but I assumed it was a family name."

"What is your real name?" Eluned asked.

"Shangshung," Bonpo said. "I haf one son, Sherab, and one daughter, Dalha. Dey plobry haf chirdlen dere own now."

"I'm so sorry," Eluned said, "but I'm glad I know. What a tremendous sacrifice you had to make."

"Arr my faurt," he said. "Nevel light take rife, or put Yeti in danger."

Jabberwock snorted, and Eluned glared at him.

"I apologize," the Bandersnatch said. "I just find it surprising that one of the ways that both Bonpo and I have dealt with our loss is by giving ourselves new names for our new lives as if a new name could wipe out the past."

"Vely tlue," Bonpo agreed. "Name armos' make pas' mole plesent."

"Exactly," Jabberwock said. "My new name constantly reminds me of what I left behind."

"Hmmmm," Eluned mused. "I think Njima and I are the only ones who haven't used assumed names."

Gwrhyr ran the others through his head, and nodded. "We don't know the name Faolan used as a spy for King Cian, but I'm sure he used one if Olcan did."

"And I just realized I haven't asked you why you chose the name Gwrhyr?" Eluned said.

"It was a private joke with myself, Fy Drysor," he explained. "It comes from the same language and means something like 'translator'."

Eluned laughed. "And that's exactly what you did for me that first night in Mjijangwa. Of course, you set that up, but you didn't know at the time we'd be seeking the Hallowed Treasures, right?"

"Not that soon, no, although Jabberwock and I suspected that might be what Omni had in mind," he said.

"Well it looks as if we may have to choose names for ourselves once we head off to search for the last Treasures," Eluned said. "And where are we going, Jabb? I know you've thought about this. Kamartha or Dziron?"

"I was leaning toward Dziron for the two of you," he said.

"I'd like that," she said. "Wouldn't you, Gwrhyr? I'd love to see Jabb's and Bonpo's home."

Gwrhyr nodded his assent.

"We can discuss further details once the others arrive," Jabberwock noted.

Eluned attempted to get Bonpo to reveal more about life in the Peaks of Vulpecula but all the yeti would say is, "I no rike tark 'bout it. Vely painfur."

"I don't know about the rest of you," Gwrhyr stood, making an attempt to rescue Bonpo, who looked very uncomfortable, "but I could really use some cognac. Weren't you saying you had some in your cellar, Bonpo?"

Bonpo stood, relief washing over his face. "Yes. We go get."

28ᵗʰ Beth

Curled up on the sofa in front of the fireplace in Rose Cottage, Chokhmah put down her knitting to adjust the wool shawl wrapped around her shoulders. The wrap was her first attempt at knitting, and had turned out rather well she thought. Faolan's sister-in-law, Beibhinn, had instructed her on the process not long after she and Faolan had returned to Bogaine in the Kingdom of Dyfed. Beibhinn had even provided her with several skeins of pale lavender yarn. Chokhmah had spent the next several weeks, as time permitted, working the yarn into a shawl—proceeding slowly so as not to make any errors.

Once her project was completed, she had rounded up some sea green yarn so that she could knit a fichu for Eluned— a belated birthday gift to present to the Princess when they arrived at Castle Mykerinos in the spring. Before returning to her knitting, she reached for the cup of tea sitting on the table in front of her—a relaxing blend of mint and rose hips, plenty of which were to be found at Rose Cottage. The fire crackled cheerily and she gazed into the flickering flames for a moment.

Faolan was out in the barn caring for the horses, and although Beibhinn would more than welcome the gypsy in her home, Chokhmah enjoyed the peaceful silence within the cottage. Quiet was something to which she had grown accustomed in the year following Yitzak's death.

The month or so since they'd returned to Rose Cottage had been nothing less than idyllic. She and Faolan had spent much of that time alone—preparing their home for winter and getting to know each other better. Although they had roomed together at both Castle Indalo and the Shamash Palace, there had always been an uncomfortable feeling of having to be careful about what they did and said. Silly, now that she looked back on it. If they had just been themselves, the events that had precipitated the death of the donkey, Derry, would probably have never happened. They had been so concerned about making the others uncomfortable that they had caused a catastrophe.

In hindsight, she thought, they should have just behaved normally. The remainder of the group would probably have soon come to terms with the fact that they were a couple and would want to do the things couples like to do together. After all, Yona and Njima had managed to pull off being together without making any waves, and even Eluned and Gwrhyr had grown closer during that time. If she hadn't begun her relationship with Faolan by feeling so much guilt about Eluned being jealous, things might have gone differently.

She and Faolan chose, instead, to go out of their way to be careful, and had lived those months more shallowly than now seemed possible. As a matter of fact, she grimaced, it was not until they were safely ensconced in Rose Cottage that Faolan had finally told her the truth about why he had remained single for so long.

It was not long after they first arrived, and they had been cuddled up on this same sofa enjoying some brandy in front of a roaring fire.

After staring into the flames for a few moments, he had cleared his throat. "I haven't been completely honest with you," he had said, which naturally made her stomach drop and her heart race. Was he going to tell her that he actually had a wife and children in another kingdom?

He stared at the fire for another minute or so, and she tried to wait patiently to find out what was troubling his soul.

"It's not true that I never found anyone with whom to share my secret," he had finally admitted, his voice hoarse with emotion. He'd swallowed audibly and gone on. "I've never told anyone this, not even Olcan. They think I returned from Tartessos because my time there had expired."

He'd scrubbed his face with both his hands. "I didn't know this would be so difficult."

Chokhmah had taken his hand in hers and squeezed it encouragingly before retrieving his brandy snifter from the table and handing it to him. "Start at the beginning," she'd said.

Taking a hearty gulp, he continued. "I was sent to Tartessos to work in King Dodi's stables at Iqbal Palace," he'd begun. "This was about ten years ago. I was twenty-five. Obviously I couldn't be from Dyfed, and I didn't look like I was from Tartessos. At that point, we decided it would be best for me to be from the Awen Alliance as it would be misleading should anyone suspect me. That pretty much narrowed it down to me being from the Kingdom of Simoon or Annewven. We decided on Simoon as it was more distant, and I spoke the language better than Annewvenese."

Chokhmah had nodded. Despite the fact that their king was dark-eyed and dark-haired, Simoon was know for its fair-skinned, light-eyed people. "But in Tartessos, at the palace, you would have spoken the Common Tongue, correct?"

"For the most part, and of course, the language of Tarshish," he'd said. "Unfortunately, when you're a spy, you never know when you might run into someone who is from the Kingdom you claim to be from. So, I arrived in Tartessos as Wulf from Simoon."

Chokhmah had chuckled, and Faolan had laughed as well.

"I couldn't resist," he'd admitted. "I wasn't there long before I met Fatimah. She arrived shortly after I did, and was newly apprenticed to the kitchen."

He'd taken a deep breath and another swig of brandy. "I won't deny it. I was smitten at first sight. She was beautiful—long dark hair that she wore plaited down her back, huge brown eyes—just breathtaking." He paused, remembering.

"So you like dark women," Chokhmah had stated, taking his chin in her hand so that she could turn his face to hers.

"I guess I do," he'd agreed before kissing her.

"How old was this woman?"

He'd bitten his lip, and shook his head. "Too young for me. No more than sixteen."

"That is nearly a decade Faolan," she admonished him.

"We're a decade apart in age," he'd countered.

"Yes, but a decade between two mature adults is different than a decade between a child and an—"

"Immature adult?" he'd interrupted her.

"You know it is true," she'd said, voice soft.

"I will admit it," he sighed. "She was a child, and I was old enough to know better. And yet I didn't try to resist her."

"And, no doubt, she was flattered by your attentions," Chokhmah had murmured. "Young women want to be admired by older men. It makes them feel sexually powerful. Unfortunately, they are not old enough to exercise that power."

"I wish I had known that then," he'd shaken his head again. "But Fatimah overpowered my common sense with her professions of love. In hindsight, I think that she thought being connected to a stable hand would give her access to Dodi's son, Aahil, who was eighteen at the time. Or, at the very least, one of the minor lords. I was blinded by love. I really believed that she loved me for who I was and not to whom I was connected while working in the stables."

"I am so sorry, my love," Chokhmah had snuggled closer to him. It seems that no one makes it through life unscathed, she thought. Did every human carry around a pain that they either kept locked in a chest in the back of their mind or talked about incessantly, refusing to let it go? No, she had mused, some were capable of letting their past hurts go. She would like to think that she had moved on with her life after Yitzak. Maybe confessing his pain about Fatimah would allow Faolan to move on as well. Clearly it had been festering in his heart for a long time.

"Tell me what happened," she'd said, taking both his hands in hers.

"I miscalculated," he'd told her. "I thought she loved me enough to hear the truth about me."

"You told her you are a Shapeshifter."

"At first she didn't believe me. She laughed at me and told me I was being silly." His face had flushed at that memory. He'd entrusted her with his deepest, darkest secret and she had laughed.

"So you showed her," Chokhmah had winced. There was only one outcome to this story.

"She screamed and threw the nearest thing at hand at me."

"The scars on your chest. You said a boiling pot had tipped over on you." Chokhmah had been horrified.

"A pot of boiling water, yes," he'd said, "but hurled at me by a frightened little girl. That's what my wolf eyes finally saw that my human eyes couldn't. So, I did what any wolf would do in that situation. I ran."

Faolan had run northwest to the coast and then followed the coastline of Tarshish to Adamah and finally reached Dyfed. He figured they would be searching for him, assuming they felt the need to do so, toward the northeast along the road that led to the border crossing over the Panavhadesh Mountains.

"Unfortunately," he'd said, "I still had yet another month in my deployment, but more importantly, I still needed time to heal. As a child I had heard stories of a witch that lived in the forest that bordered the cliffs east of Thírnagall. They said that she could talk to the animals; that they would come to her when wounded. I didn't know if it was true, but I sought her out."

"Did you find her?" Chokhmah had been intrigued. She had not pressed him on his scars as she assumed it was a painful memory for him.

"I did," he'd smiled, "and she was not at all what I expected."

"How do you mean?"

"She was young, for one thing."

"Young?

"She was probably about forty," he'd said, "and like you, she looked young for her age. She was also quite beautiful—hair the color of burnished copper and eyes as green as the yew trees that stood around her house."

Chokhmah had nodded in understanding, a knowing smile on her lips. "I see you are a poet. I am thinking that she did more than heal you."

Faolan had blushed, but admitted that they had been lovers for the month he had spent with her.

"And I am thinking," Chokhmah had continued, "that it did not take you a full month to heal."

"You're right," he'd said, "I could have left sooner, but she was the first woman to know who and what I was and not care."

"So, my love, why did you leave?"

"I would have stayed longer, but Lori didn't wish it so. It wasn't the age difference so much as the fact that she truly enjoyed living alone. A month was probably longer than she desired for me to stay there, but I think she was trying to be kind after what had happened to me. She understood how much I'd been hurt, which is to say she understood how very young I was in so many ways, and that I wouldn't continue to mature if I stayed with her. I think after a month, she decided that I'd stayed as long as necessary."

"A wise woman, Lori," Chokhmah smiled. "I am glad that she made you go."

Faolan had caressed her face, and kissed her again. "So am I," he'd said, "because I can no longer imagine a life without you. I've really grown a lot in the past ten years, and had even grown content with the fact I'd never find love."

"Which is always when you discover it," Chokhmah had smiled.

After leaving Lori's, Faolan made his way back to Bogaine arriving about the time he would have been expected. He managed to keep his scars hidden for several months, and by the time his brother noticed them, he was able to play down how bad the burns had been.

The stamping of boots outside the cottage interrupted her reminiscing—Faolan was finished with his chores in the barn. She looked down, and was surprised to discover that she had been knitting automatically while her thoughts wandered. She picked up her teacup to find that it was now stone cold. She shook her head, marveling at herself. She was not one to woolgather. How much time had passed? She had not even begun the preparations for lunch.

The door opened and Faolan walked in, dropping his boots in the entryway.

"Is everything all right?" he asked, hurrying over to the sofa.

"I completely lost track of time," she admitted. "Is it already time to make lunch?"

He sat down next to her. "No hurry. Eluned's shawl is coming right along." He paused. "Is there a reason you're in a hurry to finish it? It's still nearly a month before we need to leave."

Chokhmah's eyes suddenly filled with tears, something else she rarely did.

"Sweetheart, what is it?" Faolan pulled her into his arms.

She angrily swiped away the tears. "I do not know why I am crying, but I think it is because I feel I cannot settle in here until the Quest is completed. I feel like something has been left unfinished."

Faolan nodded. "It's the threat of the Awen Alliance. What if they pursue war before we gather the remainder of the Treasures?"

"Yes," Chokhmah agreed. "Eluned began the Quest before spring last year. I think we can all bear a little cold for the greater good." She paused for a moment before continuing. "No, it is more than that. When we were still at Castle Indalo, Eluned told me that every day she sat waiting in the glade she would fret about what was happening back at camp. She was worried that while we were doing all the work, she spent the entire day figuring out ways to waste time. She missed being a part of what was going on, and she worried that we would resent her because she was not participating in the daily chores."

"That's silly," Faolan said. "I don't think a single one of us would have traded places with her. I can't imagine being confined to one spot for days on end. And nothing made that more clear than the days we were stuck in our tent because of rain."

Chokhmah chuckled. "You could not even bear it then, my love. As I recall a certain wolf needed a quick run through the forest on those days."

Faolan smiled. It was true. Despite the cold and wet, he had to get out and stretch his legs, so to speak.

"I told Eluned that she was mistaken. That we all appreciated the fact that she had made a great sacrifice for us. But what is worrying me now is this: If we arrive at Castle Mykerinos on the vernal equinox, we will almost immediately split up into twos and begin our personal quests. I have been thinking about this, and I know that Jabberwock will send the two of us to Simoon." She stopped, and smiled at Faolan. "Shall you be Wulf again?"

"How ironic," he laughed.

"King Hamartia has never met me nor do they know you.

If the Treasure is in Castle Rodolf, and we must assume it is, then we will probably have to face him or the Queen at some point."

Faolan considered this for a moment. It was true that Bonpo and Jabberwock not only stood out too much, but would also face certain death there. This was also true for Yona and the Princess. And, of course, Gwrhyr. He shook his head. Njima was also not welcome in Simoon. They were the obvious choice. "You're right," he admitted. "I can't see any other choice. Which Treasure is there?"

"The Whetstone. But that is unimportant at the moment. What is important to me is that if we do not leave soon for Zion then we will have very little time with our friends before we leave."

"When are you suggesting?"

"As soon as we are able to make the preparations to leave. I also think that we should send a letter or pigeon to Yona and Njima informing that we plan to arrive early. If we leave soon, we can be in Goshen in time for Eluned's birthday, and you know how important that is to her."

"So the plan is to tell Yona and Njima that we would like us all to be there for her birthday?" Faolan asked.

"Yes, and that we intend to surprise the Princess," Chokhmah smiled. It felt as if a great weight had been lifted from her shoulders. "Eluned would like that."

"Should we send a pigeon to Bonpo, as well?"

"If I know Eluned, she has already been in contact with him," Chokhmah said. "She has probably even invited him to celebrate her birthday with her as he is less than two days away."

Faolan nodded. That made sense. "What about Gwrhyr?"

That was more troubling. Had Eluned already broken her engagement with Uriel? She had intended to do that immediately, and Gwrhyr was supposed to leave for Zion once she had. "We will have to trust that he is already on his way there."

She paused. "Do you realize, Faolan, that we do not even know how to get in touch with him? We know Yona and Njima are at Castle Indalo, and that Bonpo is at the Crossroads Inn, and that Eluned and Jabberwock are at Castle Mykerinos. But, we know only that Gwrhyr is in Ponike."

"I hadn't thought of that. It just never came up. You're right. We will have to trust Omni in this. It hasn't failed us so far." He thought about that for a second before continuing. "If we arrive by her birthday, that will give us three weeks in Zion if we still leave on the equinox. It will also allow us to be more flexible about our parting time in case we all feel the need to return to the Quest sooner than that." He paused, forehead creased in concentration. "Okay," he said. "I'll talk to my brother. I think with Olcan's help we can be ready to leave by the third or fourth of Luees. I'm going to need at least three days to get everything in order."

If they took some cross-country trails northeast of Bogaine, they could hit the trade road near the river border with Adamah more quickly than returning to Thírnagall. It might shave a couple of days off their time. It was a five-week trip from Bogaine to Goshen. And, it was winter. Fortunately, Chokhmah didn't have a problem with camping nor was she wont to complain about the cold. She would put her discomfort aside for the greater good. It was one of things he loved about her. "You'll see to getting in touch with Yona?"

"Of course. Thank you, my love," she kissed him tenderly. "Even a week with our friends would be nice to have before we part again." Chokhmah stood. "Lunch?"

2ND Luees

It had been one of those mind numbingly boring days that always seemed to follow Deethseel, Yona reflected. There is something about returning to routine following a brief break that is difficult to wrap your head around despite the fact it happens every week, she thought, taking another sip of her wine and sighing. They were seated in Njima's sitting room attempting to keep warm. It had also been a brutally cold winter's day, and Yona had her feet as close to the brazier as safety would permit.

"What is it my dove?" Njima turned to her, brushing back a lock of auburn hair from Yona's face. It was now down to her shoulders, but Yona was sorely tempted to chop it off again. Yet, they were not sure what the future held, and how they might need to disguise themselves so she continued to let it be.

"It has been more than nine weeks."

"Yes?" the Queen's brow creased in confusion.

"That's more than twice as long as it took me to steal the hamper and reach Favonia."

"Where are you going with this, sweetheart?"

Yona couldn't hold back the tears any longer. "I miss them, Njima," she cried. "I'm beginning to feel like I'll never see them again. That we'll never finish this quest."

It was true, Njima mused, that it was another eight weeks before they had to be at Castle Mykerinos, or a maximum of five weeks for Yona to have to wait before they departed for Zion.

They were interrupted by a knock at the door.

"Enter!" Njima called, and she turned to see her Lord High Steward walk in. "Eremias." She stood, tensed. Had something happened?

"Your majesty," he smiled, and she relaxed. "Please do not be alarmed. It is only that as I was returning from a meeting with Kess, I noticed a page hurrying this way. When I asked her why, she informed me a pigeon had just arrived with a note for your Majesty. I offered to bring it to you, that is all."

Njima strode over to the door where he stood and extended her palm. "Thank you, Eremias, I appreciate it. All else is well?"

"Yes, your Majesty." He placed the tiny piece of rolled up paper in her palm, bowed, and left the room.

Njima unrolled the scroll, and read the brief message squeezed onto its surface. "I think you have your answer." She handed the note to Yona.

My dear friends,
Faolan and I have decided that we are ready to return to the Quest. It is our intention to leave on the 4th of Luees for Zion. We plan to be there to celebrate with Eluned her 19th birthday on the 11th of Neeon. It is our hope that the two of you might join us then. We miss you and cannot wait to see you again.
With much love, Chokhmah and Faolan.

Yona looked at Njima, eyes filled with hope.

"Yes, my dove, I think that is something we can do. When do we need to leave?"

Yona pulled a calendar from her bag. She had been crossing off the days until they could leave for Zion. She was so excited that her hands were shaking as she calculated the latest they could leave in order to make it in time for Eluned's birthday.

"No later than the thirteenth or fourteenth of Luees," she told Njima.

"We will begin preparations on the morrow," she promised, raising her glass. "To the Quest."

"To the Quest," Yona laughed.

Eleven days later, Njima informed Yona that everything had been set for their departure. "We can leave on the morrow," she said. "I trust Eremias and Kess to keep things running smoothly just as they did when we went to Kamea."

"Why tomorrow?" Yona asked.

Njima blinked in confusion.

"It is only noon," Yona explained. They were eating lunch in the dining room, which seemed much emptier without Bonpo and the others.

"Are you suggesting we leave today?"

"Why not? We can get a decent start on the trip, and camp tonight if we don't find an inn by sunset." Yona's eyes shone with the thought of returning to the adventure of the road.

The Queen chuckled. "What am I going to do with you once this quest is over?"

Yona laughed. "I promise I will feel more settled afterward. It's not knowing the outcome of this quest that keeps me anxious."

THEY SET OUT FOR ZION in the late afternoon, their gear and weapons strapped to Aine and Makeda. They hoped to spend as many nights as possible lodging in inns because it was still winter, and as romantic as cuddling in a tent might seem, getting ready for the day in the frigid air of dawn was always a daunting task.

"As I've had a lot of time to think," Yona broke the silence once they were a few miles out of Jazeel, "I've come to the conclusion that Jabberwock will send us either to Dziron or Kamartha."

Njima nodded. "It is true that we cannot go to Simoon although we could go to Pelf."

"I just don't see Jabberwock doing that," Yona said. "It's dangerous, and I find it difficult to believe that he would risk the life of a queen. Or a princess, for that matter."

"It does seem irresponsible," Njima agreed.

"Speaking of which, I wonder what happened with Gwrhyr. I can't wait to find out whether she was able to break her betrothal."

"Something we've both accomplished," Njima laughed. "I hope that she is also successful.

"Anyway," Yona returned to the subject at hand. "I can't decide which it will be as Eluned has reasons to go to both Dziron and Kamartha."

"Why Dziron?"

"It is where both Bonpo and Jabberwock are from, and Eluned is sentimental enough that she would want to see where they were born and raised even if she couldn't actually make it to the Peaks of Vulpecula," Yona explained.

"And Kamartha because that is where her great grandmother was from?"

"Yes," Yona said, and paused in thought. "What am I thinking?" she blurted a couple of minutes later.

"I don't know, sweetheart. What are you thinking?"

"She can do both! The only way to get to Dziron is through Kamartha. She and Gwrhyr can travel with us to Kaumari, and then go on to Jungnay."

Njima smiled. "I like the idea of travelling with them."

"So do I," Yona smiled, "because once they leave, we don't know when we'll see them again."

"I've been wondering what we are supposed to do once we get the Treasure."

Yona shook her head. "That's a good question. Do we meet back in Zion? Or, do we travel to Favonia where the Phaeton and Chessboard are being hidden? If we manage to gather the remaining Treasures, will Arawn just shrug his shoulders, and say: Okay guys, you win? I find that very difficult to believe. He's probably even angrier now than he was when I last saw him."

"I would be if someone removed my right hand," Njima said.

"Exactly! The fact that Eluned did it in self-defense would not make a difference to him. Believe me, that man is evil incarnate." She shuddered, remembering the lifeless corpse of the jewelry vendor and all the nameless maidens who had their lives taken during Arawn's sacrifices to the Sacred Three. "Treasures gathered or not, he won't accept peace willingly. And I imagine that King Hamartia will support him fully. Hevel, I am not so sure about. I suspect he's in the Awen Alliance for his own vanity, and if it no longer offers him power and prestige, he might look elsewhere for it."

"You know him better than the rest of us," Njima said. "I will take your word for it."

They rode in silence for a while before Yona spoke again. "I never got around to what I was originally thinking."

"And what is that?"

"If we're going to Kaumari, what will be our reason for travelling there? Do we go as ourselves, or will we be entertainers, or what? How do we ingratiate ourselves at Lamaxana

Palace? If King Janak and Queen Lakshmi know about the Horn of Bran, then I am sure it is inside their palace, perhaps even guarded."

"That would make the most sense," Njima agreed, "unless they have it in some sort of museum."

"I guess that's also possible," Yona sighed. "There's so much we don't know."

Njima was silent for a moment. "The question about how we intend to present ourselves is going to take some thought."

With the rapidly descending sun at their back, the women emerged from a bend in the road to see a dilapidated travellers lodge about a hundred yards ahead. Had the roadside not been planted with trees to provide a much-needed windbreak on Naphtali's high plains, they would have seen it sooner. Njima reined in Makeda, and Yona stopped beside her.

"An inn," Njima said. "Why don't we go ahead and stop for the night?"

"It's probably still a couple of hours until sunset," Yona replied.

Njima acknowledged that this was true. "But, we already have an excellent start on the journey, and I for one will be able to make an early start in the morning if I am already warm and well rested."

"You don't think it looks a little dicey?"

"Dicey?"

"I don't know—seedy? Run down?" The building didn't look exactly reputable with its peeling paint and sagging front porch.

Njima laughed. "Says the woman who is a friend of pirates and smugglers!"

Yona giggled, before sobering.

"What is it?" Njima asked when she saw a shadow slide across Yona's usually cheerful countenance.

"I guess it's just that the inn reminds me of why it was I came to be friends with pirates and smugglers."

"And why is that?"

"I'll tell you when we're in our room, but I'll need plenty of wine." Yona clucked to Aine and started toward the lodgings, but her face was grim.

THE INN WAS NICER ON THE INSIDE than they'd been led to believe by its outward appearance. Clearly all the owner's resources went toward making sure the furniture and bedding remained clean and comfortable.

The manager was friendly and accommodating, and soon Yona and Njima were comfortably ensconced in their room. They removed their boots, and settled down on a plush sofa in front of a roaring fire, and Njima poured them each a mug of mulled wine.

After a few sips and some contemplative staring into the flames, Yona finally spoke. "Remember when I was telling you about meeting that vendor from Naphtali in the marketplace in Hagafen?"

"I do," Njima said. "You said you thought he might be a spy."

"I still believe that to be true. I told him that I was in Seagirt caring for a dying innkeeper when I had to care for Libni, although I think I told him 'a pirate' and not her name. I wasn't just making a story up on the fly." She stopped for a moment and took another gulp of wine. She didn't want to get too choked up to tell the story. Njima moved closer to her and put an arm around her shoulders.

"Take your time," she said.

Yona closed her eyes for a moment, remembering, before continuing. "The truth is that I wasn't taking care of Libni. Libni was taking care of me."

That day still gave her the occasional nightmare when she was under a lot of stress. "It was my sixteenth birthday, and I was wandering the wharves in Seagirt, which was one of my favorite things to do at the time. I ran into some of my sailor friends, and they offered to buy me a couple of celebratory drinks at one of the dockside pubs—The Bloody Harpoon."

Njima wrinkled her nose. "That is a horrible name!"

"But somehow appropriate," Yona murmured. "I will freely admit I had one too many drinks. Maybe several too many. I was pretty drunk by the time I realized it was getting dark and my parents would be worried that I wasn't home yet. I thanked my friends and stumbled out the door. I hadn't gone very far before I had to duck into an alley to vomit. I was so sick. When the nausea and dizziness passed enough for me to try to stand, I realized there were three men blocking the entrance to the alley."

"Oh no," Njima's breath caught in her throat. She had a feeling she knew where this was going.

"I couldn't get past them, and I realized that the other end of the alley was blocked by the back of another building."

"They raped you," Njima stated, mouth thinning in anger.

Yona began to cry, and Njima pulled her into her arms. "And they beat me when I struggled. I was lying in the alley bleeding and weeping when Libni happened upon me. She actually picked me up and carried me to the nearest inn where she got me a room. Then she cleaned me up and bandaged my wounds and waited with me until I was sensible enough to tell her who my parents were. She sent a messenger to my father, and within half an hour he was at the inn, and Libni was gone.

"But she told me her name, and the name of her ship, and when I was able I found her and thanked her. And that's how we became friends, and eventually lovers."

"Did they find the men who attacked you?"

"I don't know for certain, but I am willing to wager that either my father or Libni took care of them. Nothing was said, and I never asked."

Njima took Yona's chin in her hand and turned her head so that she could look directly into her eyes. "Is that why you prefer women?"

"What?" Yona looked shocked. "No! I've known since . . . well, I've just always known, and it became even clearer to me when I entered puberty. I just had no interest in boys. And I don't hate men because of that, either. Most men aren't rapists."

"Enough of them are," Njima said. "I will never completely understand what you've been through, but I came close to knowing."

"I don't understand. Are you saying that you were raped as well?"

Njima's eyes flashed with anger. "No, not that. When I was thirteen I was molested." She closed her eyes and waited for the anger to fade. "By my uncle. Perhaps it would have gone farther, but as soon as he grabbed my breasts, I kicked him in the balls. And then I started screaming."

"By Omni, Njima," Yona cried, "I'm so sorry."

"Fortunately, my father believed me. He sent his brother on a diplomatic mission to Sheba, and when he returned nearly a year later, he was no longer allowed to live in Castle Indalo."

"Seems a small price to pay for what he did," Yona remarked as she leaned forward to refill their mugs. "Does anyone escape life unscarred?"

"I seriously doubt it." She accepted the mug Yona was handing her. "It is all just a question of scale, is it not? Some people are only bruised, others beaten to a pulp."

Yona took another sip of wine, pondering. "Then I suppose the same question applies to you."

"Like you, I was already old enough to know what I preferred, and it wasn't men. Perhaps that sealed it for me, and made me even more determined to break my betrothal to Prince Aahil. I decided then that I would rather remain single for the remainder of my life than live a sham marriage."

"And for that I am eternally grateful." Yona leaned forward and gave her a tender kiss. "I have never been as comfortable with another human as I am with you."

"Not even Libni or Eluned?" Njima teased her.

"There will always be a special place in my heart for them," Yona said. "But, no one can ever replace you."

THREE DAYS LATER IT WAS NEARING the end of a cold, grey, and drizzly day, and Yona was praying fervently that they would find lodgings before they were forced to set up camp for the night. There was nothing worse, she'd learned, than trying to pack up a wet tent in the frigid morning air.

Not that she could actually tell it was nearing sunset—the day was just as dark and grey as it had been when they awakened that morning in their hastily made camp—she just knew that she was miserable and could really use some warmth.

A few minutes later, a rider coming from the opposite direction appeared from around the curve in the road. As he approached, they waved him down.

He looked wet and uncomfortable himself, but he stopped.

"Can you tell us if we can reach an inn before sunset?" Njima asked.

"There's lodging about five mile back," he surveyed them with obvious doubt. "But it looks to be quite expensive. Might be cheaper to push on another five miles past that to the travellers' shelter."

"Thank you so much," Yona said. "That's good to know."

"You're most welcome," he replied over his shoulder as he spurred his horse onward.

When he was gone, Yona turned to Njima with a wide smile and hopeful eyes.

"Yes, darling," the Queen laughed. "We'll stay at the inn."

"Praise be to Omni," Yona giggled, urging Aine into a trot, "and thanks be to Queen Njima."

Within half an hour, they reached the outskirts of the village of Shillem where they found the inn the horseman had informed them about—The Gorgon's Head. It wasn't long before they were soaking in a hot tub in their own private room, washing away the dirt and cold of the past couple of days of camping.

Afterwards, Njima arranged for food and wine to be brought up to their room so that they might refresh themselves without having to get dressed for the dining room. A low couch scattered with numerous throw pillows sat in front of a combination table and brazier, and they settled themselves there while they waited for their food to arrive.

"I've been thinking these past few days about what we could do that might have us invited to the palace," Yona said.

"And have you come up with anything? I certainly haven't. I was taught to be a queen, and at this point my greatest skill is diplomacy."

"Don't underrate that," Yona said. "It might come in handy if we have to admit who we really are."

"And, I ask again, have you had any ideas?"

"I'm afraid to suggest it, honestly," Yona grimaced.

"Why is that?"

"Because it's scary and dangerous."

Njima frowned. "Scary and dangerous for whom?"

There was a knock on the door, and Yona jumped up quickly, thankful for the interruption. She rushed to the door, and ushered the servant in.

"You can place the tray right here on the table," Njima said.

The servant did so, bowed briefly, and exited the room, as Yona busied herself ladling a thick curried lentil stew with potatoes, carrots, and peas into their bowls. "This smells really good," she said, handing a bowl to Njima who had filled their goblets with wine. "To warmth!" she said, raising he glass.

"To warmth," Njima agreed, smiling inwardly. Yona was clearly stalling for time.

But they couldn't eat forever, and it wasn't too long before the tray was placed in the hallway and they were once again settled on the sofa, sipping their wine.

"Now perhaps you will finally tell me," Njima had to force herself not to smile.

Yona sighed. She couldn't avoid this forever. "Well, you know how I've been working on my archery skills while you've been busy in meetings?"

"Yes?"

"It's pretty much my only real skill," Yona continued, "and all I've been able to come up with is something that employs that skill."

"I feel strongly you're not talking about shooting at targets."

"In a manner of speaking," Yona said. "It's just that the target would have to be small."

"Or the skill would not be evident."

"Exactly."

"But what makes shooting a small target 'scary and dangerous'?"

"I think the object would have to be on someone's head," Yona finally admitted.

"That someone being me," Njima stated.

Yona felt as if she were swallowing a peach pit. She nodded but said, "Of course, we can always arrive as who we are and attempt to seek an audience with their majesties."

"True," Njima said, "but we need to be prepared to do otherwise. Why don't we start practicing before we make a final decision?" Yona's eyes widened in fear, before Njima continued, "And by practice, I mean you need to make sure you are adept at shooting small stationary objects before you attempt shooting them off my head. Did you have something in mind?"

"Perhaps some sort of fruit? I don't want to shoot anything live."

Njima laughed. "Yes, that is the most important. You don't want to shoot anything that is living." She paused. "Unless, of course, that living thing is threatening our lives."

"Like cobras?"

"Exactly. Or Aberrations, or something we have yet to meet."

Yona finally allowed the wine to relax her, leaning her head against Njima's shoulder. "Thank you." Her sigh of relief was genuine. "I was terrified that you'd think I'm insane."

"Oh," Njima laughed. "I was already well aware of that. It's one of the reasons I love you."

Yona giggled, and gently nipped Njima's ear lobe. "Insanely in love," she murmured.

THE FOLLOWING DAY WAS COLD but sunny and clear. It was decided that they would begin the routine of getting up and out as early as possible and stopping early enough that Yona could get in a half hour or so of archery practice before they had to settle down for the evening whether it be in camp or at an inn.

Inclement weather notwithstanding, she managed to become quite skillful at shooting small objects during the next three weeks. She was looking forward to demonstrating her newly acquired skills to Gwrhyr and Eluned.

But, Yona worried as they reached the outskirts of Goshen midmorning on the tenth of Neeon, the day before Eluned's birthday, what if all had not worked out as planned with breaking her betrothal with King Uriel? She prayed to Omni that it had—she just wanted her friend to be happy.

"I hope we arrive to find Gwrhyr here," Njima voiced her unspoken thoughts. "I can't imagine how the Quest can continue without him."

Yona hadn't considered that aspect of the Gwrhyr dilemma. If King Uriel, or even Eluned's father, had forbidden her to break the betrothal, the entire quest would have to be rethought.

10ᴛʜ Neeon

Eluned surveyed herself in the mirror, eyes wide and cheeks pale.

"What is it, darling?" her mother asked as she noticed the expression on her daughter's face. Ceridwen had been arranging Eluned's veil, but paused as she waited for an answer.

"I know that I was the one to suggest this, Mother, but now the idea of getting married is suddenly terrifying."

"As it should be," her mother said. "Otherwise, I might worry that you didn't know what you were about to do. Marriage is not easy."

True enough, the soon-to-be Queen of Aden mused as her mother finished adjusting the short veil, which had been a compromise on Eluned's part. She had really just wanted to wear a simple crown of flowers. Everything was wonderful at the moment because they were still blindly in love, but she knew that feeling would eventually pass. There was still so much more to learn about each other, and there would be the added burden of being a queen.

"Perfect," her mother said to the seamstress, who was putting the final stitches along the hem of the dress. "One final pressing, and it should be just right for tomorrow." The layered tea-length dress of embroidered handkerchief linen also featured an embroidered mesh overlay, a scalloped V-neck, and detailed accents of seed pearls and opalescent tube beads fashioned in the shape of flowers.

The dress was also a little more than the Princess had bargained for. It was supposed to be a simple wedding. If this was simple, she couldn't begin to imagine the spectacle the public wedding would likely be. She inwardly rolled her eyes while acknowledging that as Ceridwen's only child, she would allow her mother to enjoy this as much as possible without completely sacrificing her integrity.

Eluned removed her dress, handed it to the seamstress, and thankfully pulled on the simplest outfit in her armoire—a long, pale pink silk skirt and a chunky cable knit sweater of cream wool. It was still winter, after all, and she spent most of her time fighting the cold. And she had promised her mother that she would forgo sword practice the day before her wedding so she wouldn't risk adding any new bruises to her skin.

"You're looking a little more chipper," her mother noted once she had dressed.

"Maybe it was the dress," Eluned joked, "and the burden of what it represents."

"Very amusing, darling."

"Seriously, Mother," Eluned said, taking her mother's hand, "I do love Gwrhyr, and I do want to spend the remainder of my life with him. It just that it's an incredible responsibility." She sighed. "On the other hand, I suppose it is a responsibility that most everyone undertakes at some point."

Her mother hugged her. "That's my girl. I'm sure everything will work out exactly as it's supposed to do."

"Especially if we could get back to this quest. I know I agreed that taking a break for winter was a good idea, but now it seems like we'll never return to it."

"Patience, my dear," her mother cautioned. "Spring is but three weeks away."

"You do understand that feels like an eternity to me?" Eluned said as they left the room. When she'd set out a year ago, in three weeks she'd been attacked by a barrow wight; met Bonpo, Gwrhyr, and Chokhmah; been led to Dyrnwyn; and spent a week on the faery isle. Alternately, she had sat in a clearing for three weeks and waited on Nyx, and spent almost as long in Shamash Palace digging for the crock and dish. Amazing what might or might not happen in three weeks, she thought as she descended the staircase.

They were meeting her father, Gwrhyr, Jabberwock, Bonpo, and Brother Columcille in the sitting room to finalize plans for that evening's rehearsal and dinner. Her mother had insisted on that, as well. Bonpo had offered to prepare the meal, but Eluned said that she'd rather him be a member of the rehearsal party.

The conversation had devolved into small talk when there was a knock at the door.

Eluned glanced at the huge grandfather clock that stood adjacent to the fireplace, and her brow creased. "It's too early for lunch."

"Enter!" King Seraphim commanded, and a page scurried into the room carrying a note.

The little boy bowed, and said, "A message for the Princess Eluned, your Highness."

Eluned extended her hand, and the page approached her, holding out the note. "Thank you, Bryn," she said as she took it from him. A second later she shot to her feet with a squeal. "Yona! Njima! They're here!" She turned to Gwrhyr, eyes shining. "I am so glad they decided to arrive early. Let's go welcome them!"

Gwrhyr stood, and taking her hand, they followed Bryn out of the sitting room.

"We'll wait here until you return with them," her mother called after the couple.

Eluned was practically jogging as she made her way down to the castle gates. "What perfect timing," she told Gwrhyr, eyes still glowing with happiness. "Just in time for my birthday and our wedding."

"Nice to keep your priorities straight," Gwrhyr chuckled.

"What?" Eluned looked confused for a moment, and then laughed. "Sorry! Of course I should have named our marriage first. It was only that I was thinking that they know when my birthday is, but not about the other."

"Good point."

Yona and Njima were waiting just inside the gates, and watched their approach with joy.

"I guess that answers our question," Njima murmured as the couple, still holding hands, rushed towards them.

"He cleans up nicely," Yona remarked, noting the opulent cloak about his shoulders.

Eluned nodded to guards, and the women advanced toward them, horses in tow.

"Yona!" Eluned exclaimed, throwing herself into her friend's arms. "I can't even begin to tell you how happy I am to see you."

"I see that things worked out with you and Gwrhyr," Yona whispered.

"If by Gwrhyr, you mean King Uriel," Eluned said, stepping back, "then yes, yes it did."

"What?" Yona looked shocked, but Njima started to laugh.

"I knew something wasn't quite right," Njima said, "but Eluned was so convinced you were the son of one Uriel's lords that I couldn't not believe her."

"I never did understand," Uriel smiled, "why she didn't think, at the very least, that I was one of his lords."

"You have to blame my limited experience for that," the

Princess said. "Between my father's lords and King Arawn's, I'd only ever seen older men and women."

"Arawn doesn't have female lords," Yona said.

"No, he doesn't," Eluned frowned, 'but my father does."

"I do as well," Gwrhyr said.

"Bryn!" Eluned called to the page. The boy had led them down to the gate and was now returning to the castle just ahead of them. He turned around.

"Yes, your Highness?"

"Can you see that Aine and Makeda get taken care of?"

"Yes, your Highness." He began to walk back towards them, and Yona and Njima removed what they needed from their saddlebags.

"The rest is just camping equipment," Yona explained. "We won't need it again until we return to the Quest."

As Eluned and Gwrhyr led them towards the castle proper, Yona whispered to Njima, "Should we keep Chokhmah and Faolan a secret?"

Njima winked at her. "It's going to be her best birthday ever."

Once Yona and Njima got over their joy of seeing Jabberwock and Bonpo again, Eluned made introductions.

"That was a brave thing you did, young lady," King Seraphim told Yona after he hugged her.

Yona blushed and stuttered her thanks as Eluned agreed with enthusiasm, "Papa's right, you are the only one of us, so far, that put their life on the line to acquire one of the Treasures."

"But you were nearly sacrificed!" Yona exclaimed.

"That was incidental," the Princess argued. "Arawn didn't even know we were intending to steal the Phaeton or Chessboard or they would have been heavily guarded that day."

"She's right," Jabberwock said. "That alone gives me faith that you and Njima will be able to retrieve the Horn of Bran from Kamartha."

Yona punched Njima playfully in the bicep, "See, I told you that's where we'd be sent."

"Wat make you tink dat?" Bonpo asked.

"She said that neither you nor Jabberwock could return to Dziron, and that Eluned would probably want to go there because that's where you two are from. And, Yona surmised that Eluned would be able to kill two birds with one stone if she went to Dziron."

"What do you mean?" Eluned asked.

"Just that if you go to Dziron, you will have to travel through Kamartha," Yona explained, "and that way you'll get to see where your great grandmother was from, as well."

Queen Ceridwen looked stricken.

"I'm sorry, Mother," Eluned ran to her, and hugged her. "I was so focused on finding Nyx when we were in Dyfed that I didn't even consider making it to Portuma."

Yona looked puzzled, and Gwrhyr explained, "Queen Ceridwen is King Cian's sister."

"I see," Yona nodded in understanding. "So, he's Eluned's uncle."

"And Gittan and Bryan are her cousins," Njima filled in.

"I understand, darling," Ceridwen said to Eluned. "Both my grandmother and mother have passed on," she explained to the others, "but her interest in Queen Fuchsia always comes with a bit of a shock."

King Seraphim laughed. "I'm sorry, my dear," he told his wife before turning to the others with a wink. "My daughter seems to have inherited more of my grandmother's characteristics than her maternal grandmother's."

Queen Ceridwen sighed dand rolled her eyes, "But I love my child dearly despite that." She smiled at her daughter.

Eluned hugged her mother again. "I love you too, Mother. And I am sure that your brother bond his family will travel here for my second wedding."

"Second wedding?" Yona asked.

"I was so excited to see you that I forgot to say," Eluned hurried over to Yona and hugged her. "Gwrhyr and I are getting married tomorrow!"

"I don't know what to say," Yona looked nonplussed. "I'm still coming to terms with the fact that Gwrhyr is Uriel."

"Eluned had to come to terms with it, as well," Gwrhyr said.

"Yes, I did," the Princess agreed, "but once I realized that Jabberwock," she slid him a mock glare, "had planned it all, and that Gwrhyr was reluctant to go along with it, I forgave him.

"Because you love me," he said, and smiled at her.

"Because I love you," she repeated.

"And there were so many times I wanted to tell her," Gwrhyr added.

"Well, you certainly tried to give me some hints," she said.

"No wonder things went so smoothly in Ponike," Yona said, remembering how effortlessly they had enjoyed their visit there.

A knock on the door interrupted them. Eluned glanced at the clock again. "This time it's lunch," she said. She glanced at her mother, who nodded. "And of course you two are expected to join us." She linked arms with Yona and led the way to the dining room.

Following a warm and hearty lunch of root vegetable stew, Eluned showed Yona and Njima to their room.

"I'm heading back down to the sitting room," the Princess rolled her eyes. "I've been forbidden to do anything that I might normally do such as sword play or the like. I promised my mother that I would socialize with more than just Gwrhyr today." She laughed. "Fortunately, you have made that easy to do! Feel free to rejoin us once you've refreshed yourselves. My rehearsal will be at six o'clock tonight followed by a formal dinner."

An hour or so later, Yona and Njima were ready to return to the sitting room.

"I guess I can go one day without practice," Yona murmured as they descended the staircase.

"I agree," Njima said. "I don't think that one day will set you back that much. I'm sure there will be time tomorrow to show off your new skill."

"Very funny."

Njima laughed. "Don't listen to me. I'm just jealous."

"Jealous that I'm going to shoot something small off your head?"

"Silly! No! That I'm not that skilled at weaponry."

"I am willing to bet that if you practiced more with your throwing axe, you would become just as skilled," Yona said.

Njima shook her head as if to say she wasn't convinced.

"Seriously, Njima. You could throw axes at me. Make it look like you're going to hit me but just get really close."

"I'd rather trust you to shoot something off my head."

They reached the sitting room where Bryn stood outside, ready to open the door for them.

Eluned jumped up from the sofa she was sharing with Gwrhyr when they entered the room. "I'm so glad you're back," she said as she made her way to them. "I was trying to explain how to play tarok, but I only know how to play using tarot cards, and not an ordinary deck. I just sent Ellie down to Goshen to see if she could find us some tarot cards in town."

"Ellie?" Yona asked.

"She's one of the servants Brother Columcille is teaching."

Njima raised an eyebrow. "Teaching?"

"Yes, Gwrhyr and I discussed this back when I was waiting on Nyx. We thought it might be a good idea to offer instruction on reading and writing to those that are interested," Eluned explained.

"Interesting." Njima nodded, reflecting on that idea. "Is she the only one taking part?"

"I have eight students," Brother Columcille spoke up.

Njima turned to him. "And how is it going?"

"Rather well," he replied. "The nice thing about offering classes to those who are interested is that they are all eager learners."

Njima turned to King Seraphim. "You are comfortable with this?"

"I wasn't at first," the King admitted, "but Eluned and Gwrhyr, and even Ceridwen, convinced me it was a good idea."

"And I agreed, as well," Jabberwock said.

"Me tink so too," Bonpo added.

"It could definitely have its advantages." Njima was thoughtful. "They would have to sign the pact, of course?"

"Absolutely!" King Seraphim and King Uriel answered simultaneously. The pact was essentially a promise that knowledge wouldn't be used to the detriment of the Thirteen Kingdoms, and included a statement that using such knowledge to create anything that might harm the environment or any of the creatures living within the Thirteen Kingdoms was forbidden. Obviously, the remaining humans that populated the earth, and in this case specifically the Thirteen Kingdoms, were forced to do some things that were essentially destructive such as burning wood and coal, but limits had been set, and balance was attempted.

There was a knock at the door.

"That was quick!" Eluned exclaimed over her shoulder as she went to the door to open it for whom she assumed would be Ellie. But it was Bryn again—with another note.

She read it, and turned to the others, eyes bright. "This is going to be the best birthday ever!" She rushed out the door, Bryn scuttling after her.

Everyone looked puzzled, but Yona and Njima started laughing.

"What?" Gwrhyr asked.

"It's Chokhmah and Faolan," Yona explained. "They were supposed to arrive here today, as well."

Gwrhyr stood up and followed after Eluned, and Njima and Yona followed after him. Bonpo and Jabberwock looked at each other. Bonpo shrugged and stood.

"Fam'ry leunion," he explained to King Seraphim and Queen Ceridwen as he departed the room.

Jabberwock jumped down from the sofa he was sharing with Brother Columcille. "And it would be amiss for me to miss it," he chuckled and trotted out the door.

As with Yona and Njima, Chokhmah and Faolan waited patiently just inside the gates, bursting into wide smiles as they saw Eluned rushing towards them followed by their other compatriots.

The Princess threw herself into the Gypsy's arms when she reached the gatehouse, hugging her fiercely. "I missed you so much."

"I missed you too, my love." Chokhmah returned the hug.

As Gwrhyr was embracing Faolan, Chokhmah murmured, "I am so glad things with Gwrhyr worked out."

Eluned opened her mouth to speak, but Yona had arrived and answered for her. "If by Gwrhyr, you mean King Uriel," she repeated Eluned's words.

"What?" Faolan took a step backwards and glanced up at the taller man. "You're King Uriel?" He looked as if he'd been punched in the gut.

"It's a long story," Gwrhyr's voice was apologetic as he stepped to the side so that Eluned could greet Faolan.

"Yes, it is," Eluned hugged the Shapeshifter. "And I promise to explain everything once we are all back in the castle."

After the others had a turn to greet Chokhmah and Faolan, Eluned turned to Bryn who was already holding Fiachdubh's and Halelu's reins. "Thank you," she said, and turned to

Chokhmah and Faolan. "Grab what you need and come with us."

As they began to make their way back toward the castle, a voice rang out.

"Yer Highness!"

Eluned turned to see Ellie hurrying towards her, a small box clasped in her hand. She looked sternly at the young woman.

"Eluned," Ellie stuttered and blushed.

"You found the tarot cards," Eluned extended her hand, laughing. "Thank you so much!" She turned to Chokhmah who was gazing at her with bemusement. "If I had known you'd be arriving, we could have used yours, assuming you brought them, of course."

"They are always with me," Chokhmah patted the pouch strapped around her waist.

Faolan nodded, face serious. "I think she's married to them."

Eluned laughed. "I love you, Faolan, but I can't say that those cards haven't had a serious impact on my life."

"And on mine as well," Yona added.

"But, I really only wanted them to teach everyone how to play tarok." Eluned opened the box. "The game was a lifesaver when we were stuck in the castle at Arberth or the tent in Hardaigh, wasn't it Yona?"

"We definitely whiled away many hours playing tarok," Yona agreed as Eluned opened the box of cards.

"Look at these," the Princess said. "They're works of art."

Yona and Chokhmah moved closer to see the cards.

"Lovely," Yona agreed.

"Very beautiful," Chokhmah said.

"So yer pleased, yer, uh, Eluned?" Ellie asked, pale blue eyes wide.

"They're perfect," the Princess assured her. "How go your classes with Brother Columcille?"

"Very well," Ellie's face was glowing. "I never thought to learn so much."

"Excellent," Eluned replied. "Now, run ahead, please, and let them know we're going to need another room made ready."

"Yes'm," Ellie curtseyed and scurried away.

"She's one of the students?" Njima asked.

"Yes, she was filling in for her mother the night I met her," Eluned explained. "She seemed the perfect place to start with our plan."

Gwrhyr smiled, happy that his soon-to-be-wife had acknowledged that it was a shared vision. "Were you thinking 'our plan' when you talked to Ellie about it?"

"Of course, silly," she smiled up at him, deciding that a little white lie wouldn't hurt. "By that time I had gotten over being angry with you."

"Angry?" Chokhmah asked.

"I had already come to realize that Gwrhyr would never have deliberately misled me," Eluned explained. "He loved me too much. I knew that there must have been a reason."

"And you are going to tell us this reason?" Chokhmah asked. "I admit I realized that something was not quite right, but I could not figure out what it was other than the fact that you two were clearly meant to be together."

They had reached the entrance to the castle. "I'll tell you," the Princess said as a guard opened the door for them, "when we get back to the sitting room." She glanced down at Jabberwock, who was to her left. She tried to look angry but failed.

"I think this is unprecedented," King Seraphim said once the story had been told.

"What do you mean, Papa?" Eluned asked.

"Look at the people gathered here," he said. "We have two kings, three queens," he paused. "Rather, soon-to-be four queens, a Janawar, a Dzu-tch, a Shapeshifter, and, and I apologize, Yona. She is apparently the only non-titled and entirely human person here."

"There had to be at least one!" Eluned hugged her friend.

"Only Omni could have put this group together," Brother Columcille noted.

"I can't deny that," Jabberwock's voice was dry. It was a continual wonder to him—the variety of his fellow compatriots in the Quest.

"And," King Seraphim added, "Ceri's brother is King of Dyfed."

"My aunt is Queen of Favonia," Chokhmah said.

"It looks like all we're missing is a connection to Sheba," Yona said.

"My aunt is Queen Yobachi," Njima replied. "I should have told you that. We had a bit of a clash between our family and Adeyemi's years ago, and the betrothal between Yobachi and Adeyemi was an attempt to amend that."

"I guess it didn't work," Faolan said.

Njima shook her head. "I haven't seen Yobachi in years."

"But, we do have connections to everyone in the Triquetra Alliance," Gwrhyr said. "Too bad we don't have a connection to Tarshish."

"The only remaining neutral kingdom," Eluned murmured. "And what is the likelihood of convincing Dziron and Kamartha from withdrawing from the Awen Alliance?"

"Good question," King Seraphim said. "We may not know until the Treasures have been gathered."

Eluned glanced at the clock. She felt like the timekeeper that day, but maybe it was because she was so aware of what was going to happen the following day. "I see it's getting towards late afternoon. It may be a good time for us to rest and refresh ourselves before dressing for the rehearsal."

Queen Ceridwen nodded and stood, and Eluned opened the door, directing Bryn to show Chokhmah and Faolan to their room.

"Is that what we're calling it now?" Gwrhyr whispered in her ear as they headed toward the stairs. "Refreshing ourselves?"

Eluned's grin was positively wicked. "I haven't had a moment alone with you today."

"The rehearsal is at six o'clock in the chapel," Queen Ceridwen reminded them as they ascended the stairs.

"We'll wait at the bottom of the stairs for you, Chokhmah and Faolan, Yona and Njima, and take you there at what, a few minutes till? It only takes a minute to get there."

FOLLOWING WHAT ELUNED CONSIDERED to be the most boring hour of her life—it seemed silly to practice something so simple—the rehearsal party were finally seated in the formal dining room to enjoy the celebratory dinner. The room was far too big for their small number.

"I don't believe it," she grumbled to Gwrhyr under her breath, "it took all that just to prepare for tomorrow, and this isn't even the formal state wedding."

He kissed the top of her head. "You don't know how much it pleases me to hear you say that. I wish we could drop the second wedding."

Eluned nodded, and then smiled as a servant filled her champagne flute. She picked it up. "To the Quest! May Omni bless it!" she said once everyone's glasses had been filled.

"Omni be praised!" everyone responded.

She took a sip of the dry and icy sparkling liquid and turned to Gwrhyr. "And here's to our being together forever," she toasted him quietly.

"Omni be praised," he whispered before kissing her.

As they sipped their champagne, a small plate containing an artichoke bottom with salmon caviar, smoked salmon and dill topped with a crème fraîche was placed in front of them.

"If it seems like a salmon heavy meal tonight," Eluned

apologized in advance, "it's because that's what I requested. I love salmon."

"Not a probrem," Bonpo smiled. "I rike salmon too."

They ate their appetizers, making small talk amongst themselves, and the plates were whisked away when they were done only to be replaced with a salmon consommé, clear as the waters of the River Musk as it flowed south out of the Northern Waste.

Champagne was traded for a fruity light red wine of recent vintage. Eluned lifted a spoon to her mouth and sipped before nodding to her mother. Perfect. The light consommé was subtly flavored with salmon, asparagus and dill. The Princess had informed her mother when they were planning the event that she would be happier with light fare. Being on the road, she had said, makes you learn to appreciate needing less, and the only thing I'm craving is salmon.

Eluned sat back, already starting to get full, and knowing that they still had the main course and dessert to go. She had grown so accustomed to light rations while on the road that she had struggled for weeks with the abundance of food. The Princess had a feeling the wealthy were repeating a noxious cycle—one that would lead to unrest in those who lived on much less.

But, she tried to shrug that thought aside as it was the eve of her wedding. She had uncomplicated the meal as much as possible, but she didn't want to seem unappreciative. Her parents were happily hosting her friends after all.

As the soup dishes were removed, new glasses were filled with an oaky and buttery red wine.

"Mmm," Eluned murmured as she tasted it. "Main course next!" she announced.

But it was a light main course—a slow-cooked salmon with turnips and chard—decent winter-grown foods.

Despite the lightness of the fare, once they'd finished the

main course, most of them were inwardly groaning at the thought of dessert.

"I'm not sure I can do this," Eluned whispered to Gwrhyr.

"Welcome to being a queen," he raised an eyebrow at her. "The key is learning to eat smaller portions."

She sighed, but was polite as the sponge cake, flavored with bourbon and peaches and topped with a raspberry peach sauce, was served.

"What do I want with this?" she asked Gwrhyr. "More champagne or bourbon?'

Gwrhyr looked into her eyes, which were getting a little bit droopy. "Champagne," he said. "Bourbon will lay you out on the floor."

The Princess smiled. "And we don't want that."

"No. I never want that."

Despite the fact the temperature was leaning toward frigid, the newly reunited friends decided to take a stroll around one of the inner courtyards before retiring for the night.

"That was a wonderful dinner, Eluned," Yona said. "Thank you so much."

"So, it looks like Chokhmah and I will be heading to Simoon for the Whetstone," Faolan said, apropos of nothing.

Everyone stopped in their tracks and looked at him. His cheeks colored, but he continued, "I'm sorry, but we all know it's the only thing we've been thinking about."

"Yes." Jabberwock began to walk again, and they followed. "Obviously, you two are the only ones who can go there. And I'm sure everyone else has figured out where they're going, particularly as you all seem to be assuming that you will be travelling in your self-assigned pairs."

No one said anything because, of course, they had. Once they had figured out that Chokhmah and Faolan were the only two that could risk going to Simoon, they had naturally decided they would be travelling to the other kingdoms with their part-ners.

"You're right," Eluned stopped walking. "It was an assump-tion." She swallowed hard because she was marrying Gwrhyr, in part, the next day just so they could travel as a couple. "Of course, I could travel with Yona or Njima or even with you or Bonpo." She was trying very hard to keep the self-pity from her voice—an excess of alcohol always made her maudlin.

Jabberwock barked with laughter. "There is absolutely no reason to do that my soon-to-be-queen. Bonpo and I can nei-ther go back to Dziron or even Kamartha. No, we have to go to Pelf. And in that case, why not let you and Uriel go to Dziron or Kamartha, if you prefer."

"Actually, Njima and I would prefer to go to Kamartha. If Eluned doesn't mind?" Yona looked at her friend with plead-ing eyes.

"She's been working on her act," Njima interjected.

"But of course," Eluned said. "Act?"

"I've been working on shooting a small object off of Nji-ma's head," Yona explained.

"Smarr objec'?" Bonpo asked.

"I've been working with fruit and vegetables," Yona said. "I can show you tomorrow."

"Yes!" Faolan exclaimed. "Definitely want to see that."

Eluned stumbled, and apologized. "Sorry, I am so tired. Maybe it's time for bed? The wedding isn't until six o'clock to-morrow. We have all day to talk. And see Yona's new talent." She swayed again and Gwrhyr caught her.

"I think my beloved is feeling the effects of the day," he said. "Let's turn in, what do you say?"

"You sound like you're turning in together," Faolan was blunt.

"I love you, brother," he told him. "Never one to mince words. And you're the guy who couldn't wait to show Chokhmah your cottage."

"It's the wolf," Faolan said.

Everyone laughed.

"We talked about being apart the night before our wedding," Gwrhyr admitted, "but we decided it was ludicrous. Had we been together for months—perhaps. But it has only been weeks. It would be a shallow gesture."

"Fair enough," Faolan agreed. "So," he yawned, "I think we're all ready to turn in." And he winked at Gwrhyr.

Eluned was smiling as she linked arms with Gwrhyr and led the way back to the staircase that would take them to their rooms.

"So, is it a wolf thing or a guy thing?" she asked once they were alone in her chamber.

Gwrhyr laughed. "It's probably as much a guy thing as a wolf thing. Most of us know when to keep our mouths shut, though."

Eluned giggled. "You've got to love him, though. You always know where you stand with Faolan. I imagine he and Chokhmah are turning in about now."

"Would you like to turn in?"

"Always," she said allowing him to draw her closer.

11ᵀᴴ Neeon

"Happy Birthday, Fy Drysor," Gwrhyr said as soon as Eluned opened her eyes. "It's a beautiful day, we're getting married, and all our friends are here. Who could ask for anything more?"

"Oh, I think I know of one thing that could make this day even better."

"Yeah?" He pulled her against his chest, and whispered in her ear. "What might that be?"

She whispered something back.

THE PRINCESS FOUND HERSELF GRINNING as she dressed for the day. She hadn't yet had her first cup of coffee, but the day was already off to a good start. It was wonderful to have everyone back together again. Chokhmah seemed to wear peace and contentment like a cloak, Faolan never failed to raise a smile, Yona was so loyal in her friendship to her, and Njima approached everything with determination and certainty. "You know," she said to Gwrhyr, "I am really going to miss not being able to travel with Faolan and Chokhmah. At least we'll be with the others for awhile before we have to separate."

"I imagine we'll have to leave Bonpo and Jabberwock

when we reach Jazeel," Gwrhyr said. "I would think the easiest route to the ruins of Buta would be to get back to Kamea and head southward."

Eluned stopped in her attempt to tame her curls, and turned to look at him. She hadn't considered that. He was right, of course. It made much more sense than going through Kamartha.

"What happens once we get our designated Treasures?" Her brow creased in worry, and her voice rose an octave. "And how will we know when the others have retrieved the Treasures they're seeking?"

Gwrhyr walked over to her and put his hands on her shoulders. "Calm down, Fy Drysor. Today is not the day to worry about this."

Eluned's eyes narrowed dangerously. "Don't tell me what to do."

"I apologize," he cupped her chin in his hand and tilted her head so he could look into her eyes. "I love you, and I hate to see you getting upset on our wedding day."

Sighing, she leaned her head against his chest, and let him stroke her hair—the mother cat calming the fretful kitten. She sighed again and he kissed the top of her head.

"Is that a purr?" he teased her.

"Mmmmhmmm." She withdrew from his arms with regret. "I imagine most of our guests are waiting for us in the dining room."

"True, and this is our chance to spend as much time as possible with Faolan and Chokhmah before they head east and we head west."

"Good point," she said, pulling her hair back into a ponytail. She would have to bathe before getting ready for the wedding so no need to groom herself extensively this morning. "We don't know how long it will take us to get ready to set out."

"I think we should give ourselves at least a week to plan and prepare and spend a little time with our friends," he said.

She nodded. "I don't know why I get so frantic about this. Jabberwock thought it might take three years and it's only been one so far."

"And who would've thought," he opened the door for her, "that in one year we'd have nine of the Treasures?"

"Or that we would be getting married two years earlier than planned?"

He laughed. "Exactly. So, how can we possibly know what's in store in the coming year?"

Chokhmah and Faolan were already in the dining room when they arrived.

"Are you the first ones here?" Gwrhyr asked, but Eluned was focused on the glint in Faolan's eyes.

"I think the others have already come and gone," Chokhmah said.

Eluned pointed at Faolan. "I see that look. I know this is new to you, but it's been weeks for us."

Gwrhyr handed Eluned a cup of coffee. "What's new?"

Chokhmah chuckled. "I believe you misunderstand that sparkle in his eye, my love. We just feel as if in the short time we have been apart our little girl has fully joined the adult world. To see you two so comfortable and happy together is absolutely wonderful."

"I guess that means you're enjoying this new experience?" Faolan made an attempt at being coy.

Eluned guffawed. "I'm not sure you can say something like that!"

"Say something like what?" Yona asked as she and Njima entered the dining room.

"Faolan was intimating that I'm delighting in the fact I can no longer catch unicorns," she explained.

"Faolan!" Yona admonished him.

"What was it Leleua and Talei liked to say?" Eluned asked Chokhmah. "Hana okolele?"

Faolan looked puzzled.

"It means something like 'you are in trouble,'" Chokhmah informed him.

Laughing, Faolan shoveled up a forkful of scrambled eggs.

"And this time you can't use the wolf excuse." Eluned picked up a plate and headed to the sideboard for some food.

"I wouldn't dare," the Shapeshifter promised her.

"Would you like me to ask the kitchen to prepare you a steak?" She turned to ask him. "I'm not sure you've been eating enough protein. You're bestial tendencies are showing."

"Touché," Faolan groaned, hand over his heart, watching as Eluned carried her plate back to the table where she sat down next to Gwrhyr.

"So, what's the plan for the day?" Yona pulled out a chair next to Eluned, and moved it to the left a few inches so she and the Princess wouldn't bump elbows.

"Well I'm looking forward to seeing your new and improved archery skills," Faolan said.

"Me too," Eluned agreed as Njima took a seat across the table from Yona. "Do we need to grab some apples and pears from the sideboard?"

"That's probably a good idea," Yona said.

"Happy Birthday, Eluned," Chokhmah said. "We cannot forget that the reason we travelled here early was so we could celebrate Eluned's nineteenth birthday with her."

"Happy Birthday!" The others chorused.

"I'm so glad we could be here," Yona leaned over and hugged her friend.

Chokhmah pulled a bundle from beneath the table. "I made this for you while at Bogaine," she said, handing it to Eluned. "I know how easily you get cold."

Grinning broadly, Eluned wrapped the sea green shawl

around her shoulders. "Thank you so much Chokhmah. I love it."

A servant entered the room to refill the coffee pot, and Eluned asked her if she could round up Bryn. She wasn't sure if it was wise to favor him but he reminded her of an older Rhys, the cherubic little page who'd often waited on her in Annewven. Besides, she would be gone soon enough.

When the young man arrived, she instructed him to run to the archery range and inform the master there that they would arrive in half an hour, and would need a shooting station. "Oh, and collect Yona's archery gear from the barn on the way and leave it with the master," she said as Bryn was turning toward the door.

"Yes'm!" He bowed and retreated.

"Doesn't he remind you of Rhys?" Eluned asked Chokhmah.

Chokhmah's eyes lit up. "Yes! I was trying to figure out who he reminded me of."

"Who's Rhys?" Faolan asked.

"The page who was supposed to spy on us for King Arawn," Chokhmah explained, "but I convinced him to do otherwise."

"One of the few good memories from our time in the Court of the Crimson King," Eluned said.

"Well, I implessed!" Bonpo clapped a meaty hand against Yona's back after she had neatly skewered three apples and two pears.

"Yes," Faolan agreed. "That trick should definitely get you some attention."

"We just need to get inside the palace," Njima said. "I'd go as myself, but I am afraid that it would elicit even more attention than pretending we're performers."

"Very possibly," Jabberwock agreed. "We just don't know how tied King Janak and Queen Lakshmi are to King Arawn.

I would imagine that everyone in the Awen Alliance is on the lookout for the culprits who stole the Treasures from Arawn and Hevel."

"Dis is definry someding we mus' discuss," Bonpo said. "But right now, I 'af wedding feas' to plepale."

"Feast!" Eluned looked horrified.

Bonpo laughed. "Leally jus' anudda dinna."

"Like last night?" the Princess pressed him.

"Yes, even same people." He hugged her. "Don't worry, Plincess."

"Won't be calling her Princess for much longer," Gwrhyr said.

"Queen Eluned," Eluned grimaced as she said it. "Why does that sound so weird to me?"

"Queen 'Leened," Bonpo chuckled. "Queen 'Leened, Queen 'Leened. It rike one word."

"The way you say it, yes," Eluned agreed. "It sounds stilted when I say it."

Yona giggled. "It's almost like a tongue twister. Say it ten times fast."

Several of them tried and all failed miserably.

She couldn't help but laugh at their attempts. "Fortunately, I am perfectly fine with all of you continuing to call me Eluned."

"So, Bonpo," Faolan changed the subject, "what are you making for the wedding feast?"

The giant bellowed laughter. "You don' know," he quipped using one of Jabberwock's favorite expressions.

"Really?" Faolan was flabbergasted. "It's a secret?"

Eluned punched him playfully in the bicep. "A surprise, not a secret! Bonpo and I discussed it, of course, and we decided to keep it simple but different. You'll just have to wait and see."

"As long as it's meat," he attempted to sound grumpy, but he couldn't hide the slight crinkle around his eyes.

"Seriously, Faolan, we can get you some meat right away if you need it," Eluned said.

Faolan blushed, and Chokhmah rushed to say. "It might help, actually. He hasn't had the chance to hunt in a couple of days."

"Why didn't you say so this morning when I offered? The cook would have been happy to fix you some beef or lamb. Considering you eat it rare, it wouldn't have taken any time." Eluned scowled at him.

"I thought I was fine, honestly," he admitted, "and I knew we needed to be at the range within half an hour, but yes, if you could arrange that for lunch I would be eternally grateful."

"Ask and thou shalt receive." Eluned winked him. "Let's head back to the castle," she announced. "I can put in that order, and show you around before lunch."

"Do we get to see the legendary clearing where you met Jabberwock?" Yona asked.

Eluned snickered remembering Gwrhyr's first impression of the giant boulder. "Absolutely, but let's just say the rock he was sitting on has shrunken over time."

"Nothing ever appears the same as it did when we were children, does it?" Chokhmah mused.

"Even our favorite flavors change," Eluned agreed.

"That is so true," and variations thereof issued from the mouths of her friends.

"I am absolutely appalled at some of the things I was willing to eat when I was young," Gwrhyr said.

"Me too!" Njima agreed. "I was addicted to these incredibly sweet cookies the kitchen produced." She paused, rethinking what she had just said. "That sounds terrible. The Kitchen. But unlike some royalty, I was absolutely not allowed there. It was unseemly. I would change that in a heartbeat . . ."

". . . if we had our own kids?" Yona said.

"Yes," Njima agreed, taking her hand. "If we have our own children."

They wandered back to the castle proper, and the Princess signaled Bryn to her side. "You have been so helpful these past couple of days," she told him. "Can you do something else for me?"

Bryn's eyes widened in surprise because one did not turn down Princess Eluned of Zion.

"It's not difficult," she assured him. "I just need you to let, by Omni, what's her name, um . . ."

"Sh," Bryn began to speak.

Eluned clapped a hand over his mouth. "No, I can remember this. Sioned. It's Sioned. Can you ask Sioned to make sure that a steak," she glanced at Faolan. He nodded. "A steak cooked rare is prepared for Faolan at lunch?"

She had already removed her hand and Bryn answered in the affirmative before trotting off towards the kitchens.

"I've spent a lot of time in the kitchens over the years," Eluned explained, "but it's been awhile."

"Too much time in the kitchens, I think," Jabberwock muttered remembering when he learned just how foul her mouth could get when they had crossed the Mountains of Misericord the previous year.

They spent the next couple of hours touring Castle Mykerinos before meeting the King and Queen and Brother Columcille for lunch.

Following lunch, Queen Ceridwen suggested that the soon-to-be-not-princess take a nap before the evening's festivities.

"Seriously, Mother? Nap? My friends are here!" Eluned complained. "What are they going to do?"

"Honestly," Queen Njima said. "I could use a bit of down time, myself. It might be wise for all of us to take a break for a couple of hours. You're getting married tonight, Eluned. That's a once-in-a-lifetime event."

Eluned sighed. "You're right. We have time. It's just that I'm so excited that you're here.

"And we are truly happy to be here," Chokhmah said.

"That's an understatement," Faolan interjected. "The four of us are here because Chokhmah missed you so much." He looked at her as if to dare her to say he was wrong.

"Faolan is correct. I was ready to see you all again. It felt as if we had been apart for a very long time," Chokhmah said. "Yet, in saying that, I also know that it would be wise to rest and prepare ourselves for this evening. You are getting married, my loves," she looked at Gwrhyr and Eluned, "and that makes me very happy."

"As long as you all are fine with it," Eluned stood, "then I am. See you at the wedding?"

THE GROUP MET AT THE BOTTOM of the stairs and reached the Chapel just prior to six o'clock. Eluned and Gwrhyr were nowhere to be seen.

"Should we start calling him King Uriel?" Yona whispered to Jabberwock.

"Gwrhyr is fine for now," he whispered back.

They seated themselves close to the front because it was a small wedding. Other than the six of them, only Eluned's parents were in attendance as Brother Columcille was performing the service.

Chokhmah smiled to herself. Two of her closest friends were getting married and the Questers were lucky enough— Omni again?—to share in the experience. Her own marriage to Yitzak had been one of the happiest days of her life. She barely remembered the ceremony, but the bliss that followed was something she would never forget.

Soon an acolyte entered the incense-scented chapel. Bowing before the altar, she approached it and lit the candles before quietly retreating back down the aisle.

Jabberwock jumped down off his seat and trotted to the back. A few minutes later, Gwrhyr entered the chapel dressed in a crimson jacquard jacket with long tails over fitted black trousers, a golden crown in a knotwork pattern studded with rubies on his gleaming dark brown hair. Jabberwock walked down the aisle at his side, and they stood at the front, and waited. Brother Columcille soon made his entrance and stood in front of the small congregation.

Music began to play. Something ancient, Chokhmah thought. Perhaps Pachelbel's Canon in D? They turned to see Eluned processing down the aisle in a handkerchief linen tea dress with the half veil held in place by her Princess tiara—a delicate concoction of platinum encrusted with diamonds and seed pearls. She held onto King Seraphim's strong arm with one hand while the other clutched a small bouquet of hothouse flowers—fragrant creamy gardenias, pale pink roses, and lavender. They waited a couple of beats as everyone stood, and then walked slowly down the aisle. Both Eluned and Gwrhyr appeared to be struggling with their emotions.

"DEARLY BELOVED," Brother Columcille began, "we are gathered together here in the sight of Omni, and in the face of this congregation, to join together this Man and this Woman in holy Matrimony; which is an honorable estate, instituted of Omni in the time of man's innocency," he began the service.

Gwrhyr gazed down at his beloved. He missed some of what was being said, but Brother Columcille continued, "I Require and charge you both, (as ye will answer at the dreadful day of judgement, when Yeshua shall return, and the secrets of all hearts shall be disclosed) that if either of you know any impediment, why ye may not be lawfully joined together in Matrimony, ye do now confess it. For be ye well assured, that so many as are coupled together otherwise than Omni's Word doth allow, are not joined together by Omni, neither is their Matrimony lawful."

The couple looked at each other, eyes wide. They had been through this, and though they felt secure that the answer was

NO, the seriousness of what they were doing made them waver a second. Then Gwrhyr smiled and nodded, and Eluned grinned at Brother Columcille, who smiled broadly in return. He had always been fond of the Princess.

"Wilt thou have this woman to thy wedded wife, to live together after Omni's ordinance in the holy estate of Matrimony? Wilt thou love her, comfort her, honor, and keep her, in sickness and in health; and, forsaking all others, keep thee only unto her, so long as ye both shall live?" he asked Gwrhyr.

"You don't have to ask me twice," King Uriel improvised, and turned to the Princess. "And you?"

"You don't have to say it," she told Brother Columcille. "The answer is yes, I do, I will."

Brother Columcille shook his head, trying not to laugh. "Who giveth this woman to be married to this man?"

King Seraphim announced that he did, and released Eluned's arm, and returned to the pews.

"This is it," Eluned whispered.

"Are you ready, Fy Drysor?" Gwrhyr asked

"Yes." Her green eyes were opalescent as he lifted her veil.

After joining their right hands together, Brother Columcille began, "Now, repeat after me: "I, Uriel, take thee Eluned to my wedded wife," he paused and Gwrhyr repeated what he'd said. "To have and to hold, from this day forward, for better for worse." Pause, repeat. "For richer for poorer, in sickness and in health, to love and to cherish, till death us do part, according to Omni's holy ordinance; and thereto I plight thee my troth." As Gwrhyr finished the words, they loosed hands briefly before Eluned took Gwrhyr's right hand with her right.

In the pews, Faolan glanced at Chokhmah out of the corner of his eye. She seemed entranced, and he wondered, not for the first time, if he should ask her to marry him. It was only the uncertainty of the Quest that had prevented him from doing so. They would soon be heading into real danger, and he didn't want to risk making her a widow once again.

Eluned was repeating the words Gwrhyr had said, and Faolan was drawn back to the ceremony as they unclasped hands again. Gwrhyr pulled the engraved gold band from his pocket.

Brother Columcille nodded at Gwrhyr who spoke, "With this ring I thee wed, with my body I thee worship," Gwrhyr paused as Eluned bit her lip and tried to control herself. He smiled, and continued, "and with all my worldly goods I thee endow." Eluned grinned at him. She couldn't care less about his 'worldly goods'. He continued: "In the Name of the Omnipotent, and of the Omniscient, and of the Omnipresent. Amen."

As the Princess repeated the same words, sliding a similarly engraved band onto the ring finger of Gwrhyr's left hand, Njima chanced a look at Yona. If they made it through this quest, would she be allowed to marry this woman, she wondered. Could she as queen set that precedent?

Yona felt herself being watched and turned her gaze to Njima. "I love you," she mouthed.

Njima smiled at her and squeezed her hand.

At the altar, Gwrhyr and Eluned knelt. "Let us pray," Brother Columcille said. "O Eternal Omni, creator and preserver of all mankind, giver of all spiritual grace, the author of everlasting life; Send thy blessing upon these thy servants, this man and this woman, whom we bless in thy Name; that, as Yitzak and Rivkah lived faithfully together, so these persons may surely perform and keep the vow and covenant betwixt them made, whereof these Rings given and received are a token and pledge; and may ever remain in perfect love and peace together, and live according to thy laws; through Omni, the Three-in-One. Amen."

The congregation murmured 'amen' and Columcille continued, "Those whom Omni hath joined together let no man put asunder."

Yona pressed a finger alongside her nose in an attempt to keep from shedding tears. This could be her wedding to King

Hevel, but instead she was sitting next to the woman she loved. It seemed too good to be true, and she said a silent prayer to Omni that It would keep her and her beloved safe while they finished the Quest.

"Forasmuch as Uriel and Eluned have consented together in holy wedlock," Brother Columcille was saying, "and have witnessed the same before Omni and this company, and thereto have given and pledged their troth either to other, and have declared the same, by giving and receiving of a Ring, and by joining of hands; I pronounce that they be Man and Wife together, In the Name of the Omnipotent, and of the Omniscient, and of the Omnipresent. Amen."

"Amen!" shouted everyone in the congregation. And before Brother Columcille proceeded with the final blessings, Bryn appeared carrying a small satin pillow upon which sat a sparkling coronet. Uriel removed the tiara from Eluned's head and replaced it with the crown that signified that she was now Queen of Aden. The gold and platinum coronet shimmered with diamonds and rubies and featured a phoenix crafted of the same jewels at its apex.

An organ began to play, and taking each other's hand, Eluned and Gwrhyr recessed down the aisle stopping at the door of the chapel to speak to everyone as they left.

Bonpo was the first to hurry out, stopping to clasp each of them in a quick bear hug. "Conglaturations! I go see if dinna leady. Champagne an' fluit in sittin' loom," he said in a rush, and started to leave before turning around and pointing a finger at Eluned. "Don' eat too much!"

"Yes, sir," she smiled at him. "I am anticipating what you've been working on all day. I'll only have a strawberry or two."

"Good," he said and disappeared down the hallway.

King Seraphim and Queen Ceridwen were next. "My daughter the queen," Seraphim hugged Eluned. "Who knew it would happen this soon!"

"I might be more surprised than you are, Papa," Eluned laughed.

Gwrhyr reached out a hand for a shake, and Seraphim hugged him as well. "I now have a son," he said, "and one that I have the utmost respect for."

"Thank you, Sir," Gwrhyr said. "I appreciate that."

"And I echo those feelings," Queen Ceridwen said. "I have to finally admit that Jabberwock was correct; that this was something my daughter needed."

Eluned nodded. "Yes, Mother. I did need it. Never in my wildest dreams could I have imagined what has happened in the past year."

"Neither could I," Gwrhyr said.

The rest of their friends agreed. They were all in far, far different and much better places than they had prepared to be a year previous.

A year ago, Chokhmah had been looking forward to her Pomona and finally releasing Yitzak and mourning for him so that she could go on with her life. But what did that mean? Where would she be today if she were still with her gypsy family? She had no idea, but probably sitting lonely in her vardo as none of the few single men in the tribe appealed to her.

Yona had been preparing to go to Arberth and Castle Emrys where she would be forced to socialize with people she didn't particularly like. By now, she would have set a date for her dreaded wedding to Hevel. How easy would it have been, in actuality, to find a lover or love once she was married? She was so glad she hadn't had to find out. There was very little chance she would have met Njima had she married Hevel.

Faolan would have continued his shifts of spying and working at the Bogaine horse farm, retiring each night to his lonely Rose Cottage. Would he have found someone he trusted and desired and loved as much as Chokhmah? He seriously doubted it. Would he have made friends with people that he now felt tied to for life, who loved him for who and what he was? An icicle on a Favonian beach had a better chance.

Njima, too, felt the force of the special comradeship. She'd never had friends, never truly hoped to fall in love. And yet here she was—on a quest that was exquisitely exciting compared to the responsibilities of being a queen, and she was travelling with a woman that loved her, that trusted her, and whom she was growing to love more and more each day as she let go of her fears and put her faith in Yona's love for her.

"Let's retire to the sitting room," Eluned announced as soon as everyone had been properly hugged. "There's champagne and fruit there, and we will be informed when Bonpo's scrumptious dinner is ready."

NOT HALF AN HOUR LATER they were sitting in the much more comfortable private dining room. Eluned had complained the previous night that it felt like they were eating in a cavern and as the wedding party was so small, Queen Ceridwen had acquiesced to her daughter's request to host the wedding meal in a smaller, more family-like, room.

"I'm so excited," Eluned raised her glass of champagne to Gwrhyr. It was her intention to drink nothing but champagne that evening. "This meal should be lighter than last night but probably taste even better."

"I trust you and Bonpo," Gwrhyr clinked her glass with his. "You two have great taste."

Servants soon entered the room and began filling their plates with thin slices of roasted duck with crispy skin, steamed pancakes, sautéed scallions, fresh cucumber sticks, pickled radishes and a sweet bean sauce.

Once it was served, Bonpo took his place and explained how they were supposed to consume this delicacy.

"Put rittre bit in each pancake. Loll up and eat," he said, demonstrating.

They all constructed a stuffed pancake, and Bonpo, who was waiting, said, "To Gooheel and 'Leened, may dey rove arways!"

"Thank you, Bonpo," Eluned smiled at him and took a bite, nodding her approval as she chewed.

After they had eaten for a while, chattering amongst themselves, Eluned spoke. "Save room for dessert. It's very rich, but it's my special request—not your traditional wedding cake."

Faolan took another couple of bites of duck, winked at Eluned and pushed his plate away. "I trust you, Princess. Wait! I mean Queen. Queen Eluned! How about that? I would never have guessed that Gwrhyr is a king. But then, neither did you."

"I love you, too, Faolan," Eluned winked back. She was a queen now. Queen Eluned of Aden. She was fine with it, but she didn't want to think about it too much until after they'd retrieved the Treasures.

A couple of servants entered and removed their plates as two more replaced them with smaller dessert plates. Then the pièce de résistance was brought in and placed in front of the new Queen.

"Oh, Bonpo," she bit her lip to keep it from trembling. "You even made it in the shape of a heart!" Before her sat a magnificent Coeur a la Crème dripping with a raspberry and orange liqueur sauce.

Gwrhyr leaned over and whispered into her ear. "I should have known it would involve raspberries."

Eluned laughed. "How many nights did we eat raspberries in our camp at Ardaigh?"

"Until they ran out." Faolan's voice was dry.

Eluned giggled. "I know you weren't thrilled, Faolan. Not everything is protein. But I adore raspberries and it is my wedding—so let us partake of this Coeur a la Crème that Bonpo has so graciously constructed for me. And may all of our loves stay true."

"Amen!" Everyone agreed.

12ᵗʰ NEEON

"Well, at least Faolan won't be able to harass us about our wedding night," Eluned said as they wandered downstairs the following morning for breakfast.

Gwrhyr chuckled. "I'll admit that when it comes to sex, he has a tendency to err toward his inner adolescent."

"Doesn't he seem a little old for that?"

Gwrhyr glanced around before answering quietly. "We know he said he had never been in love before he met Chokhmah, but we don't really know what might have happened to him before we met him. Not everyone gets raised like you did. Even I lost my parents before I was fourteen."

Eluned bit her lip. She hadn't thought of that. "Perhaps it was something too painful to admit." She paused for a second, reflecting. "I've never lost anyone dear to me, never had my heart broken." She glanced at him sharply, and said pointedly, "And I hope I never will."

"So do I," he agreed, "so do I."

WHEN THEY ARRIVED, everyone was in the dining room except for Faolan.

"Good morning everyone!" Eluned said, surveying the dining room table. "Where's Faolan?"

"He is not yet back from his run," Chokhmah said.

"Run?" Eluned asked, and then understood. "Oh. Run. As in wolf run."

"Yes, there is not enough room within the walls of the castle so he must go to the forest outside of Goshen," Chokhmah explained.

Eluned nodded, and headed toward the sideboard where Gwrhyr was pouring their coffee. Other than the acre or so of forest that contained the glade where she once met with Jabberwock, there wasn't much unused land within the walls of Castle Mykerinos. Even her father's soldiers did their more extensive training at a facility between Goshen and the village of Roodspire to the southeast.

Faolan would probably be glad to return to the road although Eluned really hated that he and Chokhmah would be heading in the opposite direction from them. She understood that splitting up to retrieve the remaining Treasures made the most sense, but she was going to miss the camaraderie of travelling together. She didn't even want to think about what would happen once they finished the Quest—when they would once again go their separate ways and return to normal life, whatever that might turn out to be.

Eluned looked down at the gorgeous spread of food on the sideboard, and her stomach twisted. Suddenly she didn't have much appetite. She put her plate down and returned to the table with just her cup of coffee.

Gwrhyr frowned at her. "You're not eating?"

"I'm not hungry yet," she said. "Maybe after I've had some coffee."

Jabberwock surveyed the Princess. No, he thought with amusement, Queen. He had seen that petulant glint in her eyes many times over the years. "Life can't be a constant adventure," he remarked to the table in general although his comment was clearly aimed at Eluned.

"I know," she sighed, "but when the Quest is over and we all return to our various Kingdoms, we won't have anything to look forward to."

Yona and Chokhmah nodded in understanding. Their lives had been the most affected by this journey—they could not return to their past lives and had yet to establish a new normal.

"That in itself could be an adventure," Jabberwock said.

"What could be an adventure?" Faolan asked as he entered the room, cheeks and nose red from the cold.

"Creating a new life once the Quest has ended and peace is restored," Jabberwock explained. "Some of us have lives to return to—Uriel and Njima must return to ruling their Kingdoms, Faolan to his horse farm, and even Bonpo to his inn. Eluned is going to have to learn what it means to be Queen, but Chokhmah, Yona and I will need to decide how to proceed with our lives."

Njima glanced at Yona, eyes wide.

"Don't worry," Yona assured her. "If we survive this, of course I will want to remain with you. I will just have to figure out what my role is. I'll have to do something—sitting around all day is out of the question."

Njima nodded. "Fair enough. That is certainly something we can look into once we return to Naphtali."

"I assume you feel the same way?" Faolan asked Chokhmah.

"Knitting in front of the fire is a pleasant distraction, but not a way in which I can spend the remainder of my life," she said. "So yes, as Yona noted, if we survive this, then I must find a place at Bogaine that involves more than waiting."

"Chokhmah makes a good point," Jabberwock said. "We are all about to set out on the most dangerous part of the

Quest, and I hate to say this, but I am fairly certain that not all of us will return."

The Questers digested this news silently for a moment.

"That may be true, Jabb," Eluned finally spoke, "but if we head off assuming that we might die won't it be more dangerous than assuming we will all live?"

"Yes, definitely, assume that you will live," Jabberwock agreed, "but remain alert to the fact that something could go wrong, and you will greatly increase your chances of living."

"Then assuming we all live," Gwrhyr said, "we would love to have you at Castle Bennu. It is our hope that someday we will have children, and we would love for you to be a part of their lives. Not to mention the fact that I can always use your wise council."

Eluned agreed. "I can't imagine you not being a part of our lives, Jabb."

"And I fine wid letulnin' to da inn," Bonpo said. "P'laps leady fol mol peacefur rife by den."

"Then maybe it's time we talk about the next part of the Quest," Eluned suggested. "Do we want to do that now, or should we meet in the sitting room in half an hour or so?"

"The latter," Gwrhyr said. "You still need to eat something, and I want another cup of coffee."

A spark of anger ignited in Eluned's eyes, and Gwrhyr took her chin in his hand. "I'm not telling you that you must eat something," he explained. "I'm just saying that you need to eat some breakfast, Fy Drysor. We will begin travelling again soon, and you know that it's not always possible to find food. It would be best to start out as healthy as possible."

"He is correct, my love," Chokhmah smiled. "You and Gwrhyr have the farthest to travel, and not one of us knows what we will face when we enter kingdoms in the Awen Alliance."

"And we'll only have Bonpo to cook for us as far as Jazeel,"

Yona added. "With six of us travelling together, we can't guarantee that there will always be space for us at the inns along the way."

Eluned rolled her eyes and raised her hands in surrender. "All right! All right! I'll eat something." She stood and approached the sideboard again. This time, the sight of all the food didn't turn her stomach, and she filled her plate with smoked salmon, scrambled eggs, and toast before refilling her coffee.

"Is this satisfactory, Sir?" she asked her husband, setting the plate down on the table.

Gwrhyr laughed and stood. "I love you too, Fy Drysor." He was still chuckling as he refilled his mug. He hoped that he would always find humor in his wife's rebellion against even minor authoritarianism. He really needed to learn to phrase his demands as a question. Perhaps he should have said, 'wouldn't you like to eat some breakfast?' or 'don't you think eating something would be a good idea?'

THE GRANDFATHER CLOCK in King Seraphim's sitting room was just chiming nine o'clock as the group slowly drifted into their new meeting space. There were too many of them now to meet in Eluned's room. The final meeting in her room at Whanga Palace had been tight. She and Yona had needed to sit on her bed. The addition of Faolan and Njima had shifted the balance.

As soon as everyone was settled, Eluned began to speak. "We know that everyone has been thinking about this, right? Not only have we seen what Yona and Njima plan to do, but we've all figured out where it is we'll be going."

"It didn't make sense to split up any of the couples," Jabberwock said, "because we all know how dangerous it's going to be to seek the Treasures within Awen Alliance kingdoms, with the exception of Pelf, of course."

"And that Kingdom has its own dangers," Eluned said, remembering the Aberrations they had faced in Kamea, and the fact that Jabberwock had lost his mate, Kamali, in the Devastation of Pelf.

"It may be cliché but it's a fact," Jabberwock said, "forewarned is forearmed. Kamali and I were so frantic to escape Dziron that we let down our guard in Pelf. We knew it was supposed to be dangerous, but we didn't take into account just how dangerous."

"Dis time, betta plepale," Bonpo said. "Now we know what ta rook fol."

"And obviously, Chokhmah and I are the ones who need to go to Simoon," Faolan said. "Plus there's the added advantage that I speak the language, which I've been teaching to Chokhmah since we realized that we have to go to Sigwald."

"I still think it prudent that I disguise myself as much as possible," Chokhmah added.

"We thought long and hard," Faolan began, and stopped as Eluned raised an eyebrow. He stifled a laugh. "And you make fun of me!"

Eluned found herself blushing. "I've spent too much time around you, Faolan."

"Blame me if you want to," he laughed, "but I think your great grandmother's novels are to blame. Poker faces and gunslingers and whatnot."

Eluned giggled. "You could be right."

"As I was saying," Faolan continued, "before I was so crudely interrupted,"

"I would hardly call a raised eyebrow crude," Eluned cut him short for real this time, "or an interruption. You could have ignored it."

Faolan regarded her silently for a moment. "Seriously? Me?"

Eluned laughed.

"Children, children!" Jabberwock admonished them.

"They are acting like siblings, are they not?" Chokhmah turned to Jabberwock with a smile.

"He's the older brother I never had," Eluned laughed, "and I wouldn't trade him for anything!"

"Nor I, you," Faolan said. "Anyway, after thinking about it," he rushed on. "Chokhmah and I decided that we would try to enter Simoon in character."

"And what would those characters be?" Njima asked.

"I would be a blind healer," Chokhmah said, "and Faolan will be my guide wolf."

"Why blind?" Yona asked.

"Because we decided it would be safer if I was in wolf form when we arrive in Simoon," Faolan explained. "That way I don't risk getting caught shifting."

"If he is discovered with me while in man form," Chokhmah said, "it is less suspicious than if he is discovered with me in wolf form."

"I see," Njima was nodding her head. "You are much more likely to meet a man than a wolf once you have entered the kingdom."

"Exactly," Faolan said.

"So, I will be a healer," Chokhmah continued, "because that is something I can do, but if I am blind it will necessitate that I wear dark glasses."

"Which will help disguise you," Eluned said, "just in case Hamartia, Foehn, or Hilya saw you the brief time they were in Prythew."

"I am fairly certain that they did not," Chokhmah said, "but still I do not wish to give them anything that might make them have associations with gypsies."

"Whom I'm pretty certain they don't tolerate in Simoon," Jabberwock agreed.

"Among others," Njima's voice was cold.

"They are definitely not known for their tolerance," Gwrhyr agreed.

"How we'll get into Castle Rodolf is another question entirely," Faolan said. "We will find a place in Sigwald, and hopefully Chokhmah will make a name for herself as a healer, and in the meantime, we'll be surveying the lay of the land."

"There is so much we will not know until we arrive there," Chokhmah agreed.

"I guess you'll also have to change your name," Eluned mused.

"Yes," Chokhmah agreed. "They may not have seen me, but they will most definitely have heard my name. I will probably use Parisa."

"It is your name, after all," Yona said. "I guess all of us, excluding Jabberwock and Bonpo, will have to use assumed names."

"At least until we know how Kamartha and Dziron are disposed to the Triquetra Alliance," Gwrhyr said.

Njima agreed. "We can't take the risk of letting them know who we truly are unless they seem willing to negotiate. I pray only that our performance draws the attention of someone in Lamaxana Palace or we, too, will have to devise an alternate plan."

"I'm really hoping," Eluned began but was interrupted by Faolan raising a hand and shushing them. "What is it?" she whispered as he stood and made his way quietly toward the door. Just like a wolf, she thought, as he pointed to the doorknob, which was turning very slowly.

When he reached the door, Faolan pulled it open quickly to reveal a tall, slender man in the act of taking a step backwards from the door. Eyebrows arched and overly widened eyes revealed his surprise.

Dressed in the garb of a deliveryman, he stuttered, "I was trying to find the kitchens."

After giving him directions, Faolan shut the door before turning to his friends with a frown. "That was odd."

Njima was scowling. "Especially considering I told him how to get to the kitchens when I came down for breakfast this morning."

"That's right," Yona said. "I thought he seemed kind of scrawny for a deliveryman."

Faolan pulled the door back open and looked out into the hallway—the man was nowhere to be seen. Turning back towards the others, he said, "Keep your eyes peeled. Something isn't right about this."

"Did you see how dark his eyes were?" she asked Gwrhyr who was sitting next to her. "He reminded me of the scullion the night we arrived at the inn in Mjijangwa. Wasn't he Annewvenese?"

"Yes," it was Gwrhyr's frowned, remembering. "We'd better keep an eye on him."

"Do you think he's a spy?" Yona asked, taking Njima's hand, brow furrowing with worry.

"I wouldn't be surprised," Jabberwock said. "If you see him again, call for a guard."

Bonpo grunted. "Dis not good."

"It's hard to believe we have a spy in the castle," Eluned said. "How do we know who to trust?"

"I'll speak with your father," Gwrhyr said. "We need to make sure that only people known to those who work within the Castle are allowed to enter it."

"At least until we leave," Jabberwock agreed.

"I suspect he is trying to find out where we're going next," Faolan said.

"Do you think he was listening at the door?" Njima asked.

Faolan shook his head. "It seems risky to loiter by the door, but maybe he couldn't think of any other way. I believe this room is pretty sound tight. I've never heard the approach of someone, just the knock, and my hearing is excellent."

"'Ow you see dolnob movin'?" Bonpo asked.

"I heard someone rattle the knob," Faolan said.

"Even I didn't hear that," Jabberwock said, "nor did I sense anything."

"Probably warned about your abilities," Gwrhyr said.

"Just in case," Eluned said, lowering her voice, "we can talk more quietly. Agreed? Back to business?"

Everyone nodded.

"Now what was I saying?" She closed her eyes trying to remember. "Oh, yes, I was hoping that I can somehow gain the confidence of Princess Xiang," she said. "I feel certain a sixteen-year-old will not want to get married to a man more than twenty years her senior. It's difficult enough being told you must marry someone near your own age. Sorry Gwrhyr," she patted his arm. "I was lucky, but that type of age difference seems almost abusive to me. I also recognize that I could be wrong. Perhaps Xiang has met Aahil, and simply adores him. Either way, I hope to find out. It might be that I will have to be someone else when I do, and not Queen Eluned of Aden."

"Why do you have to gain her confidence?" Yona asked.

Eluned thought for a second. "I have to gain her confidence in order to find out how she really feels. If she is rebelling against the idea of marrying Aahil, I can confess who I am, and offer to help her break her betrothal."

"You were willing to do it for me," Gwrhyr said. "That is, me as Gwrhyr. Are you thinking as Queen of Aden you can negotiate with King Zhang and Queen Ling?"

"Not them, no," Eluned made another attempt to explain. "But I think I can go to Aahil, first, and then perhaps his parents, and negotiate with them. Was it Aahil or King Dodi and Queen Chahindra who were upset when you broke the betrothal, Njima?"

"It was his parents," Njima said. "I never heard from Prince Aahil."

"He may not be interested in marrying a woman that

much younger than he is," Eluned continued. "Obviously it will all be a moot point if Princess Xiang is anticipating marrying him."

"That's all well and good, Eluned," Jabberwock said, "but I'm not understanding just what this has to do with the Treasure."

"Absolutely nothing," she admitted.

"Then why are you discussing it?" Jabberwock bared his teeth at her.

"Because it's important to me, and it has the added benefit of finding an ally inside the palace assuming it works," she explained.

Jabberwock rolled his glassy eyes, and snorted. "That is neither here nor there to us. I think . . ."

"Wat da pran to get Tleasule?" Bonpo interrupted their spat.

"The Mantle of Arthur and Eluned's ring," Gwrhyr replied.

"Why not?" Faolan agreed. "You can do just about anything when you're invisible. "Wouldn't it make more sense, though, for you to lend one of us either the mantle or the ring?"

"I see your point," Gwrhyr said. "I guess I was so wrapped up in it being a team effort to retrieve the Treasure that it didn't even occur to me. The only drawback is that it would put the entire responsibility into one person's hands."

"In that case, we would have to take the cloak," Eluned said.

"Why is that?" Faolan asked.

"Because we have to steal the Cauldron," Eluned began before standing abruptly, and pulling her leather pouch out from under her sweater. "Watch this." She removed the moonstone, and held it in the palm of her right hand, disappearing before their eyes. She walked over to one of the coffee tables and lifted Chokhmah's teacup.

There was a collective moan of understanding. The cup

appeared to be floating in the air. Eluned put the teacup back on the table, and then deposited the moonstone back in the pouch. "It would look pretty strange to see a floating cauldron, wouldn't it?" she said when she reappeared.

Chokhmah nodded. "Yes, I see. The Whetstone or the Horn might be hidden in one's clothing, but not the Cauldron."

"But, I imagine if you hid it beneath the mantle, it would remain invisible," Eluned said.

"Are you willing to part with the ring, Princess?" Jabberwock asked.

"That's Queen Eluned to you," Eluned said, face stern, then laughed. "Am I willing to part with it? No, of course not. Will I part with it? Absolutely. It would be selfish not to, and I know that whomever carries it with them and wears it, will treat it with care."

"Then I suggest lending it to Chokhmah," Yona said.

"I agree," said Njima. "She and Faolan are heading to the most dangerous kingdom. They need every piece of luck they can get."

"Despite the ability to be invisible, I still strongly recommend that each of you come up with a backstory and new identity," Jabberwock said.

"Yes, bes' not be suspicious," Bonpo said. "Udderwise, dey watch you rike hawk."

"But I don't even know what kind of backstory to come up with," Eluned complained. "Unfortunately, my talents are those of a princess and not someone who might wish to procure a job."

"That is not completely true, my love," Chokhmah said. "You undersell yourself. I have heard you play the harpsichord. You could give lessons."

"Or even harp or drawing lessons, " Gwrhyr added.

"Or," Eluned's eyes lit up. "We could be wandering minstrels. I play the harp much better now." At Gwrhyr's insistence, she had continued to practice since leaving Hardaigh Forest behind. She sighed. Now that was a romantic image—two wandering minstrels, young and in love. Much better than giving lessons. "Besides," she added, "then it wouldn't seem so strange when we disappeared, hopefully not long after we arrive." She was grinning now. "Ivanhoe and Rowena. I will start working on songs about faeries and unicorns and magic forests today."

Gwrhyr chuckled. "Looks like we have a backstory after all."

"So what about you two?" Eluned addressed Yona and Njima. "Have you come up with anything other than your act?"

"Fortunately," Njima said, "I don't have to do anything other than look stunning and keep incredibly still. But, yes, we have discussed disguising ourselves a bit more and we even have a name for our characters—Zenobia and Skaði: The Luscious Lesbians."

Jabberwock barked with laughter and was soon joined by the others as Yona struggled visibly to maintain a straight face.

"Okay, okay, obviously I'm joking," Njima couldn't help but chuckle herself.

"Really," Yona smiled, "we intend to be Zenobia and Skaði, but we haven't named our act."

"It's true," Njima said. "It seemed pointless to name an act that is limited to shooting a piece of fruit off of my head. We're praying that we don't have to expand our offering."

"Which one of you is Zenobia, and which one is Skaði?" Faolan asked.

"Playing the part of Zenobia will be Queen Njima of Naphtali," she laughed.

"And to make ourselves even more difficult to recognize, I'm going to cut my hair short again," Yona said, "and we are going to bleach our hair as blond as possible."

"Yikes! I hadn't thought about my hair," Eluned put a hand

to her telltale black curls. "Do you think anyone will make the connection?"

"You do stand out," Gwrhyr admitted. "We need to think about that."

"She can do like I had to do when Faolan and I were travelling on Adam's Way," Yona suggested.

"What was that?" Eluned asked.

"I was no longer in the nun's habit, but my hair was still short so I had to hide it with a headscarf. If you wear your hair up and cover it with a scarf, you'll look a bit different. Like me, you can't disguise yourself as male—your face is too feminine and your figure just a tad too curvy. Besides, I don't think you want to cut off your hair, right?"

"I'd prefer not to. I'll experiment with scarves tonight," Eluned said.

"Actually, what I would like to suggest is that we spend the mornings working on preparing to leave," Gwrhyr suggested, "and spend the afternoons together. The truth is, once we set off and have all gone our separate ways, we don't know when we will meet again."

"Yes, Jabb," Eluned said. "How are we going to handle that?"

"As gathering the Treasures is the most important thing," Jabberwock said, "I would suggest that once we have them, we bring them here to Castle Mykerinos. We will leave all the Treasures here except Eluned's ring and the Mantle of Arthur, of course . . ."

"And Dyrnwyn," Eluned interrupted him.

Jabberwock shook his head. "I'm sorry, my dear, but it is highly unlikely that a travelling minstrel would be carrying a sword as spectacular as Dyrnwyn."

"He's right," Gwrhyr said. "I know you feel safer when you have your sword with you but as Jabb said, it is highly unlikely that we will need that kind of protection. Musicians are notoriously poor. It would look very suspicious."

Eluned pondered that for a moment. She supposed they were right; she might put the entire quest at risk because she insisted on bringing along her sword. "All right," she admitted, "I would hate to put us in danger because someone coveted Dyrnwyn, and it would only get worse if we had to defend ourselves. Plus, if the Sword was stolen or one of us injured or killed trying to keep it, I would never forgive myself."

"Anyway," Jabberwock continued, "Dyrnwyn, the Red Coat, the Hamper, the Halter, and the Crock and Dish will remain here in a vault beneath the castle. Chokhmah will guard the Ring and Moonstone with her life. As a matter of fact, Chokhmah, I would recommend that you don't wear the Ring until it's absolutely necessary. Do you have somewhere to keep it safe?"

Chokhmah patted the little leather pouch she always wore at her waist. "This leaves my person only when I am without clothing or sleeping, and then I can make sure that it remains in my presence."

"And no one is going to be interested in a moth-eaten cloak," Gwrhyr said, "but I will trade the phoenix breastpin for something a little less eye-catching."

"Good idea," Jabberwock said. "If someone rifled through your luggage, a gold pin would definitely draw notice."

"I'm sure we can find something made of pewter or brass in Goshen," Eluned said.

"Once all the Treasures are gathered, we will have to arrange to go to Favonia and get the Phaeton and Chessboard," Jabberwock said.

"I would like to help with that," Chokhmah said. "I wish to speak with Miryam and see just how much she knows about my origins."

"At least it will only be a one-way trip," Yona said.

"Poor Halelu," Chokhmah said. "I hate to subject him to the voyage to Paliaina, but he has been attached to the Phaeton once already."

"Are you going to leave Fiachdubh here when you go to Simoon?" Eluned asked. "You said Faolan is going to enter Simoon as a wolf?"

"Yes," Faolan said, "but we were hoping we could leave him in the stables at Salama Palace before crossing the border into Simoon. We thought it would be better to make the final transformation to blind healer and guide wolf in Mwezibarafu. It seems too risky to draw attention to ourselves before then."

Bonpo was nodding. "Yes, dey might want you stay in dere kingdom. 'Earels arways needed."

Chokhmah nodded. "Healing is important."

"I'm sure either I or King Seraphim can arrange for that to happen," Gwrhyr assured him.

"It is possible that I will have to travel invisibly once we leave Sigwald," Chokhmah said. "It is easier for a wolf to travel unseen, and with the Ring it will now be less risky for me. But that would make Halelu a problem because I cannot be invisible on a horse. Perhaps we should leave Halelu at Salama Palace as well?"

"Good point," Faolan said. "He would most likely really stand out in Simoon as the type of horse that is unique to gypsies. If we enter Simoon on foot, it will be easier to keep off the roads when we leave."

"There is so much to think about," Njima sighed. "Yona and I need to consider what is normal for performers. We don't want to draw the wrong kind of attention either."

"So the plan is once we have the Treasure, bring it back to Castle Mykerinos," Yona re-stated to make sure she understood. "Then what?"

"Then you may return to your lives until we decide what the next step is," Jabberwock said. "We are hoping . . ."

"We?" Eluned interrupted him.

Jabberwock rolled his eyes. "I can never even finish a

sentence," he groused. "King Seraphim, King Uriel, and I, at this point. We are hoping to contact the other monarchs in the Triquetra Alliance to discuss a plan once we have all the Treasures."

"The real hope," Gwrhyr made an attempt to explain, "is that with the power of the Treasures behind us, a delegation can approach Kings Arawn and Hamartia, at a minimum, and request them to refrain from any future aggression towards the Triquetra Alliance."

"In other words," Njima said, "ask them to stop preparing for war?"

Jabberwock nodded. "Exactly."

"It's funny," Eluned mused, "we've been away from the Quest for so long that it almost feels surreal. Is Omni really guiding us? Will we really be able to retrieve all the Treasures? For awhile it all seemed so possible, but now it feels like a dream."

"I'm sure it will soon seem very real indeed," Gwrhyr pulled her close and kissed her forehead. "I would bet that Chokhmah and Faolan, and Yona and Njima don't feel as distanced from the Quest as we do." They all murmured their assent. Gwrhyr continued, "The brief trip to the Crossroads Inn and back wasn't enough to return to that sense of 'being on the road.'"

"He is correct, my dear," Chokhmah said. "We travelled for weeks to get here. It will not be long once we start travelling that you will find yourself fully immersed in the experience again."

"Thank you, Chokhmah," Eluned said. "I'm sure you're right. And there is a fair amount to do to prepare in the coming week. That will help as well."

Gwrhyr stood up. "Why don't we meet back here in half an hour? I need to find King Seraphim and talk to him about that deliveryman."

"Do you really think that man is a spy?" Chokhmah asked Faolan as they made their way back to their room.

"I can't imagine," he stopped, pulling Chokhmah back around the corner they'd just turned.

"What is it?" she whispered, amber eyes wide.

Faolan peeked around the corner. "Damn it," he said under his breath, "it's that man."

"What do we do?"

"Wait," Faolan whispered, "he's heading this way."

When the spy rounded the corner, Faolan reached out and grabbed his arm. "Who are you?" Faolan demanded, but the man dipped and twisted his arm from Faolan's grasp and began to run.

"Stop!" Faolan yelled, chasing after him. The spy was fast—lean like a long distance runner. At the top of the stairs, Faolan called to the guard below. "Stop this man! Don't let him leave the castle!"

The guard unsheathed his sword and ran toward the staircase. "I order you to stop!" he yelled as the spy sped down the stairs.

When he was three steps away from the bottom, the man launched himself into the air. Afterwards, Faolan couldn't testify whether it had been the spy's intention to jump past the guard or to impale himself on his sword, he only knew that the latter had occurred.

Seraphim, Jabberwock, Gwrhyr, and Eluned hurried into the entry hall from the direction of the study as Chokhmah, Njima, and Yona descended behind Faolan. Bonpo, who had gone to the kitchens after their meeting, missed the disruption.

"I didn't mean to kill him," the guard was telling Faolan. "He landed on my sword."

Faolan knelt next to the man who was barely breathing as the blood pooled around his body. "Why are you here?" But the spy refused to speak and within minutes, his life had ebbed away.

A thorough search of his pockets and clothing revealed nothing but a few coins, all from Zion.

"We'll never know," Gwrhyr's face was grim.

"No," Faolan said, "but he was clearly a spy. Let's just pray that he never had a chance to reveal anything he might have learned."

"Something else we'll never know," Jabberwock said.

"Yet another reminder just how careful we are going to have to be," Njima said.

Part Six

"Nature does not hurry,
yet everything is accomplished."

-Lao Tzu

"All shall be well, and all shall be well
and all manner of thing shall be well."

-Julian of Norwich

19ᵀᴴ Neeon

Eluned glanced over her shoulder and sighed. Chokhmah and Faolan had disappeared from view as they took the trade road that curved north around Goshen and Castle Mykerinos before paralleling the River Musk toward the town of Muskroe.

Eluned and the rest of her comrades were travelling south-west toward Jazeel. It was still nearly two weeks until the first day of spring, and a frigid breeze forced Eluned to pull her hood up to protect her ears from its bite. It wasn't quite the auspicious beginning she'd hoped for, but at least they were on the Quest again.

The two couples had decided to leave their 'transformations' until they reached Jazeel. Njima had suggested that it might be safer to arrive at Castle Indalo as they did when they left Castle Mykerinos, and leave for Kamartha in their disguises.

"The fewer people who know the Queen of Naphtali is heading to Kaumari, the better," she had said.

They had all agreed.

"We can't be too careful," Jabberwock had said, his glassy

eyes shining with secret knowledge that no amount of badgering could get him to reveal.

And so they would travel to Jazeel as themselves, but when they began the real journey they would go as Ivanhoe and Rowena and Zenobia and Skaði. They would remain in character as long as it was in their best interests. Jabberwock and Bonpo were the only ones that didn't have to hide who or what they were.

It was also in Jazeel that the four travelling to Kamartha would purchase the clothing necessary to make them appear to be poor wandering minstrels and travelling performers.

As the day progressed, it seemed to be growing darker rather than lighter, and the breeze became an icy wind blowing in dark clouds from the north. They ate a hurried lunch as the clouds continued to pile up overhead, and by one o'clock, the day had grown strangely quiet. It was clear they were experiencing the calm before the storm as the cinereous clouds threatened to release torrents of rain on the poor riders.

"Legion is about an hour away," Eluned said, glancing nervously at the sky. "I know they have an inn. Perhaps we can stop early and spend the night there? Let this storm pass?"

As the others murmured their agreement, a flash of lightning, followed shortly by an emphatic clap of thunder, split the atmosphere. The air took on the peculiar aroma of ozone and impending rain.

Urging their horses into a trot, they hurried toward Legion with Bonpo practically dragging Tikvah in their wake. The sky opened up a few minutes later and released buckets of freezing water on the travellers as the wind whipped the hoods from their heads. Eluned decided that it was safer to keep her hands firmly on Ronan's reins rather than risk tumbling from her mount while attempting to hold her hood to her head. Wet hair and clothing would dry. Broken bones were something she wasn't willing to risk.

They arrived at the inn in Legion, which was called very simply, Jeremiah's, soaked to the skin. The rain had still to let up as Gwrhyr hurried into the long low building to arrange for rooms. While he was gone, everyone else removed the necessary gear, and helped get the horses and Tikvah situated in the barn where several stable hands promised to thoroughly dry and feed them.

Jeremiah's was Spartan but warm and apparently well sealed against inclement weather. As soon as they were in their rooms, the bedraggled bunch set about getting warm and dry with the agreement to meet for dinner in the dining area.

"Well that was hardly a propitious beginning to the Quest," Eluned groused as she handed her cloak to Gwrhyr so that he might wring the water out of her clothing. Her boots were drying by the fire, and she was draping their wet clothes around the room in the hope they would dry out some before they had to leave the following morning.

"You can say that again." He handed her the cloak, and began squeezing the water from her cream wool sweater. She had pulled on her grey cotton sweater, which would be fine in the inn, but might not be quite enough to keep her warm if it was cold again on the morrow. "Although," he continued, "we were fortunate that we weren't that far from Legion. I would have dreaded camping tonight."

Eluned shuddered, chilblains prickling her arms at the thought of setting up tents and preparing a camp while wet and cold. "And it would have been even worse if it had still been raining!"

Gwrhyr nodded, handing her the sweater, and drying his hands on one of the inn's towels. There wasn't a couch in the room, just a couple of rocking chairs in front of the fireplace. Not very enticing. He turned to Eluned with a wicked grin.

"What?" she exclaimed.

A meaningful glance was cast at the bed, and he turned

back to her with raised eyebrow. "Or we could sit in the rocking chairs."

Eluned giggled. "You're incorrigible." She pulled off her sweater and moved towards the bed. Truthfully, she couldn't think of a better way to get warm.

GATHERED AROUND THE LONGEST TABLE that was also closest to the fire, the group was eagerly awaiting the arrival of their pitcher of mulled wine and whatever stew was being served that evening.

A cauldron of a thick chicken and potato stew had just been placed on their table when the inn's door was flung open and a tall, lean man in leather pants, long coat and hat that almost entirely hid his face, rushed in.

"Jeremiah!" he called out, eyes scanning the room for the eponymous proprietor, as rainwater puddled around him on the wood floor.

"Saul?" Jeremiah stepped out of the kitchen, drying his hands on the apron he wore around his waist. He was a stocky man with a full head of silver grey hair and piercing blue eyes. "What is it?"

Saul removed his hat, revealing a long narrow face and scalp as smooth as an egg. Gwrhyr watched as he glanced around the dining area, noting that other than the large table at which sat the unusual group of travellers he was a part of, there were only two other tables, each with a single man. His hurried entrance and the timbre of his voice as he had called out for Jeremiah had gained him the attention of every person in the room. He gulped, but pushed on. "I've just had news from Sheba," he said. "Three border towns were raided simultaneously."

"Which border?" Jeremiah's voice was troubled.

"Not Zion," Saul rushed to explain. "It was Opari on Simoon's border, Wajir on Annewven's and Badda on Adamah's."

"What do you mean raided?" asked one of the men who sat alone.

Removing his coat, Saul walked over to the fireplace, and then turned to face the room. "Just small raids—cattle stolen and barns burned—in Wajir and Badda. But, two farmers were lynched in Opari."

"Lynched?" Njima exclaimed. "Was it King Hamartia's soldiers?"

Saul shook his head. "No one can say. They were dressed like common folk."

"Terrorists," Gwrhyr stated. "Although I'd wager they were soldiers acting on orders from the kings."

For a moment the only sound was the sibilant hiss of the rain against the roof and the crackle of flames in the fireplace. This was not good news. Apparently the Awen Alliance was stepping up its efforts to heighten fear in Sheba, which in turn would cause Sheba's allies to go on alert if not come to that kingdom's aid.

"Has King Seraphim been informed?" Eluned finally broke the silence.

"King Adeyemi dispatched a messenger to him as soon as he was informed," Saul said.

Eluned fought against the rising tide of panic. How far would those three kings go to press for war? And would Kamartha and Dziron follow suit?

"Thank you, Saul," Jeremiah spoke. "Have a seat, and I'll join you with some wine." Jeremiah disappeared into the kitchen as Saul settled down at a table on the opposite side of the fireplace from the Questers.

Bonpo began ladling stew into their bowls as Gwrhyr filled his mug with wine, and then Eluned's, before passing the pitcher to Yona.

"To finding the Treasures as soon as possible," Gwrhyr spoke quietly, raising his glass as soon as all had been filled.

Njima shook her head in dismay, keeping her voice low. "I suppose I had grown accustomed to the quiet, and yet, deep down, I think we all knew it was only a matter of time."

"I wonder what the kings know," Eluned said, glancing over her shoulder to make sure they weren't being listened to. But, one of the single men had joined Jeremiah and Saul, and the other had left the room. "I'm still certain that they don't suspect we went to Favonia. Surely they presumed that we took the Phaeton back to Zion?"

"Perhaps, but I'm certain they have spies," Jabberwock said, "The question is what have they seen since we disappeared?"

"They could have thought we were inside Castle Mykerinos all those months, but they were bound to see our return to Goshen in Rees," Eluned mused.

"Dat'd be vely confusin' to dem," Bonpo said.

Jabberwock nodded. "It might have seemed as if we appeared out of nowhere."

"And without Gwrhyr, Chokhmah, or Yona," Eluned added.

"Would they have noticed our arrival at Castle Mykerinos?" Yona wondered.

"Two very dirty women arriving unceremoniously at the castle's gates?" Njima said. "Probably not. We were completely out of context, and they don't even know about me."

"That we know of," Jabberwock corrected her, "and it is also possible they knew Bonpo, Eluned, and I were on our way back to Zion."

"You mean spies in Naphtali?" she asked him.

"It is very possible," he said. "We didn't exactly keep our presence a secret."

"We did manage to get to Kamea and back without being spotted," Njima continued. "I think we can be relatively certain of that."

It was true that when they had arrived at the barricade, everything looked much as they had left it, though a bit more overgrown.

Had their departure from Jazeel been noticed, if they had indeed been seen there? Faolan, Chokhmah, and Uriel could have easily become lost in the crowds heading southward from Jazeel, but it was more difficult to hide a giant. It was also highly unlikely that the three kings had guessed that Gwrhyr was actually King Uriel. Most of the focus would have been on Jabberwock, Eluned, and Bonpo.

"We did leave incognito and unannounced for Zion, though," Yona said, "and we posed as travellers. I never gave my real name at any of the inns we lodged at. I was always Miryam, and I said Njima was Libni."

Njima chuckled. "You never told me that."

Yona blushed but laughed, "I didn't think to. We always remained in our room until morning so we were never overheard talking."

"So they may know that we are all now on our way to Jazeel," Gwrhyr said, "and by now they have, no doubt, heard that the Princess Eluned was married to King Uriel. They may or may not put two and two together." Gwrhyr stood. "I'm going to ask Jeremiah who the man was that left. Just in case."

They waited as he walked over to the table Jeremiah was sharing with Saul and the other single man. He was speaking quietly, and they had to wait until he returned before they learned anything.

All eyes were on him as he returned to the bench. He shook his head as he sat down. "He's a regular. Jeremiah said that he's been coming here for his evening meal since his wife died about a year ago."

"That's a relief," Yona said. "Anyway, I think the key is going to be departing Jazeel in disguise and with as little notice as possible."

"Yes, we'll figure that out when we get there," Njima said. "No one, not even Eremias and Kess," she paused as she noted the confused look on Bonpo's face. "My Lord High Steward and Chancellor."

"Tanks," Bonpo said.

"Anyway, not even they can know what we look like when we leave."

Everyone nodded, faces solemn. The spy in Castle Mykerinos, and the attacks in Sheba, had made the Quest even more dangerous. It also made it that much more important to acquire the Treasures as soon as possible.

Eluned found herself worrying about Chokhmah and Faolan. They were in the most danger—their only advantage was the fact they were the least known of the group. She was really thankful now that she had entrusted her ring to Chokhmah, glad that Faolan could shift into a wolf. They would need all the help they could get.

"From now on," Gwrhyr said, "regardless of the weather, we need to make as many miles each day as possible."

"An' camp much as possibre too," Bonpo added. "Ress people to see us."

By waking before dawn and leaving camp shortly after daybreak, and pushing until sunset before camping again, the travellers were able to shave three days off their time and arrive on the outskirts of Jazeel on the eleventh of Feharn, three weeks after leaving Castle Mykerinos.

They had agreed earlier on two things—Queen Njima and Yona would enter the city just before the gates closed on whichever day they arrived. They would then arrange for the remainder of the group to be admitted in the wee hours of the morning where they would be led to Castle Indalo in pairs separated by a half an hour's time. With Jabberwock curled up in his basket seat atop Tikvah, it would look like Bonpo was walking alone should he be spotted. And, despite his height, the fact that he was moving about the city in the predawn hours might make him look more like a tradesmen heading to market to set up for the day.

Eluned and Gwrhyr would use their cloaks to conceal as much of themselves as possible, and would be taken on a circuitous route to the castle, also in an effort to appear less suspicious—the theory being that they would be more likely to be spotted should they ride there directly.

They had arrived mid-afternoon on the outskirts of Jazeel, and Yona and Njima had been forced to wait nearly three hours until they could pass through the city gates before they were closed for the day. The rest of the group had then waited another nine hours prior to approaching the city gates.

And, while they could have used that time to catch up on their sleep, they had all been too anxious about being seen and making it to Castle Indalo unnoticed. Instead they'd spent most of that time sitting quietly and staring into the flames of the small campfire they'd built because they'd needed its warmth. The day had been cold and grey, and once the light faded, the temperature had continued to drop. Eluned had Gwrhyr's warmth at her back and the fire at her feet, and she still found herself shivering.

It was with great relief that they'd put out the fire and prepared to leave their little campsite when Gwrhyr's pocket watch finally informed them that it was half past two in the morning. Saddling Ruari and Ronan, and settling Jabberwock in his basket atop Tikvah, they headed for the city gates.

Once inside the town, Eluned and Gwrhyr parted ways with Bonpo and Jabberwock, following another heavily cloaked horseman who spent the better part of an hour leading them through the winding streets of Jazeel before they finally reached the gates of Castle Indalo. They entered the castle to find that Jabberwock and Bonpo had reached the Castle nearly half an hour before them.

ONCE SAFELY ENSCONCED BEHIND the protective walls of Castle Indalo, the group met briefly to confer on how their plan had worked. Njima and Yona had spent a sleepless night worrying about their friends just as the others had spent a sleepless night worrying about being discovered.

"I dink we successfur," Bonpo said when everyone had arrived. "I no see anyone forrow us."

"I don't think I saw anyone at all," Eluned said. "Everything was quiet. It was as if the entire town was still asleep."

"That dark and silent time just before dawn," Njima said. "It seems to be the time when people sleep the hardest, as if it takes them nearly an entire night to fully release their worries."

"But there are always exceptions," Yona yawned. "Those people whose worries are just too great to let go—like ours last night."

"It is entirely possible that someone awake at that hour glanced out a window and noticed our passing," Gwrhyr said, "but I find it unlikely that they connected us with anything other than early travellers."

"And in order to keep it that way," Jabberwock found himself yawning as well, "none of us can venture outside the castle walls with the exception of Yona and Njima."

"And I can only do so in my capacity as Queen," Njima added.

"And even I would have to be careful about why I ventured out," Yona said. "I think we are going to have to make lists of what we need to proceed on this quest, and enlist servants to purchase what we've decided on. If we use different people to buy different items then no one should suspect we are preparing for a journey."

"That makes sense." It was Eluned's turn to yawn, "but I am not even going to be able to think clearly until I've had a little sleep. Can we nap for a few hours first?"

"Oh, I definitely could use a few hours shut eye," Yona agreed, rubbing her eyes.

"I've had your previous rooms prepared for you," Njima said, "although I assumed Gwrhyr would now be sharing your room rather than returning to his."

Eluned smiled. "Thanks. As I recall it was a beautiful room, and Gwrhyr and I spent many wonderful hours in it."

Njima glanced at the pendulum clock that hung on the wall. It was almost four o'clock on the morning of the 12th of Feharn. "What if we meet in the dining room at noon. That won't give us quite eight hours but it should be enough time to wind down, sleep for a few hours and then get ready. I can make sure we're awakened at eleven o' clock?"

"Sounds good to me," Gwrhyr said.

"Please tell me there is some wine or something like that in the room," Eluned added. "I'm exhausted, but I still feel on pins and needles."

"There should be a decanter of cognac," Njima assured her.

"You're a savior," Eluned said, taking Gwrhyr's hand. "Goodnight everybody, see you at noon."

She led the way down the tiled hallway to the staircase that led to the bedrooms upstairs. Eluned stopped in front of the familiar arched doorway, and smiled up at Gwrhyr. "How quickly things change. Last time we were here, we had to beg Jabberwock to let us spend a night alone together."

She opened the door. Nothing had changed since she'd last been in the room. The big wooden bed with its hand tooled silver and gemstones still sat to the right of the door, and the sofa still sat in front of the four arched windows. Eluned headed immediately to the closest brazier and extended her hands toward its warmth.

"I don't think I've been warm since we left Jeremiah's three weeks ago," she shivered, "and I hate that we're going to have to continue the journey so soon. I feel like it could take weeks to thaw my marrow."

While they'd been talking downstairs, their saddlebags and necessary gear had been deposited in the room. On one of the barrel tables adjacent to the sofa sat a ceramic decanter, hand-painted in an intricate design, and a couple of matching goblets. Gwrhyr walked over and poured them a good inch or two before settling into the large and comfy sofa. He took a long sip of his cognac before speaking. "We could take a hot bath," he said thinking of the sunken tub in their bathroom.

Removing her boots and placing them next to the brazier, Eluned then walked over to the sofa, sat down next to him, and leaned against his left side, stretching out on the sofa. Taking a sip of her cognac, she moaned softly. "I feel disgustingly dirty," she admitted, "but I'm too tired to take a bath."

Gwrhyr yawned. "I know what you mean. These past three weeks haven't exactly been leisurely."

"And the stress of the past, what, more than twelve hours?" Eluned said. "I feel completely wrung out." She sighed and leaned her head back against his shoulder. Now, with the heat from the braziers, the warmth of the cognac in her belly, and her husband's solidity at her back, Eluned found her eyelids beginning to droop. "I'm not sure how much longer I can keep my eyes open," she yawned although her eyes were actually closed as she spoke.

"Then why don't you finish your cognac and take off those filthy clothes?" Gwrhyr asked. "It's time for bed." He stood after Eluned tossed back the remainder of her cognac and handed him her goblet. "But, it's not going to be like the last time we were here," he chuckled. "That night it was all I could do to restrain myself knowing that there was every chance we might not be together again."

20ᵀᴴ Neeon

Chokhmah reined in Halelu, extended her left arm, and lined her fingers up with the horizon.

Faolan stopped beside her. "What are you doing?"

"Taking advantage of the fact that we can see the sun today," she explained. "Surely you know this trick?"

"Guess I spent too much time in the woods."

"Four fingers," she turned to Faolan, dropping her arm.

"Four fingers?"

"Yes, four fingers between the horizon and the bottom of the sun. That means we have an hour, give or take, before sunset," she said.

"Hmpff," Faolan seemed unimpressed. "I could have told you that just by looking at the sun."

Chokhmah regarded him silently before shaking her head, and then clucking to Halelu to get him moving again.

"What?" Faolan called after her.

"Nothing, my love," she smiled to herself. Sometimes Faolan's need to be more knowledgeable than she left her completely bemused. Chokhmah was completely at peace with him knowing things that she did not and vice versa. But there were times when she sensed that he felt as if his masculinity was being threatened by the fact she might know something that he did not know. Or, perhaps, it just came from being the younger brother and the competition that might engender.

Fiachdubh was urged to a trot so that Faolan could ride alongside her. He studied her for a moment. "Good, I thought you were mad at me for a second."

Chokhmah smiled at him. "I find it very difficult to be angry with you. If you say or do something to perturb me it is like throwing a pebble into a pond—the ripples disappear very quickly."

He reached over and squeezed her thigh, chuckling. "And that is why, my beautiful gypsy, I love you."

"That's Queen Parisa to you." She tossed her head and gave him a sidelong glance. Her voice was stern but a moment later she threw back her head and laughed before worry clouded her face. "No, I am Chokhmah, your gypsy. I will be Parisa soon enough and I do not relish that idea."

Faolan's face hardened as well, lips thinning and brow creasing with worry. They had to go to Simoon. It was necessary, and yet he dreaded it with every fiber of his being. He heaved a deep sigh and changed the subject. "We need to start looking for a likely campsite."

"Exactly," Chokhmah smiled to herself again. That had been the whole point of stopping and judging how long it was until sunset.

They had been paralleling the River Musk for the past couple of days—the previous day in the rain and today, colder but sunnier. She would like to find a camp early enough to start a big fire, which had been impossible the previous day. Their tent was still damp from the past night, and she thought the warmth of a fire might finish drying it out. Although a little heat to thaw her numbed fingers and toes would be nice, as well.

They weren't far from the Spruce, a tributary that flowed westward into the River Musk from the Mountains of Misericord. On the northern side of the Spruce, they would find the trade route that would take them eastward over the mountains and into the Kingdom of Sheba. It would be nice to be able to find a spot somewhere along its banks, preferably the southern side.

They continued to ride. The ground was rocky and exposed at this point. They were hoping that when they got closer to the Spruce, they'd find some forest to help shelter them. About half an hour later, they could see the gleam of the Spruce up ahead.

Chokhmah narrowed her eyes. "What is that? That looks like a pretty large encampment to the east."

Faolan heaved a sigh. Camping around strangers was not his favorite thing to do as he had to be even more careful about shifting. "It looks like we're going to have company tonight."

Chokhmah chuckled. "Technically, they will have the company, but perhaps we can find a space to ourselves."

A minute later, Chokhmah reined in Halelu. "I don't believe it." Her voice was barely above a whisper. She would recognize those colorful vardos anywhere, and that peculiar double clang of her brother's when he was working at his forge.

"What?" Faolan looked at her, wide-eyed, bringing Fiachdubh up short.

Her eyes filled with tears, and she swiped them away, angrily. "It is silly," she choked, "but it is my people—Moshe, my brother. My Roma."

Faolan squinted into the gathering darkness. "Then what are we waiting for?"

Urging their horses into a light canter, they were soon outside the gypsies' makeshift village.

As was usual, it was Moshe and Daniel who approached the strangers on horseback.

"Peace be with you!" Chokhmah called out as they neared her and Faolan.

"And also . . . by Omni, is that you Aunt Chokhmah?" Daniel's voice broke.

"It is!" Chokhmah swung out of the saddle, and raced towards them knowing Halelu would follow. "I am so glad to see you!"

"You said you would see us again," Moshe grunted in an attempt to keep the emotion from his voice. "Who is this?" he changed the subject as Chokhmah threw her arms around him.

"Always so gruff," she chided. "This is Faolan. My . . ." What should she call him? "My helpmeet."

Moshe and Daniel looked at him appraisingly, trying to see if this clearly gaje man was worthy of their sister and aunt.

Chokhmah laughed. "No, he is not Roma, this is true, but he is a good man."

At this point, Faolan thought it wise to dismount. He approached the two men slowly.

"She's right. I would never hurt my family nor Chokhmah's, and I love her as my soul," he said, trying to remember the phrasing Chokhmah used when she spoke of her love for him.

"Come," Daniel invited them. "I will even sacrifice my beautiful little vardo for the night."

"Oh, Daniel, you do not have to do that. I gave that to you," Chokhmah objected.

"Yes, but I sense that you will not be with us long. You appear as if you are on a journey." Daniel said.

Chokhmah sighed. "You sense correctly. We are on a mission."

"The Treasures," Moshe's voice was grim.

"Yes," Chokhmah affirmed.

"So the rumors are true." He scowled. "I thought the Princess' story did not add up—a diplomatic mission to Annewven. Harah." He spat.

"I knew we were searching for the Treasures when I left last spring, but I had been sworn to secrecy. Now, we lack only four. Faolan and I have been tasked to retrieve the Whetstone from Simoon."

Daniel's face paled and Moshe, if possible, grew grimmer. "Then you have not heard the news."

"What news?" Faolan asked.

"First things first," Moshe answered. "Let us get you settled for the night, you and your horses. Glad to know Halelu is still with you, by the way. I would hate for a Roma horse to have fallen into the wrong hands. Once we do that, then we will discuss everything in The Circle."

Chokhmah nodded. The Circle was where they met to discuss important business.

After removing what they needed, Daniel led Halelu and Fiachdubh away, and Faolan and Chokhmah entered her wagon. It looked essentially as if she had never left it. Daniel had honored her memory. There were more male-related items scattered around, but very like how she had turned it over to him.

Chokhmah looked at Faolan searchingly. "You do not mind that this was once the vardo that Yitzak and I shared? We can camp if you are uncomfortable."

Faolan pulled her into his arms. "That was nearly two years ago," he kissed the tip of her nose. "And from what you've told me of Yitzak, he would be very happy to know that you are happy. You are happy, right?"

"I am, my love," she kissed his mouth. "More than I ever believed possible. Despite the danger we are heading into, despite an unknown future. Yes. I want that future to be with you because you make me happy."

"So," he nuzzled her neck, "how soon do we have to be in The Circle?"

Chokhmah chuckled. "I am sure we could spare a couple of minutes."

Faolan laughed, "Maybe three or four," and led her to the bed.

Heading to the Circle, Chokhmah stopped and said quietly, "Do you mind if I let them know that you are a Shapeshifter? I think they might be shocked, but in the end, I believe it will make them feel much safer about our travelling to Simoon."

"Can we trust them?"

"With our very lives," she said quickly. "It is part of our code."

"In that case, I will let you say whatever you think best," he took her hand and they began walking again.

Sitting in the circle, blazing campfire in the center, bowls of rabbit stew with carrots, onions, mushrooms, and potatoes seasoned with thyme, cloves, and red wine in their hands, The Circle began.

"First the news," Moshe said as the couple spooned the thick soup into their mouths. It had been a long time since their meager lunch. "I know you do not know this," he continued, "but a day or so ago there were three attacks on the borders of Sheba with Simoon, Annewven, and Adamah."

Chokhmah put down her bowl, face draining of color. "What?"

"The towns near Annewven and Adamah, Wajir and Badda, suffered only stolen livestock and burned buildings," Moshe said. "Bad but reparable. Opari, on the other hand." He stopped. Not sure how to go on.

"Two farmers were lynched," Daniel rushed to say, "and now you are heading that way."

"But they will not know that I am a gypsy when I enter," Chokhmah assured them, and was greeted by uncomprehending stares. "I intend to disguise myself."

"How?" Daniel asked. "It is difficult to hide those eyes, that hair, your coloring."

Chokhmah paused. Should she tell them that she was not Roma by birth?

"What is it?" Moshe pressed. "I sense you are hiding something."

Faolan squeezed her hand and nodded encouragingly. If they were to know he was a Shapeshifter they might as well learn that Chokhmah was Pelfan.

"The truth is that as far as blood is concerned," she paused, and swallowed hard. "I am not Roma at all."

There was a collective gasp.

"What do you mean?" Moshe asked.

"Moshe, I am not actually your sister," Chokhmah said, and paused again. "May I have another glass of wine? I think I will need it. I know we can trust all of you, and I think that it is time that we tell you the story beginning from the day we left this camp for Annewven nearly a year ago."

It was just a little over two hours later when Chokhmah, with the help of Faolan, finally finished the story of what had transpired up until that point, having been interrupted repeatedly by questions from her fellow Roma.

"We cannot allow these three kings to destroy the peace we have worked so hard to maintain just because they want to decide what is wrong and right for everyone else," Chokhmah said. And that is why it is important that all these Treasures be gathered."

"Or who is acceptable or not," Faolan said under his breath.

"Queen Parisa," Moshe grumbled. "I always knew you were odd, but I cannot believe our parents kept your true identity a secret."

"I am sure they had their reasons, but I am also sure that Aunt Miryam is aware," Chokhmah said. "I am looking forward to asking her."

"She sent us a letter," Daniel said, "not long after you departed for Dyfed. Of course, she did not say that. She just told us you were safe and that she could not impart any more information. But she intimated that perhaps things were not as safe for us as we might choose to believe."

"That is why we are here in Zion and not in Sheba at this time of year," an old man, grey grizzled hair hanging lankly on his shoulders, interjected.

"It is true," Moshe agreed. "Sheba has become more and more dangerous because of its proximity to Simoon, Annewven, and Adamah. We sensed that Miryam was right—that something bad might happen if we remained."

"Well, you can trust King Seraphim, and for that matter King Uriel, Queen Njima, and King Cian. They are all firmly committed to the Triquetra Alliance," Chokhmah said. "As is King Adeyemi, of course, but his geographical proximity to the Awen Alliance countries . . ."

"And the color of his skin," Faolan interjected, frowning.

"And that," she agreed. "It is also true that we could not risk any letters being intercepted. No one could know where we were heading. Even the parents of Pri—I mean Queen—Eluned did not know where she was or what Treasure she was seeking next."

"And that is why we are forced to be so careful now," Faolan said. "We are ourselves at the moment, but as soon as we reach Mwezi-barafu we become different people. Actually we become a blind healer and a wolf."

Moshe nodded solemnly. "I see the wisdom. Who would not trust a blind woman with her dog?" He paused and looked around the circle. "I say enough with this prikaza." He cleared his throat and spat. "Chokhmah is returned, and I have only one question. Can a wolf dance?"

AND DANCE THEY DID, for the next hour or so, until Chokhmah pleaded exhaustion and the need to head out early the next morning.

"Must you leave so soon?" Moshe asked.

"I am afraid so," she told him. "The knowledge that things

have begun to escalate with that terrible trio makes it even more imperative that we find and steal Simoon's Treasure as quickly as possible. The sooner we are there, the sooner we can leave. I did not tell everyone this, but I can entrust it with you because it should give you some ease—Eluned has lent me her Treasure. It is a ring that makes the wearer invisible when they hold the accompanying moonstone in their hand. You are familiar with this, correct?"

Moshe nodded. "I made some inquiries on these so-called 'Hallowed Treasures' when rumors emerged that a certain princess was seeking them." He paused. "I even knew that King Arawn lost his right hand and his lord high steward, and that King Hamartia's chancellor had been killed as well."

Chokhmah continued, "We feel sure that we can use this ring to enter the palace, ascertain where the Treasure is kept, and remove it without anyone noticing, but we must do it quickly."

Moshe nodded again. "Yes, it is a good plan. Are you sure that they will not recognize you?"

"I never met King Hamartia nor his wife," she said. "They left the day following the dinner party and had departed the castle by the time Yona and Eluned woke up the following morning. As I was playing the part of Eluned's handmaid, I did not leave the room until they had awakened."

Moshe grunted.

"But, I have dark glasses with which to hide my eyes, just in case," she said.

"Yes, they are a distinctive color," Moshe noted.

"They are Pelfan eyes." Chokhmah smiled remembering Jahan, the little boy she had met in Kuna in Naphtali. They had bonded immediately because he had been drawn to their similar appearances—the thick-lashed amber eyes and dark hair. She had later discovered that everyone in Kuna shared those same traits. She shook her head and refocused. "Will you be moving on soon?" she asked.

"Within the next few months, but if you have not returned by then," he took her hands in his, "Daniel, Chelli, and I will remain behind until you return or we know why you have not."

"Thank you, brother," Chokhmah felt her eyes pricking with tears again. "Despite everything, you will always be my family."

He pulled her into a hug. "Yes, baby sister, I do know that."

She hugged him back, fiercely, before pulling away. "We will be out early but I imagine you will already be awake. Faolan and I will stop by and say our farewells before we leave in the morning."

"Good night and sweet dreams," Moshe's voice was formal. "Because you will need every ounce of strength you have to complete this quest."

"Thank you," Chokhmah's voice was barely a whisper, "thank you very much." She turned and saw Faolan waiting for her at a discreet distance. She joined him.

"You have a wonderful family," Faolan said. "And I mean everyone here. It's like you're one, very large, extended family. Ours was always so small—just me and Olcan and our parents, and now it's just me and Olcan and his family."

Chokhmah emitted a noise of disbelief. "What about me?"

"Do you want to be a part of my family?"

"Faolan, what about us would make you think that I would not?"

He swallowed hard. "I guess I just can't believe that I'm lucky enough to have won your love."

"Won?" Chokhmah laughed. "Faolan, I feel as if we have loved one another since the beginning of time. Not only do I feel as if I am part of your family, I feel that you are a part of mine."

"I'm a part of your family?"

"Did you not feel accepted, unconditionally, tonight?" She took his chin in her hand and stared into eyes that seemed more grey than blue in the darkness.

He swallowed hard, and nodded. It was true. Everyone had seemed to accept that Chokhmah, appearing with a new man, a Shapeshifter no less, who was not even gypsy, was somehow natural. They had approved of her choice because she was one of them and known to be wise and they loved her.

"Darling," Chokhmah said, "I know that you have faced so much prejudice because of what you are, but I, no we, do not care. You are the man I love and that is all that matters. We deserve to be happy."

He took her into his arms. He knew she was right. They could do anything they chose to do together, especially if she had a way in which to use her talents when they returned to Dyfed. He couldn't deny her that. "I want to spend the rest of my life with you," he told her. "I want your family to be my family. They can come and spend as much time as they want at Bogaine. I know they can't settle there, it's not their way, but I hope that you can. I hope that we can figure out a way to spend our lives together."

"Oh, my love," Chokhmah said, taking his hand and leading him back to the wagon, "that is all I need you to say. But of course we will figure out a way. We can conquer any adversity when we are together."

THEY HAD BEEN RIDING for about two hours, and were slowly ascending toward the pass through the Mountains of Misericord when Faolan finally broke the silence.

"You've been awfully quiet this morning. Are you regretting agreeing to go after the Whetstone?"

"What?" She sighed. "No, it is not that. It is the dream I had last night."

"You dream every night," he laughed. "Sometimes more than once."

"I know, but when I dream like I dreamed last night, it often presages the future."

Faolan's brow creased and he studied her for a second to make sure she wasn't about to tease him. Sometimes it was hard to tell. "Are you serious?"

"Yes, it does not happen often, but when it does I try to take it seriously."

"What did you dream?" There was a note of worry in his voice. If she had dreamed that something happened to either of them, that for some reason they didn't end up together, he wasn't sure he could take it.

"I dreamed that the Knife of the Horseman is not in Buta."

Faolan was relieved for a moment before he remembered that Jabberwock and Bonpo were headed there. It was said to be a dangerous place. No one ventured there for fear of the Aberrations. "Not in Buta?"

"Not in that Buta."

Faolan's eyes widened in understanding. "In the new Buta," his voice was rough. But of course, any man who was determined to see his family line remain pure throughout the centuries after the devastation of his kingdom—the Devastation of Pelf—would make sure that he brought the family's Hallowed Treasure with him to his new home. "But he left Buta as a child. Did they bring it with them then?"

"Clearly they had a stronger nationalistic sense than that of Naphtali," Chokhmah said. "Unlike many of the other kingdoms, they did not interbreed. They preferred to marry within their own kingdom. I think King Alborz would have insisted that Queen Jazmin take it with her when she and the children fled to Kamea."

"But the new Buta was destroyed. Do you think it's still there?"

"Either it is lying amidst the ruins of New Buta," Chokhmah said, renaming it to distinguish it from the original, "and I do not think that a little more than forty years can have changed the landscape that drastically," she said.

"Or, what? One of the attackers found it and carried it away with him?"

"Possibly. We do not know what it looks like, unfortunately."

Faolan was silent a moment, thinking. "It's true that most of the Treasures have been very plain looking although there are exceptions like the sword and the chessboard." He paused again. "So, what do we do? Do we send a pigeon to Jazeel when we arrive in Mwezi-barafu? Will they get it in time, and if they do will they believe your dream?"

"I do not know!" she almost wailed. "I have been worrying about this all morning. "I do not want to send my friends into danger, and yet, what if I am wrong?"

They continued their ascent, Chokhmah fretting silently about her dream, Faolan worrying about the rapidly dropping temperature. He wondered if it might snow. That would slow down their trip.

By the time Chokhmah remembered her dream again, more than two weeks later, it was far too late to send a pigeon to Jazeel.

16ᵀᴴ Feharn

Staggering their departure times seemed to be the wisest way for the Questers to set out on the next leg of their journey. Because Queen Njima was the most recognizable of the group in her Kingdom, they decided it would be best for she and Yona to leave when the lack of light could more easily mask their faces. Even so, they had both bleached their hair nearly white, and Yona had cropped hers as closely to her head as possible. As it was still cold, knitted caps topped their heads, and they further hid their faces in the depths of their hooded cloaks. Unfortunately, they couldn't hide the quality of their horses, but so be it. They were both reluctant to give up Makeda and Aine. The mares had served them well.

Setting out at first light, Njima and Yona, now decked out as Zenobia and Skaði, took the road west that would bring them to the trade route that travelled northwest in a gentle arc around the Sea of Blood to Kamartha. They had journeyed along this road before when they were on the way to Kamea seeking the Crock and Dish of Rhyngenydd the Cleric.

Bonpo and Jabberwock were more difficult. It was hard to mask the Abominable Snowman and his little Bandersnatch friend. They finally settled on a solution. The two of them planned to leave town in a covered cart driven by one of Njima's trusted soldiers, completely hidden inside, and with Tikvah in tow. Once they reached the trade route, the same one that the other four would head northwest on, they would emerge from the cart and then continue west through the well hidden gate into no man's land, destination Kuna.

Just to be doubly safe, they left an hour after Yona and Njima. If anyone happened to be watching, it would look like a travelling merchant heading north with his wares.

Eluned and Gwrhyr, or as they would now be called, Rowena and Ivanhoe, were to leave two hours after Bonpo and Jabberwock. The plan was to join up with Yona and Njima at the first travellers' campsite when they finally reached it. This meant that the two women would have to come up with an excuse for stopping early, but would also ensure that they had a spot to camp together by doing so.

They, too, had tried to disguise themselves as much as possible. Clad in dirty leather breeches, an equally dirty leather jerkin, and a moth-eaten wool sweater, Eluned looked the very essence of the travelling minstrel. A woolen scarf was tied gypsy-style around her head, and she had also wrapped herself in an old and very heavy woolen cloak.

The cloak was a wondrous find, and she had rewarded the servant who had discovered it excessively. The new queen had spent an entire day "staining" the article of clothing with mud, wine and even grass. It needed to seem like she had spent a lot of time outdoors among folk enjoying the music she and Ivanhoe performed. It was true enough that she had spent much time camping during her journeying, she had smiled as she ground a handful of mud along the cloak's hem. But, she had thought with a slight grimace, the entitled travel differently than the poor, and many nights had been spent in inns or other lodgings, as well.

Gwrhyr was similarly outfitted although Eluned thought it was too bad he couldn't wear the Mantle of Arthur as it already looked incredibly aged. Obviously that was out of the question, his look said when she'd jokingly suggested it to him.

"By Omni," he'd said, "don't you think it would look odd to see a riderless horse?"

"Not necessarily," she'd frowned. "Besides, I was clearly kidding. Why do you and Jabberwock insist on assuming I'm an idiot?"

"I'm sorry, Fy Drysor," he'd said. "I guess I'm more worried about going to Kamartha and Dziron than I care to admit."

Yet he, too, had managed to find a suitable cloak although his was constructed of stitched together animal skins. Eluned frowned in disapproval when she saw it until he assured her that it was made from deer that had been slaughtered for their meat.

"And you have yet to give up meat," he reminded her.

Both they, and Yona and Njima, carried very little with them on their horses—one tent per couple, bedrolls, the gear they needed to perform, a bare minimum of toiletries, and a modicum of food and money, as well as oats for the horses. The Mantle of Arthur, which Gwrhyr and Eluned needed to complete their task, was rolled up like a blanket behind Ronan's saddle. The horses, they decided, they would claim as a wedding gift from Gwrhyr's parents as they, also, were unwilling to give up the mounts that Faolan had chosen for them. They had been through so much together already.

NOT LONG INTO THEIR RIDE northwestward along the trade route, Eluned began fretting about the horses. The day had turned out to be overcast and frigid, and every time the glacial wind changed into a gale, Ronan's ears would twitch madly and he would shake his head in protest. Gwrhyr assured her that the horses were warmer because they were carrying their weight and gear, but if she was really worried they could urge them into a light canter for a mile or two.

A canter would definitely warm them up, Eluned debated with herself, but if they sweated too much they would be colder once they started walking again. And, if they cantered, she and Gwrhyr would be colder while they did so. Perhaps, it was better to practice her breathing prayer—Omni Within, Omni Without, as she inhaled and exhaled—and let the horses do what they felt inclined to do. She loosened her hold on the reins and Ronan continued along at a steady pace. So he wanted to walk. She was probably just projecting the way she felt on him as her fingers and toes were numb with the cold, and she wished she could make her nose stop running. It was going to be raw by the time they reached the campsite. Eluned leaned forward, caressed his neck and spoke to him encouragingly. They would reach the camping ground eventually, and then they could all thaw out around a nice roaring fire.

THEY FINALLY TURNED THEIR HORSES down the trail to the established campsite late that afternoon. When they arrived in the clearing, they were surprised to find more than a dozen people already setting up tents and filling out the shelters.

They spotted Njima and Yona right away and nonchalantly headed their mounts in that direction. They had to meet "by chance".

"Is this spot taken?" Gwrhyr asked, pointing to the empty space next to the women's tent.

"Well," Yona said loud enough for others to hear, "we had hoped our friends would show up, but clearly they're not going to make it this far today. You're more than welcome to that space. The camp is beginning to get crowded and I would hate to deny someone a space and have our friends never arrive."

"Thank you so much," Eluned groaned, sliding off Ronan. "The ride wasn't bad, but this cold is vicious."

"To where are you travelling?" Njima asked, resisting the urge to assist Eluned. Her nose was red and runny from hours spent in the cold.

"We're heading to Kaumari," she said. "We're hoping we can find some gigs while we're there. It's such a big city."

"Gig?" Yona asked.

"Yes, getting hired to perform for one night in several places." Eluned extended her hand. "I'm Rowena, by the way."

"Skaði," Yona said.

"My husband and I are minstrels." She leaned over to unbuckle Ronan's saddle, and was about to heft it off when Gwrhyr interrupted.

"Let me do that, Fy Drysor," he said.

"Fy Drysor?" Yona asked.

"It means 'My Treasure,'" she explained turning toward the two women. "This is my husband, Ivanhoe."

"I've studied the ancient languages in order to incorporate some old tales into my songs," he said, turning to shake hands with Yona and then Njima.

"This is my partner, Zenobia," Yona said. "We have an archery act, and we're heading to Kaumari where we also hope to find someone who wants to see what we do. A gig, you called it?"

"We were building a fire," Njima said. "You are more than welcome to join us at it. We stopped a few hours earlier because I had a severe headache, but I'm feeling better now."

"I'm glad you're feeling better." It was all Eluned could do not to wink at her. "That would be so wonderful! I've been freezing all day."

"We'll get things set up and join you soon," Gwrhyr promised, pulling the tent off Ruari's back where it was still balanced. "Ee, uh, Rowena, if you could feed Ruari and Ronan, that would help a lot."

"Sure, Ivan, my heart," she smiled at him, "I'll see right to it." Eluned took the leads in her hand and led the horses closer to where Gwrhyr would be setting up the tent. There was also more grass in this area for them to crop—mostly dry winter grass, but a Strawberry Spring the previous week had sent up early shoots of spring grass that looked much more appetizing.

In addition, she gave them each a couple of cups of oats, and while they were munching, looked for something to which to tie them. She finally spotted the hitching post and removing their bridles, one by one, replaced them with a halter and tied the leads to the post. She then cleaned the bits, rubbed what very little sweat there was off the leather of the bridles and set them down next to the saddles for the evening.

She was going to have to find them water. Should she wait and lead them to the trough that was adjacent to the shelters or go and fetch them some? She was waffling when Gwrhyr approached.

"You're standing there looking befuddled," he said.

"I don't know whether to lead the horses over to the trough or go and fetch them some water in our bucket," she lamented.

"That doesn't seem like a difficult decision," he said.

"It is, though. I'm afraid someone will try to talk to me, and I'll have to sound like a common minstrel."

"You'll be fine," he assured her. "Lead them to the trough now. No one else is near it. They'll drink their fill and be content here the remainder of the night."

"Maybe no one will bother me if they see I have two horses," she said.

"Thank you for the cover on my slip earlier, Fy Drysor. I really need to get accustomed to our new names."

Eluned, who'd been studying the campsite to make sure the other campers were fully occupied, looked up at him. "You're welcome. Kiss?"

He kissed her tenderly before continuing with his chores. She untied the horses and hurriedly led them to the water trough.

Gwrhyr and Eluned were sitting next to the campfire, spooning their meager dinner, a stew of beans and salt meat, into their mouths, along with Njima and Yona, who were eating similarly, when they were approached by some other campers.

"We hear ther's some travellin' minstrels here," a middle-aged man, face sun worn, said.

Coughing, trying not to choke on his beans, Gwrhyr put down his bowl. "That'd be me and me wife," he winced inwardly as he said it.

"Could yer give us a song or two?" the man asked.

Eluned's stomach dropped. It was the first test. They weren't musicians. She hoped the ballads they'd come up with would serve them if they were forced to play. Now she experienced severe reservations. Thank you, Omni, her thought was sarcastic, for making us perform them on our first night out.

"Sure," Eluned said, taking a final bite before putting down her bowl and standing. "We kin der that. Let me get me harp, an' werl join ye in front of ther shelters."

"But firs' we muss finish our'n stew an warsh up," Gwrhyr picked up his bowl and gulped down the remainder of his stew, then stood as well.

When they both had their harps, they found a place in front of the bigger campfire of the three pits where they could sit comfortably, and Eluned said, "Cuhvetena's song?"

Gwrhyr clenched his teeth. Eluned had written this one, and like his ballad, he wasn't sure how well it would play. True she had a beautiful contralto. He just hoped they were satisfied with the tune.

SHE STRUMMED FOR A MOMENT, tuning her harp, took a deep breath and began:

"They stood atop the stone gird hill,"

she sang, continuing to strum her harp, Gwrhyr offering up the harmony on his.

> "Flowers scenting the air.
> "Illusion revealed a hidden door;
>   they descended the stair."

She continued:

> "Through marble hall on foot they sped
>   Until the isle was met
> And dance did they all through the night
>   Until her cheeks were wet.
>
> The tears they flowed for she bethought
>   Ne're more her friends to see.
> But the Fae and Goddess alike
>   Allowed them to go free."

As she continued with a few more verses detailing the beautiful island and faeries themselves before concluding with finding their friends still awaiting their appearance a week later, Gwrhyr noted the arrival of Yona and Njima. They stood just outside the circle of campers and listened politely.

Despite the fact she thought the song subpar, they received a hearty round of applause, and Gwrhyr was forced to introduce his ballad next.

The King had spent a lot of time trying to decide what the subject of his ballad should be. He'd mentally worked his way through all their adventures—from Eluned being led to Dyrnwyn by the pwca to their battle with The Aberrations. Unfortunately, those stories seemed too real, too personal.

Eluned had chosen the night they'd met Cuhvetena just because it had nothing to do with the Treasures and seemed magical enough that it could just be a story. He sincerely doubted that anyone hearing it would tie the adventure to Ivanhoe and Rowena.

He had a flash of inspiration—what about the Treasures in general? Because there were thirteen of them, it would make for a nice long ballad. Most people weren't really familiar with the Treasures. It seemed just the thing.

It was Eluned's turn to strum the harmony as Ivanhoe began his tale of the "Thirteen Hallowed Treasures" and what would transpire should they all be gathered together again.

When he was finished there was a round of applause accented by the stamping of feet, and cries of "Amen!"

"It sure would be nice ter know that ther' all gathered together agin," one man with a heavy Adenese intonation to his voice said. "Things err gettin' right unpleasant in Sheba, I hear."

Zenobia agreed. "It is true true," she said, trying to affect a light Sheban accent, and praying no one had heard otherwise. "I am loathe to return to my Kingdom until there is peaces again."

"Them Awen Alliance Kingdoms dunna want thems of us from the Triquet' Alliance to sell our wares in thems lands no more," said another man who sounded like he was from Southern Zion, "at leas' them eas'ern Kingdoms."

"I've heard rumors that the Treasures are being collected," ventured Skaði, hoping to find out how wide those rumors had spread.

"Yes, heard that meself," the man who'd asked them to sing said. "Also heard that King Arawn lost his hand."

A number of people were nodding.

"Really don't want ter go ter war," a man who looked to be in his early twenties said. "I jus' got married, got a babe on the way."

Rowena's eyes welled with tears. "Us too," she sniffed. "An' anyone who be young an' able would haf ter fight." She tried to imitate Ellie's accent. Minstrels might sing poetically, but they talked like commoners. She really hoped that she could pull off this masquerade.

"Amen ter that!" Ivanhoe said. "Who of us here wouldna' rather be wit ther' fam'lies than riskin' ther' life onna battlefield? One more song, a happy un, to send us offn' ter bed?"

Everyone clapped their approval, and he launched into a well known ditty that anyone could sing along to.

Zenobia and Skaði drifted back to their tent before Ivanhoe and Rowena to prevent suspicion. The latter couple shook hands and accepted thanks gratefully, and turned down any proffered gifts.

"We did it fer our feller travellers," Ivanhoe said. "P'raps some day, yerl do us a favor in return."

"I DIDN'T REALIZE IT WOULD BE SO DIFFICULT to talk like that," Eluned said once they'd reached the privacy of their tent, but she made sure to keep her voice lowered. "I mean, I've listened to people speak like that all my life, but I was always punished if I ever tried to imitate it." They undressed quickly as they spoke, eager to seek the comfort of their warm blankets. It was still cold, but the temperature hadn't dropped too much, and the wind had gentled to a breeze.

"A proper Princess . . ." Gwrhyr said.

"A proper Princess speaks properly," she laughed, but quietly. "A proper Princess doesn't slouch, snort when laughing, pout, et cetera, et cetera, et cetera."

"I'm pretty sure I've seen you pout, Queen Eluned." Her king pulled her into his arms.

"And I am sure you will see me pout again, King Uriel." She shivered and pulled away from him, sliding between their blankets. She scooted over so he could join her, then snuggled against her husband. Within seconds, the warmth of his body had eased her into a peaceful sleep.

BECAUSE THEY WERE ACCUSTOMED to doing so, the four of them rose earlier than most of the other travellers and quietly set about breaking down their camp. In doing so, they were able to be on the road just as the other campers were starting their day.

When they were far enough away from the camp, Gwrhyr spoke. "I didn't want to risk saying anything while we were there, but we can't afford a repeat of last night."

"What do you mean?" Yona asked.

"I think he means," Njima said, "that he and Eluned only have the two ballads prepared, and that real minstrels would have a compendium of songs."

"Exactly," Gwrhyr said, "which means that we need to push on past the established site tonight and find someplace to camp on our own."

"Not just tonight then," Eluned added. "Every night until we reach Kaumari."

"Yes," he said. "We can't risk having our cover blown just because we don't have enough original material to play."

"And Omni forbid that anyone ask us demonstrate our act!" Yona said. "I don't want to shoot anything off Zenobia's head until I absolutely have to!"

Njima laughed. "I can't argue with that!"

"So, push ahead it is," Eluned said. "I say we make only as many stops as necessary today, including as short a lunch break as possible. That should get us well ahead of the travellers behind us."

THEY PASSED THE TRAIL to the established campsite about three o'clock and continued on for another hour before beginning to keep an eye out for a possible place to camp. The road that day, as it had the day before, passed through never-ending fields of tall golden brown grass that had yet to take on the pale green hue of the new growth of spring.

Oh for just one tree, Eluned thought as the sun began to sink toward the horizon. The idea of camping amidst the grass of the plains made her very uncomfortable. At least the established camp the previous day had been set amongst a small grove of oaks and hemlocks. As, no doubt, had the site they had passed an hour ago.

They rounded another curve and Eluned squinted into the distance hoping to see something that would indicate a forest or even plant life around a spring or creek.

"I could be wrong," she said, "but I think I see something. I can't tell how far it is." She pointed, and everyone strained to see what Eluned thought she saw.

"It could be a grove of trees," Gwrhyr said. Like Eluned, his far distance sight was better than both Njima's and Yona's.

"It all looks flat to me," Njima said.

"Let's give it another ten minutes and look again," Gwrhyr said. "If it's more apparent at that point, it may be worth pushing on to."

Ten minutes later, there was clearly a visible convexity on the horizon, most likely a copse of trees. And where there were trees on the Plains of Naphtali, one could usually find a source of water.

Eluned felt her spirits lifting, and as if sensing her joy, Ronan's gait increased to a trot. She wasn't the only one, apparently, who was ready to rest for the day. Within a quarter of an hour, the little group could make out that the stand of trees they were fast approaching was composed of birch, oak, and ash. Hopefully somewhere amidst the grove, they would find a spot large enough in which to camp for the evening.

It wasn't long before they were dismounting, and leading their horses into the stand of trees, many of which were just beginning to sprout yellow green foliage. Gwrhyr spotted a narrow trail to their left after they'd walked about twenty feet through the leaf litter, and they followed it eastward into the thicket of trees. It curved through the small wood passing around trees and shrubs before opening up into a small clearing.

"This seems a likely camping spot." Njima's voice was quiet.

"Listen," Eluned said, voice lowered, as well.

They paused for half a minute—nothing but the sound of their breathing, the whisper of wind in the branches, the swish of the horses' tails and the nearly silent trickle of water.

Makeda, Njima's buckskin mare, whickered softly, and everyone jumped.

Eluned felt the hairs on the back of her neck prickle. She didn't feel danger but it was too quiet. "Shouldn't we be hearing birds? Insects? Small mammals?"

Gwrhyr grunted his agreement.

"What do we do?" There was worry in Yona's voice. "It's quickly approaching sunset. We could return and camp on the plain, but that feels too exposed. Yet, will it be dangerous to remain here?"

They surveyed the glade, which was now lit by the amber rays of the late afternoon sun. It was flat, there was plenty of grass for their horses and Eluned could see the sparkle of what was probably a spring on the far side of the clearing. Yes, it had to be a spring or small pond, as several willows seemed to hover around it.

"I don't sense danger," Eluned said. "It just strikes me as otherworldly somehow."

Gwrhyr groaned. "Don't say faery."

"That's not fair," she frowned at her husband. "Technically, we've never had anything but good luck with faeries."

He sighed. "True enough. I was just happy to be taking a break from the supernatural for a change."

"You're just jealous because they tend to seek me out." Eluned tapped his bicep with her fist.

He blinked at her. "I, uh, you're probably right. Other than Rua, I've never seen a faery or a pwca or . . ."

"Or anything magical," Yona said.

"And you definitely can't count the Aberrations," Njima

said. "They were just," she shuddered for emphasis, "beyond scary."

Eluned studied her friends for a moment. It did seem awfully unfair that she'd had the lion's share of visitations by otherworldly creatures. Feeling guilty about that, she said a quick prayer to Omni requesting that if there were something magical in the woods around their campsite that it appear to her husband or one of her friends rather than to her.

"So, I take it we're camping here tonight," Yona said, pulling the tent off Aine's back.

"There is something unusual about this little forest." Eluned squinted into the woods before continuing. "I can't see anything but I truly don't sense any danger."

And, as if to lend credence to what she'd just said, the birds began their twilight concerto accompanied by the buzz of insects and the skittering of small animals.

"Well," Gwrhyr said, "I guess we've been accepted." He looked at Eluned. "Do you want to set up the tent or gather firewood?"

Gather firewood, she thought, but said, "I'll set up the tent." She didn't want to risk wandering into the forest and chancing upon whatever might be inhabiting it.

Gwrhyr placed the tent on the grass for her before heading into the woods. He wanted to collect enough wood for the night before it got too dark to see beneath the trees.

Arms fully loaded with logs for the campfire, Gwrhyr turned to make his way back toward the clearing. He was stopped in his tracks by the sight of a tiny man, less than two feet tall, standing in the trail, arms crossed.

His first instinct was to drop the downed branches and run, but Gwrhyr gripped his armload tighter fearful that dropping the wood might scare the little man or even injure him. Swallowing hard, he said, "Hello?" His voice came out a little too high-pitched and quavery so he cleared his throat and tried again. "Greetings."

The little man doffed his brown pointed cap, which looked to be fashioned from birch bark, and bowed. He sported a loden green woolen suit belted at the waist with twine or a vine. Gwrhyr couldn't tell. He had a full beard and mustache of chestnut brown hair and his dark brown eyes glimmered with merriment.

"Urigrim, at yer service, yer highness," the man said.

"Pleased to meet you," Uriel proffered his hand. "Apparently, you know who I am."

"'Tis true that we Gnomes can always sniff out royalty," Urigrim said.

"Gnomes." Gwrhyr smiled. "I can't tell you how delighted I am to meet you."

"The pleasure is mine," Urigrim said, voice formal.

"I want to thank you for caring for our environment," Gwrhyr said. "It seems we humans don't really excel at it."

Urigrim laughed. "Ain't that ther truth! Yee humans tend to'ard ther selfish side, if'n I can be so bold."

"I don't deny it, but I apologize," Gwrhyr said.

"Fair enough," Urigrim said.

"And if I am to be completely honest," Gwrhyr continued, "I wasn't sure you or any other magical beings existed until I met the faeries, and that called everything else into question."

"Ther's erlot ter be seen if'n yee look at things rightly," Urigrim said. "Now tell me why yee've chosen this little wood fer yer campin' spot tonight. Ther' be an official site 'bout two hour back. Looks like yee pushed to get here."

"Perhaps you should return with me and meet my wife and our two friends," Gwrhyr said. "Then we can explain everything. I need to get this wood back so we can prepare our dinner."

"What yee be eatin'?" Urigrim asked.

"Trail food," Gwrhyr said. "Probably just rehydrated beans and some vegetables. Why?"

"What if'n I bring me wife and some friends? Ther other keepers of this wood. We kin provide yee wit' some fresh food—spring mushrooms, greens, that sorta thing. And a'course, some of our mead."

"That seems more than fair," Gwrhyr said. "I look forward to meeting your wife and friends."

THE POT OF BEANS WAS JUST BEGINNING to simmer when Urigrim arrived with his friends. Eluned covered her mouth with her hands, though her eyes were wide, when she first spotted them. They were too adorable, and she didn't want to embarrass them by making a sound that might reveal that. Instead, she took a deep breath, swallowed, and said to Gwrhyr, "They're here."

They turned to watch the Gnomes make their way across the clearing. There were six of them—three males and three females—and they each held baskets containing either fresh vegetables or small casks of their mead.

After Gwrhyr had introduced Eluned, Njima, and Yona (erlot of royl'ty in this'n glade, Urigrim noted under his breath), the Gnome took his turn.

"This be me wife, Nidira," he said. Unlike his dark chestnut hair, Nidira's tresses reminded Eluned of the bark of silver birch trees although an earth-toned scarf hid most of it. "An' Mercryn an' Voza, an' Jornan an' Quegani, who help us care fer this beautiful copse."

The other two couples bowed to the humans who had decided to camp in their woods. Like Urigrim and Nidira, they too were dressed in colors of the earth. With their tree-colored hair and clothing in browns and greens, they would easily blend into the forest, Eluned thought.

After incorporating the Gnomes' vegetable offerings into their beans, the food was served, toasts were made, and the group enjoyed their dinner while getting to know each other better. Despite Gwrhyr's admonition that they keep what they were doing secret, Eluned felt it prudent to let them know that they were on a quest to find the Thirteen Hallowed Treasures because knowledge had always seemed to help the magical folk previously.

"We suspected as much," Jornan said. He seemed to be the eldest Gnome. His beard was prodigious and as white as pear blossoms.

"I guess you hear things," Yona said before taking another sip of her mead. It tasted strongly of honey and she had to force herself to drink it slowly as it was clearly potent.

"We do," admitted Mercryn.

Njima frowned. She wasn't pleased that it always seemed to be the men who spoke.

"How do you hear, Voza?" she asked, disregarding Voza's husband.

"Ther fae tell us, yer majesty." Her eyes were lowered as she answered. Njima tried to control her anger. Voza was a beautiful Gnome—hair the light reddish brown of willow, eyes the light green of their leaves. She was slender despite her height—more elvish than gnomish—and she clearly could think. Why did men have to constantly subvert their women, Njima thought.

She took a deep breath and said, "And how can we help each other?"

"I would think," Quegani, Jornan's wife, who seemed to be significantly younger than her husband, glanced sideways at him before continuing, "I would think that we can make sure you have places to camp where you will be alone. I think that would be the least we could do." Eluned couldn't decide whether Quegani was shy or afraid of what Jornan might think of her offer.

Her hair was the brown of Autumn leaves and unlike the other two women, it was uncovered and braided with strings of acorns and miniscule pine cones. She wore a sepia-toned tunic and leggings of thick wool, and her speech was more formal than the others. Eluned wondered how she had ended up here in this small grove of trees on the Plains of Naphtali.

Instead, she asked, "How is that?"

"We have ways to send word m'lady," Quegani said.

"That would be so helpful," Gwrhyr spoke. "We just can't risk blowing our cover."

"Yes, if'n yee follow our'n signs," Nidira said, "we can get yee all the way to Kaumari."

"And what about from Kaumari to Jungnay?" Eluned asked.

"It be cold ther," Urigrim said. "They get mer mischievous."

"We dunna trus' em, is what he means," Jornan said.

"What about ther Elermentals?" Voza offered.

"Aye, yee be right," Jornan acquiesced. "Them Sylphs might see yee right."

"What do we need to do?" Njima asked.

"If we pass ther word along, should be a'right," Urigrim said. "Come Kaumari, we transfer yee ta Elermentals. Canna' remember who's there."

"I believe it be Tancorin," Mercryn said.

"Yes, Tancorin," Urigrim said. "He'll lead yee to ther right Elermental. Take our'n word. We'll lead yee the right way."

"I'm assuming your stake in this is the same as all of the magical," Gwrhyr said, "because both King Arawn and King Hamartia want to bend the otherworldly to their will or kill them."

"And WE will not be bent to ther' will," Jornan was adamant.

"Never!" The remainder of them echoed.

17th Feharn

Spring's new growth had yet to choke the road the travellers had cleared back in the fall, Bonpo and Jabberwock discovered with relief. In addition, the weather, while frigid and overcast, didn't hamper their progress, and they made good time as they journeyed southwest toward Kamea.

During the late afternoon of their second day on the road, the Janawar and the Yeti recognized the changing terrain that signified they were drawing close to the little community of Kuna. They had just cleared a bend in the road that curved southwestward along the fence line when they noticed a horse thundering in their direction. Bonpo was alarmed at first until Jabberwock reminded him that Queen Njima had sent a pigeon the day the Questers left Castle Indalo. The Preternaturals were expecting their arrival in Kuna.

Bonpo chuckled. "I bet dat da rittre boy, Jahan."

"I wonder who he managed to wrangle a ride from," Jabberwock said from his basket atop Tikvah. As the rider drew closer, they sighted the brilliant white star on the horse's forehead and the bouncing braid that could mean only one Kunan.

"Azar," Jabberwock and Bonpo spoke simultaneously, and

laughed. Jabberwock was not surprised that the precocious young man had charmed a ride from the beautiful Azar.

When she spotted the giant and the donkey standing stock still in the middle of the road, Azar reined in her mare and skidded to a halt barely a yard away from them. She flipped her single braid back over her shoulder, whipping Jahan in the face as she did so.

"Ouch!" Jahan cried out, and flipped the braid back over her shoulder. "That thing is a lethal weapon," He spoke in Pelfan but his meaning was clear. Sliding down from the horse, he ran the last few steps toward Bonpo and Tikvah, and said in a stilted Common Tongue. "Good afternoon Jabberwock and Bonpo. It is good to see you again."

Bonpo bowed solemnly. "It arway honor t'see you 'gin."

"You two, or three, I should say, appear as if you're doing well," Jabberwock said in Pelfan.

Azar dismounted, smiling as she held her mare's reins, she turned and greeted them in the Common Tongue.

"I see you've mastered the Common Tongue," Jabberwock said.

"I have still much to learn," she said, cheeks coloring at the praise. She patted her horse on the nose. "This is Esfir. I cannot even begin tell you how much this horses has improved our life. And," she held her hand alongside her mouth as if to hide what she was saying from her horse, and whispered loudly, "both Esfir and Mahin are have baby."

"Blavo!" Bonpo said. "Exacry what we want."

"It won't be long, relatively speaking," said Jabberwock, "until everyone has a horse of their own."

Azar's huge amber eyes were shining. "I cannot wait for Esfir give birth! I been studying the books we has on sheep and goats so I learn. I cannot think that it will be much different from sheep."

"The books should serve you well," Jabberwock said. "And,

if you remain calm and relaxed while the mares are giving birth, that will go further than any book knowledge."

Azar smiled, and prepared to mount Esfir. "Everyone are waiting for us to return."

THE FINAL MILE PASSED QUICKLY, and as they made their way through the village, the Imperator, Nahid, Jahan's father, Cyrus, and the others greeted them warmly, although the Preternaturals also expressed their disappointment that the remainder of the group wasn't with them.

After handing off Tikvah, and depositing their gear in the Community Hall (Bonpo's size once again preventing him from sleeping elsewhere), the two ambled over to the dining hall.

Bonpo wandered back to the kitchen to see if he could help in any way, and Jabberwock found a seat at one of the tables where Nahid joined him. He cautioned her that he would save most of the news for the dinner hour as he didn't want to repeat the information. "Except," he said.

"Except?" Nahid's brow creased.

"Except that the three preeminent Kingdoms in the Awen Alliance—Annewven, Simoon, and Adamah—have stepped up attacks in Sheba," he said.

Nahid's face lost its color. "Oh, by Omni, no, please not war."

Jabberwock couldn't decide if what she uttered was a prayer or a curse. "Exactly, which is what makes obtaining these final four Treasures so important."

"Yes!" Nahid's eyes were wide. "The community backs the Triquetra Alliance in one way or the other, but obviously we would prefer not to fight."

"Exactly." Jabberwock repeated the word. Centuries of experience were exhaled in his sigh.

They sat in silence for a moment, contemplating the atrocities of war.

"Even if we manage to retrieve all the Treasures," Jabberwock continued, "we are going to have to hold some kind of accord with the Awen Alliance. They are too focused on the power they desire to be completely influenced by the combined power of the Treasures. I feel that with a greatly expanded Triquetra Alliance behind us, we can at the very least force them into submission."

"That is definitely something we should hope and pray for," Nahid said.

Nahid hid her face with her hands before rubbing it briskly, and taking a deep breath. "We, and our ancestors, have seen hell itself and faced it. We will face this. We cannot let a few bullies decide the fate of the Thirteen Kingdoms when most of us just want to survive in some semblance of contentment."

"Exactly," Jabberwock reiterated for the third time. "Exactly."

Once again the Kuna community proffered the travellers a delicious meal—chicken in a delectably spicy sauce, and a variety of root vegetables and early spring greens to choose from. Freshly baked bread with which to mop up the sauce completed the meal. Everyone settled down to eating as most of them had been physically active since dawn. And yet, an undercurrent of excitement seemed to permeate the atmosphere. Everyone wanted to know what had transpired since Jabberwock and the other Treasure seekers had left Kuna before winter set in.

After everyone had eaten, Jabberwock filled the Preternaturals in on what had happened in the Questers absence. He kept the details to a minimum because he didn't want them to be privy to every particular, but he did let them know that the Princess had married Gwrhyr. He would let them find out of their own accord that Gwrhyr was King Uriel of Aden as it seemed a bit early in their return to the Quest to make that general knowledge. That information was better kept as secret as possible. The Questers' current identities needed to remain unknown as well. Their safety depended on it. So while Jabberwock refrained from saying whom was sent where, he did admit they had broken up into twos in order to complete the Quest more quickly.

"It seemed much more expedient," he said. "I can say that Bonpo and I are travelling to the former Kingdom of Pelf. We will try to make our way to the capital, Buta, to see if we can find their Treasure there."

"It might be foor's game," Bonpo interrupted.

"Yes, it might," Jabberwock agreed. "We are only going on what we know, but it has been centuries. And looking for a knife amidst sand and ruins might be like looking for a drop of oil in an ocean."

"Yet we mus' rook," Bonpo said.

Silence followed as what was said was digested. Bonpo and Jabberwock were clearly heading into dangerous territory.

"Do you have weapons with which to protect yourself?" Nahid asked, remembering that the group had had to fight off Aberrations in Kamea.

"I 'af axe and machetes," Bonpo said.

"Unfortunately, my only weapon is to retreat," Jabberwock said.

"'E mean lun away," Bonpo chuckled.

Jabberwock glared at him. "My options are limited by both my size, and the fact I cannot hold a weapon, so yes, 'run away', if you like, but there it is. And, I have to agree that it seems highly likely that we will have to fight off Aberrations at some point." He sighed. "They are what killed my Kamali, and yet I feel I must face this rather than having sent Gwrhyr or Faolan. I am the one that got away. She didn't."

"Yes," said Bonpo and his chest rose as he took an even deeper breath and expelled it loudly. "We mus' arr letuln to our ghosts in da end."

THE TWO DIDN'T WASTE ANY TIME in Kuna. The next morning they were on their way to Kamea where they would take the coastal highway, or what remained of it to the south although they would spend a night in the relative luxury of Shamash Palace before they did so.

If they had been honest with each other, they would have admitted that they preferred to remain in Kuna for another day or so. There was a certain peacefulness to the place—the folk tended toward the introverted, barring Jahan and his father, and there was a general acceptance that life in Kuna was the best their life could be, be it as it may.

But, time was a wastin', Jabberwock thought, as he snuggled down into his blanket for the night. They needed to focus on the Treasure—in this case, the Knife of Llawfrodded the Horseman, which could carve enough food for twenty-four men to eat at table. Jabberwock snorted quietly as he curled up tighter. Eluned had been correct all those months ago as she read the book about the Treasures at the inn in Mjijangwa—an awful lot of the Treasures revolved around food. Had they been created in a time of famine?

As Bonpo snored quietly on the floor next to him, Jabberwock's brain continued to race away. They knew they had clear sailing until Kamea, but once they turned southwards it was anyone's guess. And that is why the plan was to rise pre-dawn the following morning, and skip out of town with the Preternaturals being none the wiser. Or, at least they hoped so. Better to leave quietly, with little fanfare, they had decided, because Omni only knew when and if they'd return. And he despised long goodbyes.

ON THE THIRD DAY AFTER LEAVING KUNA, Bonpo, Tikvah, and Jabberwock began the descent toward the former capital city of Kamea. The journey there had been cold but uneventful. Shamash Palace was in the opposite direction of their travel, but it was difficult to resist a sure water source in the dry and barren ruins of that city. Bonpo reminded Jabberwock that it would be easier to protect themselves, if necessary, in one of the rooms off that central courtyard. As an added precaution, Tikvah would share the room with them.

As it turned out the increased security saved their lives. They had been asleep for a couple of hours, which made it close to midnight, when Tikvah emitted a worried bray. Bonpo was on his feet in seconds—machete in one hand, axe in the other.

"Wat 'appen?" he asked Jabberwock whose ears and tail were raised at full alert.

"Listen," Jabberwock whispered loudly.

They were silent for a moment. Bonpo had pulled Tikvah closer and was stroking her muzzle with the back of the hand that held the axe. A lumbered shuffling could clearly be heard on the other side of the door.

"The Aberrations," Jabberwock used his telepathy to communicate to Bonpo. "They know we are here."

Bonpo nodded as his grip tightened on his weapons. "You dink I should go out dere?" He tried to whisper.

"Wait," Jabberwock cautioned.

They couldn't barricade the entryways as there was no furniture to block the two functioning doors in each room. Bonpo could place his bulk against one door only to find they were forcing the other. He and Jabberwock moved closer to the courtyard entry as that seemed to be the location of most of the sound. But how many Aberrations were out there? His hearing was more acute than Bonpo's, but it was still difficult for him to determine whether it was two or twenty.

There was some feeble pushing and scratching at the courtyard door, which they had barred from the inside, a precaution they had built for each room when they were last here. But had the creatures thrown their combined weight against the door, the old wood they'd used for the bars would have split. They listened for another quarter of an hour before they finally heard the Aberrations shambling off.

Jabberwock silently thanked Omni for the fact that the Aberrations were not intelligent. Their advantage, when they were able to kill their prey, always came in the guise of surprise. They were capable of lying still beneath the sand for hours on end.

The three of them would need to be very careful when they travelled south that morning for it was nigh on two o'clock at this point, Jabberwock reckoned. He imagined there would be very little sleep for them until dawn as it was impossible not to continue to listen for the shuffling that would indicate another attempted attack.

Jabberwock mulled over the question of how they'd been discovered for the remainder of the night. They'd spent more than a month here and had only been attacked when the Aberrations had followed Faolan back to the palace.

Had they sniffed out their fellow monsters somehow? That seemed unlikely as the group had buried them well and months had passed since then. Or were they intelligent enough to search for their deceased friends or family until they found this well-used room? The scents of the Questers' former habitation in the courtyard might still linger here. That could have drawn them.

Jabberwock sighed, and tried to relax. They would never know for sure, but the Bandersnatch did realize that they would have to be ever so diligent if they wanted to make it to Buta alive.

As the Aberrations seemed to be most active from dusk until dawn, Jabberwock and Bonpo decided to wait to leave until after sunrise. If they were forced to face the monsters, it would be much easier in the light of day.

22ND NEEON

"You have returned!" Moshe took in his sister's disconsolate expression. "What has happened?"

Chokhmah slid off Halelu's back, handing her reins to Faolan. "The infamous Snow of Misery. Eluned managed to miss it last year, but we are farther north. The snow has yet to melt enough to make the road passable."

"Ironically, they think it'll be another week or two before travel can commence," Faolan added.

"Why is that ironic?" Moshe asked.

Faolan chuckled. "Because that will be around the time of the Vernal Equinox, which is when we originally intended to resume the Quest."

Moshe barked a laugh. "The ways of Omni are mysterious indeed. There must be a reason you needed to return to our camp."

There was a peculiar glint in her brother's eye, but Chokhmah was more concerned about what they would do and where they would stay for the next couple of weeks. She was sure they would be welcome back at Castle Mykerinos but she hated to backtrack more than they already had.

"May we spend the time we must wait here with you all?" she asked. "We will camp. I would not ask Daniel to . . ."

"Would not ask Daniel what?" her nephew said from behind her.

Chokhmah turned and hugged him. "I would not ask the use of your vardo."

"But of course you must use your wagon!" Daniel said, his offer sounding genuine.

"We may be here as long as two weeks," Chokhmah objected.

"The length of time makes no difference," he assured her, "but may I ask why you have returned?"

"The Snow of Misery," Moshe said.

Daniel nodded. "Ah, yes, I had forgotten about that. Normally we would be in Sheba now. But take my word for it, you are welcome to the vardo."

Moshe's eyes sparkled, and Chokhmah noted a little twitch at the corner of his mouth as he spoke. "I am thinking that there is a certain someone you may be wanting to bunk with."

"Who?" Chokhmah exclaimed. "That is not allowed unless . . ."

"Unless they are betrothed," Moshe completed her sentence.

"Daniel! Baksheesh!" Chokhmah hugged her nephew again. "We've only been away one night. Did you neglect to tell us this when we were here?"

"I would not forget such a thing!" Daniel returned his aunt's hug. "I gave her my scarf yesterday, and today she is wearing it."

"Ah, so you will spend a few days in the bender to see if you are suited," Chokhmah said. "You would not be needing the vardo anyway. But, you have not told me who it is."

"Avigail." Moshe and Daniel spoke simultaneously.

"Praise be to Omni!" Chokhmah smiled.

"Whoa! Stop!" Faolan finally protested. "I'm hopelessly behind here."

"I am so sorry, my love, I got lost in my excitement," Chokhmah said. "It is our tradition that if a young man is interested in a young woman, he gives her his neck scarf. If she wears it on her head, it means she is interested."

"Normally," Moshe said, "she and Daniel would begin to court before spending some time together in a wagon to see if they suit each other."

"But, I have known Avigail my entire life," Daniel explained. "We grew up together. It has only been during the past year that we have felt our friendship growing into something more."

"So no need for courtship, first?" Faolan asked. "You can go straight to co-habiting?"

"Exactly," Chokhmah said. "If in a few days, they still feel the same, we will have a pliashka or engagement feast." She turned to Daniel, smiling. "And I have no doubt that this will happen."

"It turns out the Snow of Misery might be yet another Omnincidence," Faolan said.

Chokhmah laughed. "It is true! Otherwise I would not be here to celebrate with Daniel, Moshe, and Chelli." She turned back to Daniel. "Then we happily accept your offer to use the vardo while we are waiting for the snow to melt."

THE FOLLOWING DAY, Chokhmah prepared a picnic lunch and she and Faolan, along with Daniel and Avigail, walked down to the banks of the Spruce River. There they found a broad trail that followed the river downstream where it eventually joined with the River Musk. A narrower trail ascended eastward towards the Mountains of Misericord, but they were more interested in a pleasant morning's stroll than a strenuous hike.

Conversation consisted mostly of pleasantries as they walked the three miles down river to a stretch of forest that

Daniel had told them about the previous evening. Here, the river widened, and as it flowed through an area of flat boulders, it formed shallow pools and little cascades for a quarter of a mile or so before narrowing once again. The spruce-fir forest through which they ambled perfumed the air with its delicate scent and a chorus of songbirds serenaded them. Compared to the misery of the Misericords, this late winter day almost shimmered in anticipation of better days to come.

As Faolan spread a blanket out on the flattest rock they could find, Chokhmah and Avigail retrieved the food from the baskets they'd been carrying. Cold rabbit, dried figs and apricots, as well as raisins and honey cakes were placed on the spread. Chokhmah surveyed Avigail surreptitiously as they set out the food. She and Faolan had set the pace on the hike to their picnic spot so she had, as yet, not had a good chance to study the young woman.

While she had known Avigail since her birth, Chokhmah wanted to see her through Daniel's eyes. She was a slender young woman who tended toward skinniness as opposed to being plump. Childbirth would probably not change that, although age might. One could never determine what changes would occur as one aged. Fortunately, Avigail's hips were not too narrow so there would probably be no problems when it came to having children. Like all the Roma, she had dark-lashed, deep brown eyes.

The fact that her own golden brown eyes had rarely generated comment now made Chokhmah wonder if more of her gypsy tribe had been aware of her heredity than they had let on. Her brow creased. Yet that could not be, as Moshe had seemed convinced she was his sister. Perhaps they had been told she was a gypsy child from a different group like the Calé. No one had ever let on that she was not Moshe's biological sister. He had been a toddler of four when she arrived in the camp at nineteen months. Surely he had been old enough to realize that she had appeared out of nowhere. How had her parents explained her arrival? She would have to ask him when they returned to camp that afternoon.

"Chokhmah?" Avigail's voice rang with concern. "Is everything all right?"

The older woman looked down, realizing she had stopped midway to placing the bowl of honey cakes on the blanket. She laughed. "Just woolgathering, my dear. It happens as you get older." She shook her head as if to clear her thoughts. "I was just remembering my own pliashka," she lied. She glanced at Faolan but he was preoccupied, having walked closer to the river to check out the cascades. She tried to refrain from referring to her previous husband, if possible, as Faolan was still a mite jealous of Yitzak.

Avigail giggled and slid Daniel a wicked glance. "You are jumping ahead. It has only been one night. I have yet to decide if there will be another." She winked at Daniel, who grinned and retrieved a jug of ale from his sack along with four wooden mugs.

"Do not listen to her, Auntie," he said. "I am the one that is unsure there will be a second night."

Avigail feigned anger, removing the colorful scarf from her head and revealing her glossy black hair. She extended the scarf toward Daniel. "Perhaps, you will want this back then. Who will you give it to next? Rox?"

"What? Rox?" Daniel grabbed her around the waist and pulled her closer. "Surely you do not think that I have ever had intentions toward Rox?"

Avigail smiled and kissed the tip of Daniel's nose. "Let us eat our lunch. I am starving. I forgot to eat breakfast this morning." She sat on the edge of the boulder, and held out her hand for the mug Daniel was handing her. He had filled it with ale before proceeding to fill the other three.

Daniel called Faolan over and once they were all seated,

Chokhmah toasted the couple. They clunked their cups together before taking a swallow of the refreshing liquid, and then began to fill their plates. Chokhmah closed her eyes and basked in the sensation of the sun's warmth on the top of her head. It had been a long and cold winter and she was looking forward to being warm again.

"You look content," Avigail noted, popping an apricot into her mouth.

"I have to admit," Chokhmah opened her eyes and looked at the young woman, "it is nice to have this respite before we begin the Quest again. It was a difficult trip to Zion because of the cold, and we did not rest long there before we once again began our journeying."

"Barely a week," Faolan confirmed.

She picked up some of the roasted rabbit and began to nibble on it. "I am not joking about the pliashka, Avigail, although I realize that these days it is little more than a formality."

"I thought it was just an excuse to celebrate," Daniel said.

"You mean an excuse to drink and dance," Chokhmah laughed. "Still, I am hoping that I might help you plan yours, particularly as we might be here for as long as two weeks."

"Hopefully not more," Faolan grunted.

"Why?" Daniel asked. "Do you not enjoy our company?"

"It's not that," Faolan said. "It's just that I'd like to get this trip to Simoon over with as quickly as possible."

"Yes," Chokhmah sighed. "The sooner the better. Things will soon reach a point in which we must sneak into the Kingdom, do you not agree, Faolan?"

"I think our cover is good," he said, "but it might only work if we are already residents. The way things are going, I'm not sure they'll be allowing immigrants from Sheba."

"Yes," she agreed, "I think rather that people will be fleeing the Kingdom of Simoon instead. But let us not think of that now. Today is beautiful, we are in pleasant company and we should be drinking to the happy couple."

"Absolutely!" Faolan said. "Baksheesh!"

"Baksheesh!" Chokhmah repeated.

"I did not realize that seeking this Treasure would be so dangerous," Avigail said with a shiver. "Yes, of course you may help me plan my pliashka, Aunt Chokhmah. It would be an honor."

DANIEL AND AVIGAIL'S PLIASHKA was to be held on Deethgwener evening so that the community would have a weekend to recover from the celebration. Chokhmah had spent the previous four days preparing and planning in order that everything would be perfect for the couple—engaging the help of the entire community in helping to provide them with a feast they would never forget.

Faolan decided it would be wise to stay out of her way unless he was instructed to do something.

By late afternoon on the fated day the camp was redolent with the aroma of all the foods being prepared for the feast. Chokhmah pulled out the bag into which Daniel had packed away the clothes she had left behind before leaving on the Quest, and removed a floor-length patchwork dress that was a particular favorite of hers.

The V-necked, capped-sleeve gown was pieced together from lace and silk in tones of cream, white and deep pink with a foot-long border of pink tulle at the bottom of the dress.

After pulling her hair up into a loose bun, which was much better to dance in, she thought, no detangling necessary before heading to bed, Chokhmah turned to see if Faolan was ready.

He was sitting on the bed, watching her, admiration and desire lighting his eyes. He patted the bed beside him, and she laughed

"Not today, my love," she said from the safety of the tiny kitchen. She could not risk the temptation by moving closer to him. "We will have to save that for later. We must be at Avigail's parents' vardo in just a few minutes."

Faolan sighed, and stood. He would be glad for this pliashka to finally be over. Chokhmah had been obsessed with preparing for it. He supposed it was because she would never be able to plan one for a child of her own, so he tried to remain good-natured about it. He walked over to the table and pulled her into his arms.

"I understand," he said, kissing her gently on the mouth. "Let the celebration begin."

They left the lavender vardo with its myriad paintings and walked over to a wagon that was much plainer in comparison. It, too, had art covering its sides but it had been applied directly to the varnished wood of the caravan.

Because the vardo was too small for everyone to fit inside, the closest members of each family had arranged to gather in front of it. The remainder of the Roma community would join in the festivities later, but Daniel and his parents, along with Avigail and her parents, and their immediate family would perform the ceremony in the little courtyard that had been constructed in front of the wagon.

Because it was still winter, Chokhmah had searched the forest for holly, and was happy to discover numerous bushes dripping with bright red berries. She cut some of these and used them to decorate the archway Faolan and Moshe had built for her. It would be a lovely backdrop for the ceremony.

Eliav and Mikhal, Avigail's mother and father, were already waiting in front of the wagon with her younger sister, Hadassah. As Chokhmah and Faolan joined them, Avigail's brother, Shaul, and his wife, Hagit walked up. The latter was well advanced in pregnancy.

A few minutes later, Moshe, Chelli, and Daniel arrived,

Moshe carrying a bottle of brandy wrapped in a turquoise and lime green silk handkerchief. A necklace of gold coins was also attached to the bottle.

Placing the necklace around Avigail's throat, Moshe hugged her warmly and welcomed her to the family. He then took a swig from the bottle and passed it to his wife, Chelli. Once the bottle had been passed around to everyone assembled for the ceremony, Moshe retrieved it. He would refill it later for the wedding ceremony.

After saying the requisite words beneath the arched canopy, it was time to leave for the feast. Laughing and singing, the two families paraded over to the communal campfire where the remainder of the community was gathered for the engagement dinner and dancing.

In some gypsy cultures, Chokhmah explained to Faolan quietly as they walked toward the campfire, it was the wedding and its accompanying feast that was most important. But, she said, in their community it had become customary to spend time in a bender prior to engagement making the pliashka acquire more importance. A low-key wedding would be held later, but tonight the camp would celebrate as if Daniel and Avigail were already man and wife.

"And you did this with Yitzak?" Faolan asked.

Chokhmah smiled, remembering. "Yes," she admitted, "we had a wonderful pliashka."

"I don't suppose we'll ever have one," Faolan said.

Squeezing his hand, Chokhmah shook her head and looked into his grey blue eyes. "I am sorry, my love. If I marry you, I will no longer be a part of this community."

"Why? Because I'm not Roma?"

"Yes, you are gaje," she explained. "A gaje woman can marry a Roma man and become Roma, but not the other way around."

Faolan frowned. "That doesn't seem fair."

"I agree, but I believe the tradition derived from the days in which a woman was the property of a man."

"I understand that," he said, "but aren't we smarter than that now? Can't a man decide whether or not he wants to become a part of the community?"

"It makes sense to me," Chokhmah said, and laughed. "I guess, now that I think about it, that I am lucky that I have been allowed to take part in all of this. After all, everyone now knows that I am not Roma at all, but Pelfan."

"Well, you are a female," he said, "and you were taken in by a gypsy family."

"True enough," she kissed his cheek and ruffled his short, light brown hair. "I suppose I will always remain Roma to them, but my heart belongs to a gaje, and always will."

"And mine to Queen Parisa even if I am a lowly gaje." His voice was hoarse with emotion, and could barely be heard over the tuning of the instruments as they passed the musicians preparing to play for the pliashka. But Chokhmah heard him and pulled his arm around her waist.

As they entered the circle that contained the campfire at its center they walked by numerous tables laden with food—roast mutton and goose, baked hams, tureens of stewed cabbage with pork, rice and tomatoes, beet soup, hare steamed with vegetables and flavored with tomato puree, paprika, and bell peppers, mutton stewed with sliced leeks, parsnips, carrots, celery, tomatoes, and more paprika.

There were also tables with breads and various potato dishes, and others with a wide variety of sweets from rich and buttery yeast cakes to cookies made with honey, nuts and cinnamon.

And alcohol, lots of alcohol. There was wine, brandy, and ale and spirits made from various fruits—plums, apples, pears. Chokhmah almost lost her appetite as the different odors battled for her attention.

She finally settled on a simple soup of lamb, potatoes, and paprika and a tankard of mulled wine. Chokhmah had to hide her smile when Faolan settled next to her with a plate piled high with various meats. Clearly he had no intention of going hunting that evening. But she had no intention of harassing him about his carnivorous ways as she was acutely aware of how much he had sacrificed his own needs during the past few days in order that she might plan this event.

And that, she realized was a type of love she had never experienced with Yitzak. They had equally shared in their love until he became ill and she spent his remaining years nursing him. What would life with Faolan be like ten, twenty years from now?

"What?" Faolan asked when he felt the weight of her gaze upon him.

She turned the full radiance of her smile on him. "I was realizing once again just how lucky I am to have found you, and I was wondering what the future might hold for us."

"I wonder that myself." He took her right hand in his left, and raised it to his mouth and kissed her palm. "At this point, I am just praying to Omni that we survive our trip to Simoon."

Shuddering, Chokhmah realized she still didn't want to think about it. She had the feeling that Sigwald was going to be even more dangerous than Buta, and she would much rather face the Aberrations than King Hamartia or Queen Foehn. She had not forgotten that they had been complicit in Eluned nearly losing her life. They had been among the inner circle that stood around the altar on which Eluned was to be sacrificed. King Hamartia had been standing right next to King Arawn when Eluned cut his hand off with her sword, the hand that had been holding the dagger that would slit her throat.

"Drink up!" she said, taking a long swallow of wine. "It is time to dance and forget about Quests and Treasures for a little while."

"Amen," Faolan agreed, taking a swig of brandy and shoveling a forkful of roasted lamb into his mouth. But he wasn't sure he could forget about the Quest for more than a minute. Even though he could shift into a wolf, even though Chokhmah could use the ring and become invisible, he felt a prickling of fear when he thought about Simoon. He could smell the scent of danger—acrid and sharp like ozone. They may have a Kingdom between them, but the scent was sharper than the roasted meats on the plate in his lap. He hoped that they could get in and out of Simoon with the Whetstone in hand as quickly as possible.

He no longer had an appetite. Setting his plate aside, he tossed back his glass of fruit brandy and stood. "I need another," he told Chokhmah before heading off to the table serving as a bar.

"Bring me back one as well," Chokhmah called after him, forcing herself to eat another spoonful of her soup so that her stomach would not be completely empty when Faolan returned with the brandy. She, too, needed to be a little more lubricated before she could forget what they would soon be heading into.

17ᵀᴴ SAITHEH

Eluned stared into the flames of their final campfire before they reached the bustling capitol of Kamartha on the morrow. Her expression was morose—lips turned down in a frown, forehead creased between her eyebrows. Between the nearly constant rain of the past two weeks, and the fact that everyday seemed as cold if not colder than the previous day, her spirits had plummeted. Add those factors to the fact it was the seventeenth of Saitheh, and it was all she could do not to cry. She took a sip of the honey mead that had been offered by their current gnome host, Skordan. He had met them alone as his wife had to remain at home with their recently born daughter.

"All right, out with it," Gwrhyr said when he could no longer stand his young wife's silence and her barely audible sighs.

"It's the seventeenth of Saitheh," she said.

He stared at her, eyes blank with incomprehension.

"Once again," she found it difficult to keep the rising note of self-pity out of her voice, "it's Chokhmah's birthday, and once again I cannot celebrate it with her."

Yona groaned, remembering. "That's right. Last year her birthday was on May Day."

"And you were with Libni," Eluned said, "and King Arawn forced me to go to every single booth at the festival with him."

"Why was that?" Njima asked.

"I think he was punishing me for returning to the castle so late on the night of the Pascha Feast," she said.

"That, and for talking to that jewelry vendor again," Yona added.

"Which he paid dearly for," Gwrhyr grimaced. Although he hadn't been there, Eluned had described the scene to him in detail. The poor man's slashed throat and blue lips still haunted her nightmares.

"I nearly did as well," Eluned said. "Do you think that was the turning point? That that night was the night he decided I was to be the sacrifice?"

"I think it was earlier," Yona mused, "but I agree that he probably decided for sure that night. He was furious with you."

"Regardless," Gwrhyr said. "That is in the past. We are here now. Skordan has provided us with some excellent mead. And tomorrow, we finally reach Kaumari. I say let's celebrate Chokhmah's birthday even though she isn't here."

"I dunna know this woman," Skordan said, raising his mug, "but may she live long and well."

"Here! Here!" Eluned drained her cup and extended it to Gwrhyr so that he could refill it. She needed all the warmth she could get, and the mead had ignited a warming fire in her belly.

THEY HAD SPENT THE PREVIOUS FOUR WEEKS arising at the crack of dawn. That often meant getting ready in the pale pink morning light. They would then push a little farther each night, arriving to set up camp, as the sun began to disappear in a similarly rosy light. All the effort expended to ensure that they stayed ahead of the travellers they had met their first night on the road.

As they left the plains of Naphtali for the undulating

terrain that bordered the Sea of Blood in the north, another gnome greeted them each evening. This usually occurred after they had climbed the steep prairie-like southern slope of a hill, ridden across its flat top where the established camp was often located, and began the descent into spruce, lodgepole pine, and aspen forest on the northern side of the hill.

Here, a gnome would be waiting trailside to lead them to a clearing near a stream or spring. When they turned eastward toward Kamartha, the pattern changed as the main road followed the valley beneath the hills. But, they bypassed the established site, and within an hour or two, a gnome would make himself known, usually at the western edge of a hill, and lead them into the forest.

It made for exhausting days, but they had managed to make it to the outskirts of Kaumari in just four weeks. Crossing the border into Kamartha had occurred without a hitch as they clearly looked like travellers who might be entertainers but certainly not like two queens and a king.

The following morning, they said their farewells to Skordan, who instructed them where to meet Tancorin, their final gnome guide. They checked themselves over before they left in order to assure each other that they were as ready as possible to play the parts of Ivanhoe and Rowena and Zenobia and Skaði. As it had been just over a month since they left Jazeel, both Yona and Njima needed to re-cut their hair and touch up their roots before they approached anyone at Lamaxana Palace.

Rather than return immediately to the trail, the group decided to ascend the last of the flat-topped hills so that they could survey the sprawling city below them before they ventured into it. Kaumari was situated on the east bank of the Qraarc, a tributary that flowed southward into the Zeuns River, which bordered the southern edge of the country at its boundary with the Devastation of Pelf.

It was in the forests that skirted the Zeuns River that Eluned's great grandmother's former home was located. The King of Kamartha at that time did not have a child who could be wed to the King of Zion, and they had offered the daughter of his Lord High Chancellor to help establish a tentative alliance. Fuchsia's home had been in the Wilds of Discord, just across the river from the Devastation. Eluned was hopeful that she and Gwrhyr might have a chance to visit there before journeying on to Dziron, although it would mean heading south before travelling north again to the main trade route. She was also really looking forward to walking down The Masala, the infamous road in Kaumari that was lined with myriad theaters, some of which Queen Fuchsia may have acted in.

After contemplating what lay before them for several minutes, they began the descent into the broad valley with its teeming capitol city. Kaumari couldn't even compare to Zion's capitol, Goshen, Eluned thought, which was small like Favonia's Seemu. Prythew, Jazeel, and even Ponike, though much larger than Goshen and Seemu, the only other capitol cities Eluned had been to, also didn't compare. She began to worry that they'd get lost and be unable to meet up with Tancorin.

"I'm afraid we'll disappear into the city and never be found again," Eluned laughed but it sounded unconvincing.

"Don't worry," Njima said. "I am sure the soldiers at the city gate are accustomed to directing visitors around their town."

"I believe that the place where we are to meet Tancorin will be well before we enter the city proper," Gwrhyr added.

"And that he will tell us exactly where we need to go to find reputable but inexpensive lodgings that will suit our characters," Njima said.

Eluned arranged her hood to more fully cover her face. She shivered in pretense because she was really trying to hide her smile. Sometimes Njima sounded so formal when she spoke. She hoped for her sake she could sound less so when the two women finally reached Lamaxana Palace.

"Thanks, Zenobia," she giggled. "You're right, of course. So far everything has worked out well for us. Things may eventually get more dangerous," she paused thinking about Chokhmah and Faolan in Simoon, "but there is no reason for them to be so at this point."

Returning to her thoughts as they continued to descend, Eluned sighed inwardly. Four weeks on the road had left her longing for the luxury of a hot bath, a good bed, and decent food. Sponge baths and quick dips in frigid streams had taken their toll. But she also knew that she would have to continue to play their game of deception until all the Treasures were in hand. They just couldn't take the risk of seeming out of character.

Njima was right, Eluned mused. She really didn't need to worry. The gnomes had taken excellent care of them so far. Regardless, that woman is fearless, Eluned thought, studying the arrow straight back ahead of her. Because of her unease, she had taken up the rear. Maybe, she thought, being a queen made you take for granted things would be taken care of the way you expected them to be. The location where they were to meet Tancorin seemed ephemeral to Eluned—"Take ther las' road 'fore yee reach ther city gates an' turn left. Tancorin'll meet yee 'neath ther second fir on ther left." Those were the instructions, and Eluned fretted about them. Would they be able to determine that it was the last road before the city gates? How do you count the trees—by the ones closest to the road?

Eluned closed her eyes and took a deep breath. She would let the others figure it out. No one else seemed to be anxious. Her gut was telling her something was wrong, but her intuition had been wrong before . . . or had it?

To distract herself, she started thinking about coming up with another ballad. The first one, in her humble opinion, was really bad. But surely her songs would continue to get better if she kept working on them?

She was deep in thought constructing a verse about finally meeting with Nyx when she realized that they were turning left. Was this the last road before the city gates? She looked around her. They had reached the wide valley that Kaumari was nestled in, although some of the town had wended its way up the slopes of the ridges like a vine.

Firs. They were ubiquitous here, she thought. How would they know which was the second tree? But Gwrhyr, who was leading, guided his stallion, Ruari, into a little picnic area almost immediately upon turning onto the smaller byway off the main trade route. It was late enough in the morning that there were no breakfasters at the half a dozen tables scattered around the clearing, but still too early for people to be eating their midday meal. All was quiet, even the insects and the birds, and that also sent warning bells ringing in Eluned's ears.

Her husband and her friends all seemed so sure of themselves, she thought. Why wasn't she? Eluned had serious misgivings about this meeting, and unconsciously her hand reached for Dyrnwyn, but her sword wasn't there. She was carrying a dagger. Dyrnwyn was safely ensconced in Castle Mykerinos. In her gut, she knew that something wasn't quite right, but she could not put her finger on why that might be.

Suddenly, she had gone from complacent to hyper-aware. And, as she narrowed in on those feelings, she knew with every fiber of her being that it was an ambush.

"Stop!" she bellowed, and her friends, unused to her putting that much force into her voice, reined their mounts in immediately.

"What is it?" Gwrhyr turned to look at her, forehead wrinkled in consternation.

"It's a trap," was all she could manage to utter.

"She knows," Yona said, seeing the expression on Eluned's

face. "Let's get the kusemmak out of here." She was already turning Aine around.

"What?" Njima's voice echoed with confusion. This was supposed to be a simple meeting.

Eluned placed her left hand on the dagger at her hip. "Look," she pointed back towards the forest with her right hand.

Several roughly dressed and dirty men were pushing a gnome, clearly under duress, out of the woods. His hands seemed to be restrained behind his back. Two of the men carried bows in their right hand.

"Tancorin?" Eluned questioned but she knew. Somehow someone had found out about them.

Perhaps the best option, Eluned thought as she realized the dagger she'd pulled was hardly the weapon to defend themselves against these armed men, is to head back to the city gates. Surely they wouldn't be challenged there? She re-scabbered the knife and said, "Let's go! There's nothing for us here!" She turned Ronan around and joined Yona. "We can lose them, right?"

"Absolutely!" Yona agreed, giving a forceful kick to Aine's ribs. "Let them try to follow us!"

Eluned looked back, Gwrhyr and Njima had already turned their mounts.

"Yes," Njima agreed, urging Makeda into a trot.

As they fled the picnic area, Eluned felt an arrow whizz by her right side, just a few inches from her bicep. A second later, she felt a sting of pain as an arrow pierced the hood she had over head, grazing her left ear and slicing a furrow through her left cheek. She clenched her teeth against the pain, and urged Ronan into a gallop. Her cheek and ear throbbed, and she could feel the warmth as a thin sheet of blood began to slide down her cheek, soaking her cloak and sweater.

A moment later, Makeda gave a piercing whinny as an arrow found its way into her right hind flank. It actually spurred the mare on to greater speed and it wasn't long before the quartet managed to lose themselves in the crowd of travellers pressing toward the city gates.

"We need a healer," Gwrhyr shouted when he saw Eluned's flayed cheek, exposed when her hood had fallen away from her face in the flight away from the clearing. The entire left side of her face, from cheekbone to just above her lip was a solid sheet of red.

"We also need an animal doctor," Yona said, glancing over at Makeda.

"Please let us through," Njima begged. "We need medical attention."

Most of the travellers looked with indifference at the horse, which infuriated Eluned, but gasped in horror when they saw the damage done to her otherwise flawless face.

The crowd helped push them toward the front of the line, and it wasn't long before they were through the gates, and being directed to someone who could take care of them.

Now that they were immediately out of harm's way, Eluned took the handkerchief proffered by Gwrhyr and held it tentatively to her face. Just the touch of the cloth against the gaping wound sent paroxysms of pain through her body. She had nearly lost her life less than a year ago, but she had never experienced this kind of physical pain. She didn't need anyone to tell her that she was going to be left with a horrendous scar.

Her eyes filled with tears and she glanced at Gwrhyr. He looked back at her, forehead creased with worry.

"Is there anything I can do?" he said.

She shook her head, and reached out a hand. He took it and squeezed it.

"It's going to be okay," he said, though the concern in his eyes made her wonder if that was true.

Eluned had insisted on someone who could help Makeda

because she knew they would be able to help her too. As they wended their way down a crowded street, they turned onto another, quieter street, and found the building they were looking for—simple but for the bright blue door decorated with myriad paintings of animals.

An elderly woman met them at the door, and her eyes were bright and kind as she quickly took in the situation.

"You first," she said to Eluned, taking her by the arm and leading her into a room with a flat table on which she was directed to sit. "Let's see about that cheek." She picked up a spotless white cloth and a container of some liquid Eluned couldn't identify.

"I won't lie to you," the woman, who introduced herself as Purva, said. Her silver hair was coiled intricately about her head and she wore a spotlessly clean black gown and a silver amulet shaped like a lotus on her ample chest.

The better to hide the blood, Eluned thought as she looked at the dress. She attempted not to focus on the process as her cheek and ear were cleared of that substance. Closing her eyes and gritting her teeth against the pain, Eluned tried not to make a sound as Purva continued to speak.

"You will have a scar," the healer said. "I can sew the ear back together and it will mend, but it will always look slightly different than the other. And your cheek," she shook her head.

She felt a brief twinge of panic. Would her husband still find her attractive? She couldn't bear the thought of his regarding her with repulsion. And she didn't even want to think about what her ear might look like. That could easily be hidden—by her hair, hats, scarves. But her face? It wasn't possible to hide one's face from one's beloved.

She glanced at Gwrhyr. His jaw was clenched and he looked angry. He noticed her looking, and shook his head.

"I wish to Omni it had been me," he said with a choked voice.

Eluned remembered Libni's scarred face. "I'll look like a pirate," she said, wincing at the pain speaking caused her. Yona burst into tears. "What, Skaði? You told me you loved your friend's scars!" Eluned tried to comfort her friend, remembering almost too late that they were also still in disguise and forgetting to change her dialect.

"I know," Yona sniffled, "but your face was so perfect, and I just hate it for you."

"We all knew that we would face risks as entertainers, right?" Eluned trying to be Rowena assured her. "I'm not sure why poor actors would be attacked, but I've never been to Kamartha. Maybe it happens all the time."

"There are some rough elements out there," Purva agreed. "You all are riding quality horses. That might have been more than enough to prompt an attack."

Eluned breathed an inward sigh of relief.

"The horses," Gwrhyr sighed. "I worried about that but they were a wedding gift from my parents, and it seemed a shame to leave them behind."

Purva had finished cleaning Eluned's cheek, and applied a numbing concoction that she allowed a few minutes to take effect as she set about sterilizing a needle. When Purva turned toward her, needle in hand, Eluned closed her eyes tight and reached for Gwrhyr's hand. It was bad enough to see the needle approaching her face, but she was sure she couldn't handle watching it pierce her skin. She liked to think she was brave, but facing off attackers was easier to confront than this.

Even with the numbing agent, Eluned could still feel the tug each time the thread was pulled tight and tied off. How fortunate she'd been, she thought as she tried to ignore what was happening. She had made it to the age of nineteen without ever having broken a bone or needing stitches.

When the procedure was complete and her wound covered in balm, Purva covered the injury with a bandage and cautioned Eluned to keep it clean. She then directed Eluned to return in a week so that she might check on the stitches.

Eluned grimaced inwardly. She wasn't sure they could remain in Kaumari for the night, much less another week. Nevertheless, she promised to do just that.

Purva then turned to administer to Makeda. "Can you hold her still?" she asked Gwrhyr.

"She is my horse, ma'am," Njima said, reaching for the reins. "I can keep her calm."

"You are?"

"Zenobia."

"Well, Zenobia, what if you both hold her? She's not going to like this."

Once again, Purva applied a numbing solution to the torn skin around the wound. "Did you see the arrows being used, what kind of tips they had?"

"I'm thinking they were broad tips," Yona said, remembering the jagged edge of Eluned's cut.

"My thought exactly," Purva said, "and not the type of point you want to pull out. I will need to cut off the fletching and push it through her flank."

The arrow was at a 45-degree angle. Purva shook her head, thinking.

"We may want to hobble her, and lay her on her left side," Gwrhyr suggested.

"We're going to have to give her a sedative, first," Purva said. "There is no way around it. Young man? I forgot your name?"

"Ivanhoe."

Purva chuckled. "Interesting. Bring me that blue flagon." She pointed to Yona. "And you, Skaði?"

Yona nodded. "Yes, ma'am."

"You artist types," the healer rolled her eyes. "See that funnel over there? Bring that to me."

Once Purva had the funnel and liquid, she had Ivanhoe and Zenobia help keep Makeda's mouth open while she poured in the tranquilizer.

"Hold her mouth shut," she warned when she removed the funnel. Gwrhyr clamped his hands around Makeda's velvety muzzle while Njima stroked her face and spoke to her softly. The horse swallowed convulsively, before shaking her head violently, but she managed to consume most of the fluid.

"That should take fifteen minutes or so to take effect," Purva said. "I will get what I need ready while we wait." She disappeared into a storeroom and returned a few minutes later with a number of items, including more bandages. She handed some of them to Eluned. "You'll need to change your bandage daily."

Makeda's eyes were starting to close and it took effort for her to hold her head up. Njima coaxed her to the floor, pulling the mare's huge head into her lap.

A little over half an hour later the arrow had been removed from Makeda's flank, washed with antiseptic, stitched, and bandaged.

"That, too, will need to be kept clean and watched closely. You can also return in a week for me to check it," Purva told Zenobia, who agreed that she would. "She probably should not be ridden for several days as well. If you can find someplace to stable her and keep her quiet, so much the better."

ONCE THEY'D MADE A SHOW of scrounging together enough money to pay Purva for her services, they led their horses to the first quiet alley they could find to discuss their options. While they had enough money secreted away to make sure they could make it to the Kingdoms they needed to reach, and back again to Zion, they didn't have a lot to spend on emergency extras.

That was poor planning, Eluned thought. Just because

they hadn't suffered any costly accidents in the previous year, didn't mean that that would continue. And now what were they to do? She and Gwrhyr would be moving on to Dziron, but Yona and Njima planned to stay in the city and hopefully make themselves known to the palace. They had no magic tricks like she and Chokhmah to obtain their Treasure—the Horn of Bran—perhaps easily hidden but not so easily obtained.

And now it was known that the four of them were in Kamartha, Kaumari even. Their only advantage was the fact that because of the cold, they had all been hooded. No one had actually seen them in disguise.

"I think our best option at this point," Gwrhyr said, "is to go ahead and split up. We just can't risk being seen together any longer."

Eluned's heart throbbed, painfully, and she gritted her teeth willing the tears not to rise in her eyes. He was right, of course, but she had so looked forward to seeing Kaumari and the Wilds of Discord.

Njima nodded. "Yes, the Treasures are all important. We must focus on obtaining them."

Yona looked as stricken as Eluned. "It's true," she admitted with reluctance. "We'll stand a much better chance of not being seen if there are only two of us rather than four."

"It's also going to be important," Gwrhyr said, "for us to not only find our own lodgings tonight, but to be careful in how we go about that."

"It would be better to ask a stranger, if possible," Njima said.

"Exactly," he said. "If we find a random stranger, say a vendor or someone just walking down the street, it will be less noticeable."

"We could even ask a waitress or waiter," Yona suggested. It was now well past noon and she was beyond hungry.

"Whatever you do, be cautious," Gwrhyr warned. "And

now we need to say our farewells. The longer we're together, the more dangerous it is."

Eluned threw herself into Yona's arms. "May Omni be with you my friend. It may be a long time before we see each other again. If you arrive back in Zion before we do and return to Jazeel, I'll send a pigeon to let you know we're safe once we return."

"It will all work out," Yona said. "It has so far. At least none of us are dead."

"And Omni willing none of us will die," Gwrhyr said, wondering how the other four Questers were proceeding. As far as they knew everyone was fine, but being in Kingdoms allied with Kings Arawn, Hamartia, and Hevel was turning out to be a lot more dangerous than originally anticipated.

The Lamaxana Palace was located in South Kaumari, the major trade route Eluned and Gwrhyr needed to get them to Jungnay skirted the city to the north.

With a final goodbye, the two couples separated, leading their horses in opposite directions.

8ᵀᴴ Saitheh

The Anoon Ocean glimmered in the distance as the plateau fell away to the west. The Sea of Blood was a barely visible glint to the north. Bonpo and Jabberwock surveyed the land bridge below them. Once they descended the plateau, they would cross the slow moving runnel that was the outlet for the former Djed Sea. From there, they would begin making their way along the coast to the ruins of Buta, once the capitol of the Kingdom of Pelf.

Jabberwock had no idea what to expect. Kamea lay under centuries of sand, and he thought it likely that Buta had suffered even worse depredations following the initial catastrophe that had destroyed it. Unlike Kamea, it was on the coast of a living sea and sea levels had risen more than one hundred feet in the past five centuries. The Zhaleh Palace, if he remembered correctly, was on a high cliff overlooking the town below. Not unlike King Uriel's Castle Bennu. If they were lucky, they would find its ruins still accessible.

A LITTLE OVER TWO WEEKS EARLIER, they had attached their gear, and Jabberwock's saddle, to Tikvah and were about to leave the palace when Bonpo stalled for time by readjusting some of their equipment.

"What is it?" Jabberwock asked.

"Wat?" Bonpo flushed.

"There's something on your mind," the Bandersnatch said, "and I can't quite read it. It seems to be taking great effort on your part to block it from me."

Bonpo heaved a huge sigh. "It jus' dat I don't feer safe for-rowin' coas.'"

Jabberwock considered this for a moment. The truth was he'd been fretting about the same thing. They had been fortunate enough the previous night to be in a room that could be made safe, and still the Aberrations had discovered them. It was very likely that they would now camp, exclusively, until they reached Buta. Not only would it be difficult to protect a tent, but also there was no way all three of them could fit in it. It was a tight fit for Bonpo who often chose to sleep beneath the stars when the weather permitted. "Do you have another plan?"

"I tink we should letuln prateau, an' forrow it as crose as possiba to da Anoon."

Pondering the idea, Jabberwock realized Bonpo was correct. On the plateau they should be able to have campfires that would scare away any animal predators. And, if Jabberwock remembered his geography, the plains of Naphtali eventually ended and transitioned into forest perhaps a dozen or so miles south of Kamea, which would provide them with greater cover.

But the most important thing to consider was the Aberrations, and it was extremely doubtful that those abhorrent humanoids would be on the plateau. They hadn't run into any up there during their previous stay in Kamea. Jabberwock nodded. "Yes," he said. "I believe that's an excellent plan, Bonpo. Next time, don't be afraid to speak up."

"I aflaid it take too much time," he explained.

"Perhaps," Jabberwock agreed, "but it will probably ensure that we make it to the land bridge, at any rate. The land is more solid up there, as well. Remember how difficult it was to find our way to the palace the first time? We'll face similar issues once we pass the road up to the plateau."

"To da prateau den," Bonpo said.

"Yes," Jabberwock said, snuggling down into his basket. "To the plateau."

ALL HAD GONE WELL FOR THE TRIO as they traversed the plateau in a slow arcing curve southwestward. Jabberwock estimated that they had likely made up some time as it was easier for Bonpo and Tikvah to travel on the flat ground of the prairie. The first day out of Kamea, they could see the landscape changing by the end of the day, and decided to push on until just before sunset so that they might camp in the woods that evening and feel less exposed than they would on the plain.

Numerous deer trails made travelling through the forest, which grew to the very edge of the plateau, easier than trudging along the sandy coast. The lack of significant undergrowth and charred sections of tree trunks caused Jabberwock to guess that a lightning strike had a caused a forest fire in the not too distant past.

Because there were deer, the forest was probably host to wolves and perhaps even wild cats, but Bonpo and Jabberwock never heard anything more than the occasional squirrel and other smaller animals as well as lots of bird song throughout the day. Jabberwock spotted a fox one evening after slaking his thirst in a small stream, but otherwise they had seen few creatures. Most importantly, and something neither of them considered as they were leaving the palace, there were continual sources of water whether it be from a spring or a brook.

"So what do you think?" Jabberwock asked Bonpo who was squinting toward the ocean.

"I dink we shourd go south, wark beach," Bonpo said.

"Because?"

"I dink safel. Onry get attack flom one side," he explained.

Jabberwock nodded, considering. "It's definitely worth trying. The further away from the Sea of Blood, the better. Will water be a problem?"

Bonpo shrugged. "Ploblem eida way."

They would still have to descend toward the west as the southern face of the plateau was sheerer and it would be more difficult to forge their own path there. The western face sloped a little more gently and would be easier to negotiate. Once down, they could turn south toward the ocean.

They reached the strip of land between the two Kingdoms shortly after the sun had reached its zenith. The river that formed the border was probably no more than a mile or two distant. After a quick lunch of a trail mix containing almonds, peanuts, raisins, dried apricots, and pumpkin seeds, the trio set off toward the outlet of the former Djed Sea. It was warmer here than it had been in Kamea, and Bonpo's black hair seemed to soak in all of the heat provided by the unremitting sun.

He pulled a voluminous handkerchief from his pocket and mopped at his sweaty face. "Can't wait to closs and get to ocean," he said. "Prenty bleeze dere."

The only consolation in this case, Jabberwock thought as they crossed the land bridge, was that the force of the explosion that had caused the two plates to collide had also supplied enough heat to turn the surface glassy. It made the surface less tricky to walk on as very little sand had covered it in the past five centuries.

Jabberwock assumed that occasional storms blowing in from the sea blew the sand northward. There would probably be some impressive dunes mounded up nearer the Sea of Blood. The blown sand had, no doubt, silted up the river as well, causing it to slow to an almost sluggish trickle.

When they reached it, they discovered that the outlet of the Sea of Blood was indeed a thick and shallow saline soup—easy to cross but it left a nasty residue. Bonpo had rolled up his pants but they hadn't walked a mile southward along the river toward the ocean before both his and Tikvah's legs were crusted in salt.

"Vely uncomfolbre, dis" was his only comment, but Jabberwock realized the giant must be suffering severely, between the sun and salt, to have said anything at all.

"But we're in the Kingdom of Pelf!" Jabberwock tried to cheer him up. "In less than two weeks, Omni willing, we'll be in Buta."

"'Ope it easia find tleasule dan in Kamea," Bonpo said.

Jabberwock sighed. So did he, but he wasn't as hopeful as he'd like to be.

THE SUN HAD NEARLY REACHED THE HORIZON in the west, staining the ocean orange and red and yellow in the fading light, when they topped a dune and finally saw the Anoon. The trio had heard the roar of crashing waves for a while and were disappointed each time they topped a bank of sand to see yet another in front of them.

Jabberwock and Bonpo had been keeping an eye out for footprints, particularly in the slack between each dune as well as on the leeward side where the wind didn't touch the sand as much. They breathed a sigh of relief each time they noted only the presence of small animals like lizards, birds, and crabs.

Bonpo was fantasizing about finding some tidal pools in which he might harvest some sea urchins, crabs, or even small octopuses to add some substance to their meals. Their continuous travel had prohibited time for hunting and what meat they carried with them was either jerky or hard sausage. Not a huge problem, but he and Jabberwock, like Faolan, were predominantly carnivorous, and the giant really longed for fresh meat.

Bonpo was thinking that Tikvah would be content with some sea oats and dried kelp when he reached the top of the dune and saw waves crashing less than a hundred yards away. He jogged all the way to the Anoon, pulling Tikvah into the ankle high water at its edge and scrubbing away the salt around her legs, then his.

The yeti knew this water would also dry to salt on their legs, but it would be nothing compared to what they'd gone through earlier.

Jabberwock patiently left him to his ablutions before recommending that they find a place to camp before the sun disappeared.

Bonpo grunted, and led Tikvah from the waves before scanning the beach. In the distance it appeared as if the dunes slowly gave way to a rising cliff face. There might be caves there or it might mean they'd have to hike inland and travel along the top of the cliff. Either way, much too far to reach tonight, he thought. They would probably reach the cliff face tomorrow afternoon.

He grunted again. "Guess we go back dune, figul' out molnin.'"

Jabberwock, who was also searching the beach for possible shelter, agreed. "It's too late to do otherwise. Hopefully, we'll be safe. Maybe we can gather some driftwood for a campfire?"

"We?" Bonpo guffawed. "Oh, Hiurau! You so funny!"

Jabberwock rolled his glassy eyes. "What I wouldn't give for opposable thumbs!"

"You and Tikvah bot," Bonpo chuckled.

They made their way back up the beach, Bonpo stooping to pick up driftwood every time they passed some, and occasionally strapping a bundle to Tikvah so that he could pick up more. By the time they topped the dune, and made it down to the trough between the next one, the light was rapidly diminishing.

The first order of business was setting up a campfire for the evening, and while Jabberwock waited patiently in his basket, Bonpo set about getting a fire of driftwood going.

Once it was blazing away, Jabberwock stared into the flame's myriad colors—blue, green, pink, orange, and yellow reflecting in his eyes as he pondered how useless he was when it came to setting up camp.

He had travelled this way once before, centuries ago, but he had been alone and suffering the ravages of grief. If he ate at all, it was only to prevent starvation. From the Devastation of Pelf, he had mostly followed the coast until he'd reached Ponike in Aden. Food was easy to scavenge on the beach—crabs, abalone, limpets, mussels, and the occasional fish trapped in a tidal pool. He was small, he didn't need much, and he was perfectly willing to eat food raw and assuage his thirst in the occasional water source. He also needed neither a fire nor a tent as it was easy for a creature as small as he was to secret himself away behind rocks, under shrubs, amidst tall grasses, whatever was handy.

Ironic that he'd been perfectly capable of taking care of himself for centuries—when he was on his own. Add humans to the mix, or even yetis, and suddenly he was relegated to the campfire while everyone else prepared the camp for the evening.

He sighed loudly, and Bonpo, who was bringing him some water and jerky, had a rare moment of insight.

"At reast you 'elp dig at Shamash, Hiurau. We no mine you can't do udder tings."

"Thank you, Shangsung," Jabberwock said. "That means a lot to me. I try to offer what I can, as little as that might be."

Bonpo laughed and settled down next to him, tossing another dry and twisted log onto the fire. "No self-pity you! You know you da backbone of dis ques'. You keep us arr focus. Udderwise we arr be stirr in Favonia. Wolse! Dead!"

Jabberwock chortled. "No hyperbole there, my dear Shangsung."

"None at arr!" Bonpo laughed. "We in Perf! Tomollow we cereblate. Stop earry, catch fish fo' dinna."

"Yes," Jabberwock agreed. "I believe we deserve a little celebration before we begin the final leg of our trek."

Ensconced safely between the dunes, with Tikvah settled right outside the door of the tent, they bedded down for the night. Bonpo was first on watch and dozed with one ear open for predators but all was quiet. When Jabberwock took over, he was wide awake but soon the sound of the waves softly crashing on the shore lulled him into the most peaceful slumber he'd had since being chased out of the Vale Vixen in the Peaks of Vulpecula in Dziron more than five centuries ago.

THEY HIT THE BEACH NOT LONG after dawn. It was almost eerie how primeval it felt, Jabberwock mused as he scanned the beach, which seemed to be empty for miles in either direction. It was as if no one had stepped foot on these shores in thousands of years.

It didn't take long for nature to return to her self, Jabberwock thought. Humans would always move toward not only the destruction of themselves, but also anything they considered Other, but life would go on. Until. Until when?

He glanced at the sun, a pale orange rising at their backs as they travelled westward along the beach. As the sun continued its path to becoming a red giant, the Bandersnatch reflected, it would continue to grow in luminosity. At some point, actually for centuries now, both flora and fauna would continue to die off until nothing existed and the planet would be composed of nothing but rock and noxious gases. Jabberwock was willing to bet that humans would destroy themselves long before the earth reached that point—they had already attempted to do so numerous times in the past millennium or two.

Only love could conquer hate. Unfortunately, far too many people chose the latter. Hate and fear. It was what had destroyed the Janawar. It was what would destroy humanity.

"You arr light?" Bonpo asked when he realized Jabberwock had been silent for quite a while. It wasn't unusual for him to be quiet when napping, but he had been sitting up in his basket, alert, surveying his surroundings.

The Bandersnatch, or Janawar rather, turned disconsolate eyes on his friend. "I just despair sometimes, Shangsung. Is it really worth it? Gathering these Treasures? Will it really change anything?"

"Omni say so," Bonpo's voice was firm. "We mus' berieve it tlue."

Must we? Jabberwock thought before realizing that there was really no other choice. He sighed and it sounded as if he exhaled every last ounce of his breath. "I know you're right. Because if we don't, who will?"

"Exacry, it our 'sponsibirity. Omni say so."

For a moment, Jabberwock wanted to rail against Omni, but in the long run what was the point? He would do as Omni required as he had done for the past five hundred years. Had he known what lay ahead of him would he still have fled the Vale Vixen with Kamali? He had no way of knowing. At the time, it was purely a question of survival, it was their very lives and the future of the Janawar that they were trying to save. Once Kamali had been killed, his life was no longer his own. Had that been the plan all along? Had he always been meant to lose Kamali? Surely Omni wasn't that merciless. It was supposed to be mercy Itself.

He shook himself as if he was trying to rid himself of water on his fur although in this case it was the questions that had haunted him for the past five centuries. There were no answers. There was only faith—faith that if he followed where he was led then in the long run all would be well.

Back to the beach, he thought. Concentrate on the present moment. He caught a glint of sunlight dancing off something to his left, and called Bonpo's attention to it. It might be a tidal pool.

It was, and Bonpo managed to gather a little over a dozen oysters and one crab. They drank what was left in one of their water bottles in order to fill it with seawater before dropping the shellfish into their temporary tank.

This would become their pattern as they made their way to Buta—troll each tidal pool for possible food, and at the end of the day find somewhere safe to camp whether it be a cave or on the pebbly beach itself. They decided not to head inland or climb to the top of the cliffs as it seemed too exposed, and they weren't willing to take the risk. Much better to face the discomfort of stones beneath the tent than to risk opening themselves up to attack by Aberrations, Jabberwock decided.

But, their first night out, as promised, Bonpo stopped early. As the yeti had guessed, they passed the point where the dunes gave way to a rising cliff face and a beach composed of wave-smoothed pebbles about the size of a quail's egg. They found a small cave to spend the night in. It had no more than a depth of ten feet and perhaps half that in height, but it had the advantage that no one could attack them from behind, and Tikvah could easily fit within it, as well. Bonpo just had to crawl when he entered.

While Jabberwock scavenged the beach for driftwood, dragging one piece at a time back to the front of the cave, Bonpo fished. By the time he caught something worthy of their dinner, in conjunction with what they had scavenged from the tidal pools, Jabberwock had acquired more than enough for a decent campfire.

Set to tend the seafood as it stewed over the flames, Jabberwock watched as Bonpo set off to scavenge enough wood to get them through the night and into the morning. Driftwood burned fast and the previous night they had awakened to a cold fire ring.

"Maybe we should just let it burn out," Jabberwock suggested when Bonpo returned with his first armload of wood. "We can start it again in the morning." Which would be better than starting off cold as they had that morning, Jabberwock thought.

"One mol' lound," Bonpo said, "an' den dinna be done. Den we can lest."

Jabberwock watched as his massive back retreated down the beach, before grousing quietly, "And by we, you mean you."

When he returned, they sat in companionable silence as they ate their dinner. While Jabberwock fretted about finding the Treasure in Buta, Bonpo found his thoughts turning to the past.

This was the closest he had been to Dziron since he had fled the Kingdom a little over two decades ago. He never dreamed it would be within reach again, and yet he knew it was impossible to return.

Shangshung was sure he had long since been written off. His wife, Karlha, had more than likely found another yeti to care for her as she was the type that needed caring for. It hadn't been a love match to begin with, and when he had been forced to leave, her father had promised to take on the responsibility of caring for her, as well as raising his two children.

The dzu-tch were comprised of numerous small communities scattered throughout the Peaks of Vulpecula, and each village was comprised of several family units. Bonpo thought back, trying to think if there was any yeti within his community that might want to take on Karlha. As far as dzu-tch women went, she was attractive with bigger than average brown eyes, a nose that was not too broad, and thick, lustrous black hair. She was definitely desirable as far as bearing a husband beautiful and healthy children. But her beauty was also her drawback as she tended toward vanity.

After much consideration, Shangshung realized that the answer was no. Everyone in his village was either settled with a mate or too young to have one. It would take an outsider. They tended to interbreed with the other families in the community but sometimes that wasn't possible, and they would have to seek mates from other villages.

Village in its most simple sense, Bonpo thought. They had no need for inns or banks or any of the other types of businesses you might find in a normal town. They had a weekly market where you could supplement if you were lacking, but they tended to be self sufficient—mostly carnivorous, they made their own clothes from animal skins. They essentially made everything they needed from toiletries to household goods like plates and pots.

Bonpo's knowledge of cuisine grew from a need to be accepted in the new world he lived in. He had stumbled upon becoming an innkeeper by accident. Chased out of Roodspire because he was so large and foreign to the simple inhabitants there, he had made it as far as the crossroads when exhaustion finally took its toll. It was the innkeeper at the time, an old man named Michael, or Mick as he called himself, who had saved him.

With the help of a few patrons they had dragged him to the inn and placed him on the floor in front of the fireplace where he was plied with broth until he was strong enough to take something with a little more substance, and slowly by slowly he regained his strength.

Thankful beyond words, he made himself indispensable to Mick, and the innkeeper taught him many things, among them how to cook. It was something he took to with joy and talent. No one, not even Mick, had ever asked him what he had done in his previous life.

It would embarrass him if his friends knew that he had been a tanner. He spent his days in the odiferous task of tanning the hides of the animals that had been killed for their food. Necessary but monumentally boring, and Karlha hated the way he smelled at the end of the day, and felt his job was beneath her dignity. He had felt the sharp lash of her tongue numerous times over the years, but counted himself lucky to have two children. Although more than two children in yeti culture was forbidden.

And, unlike the dzu-tch who stole the cattle they ate or hunted for other meat, his job was safe. Unrespectable, Bonpo frowned, remembering, as far as Karlha was concerned, which is perhaps what made it easier to leave her. But his children— Sherab and Dalha. Sherab, his son, shared his mother's disdain of his father's profession. He wanted to be a hunter, too, and was humiliated that his father was a lowly tanner. Dalha, on the other hand, she was his darling. Not a day had gone by since he fled Dziron that he hadn't thought of her, the ache in his heart still as constant as it always had been. She had loved him, as he had loved her, unconditionally. He hoped, he prayed, that she understood why he had to leave.

And where was she now? Had she been mated off? Did she have children of her own? He would never be able to answer those questions because he could not risk returning. Karlha wouldn't want him nor would the rest of the community. He had put their entire existence at risk, and he had to live with his mistake every day of his life.

Sighing, he glanced at the gear in the cave. There was a small cask of cognac packed within one of the bags that he'd purchased in Jazeel before they began their portion of the Quest. He thought tonight might be a good time to open it.

2ND SAITHEH

The guards were in the process of closing the capitol's gates when Chokhmah and Faolan arrived in Mwezi-barafu. The couple had spent the past half hour following the road that paralleled the towering walls that surrounded the city proper. The town continued, out of sight, on the other side of the road, and Chokhmah assumed it was home to tradesmen and others who were deemed unfit to live behind the walls.

Intrigued by the palisade that rose above them, Faolan tried to determine how thick it was. He guessed several feet maybe even more, but couldn't be sure until they passed through. It certainly appeared to be impenetrable.

"They really don't want anyone to breach their walls, do they?" Faolan had remarked. He wasn't sure what was on the inside or even what it was constructed of, but the outside of the walls were coated in something as slick as glass, and broken glass and spikes could be seen protruding from the top, which looked to be maybe four times his height from the ground.

"I am willing to bet that they are congratulating themselves on making the decision to build such strong walls," Chokhmah said. They had heard news of continued skirmishes along the borders with Simoon, Annewven, and Adamah during the three weeks it had taken them to reach Mwezi-barafu. Crossing into Simoon was going to be much more difficult than originally planned as they would have to do so at night in an area that was not guarded.

Chokhmah scrounged through her saddlebag looking for the introductory letter from King Seraphim she would need to present to the guards. The closer they drew to Mwezi-barafu, the more she worried. The little worm of doubt and fear had grown into a full-sized dragon. She could feel its hot breath beginning to singe her courage, and she was looking forward to a few days in Salama Palace. Chokhmah prayed to Omni that she might slay that dragon before they entered Simoon.

The guard perused the letter then signaled to another sentry, who received his orders, and led them down a wide avenue lined with fir trees. The evergreens towered so high above them that even craning his neck as far as possible, Faolan still couldn't see the tops of them.

At the end of the avenue sat Salama Palace, which also had high walls coated in the same glassy substance. They passed through another set of well-guarded and well-fortified gates before they dismounted, gathered their belongings, and handed their horses off to a waiting groomsman. The couple watched as Fiachdubh and Halelu were led away, both wondering when they might see them again.

Crossing a bridge over a moat, they finally entered the palace proper once being admitted through an iron door, also protected by armed sentries. Despite all the security, which should have made her feel safe, Chokhmah found the atmosphere oppressive. She did not like the idea of living life in fear, and that emotion was almost palpable here in Mwezi-barafu. She was overwhelmed by a sense of pity that unexpectedly strengthened her resolve. The sooner they travelled to Sigwald, found the Whetstone, and escaped with it, the sooner all this could be over and people could live their lives normally.

A page led them upstairs to their room, and informed them that they would meet with King Adeyemi and Queen Yobachi in the morning.

"Unteel then, please to makes youselves comfortable in yous rooms. A servant will brings yous dinners in about an hour, an' yous breakfasts tomorrow," the young man told them. "Do yous has any questionsa?"

Chokhmah glanced quickly around the room noting what was probably a door leading to a bathroom, and a circular fireplace with plenty of wood and tinder. "I think we have everything we need."

"We're not supposed to leave the room?" Faolan frowned.

"I am sorry sirra," the page answered. "We have beena forced to tightens our security, an' unteel yous has meet witha their Majesties, it would be wiser to remains in yous quarters."

Faolan's frown deepened, but Chokhmah sent him a look of warning, laying her hand gently on his bicep. "We will be just fine," she said. "Won't we Faolan?"

He sighed. It wasn't that he needed to go out he just hated being confined. At least their room was large. It was better than being stuck in a tent.

As the page disappeared down the hallway, Chokhmah shut the door and surveyed the room that she had only given a cursory glance previously. Faolan began to unpack their meager belongings into a large armoire that filled up the corner to the left of the door, and she walked over to the window opposite the door, smiling to herself as she did so.

It was Eluned's habit to check the view from the window every time she arrived in a new room. The only exception Chokhmah could recall was when they arrived at Castle Emrys in Arberth via the Phaeton. They had both been too ill to do anything but nap for a couple of hours before they could face the world again.

Heavy forest green drapes covered the wide window, and Chokhmah pulled them back to reveal that what she surveyed from their room in Salama Palace did not quite equal the breathtaking panorama they had in Arberth. Of course that had been a room for a princess, she thought, with a small balcony and an incredible view of the Anoon Ocean. This was probably not the palace's finest room, and if there was anything scenic to see, it was mostly blocked by more of the seemingly ubiquitous firs that lined the capitol's streets.

"Hmpff," Faolan, who was now standing by her side, noted. "Not really much to look at is there?"

"We may have to cut our visit here short," Chokhmah said. "It doesn't look as if there is any place within the walls in which you can run wild."

"I'm sorry. I know you were looking forward to taking a break for a few days."

"That is quite all right, my love," she moved away from the window to give the room a closer look, leaving the drapes open for the time being as the light the window provided helped illuminate the shadowy room. "I am eager to continue our journey and get our portion of the Quest resolved." She shivered, pulling her woolen cloak more tightly around her.

"Let me start a fire," Faolan said, walking over to the fireplace. "The room is definitely on the chilly side, and it's getting dark. We'll probably need to light some," he glanced around to see what was available, "oil lamps soon."

As he worked, Chokhmah studied the walls of the room, which were coated with stucco and painted in a shade the color of the red rock hills they had passed enroute to King Arawn's castle. An intricate design in purple, green, black, and white was stenciled near the top of the wall. The pattern reminded Chokhmah of four-petaled flowers with a four-pointed star in their centers. It was striking. A few stylized masks, intricately carved from dark wood, decorated the remainder of wall space. Scattered across the floor on three sides of the fireplace were a few floor mats woven from yucca that had been dyed in bright colors. She had seen a lot of these mats when travelling through the high desert of southern Sheba.

The bed, tucked into the corner of the room left of the door, was even more breathtaking than the masks. Constructed of ebony wood, it was carved with animals that were now nearly mythic—elephants, rhinos, and hippos among them. A heavy purple blanket covered the mattress, and another of green lay folded at the end of the bed. The nights must be cold here, Chokhmah surmised.

A small desk to the left of the window and a loveseat and small round table tucked into the far right corner completed the room.

A simple but serviceable bathroom adjoined the bedroom, and Chokhmah used the sink to wash the grime of the road off her face and hands before returning to the room. The fire had now taken hold, and Faolan had moved the black leather loveseat closer to its warmth.

An afghan, knitted in tones of green, purple, and yellow hung over the back of the sofa, and he pulled it down, indicating that Chokhmah should snuggle up next to him. They cuddled under the blanket and watched the flames, Faolan occasionally feeding the fire, until their supper arrived.

After the servant had placed a large covered tray on the round table that was still sitting in the corner and silently departed the room, Faolan removed the cover to see what they'd be eating.

"It smells like a coconut curry," Chokhmah said, and picked up the serving spoon to dish some rice onto their plates first.

"The meat looks like chicken," Faolan noted, the meat always being his first concern. He watched as Chokhmah ladled the curry over his rice. Another dish held cooked greens and Faolan shook his head, teeth bared in a grimace. There was also a bowl containing stewed apples and prunes that smelled of cinnamon and nutmeg, which she insisted on serving a portion of to Faolan.

"We cannot seem rude, my love," she admonished him while smiling. She gave herself less curry so that Faolan might have another helping, and a healthy serving of the stewed greens. There was also a pitcher of water and another of what looked to be some sort of wine.

While she took their plates back over to the sofa so that they could eat in front of the fire, Faolan poured them mugs of the wine.

"It tastes like some sort of honey wine," Chokhmah noted after taking a small sip.

"It only takes effect if you drink it," Faolan said taking a long swallow.

Laughing, Chokhmah swallowed another mouthful of the sweet wine to placate Faolan. Sweet wines weren't really to her taste, but she would definitely finish a cupful or two before heading to bed. She then set her mug down on the ledge of the fireplace, which was more than wide enough to hold a plate, and a little over knee height from the floor. "Perhaps, my love, but I want to eat this before it gets cold."

The room was warmer than when they'd first arrived, but it was full dark now, and she had a sense that they were fighting a losing battle with the cold that seemed to seep in through the window and under the door. It did not bode well for their impending two-week trek through the forests of Simoon to Sigwald.

"Oh by Omni!" Chokhmah cried out, sitting up in bed, hands clasped to her cheeks in horror.

"What is it?" Faolan rocketed out of bed and ran to the fireplace to grab the poker.

"The dream! I had it again. Oh, Faolan, I forgot to send a pigeon to Jabberwock and Bonpo."

Faolan put down the poker and crawled back into bed. The room was frigid. He needed to get dressed and start a fire, but comforting Chokhmah seemed more important.

Once he was under the blankets, Faolan pulled Chokhmah into his arms, and she lay with her head cradled on his chest.

"I feel so guilty," she admitted. "I was so wrapped up in Daniel's pliashka that I completely forgot about warning Bonpo and Jabberwock."

"Perhaps it was meant to be," he stroked her hair. "Would warning them have prevented them from going to Buta? Knowing Jabberwock, I sincerely doubt it. He would have wanted to make sure, and the only way to know for certain is to go there and see for yourself."

Chokhmah sighed. "You are no doubt right. But why then did I have the dream?"

"Maybe we're supposed to go to New Buta once we steal the Treasure from Simoon?"

"I had not considered that," she said, "but now that you say it, I can see that it makes sense. If we are successful, we will finish our portion of the Quest well before anyone else can return to Castle Mykerinos. Perhaps we can drop off the Treasure and travel to New Buta once we leave there?"

"With one caveat." Faolan's voice was grim.

"What is that?"

"That we stay as close as we can to the border of Zion as long as possible," he said. "Once we steal the Treasure, we will no longer be safe near any of the Awen Alliance Kingdoms."

"Then I will worry about that once we find ourselves back in Zion," Chokhmah said. "One step at a time."

"And I believe the next one is starting a fire," he said, sliding out of bed and pulling on his clothes.

They met with King Adeyemi and Queen Yobachi in a small parlor with walls the color of desert sand and drapes as creamy white as a saguaro blossom. Chokhmah smiled. Clearly, she thought, either the King or Queen wanted to reflect the various aspects of their kingdom throughout the palace. She wondered if she would find a room decorated with the hues of the coast in another room.

The cactus-green armchairs and dark wood of the coffee table only added to the effect that they were sitting in a desert oasis. Spines of ocotillo with their bright red flowers filled a sky blue vase in a corner of the room.

Chokhmah glanced at the ceiling to see if it mirrored the blue of the vase, but it was the same sand color as the walls although a large bronze chandelier was suspended over the coffee table. Rather than a circular fireplace, the sitting room featured several bronze braziers, coals glowing red and grey against the grating that covered them. The room was significantly warmer than theirs, and Chokhmah took a seat closest to the nearest brazier.

Once they were seated, the King drilled them with questions about the Quest.

Chokhmah and Faolan tried to maintain a balance between politely answering his questions and revealing as little as possible. The Kingdom of Sheba was in turmoil, and they had agreed while at the gypsy camp on the Spruce that the less the King and Queen knew, the safer everybody was.

Faolan explained the outline of their plan to get to Sigwald. He had yet to reveal he was a Shapeshifter and hoped not to do so. Both Seraphim and Uriel, and even The Bandersnatch had encouraged the couple to keep as much as possible about their plan to themselves.

"We think it will be safer for us to cross the border into Simoon at some location that isn't usually guarded," Faolan said. "At least, we are hoping that not every single mile of the border is under scrutiny."

"You are correct," King Adeyemi said. He was a man on the short side of medium stature, not unlike Faolan, but he was more compact and muscular with skin the color of dark chocolate. "It would be impossible to do so. You prefer to walk, then? You do not wish to take your horses?"

"I think we'll be much safer on foot," Faolan explained. "It will be much easier to melt into the background if we don't have horses to take care of."

Adeyemi nodded. "I can see the wisdom in that. When do you wish to leave?"

"As soon as possible," Chokhmah said. "Perhaps tomorrow? Can we find the way ourselves or will we need a guide?"

"I would prefer to send a guide with you," the King said. "That way we will know for sure that yous," he slipped into the local dialect for a second, "have made it safely into Simoon."

"When you return to your room create a list of the supplies you will need to take with you," Queen Yobachi said, "then a servant can assemble them for you. It would be best for you to remain in the castle." Unlike her husband, Yobachi favored her niece, Njima. She was tall and slender with high cheekbones and almond-shaped eyes. Like Njima, she carried herself with a natural grace.

King Adeyemi stood, and the others followed suit. "We look forward to your return. I do not need to say that gathering these Treasures is of extreme importance to us?"

Faolan and Chokhmah nodded solemnly.

Stating that he had another meeting to attend, he said his farewells and left the room.

"Before you begin that list," Yobachi said, "can you please tell me how my niece is faring?"

Chokhmah smiled, face reflecting the genuine affection she had for the younger woman. "She has been a great asset to our quest. We all love her dearly."

"I understand she now has a girlfriend?" Yobachi said with hesitation, brow creased.

"Yona," Faolan said, smiling broadly. "What a woman! I

can honestly say that I've never met anyone who is so unselfish. Everything she does is for the good of the group. And she adores Njima. I can't speak highly enough of her."

"Faolan is right," Chokhmah added. "Yona is one of the most genuine and loving humans I have ever met. She would never do anything to harm Njima's reputation as Queen of Naphtali."

"And they did not seem threatened or repulsed by her sexuality?" Yobachi asked.

Faolan looked nonplussed. "I, uh, not to my knowledge. I imagine if anyone had a problem with it, then they moved on to another Kingdom."

"I agree," Chokhmah said, thinking of Yona's run in with the spy formerly from Naphtali. She had spoken to him in the marketplace when she was fleeing Adamah with the Treasure she had stolen, and had wisely cut short her business at that particular stall. "I saw nothing but love and respect for their Queen from the people there."

Yobachi's face seemed to glow with relief. "I am so glad to hear this. Adeyemi insists that this is all evil, but I have never felt so myself. I hope that someday I can see my niece again."

"I am sure that will happen once all the Treasures are gathered," Chokhmah assured her. "We will have to have some kind of summit between the Alliances, and every monarch that can be there will help the cause to return peace to the Thirteen Kingdoms."

Yobachi smiled and gave a slight bow. "Please send a page with the list as soon as you have made it. You will be joining us for dinner tonight, will you not?"

"We would be happy to," Chokhmah said, "as long as it is not a problem that we have not brought any formal wear with us."

"It is not a problem at all. A page will be sent for you at seven o'clock."

Back in their room, Chokhmah hurriedly put together a list for the waiting page. As soon as he disappeared down the hallway, she turned to Faolan. "Did you feel as uncomfortable with King Adeyemi as I did?"

"I realize he's in the Triquetra Alliance," Faolan said, "but he struck me as overly suspicious."

"Perhaps it is just because it is his Kingdom that is being targeted by the Awen Alliance," she said, "but I will feel significantly more comfortable once we have returned to the Quest."

Faolan pulled their bags from the wardrobe. "I'll feel better knowing we're mostly packed. I'd like to leave as early in the morning as possible."

18ᴛʜ Saitheh

Winding their way through the streets of Kaumari, Gwrhyr and Eluned attempted to maintain as low a profile as possible. Grimacing as the dull ache in her cheek turned into a continuous throb along the arrow wound, Eluned pulled the hood of her cloak forward again. It had a tendency to slip backwards, and she couldn't risk revealing the bandages that swathed the entire left side of her face from her ear down across her cheekbone, ending underneath her chin. She needed to replace her headscarf, but couldn't bear the idea of the pressure it might place on her painful laceration.

"We might want to find a place to stock up on wine before we leave the town," Eluned said.

Gwrhyr glanced at his bride. She was clearly miserable since the medicine that had numbed the wound had worn off. Hunched over her saddle, she loosed a whimper whenever Ronan was forced to side step around a cart, a human, or another animal in the street. "Not a bad idea," he agreed. "Keep an eye out for a vendor."

The road they were on began to curve southward, so they turned right at the next street to continue their journey. If they continued to head north, they would eventually reach the major trade route to Dziron. Gwrhyr was counting on the fact that whoever attacked them would expect them to hide out in the city rather than continue on to Jungnay.

Their attackers might not be aware that Eluned had been hit, but no one could have missed Makeda's shriek of pain when the arrow struck her flank. He just prayed to Omni that Njima and Yona had found a place to stable their horses. They should have asked Purva for a recommendation but they had been so spooked by the fact they'd been discovered, it was hard to trust anyone.

"By Omni I pray that Yona and Njima are alright," Eluned echoed his thoughts.

"So do I," he said, "but we need to stop worrying about them. It won't help us. They're on their own now and so are we." He gritted his teeth, trying hard not to berate himself too severely. He was supposed to protect his wife, but she had been the one to sense something was wrong. They'd become too complacent. Not again, he thought. From now on he would stay alert. "Eluned?"

She glanced over at him.

"Next time," he said, "please don't keep your misgivings or your gut feelings or whatever it was that told you that things didn't feel quite right to yourself. Understand? If I had known you felt something was amiss, I would have been a lot more cautious."

Eluned attempted a smile but her lips twisted as the pain of doing so made itself felt. "It hurts to move my mouth."

"Because it uses the muscles in your cheeks to talk. So don't for awhile."

She nodded and had to bite her lip to keep from smiling. She pointed instead.

Gwrhyr's eyes followed its direction and he smiled for her. "Praise be to Omni! A wine seller!"

About an hour later, the road they were on dead-ended into the trade route, and they turned their horses westward.

"I thought we would camp in a designated site tonight," Gwrhyr said. There was no one in sight at the moment, and that made him nervous.

Eluned turned toward him and raised an eyebrow.

"I know, but I think it will be safer to be surrounded by fellow travellers at this point than to risk being alone."

Particularly tonight, she thought, as she hoped to drink enough to dull the pain and make sleep arrive more easily. It was rapidly heading toward dusk, the sun disappearing behind the mountains that ran along the border between the King-doms of Dziron and Kamartha.

When they arrived at the campsite, Eluned helped Gwrhyr quickly set up the tent in a small space within a grove of pines.

"Would you mind setting up things within the tent while I get everything set up out here?" he asked her. Because, he thought, I think it would be better if you showed your face as little as possible. The bandages were hard to hide and might prompt questions. He glanced around the site. Most of the campers seemed to be busy setting up their camp or preparing meals, but he preferred not to take any chances.

Eluned was also studying the site. He was probably right. There were only about half a dozen other people there, but it took a lot of effort to keep her bandaged face from being seen. It would be nice to be inside the tent where she could throw her hood back and relax. "Only if I can have some wine while I'm doing it," she said through clenched teeth.

Gwrhyr laughed and pulled one of the skins off Ronan's back and handed it to her. "Want a mug?"

Eluned smiled before wincing. "Ouch, I keep forgetting." She touched her cheek tentatively. "I think I can make do with this," she indicated the wineskin, and disappeared into the tent.

"I figured tonight was going to be a broth night," he said handing her a mug of the fragrant liquid when he finally joined her in the tent. She had been unable to eat the sandwich they'd purchased in Kaumari earlier that day as both taking a bite and trying to chew tugged at her cheek too much. Pulling the sandwich from the pocket of his cloak, Gwrhyr held it up. "I'll have this for my dinner. It will save me from having to prepare something." He unwrapped the waxed paper from the roll stuffed with chicken and cheese to reveal it was missing only one small bite.

Eluned nodded. "Liquid does seem to be all I can handle at the moment."

"Is the wine helping?"

"It's starting to." She patted the blankets next to her, and he settled down beside her. She was thankful to be able to lean against his chest. Closing her eyes, she sipped at her broth.

"Good," he said when she drained the last drop from the mug. "We need to keep your strength up. Perhaps I'll make some scrambled eggs in the morning. You should be able to manage that."

"With cheese?" she murmured.

He hugged her closer to himself. "Yes, with cheese, Fy Drysor," he whispered in her ear, taking her mug and refilling it with wine before filling his own mug. "You'll be healed in no time." He hoped that was true, he thought, as he untied the scarf from around her neck. She was going to take the scarring of her cheek much harder than he would.

The following morning, Eluned allowed her husband to remove the bandage and gently wash the wound, which was still raw and inflamed. She didn't even have to ask how it looked as Gwrhyr's clenched jaw spoke volumes.

"On the bright side," he said after applying the balm Purva had sold them, "it doesn't look infected."

"It's just angry," Eluned said.

"What?"

"My skin is angry that it was ripped apart like that."

Gwrhyr smiled. "Yes. Yes it is."

"I wish Chokhmah were here. I bet she'd know how to make something that would heal it more quickly."

Kissing the top of her head, Gwrhyr began to back out of the tent. He intended to burn the old bandages. He didn't want to leave behind any evidence that they had camped here the previous night. "Drink your coffee."

He saw the spark of anger in her eyes, and added, "Please."

"Sorry," she took a sip. "Automatic response."

Gwrhyr pointed at his heart and then at hers. "I'll go make the eggs."

As the sun approached its zenith on that partly cloudy day, they began looking for a spot where they could leave the road and have a private lunch break out of view from any passersby. The trade route wound through the hill country north of the River Zeuns, and the horses had just splashed through a shallow brook when Eluned reined in Ronan.

Eluned pointed upstream where the brook curved around the hill they were passing and disappeared from view. A narrow track ran alongside the brook.

Gwrhyr nodded and turned Ruari toward the track. Eluned followed. Once on the far side of the hill, the land flattened out into a broad meadow. Dismounting, they allowed the horses to graze, and while Gwrhyr set about getting some lunch together, Eluned excused herself.

She headed toward a small copse of trees at the base of the hill preferring to hide behind a tree rather than expose herself in the open on the off chance another traveller decided to take the path alongside the brook.

As she was turning back toward the meadow, a sparkle off

to the left caught her eye as the sun reappeared from behind a cloud. Taking a step closer, the shimmer remained and soon she determined that it was the sheen of water that had attracted her attention.

The spring was located in a tiny glade within the grove of trees, and took up most of the space therein. She glanced around the clearing, which was covered in velvety green moss and pine needles. It was pretty, but nothing remarkable stood out to her. Glancing into the spring, which was crystal clear, she could see small pebbles scattered across the fine sand at the bottom, and guessed it might be rather shallow. And then she noticed something else as she turned to leave—her reflection.

The hood had fallen back from her head and the brilliant white bandage made her pale skin appear darker than normal. She watched herself raise a hand to touch it. It was as if she was looking into a mirror. The others had seen her wound, but she had yet to find the fortitude to do so.

Kneeling next to the spring, she pulled back the bandage, stomach twisting as she saw what the others had seen. Red and puffy skin flanked a long row of black stitches. Even the glistening balm couldn't hide the ragged flesh. Choking back a sob, she hastily replaced the bandage. It was a great testament to her friends, and even more so to her husband, that they had shown no horrified reaction to what was clearly going to be a hideous scar.

Despite the fact she had promised herself she wouldn't, she was suddenly weeping uncontrollably in spite of the pain it caused. She would never be able to show her face in polite company again, she cried to herself. And she couldn't imagine making love with her husband unless it was pitch dark.

Eluned didn't even want to consider how the people of Aden would see their new queen. Would she have to spend the remainder of her life with a scarf across the lower half of her face just so she wouldn't have to subject them to looking at it?

She cried until her throat was raw and the agony in her cheek became too much to bear.

Checking her reflection in the pool, she was horrified to see that her eyes were swollen and red. She splashed some of the cold water on them, and pulling a handkerchief from her pocket, dabbed them dry before blowing her nose. Her sinuses felt tender and congested from the force of her grief. She forced herself to relax for a moment by taking deep breaths.

Gwrhyr would be looking for her soon, and she needed to be as composed as possible before returning to him. She felt a sudden flash of anger towards her husband. Why was he pretending that her disfigurement was no big deal?

As she walked out of the grove of pine trees, Gwrhyr hurried toward her. "I was beginning to get worried," he said before noting her tear-stained face, which caused him to skid to a halt. "What is it? What happened?"

Eluned touched the bandage tentatively. "I'm sorry," she said, but her tone was unconvincing. "Sometimes the pain is just too much to take. I confess that I might have cried a little."

Gwrhyr winced. What he wouldn't do to take yesterday morning back. At some point she would see her wound. He probably should warn her before she did, but he just couldn't quite bring himself to do so. Tomorrow, he promised himself. *I'll tell her when I change the bandage in the morning.*

That evening they opted to camp off the road, and not in the designated site. They hadn't seen anyone since that morning—the detour off the main route at lunch had left them behind the other westbound travellers, and they decided to take advantage of that by stopping a little early for the evening.

Eluned had been tempted to camp in the pretty little clearing with the spring where they'd stopped for lunch, but a nagging feeling that they needed to keep moving made her decide otherwise. When they passed another brook with a narrow path running alongside it, this one downstream, they decided to check it out on the off chance it led to a potential camp site.

Luck, or Omni, was with them as after paralleling the creek for a quarter of a mile, another path turned off to the left into the woods. They followed it a couple of dozen yards before reaching a space beneath the trees that was large enough to allow them to set up their tent, build a campfire and hobble the horses.

The pine boughs would diffuse the smoke from their fire enough that it would not be noticed from the main road. Eluned set about helping with the chores, enjoying the quiet disturbed only by the murmur of the breeze ruffling the tops of the trees and the songs of birds and insects.

While she was scavenging for downed wood, she stopped for a moment to listen. Her eyes immediately filled with tears, and she swiped them away angrily. She was having trouble not feeling sorry for herself, but she didn't want to return to camp with swollen eyes again. She couldn't bear the look of guilt on Gwrhyr's face.

Taking a deep breath, she focused on listening to the forest. No, she decided, releasing her breath, not even a tingle that something might be amiss. The creatures that inhabited these woods were clearly natural. There might be wolves, she thought, but all signs led her to believe that they had enough normal prey to content themselves. With the horses between their tent and the campfire, they should all be safe.

Eluned also felt certain that they had not been followed out of Kaumari. It would be a logical conclusion that the four of them were working together as they had travelled almost all the way from Jazeel in each other's company. If she were making a guess, it would be that the four of them would get the Treasure in Kamartha before heading on to Dziron. It might take days for them to figure out that they were looking for two people not four.

Feeling as if a tremendous weight had been lifted from her shoulders, she set about gathering some firewood before she returned to their campsite. As long as they travelled from dawn to nearly dusk each day, she and Gwrhyr could probably stay well ahead of anyone who might come after them.

"And if we keep finding places like this to camp," Gwrhyr said once she'd told him, "we'll remain even safer." He set a pot of water on the little rod of iron they used when cooking over a fire. It had a little crook at one end to hold the pot's handle. They would have to rehydrate some vegetables and meat for their dinner as he'd used the remainder of the eggs that morning. Worth the sacrifice, he thought, to keep his wife fed and her strength up, but he'd have to mince the meat so that she wouldn't have to chew it as much.

Eluned handed him a mug of wine as she sat down on the log he'd pulled up next to the fire. Snuggling against him for the warmth, she felt content for a moment. Then her cheek throbbed again and recalled her back to the situation—she was disfigured for life. If they succeeded in the Quest, would the wound be worth it? Honestly, she thought, she couldn't yet say. Gulping her wine, she drained the mug and waited for the anesthetizing to begin. At this rate, they would run out long before Dziron.

THE FOLLOWING MORNING HER CHEEK was still hurting, and her mood was definitely surly as she answered Gwrhyr's questions with grunts and nods until he finished breaking camp in silence. Not a good day to talk to her about her wound, he decided.

They were back on the main road as soon as the sun provided enough light to pack up and head out. There were no other travellers about when they reached the road, and as they turned westward toward Dziron Eluned was in higher spirits.

"It looks like we might get at least another night alone,"

Eluned thought. She dreaded the thought of having to face anyone ever again.

The morning ride was silent until noon when Gwrhyr suggested they find a spot to grab some lunch. He'd been wracking his brain all morning trying to think of a way to cheer his wife up, and had failed miserably.

As he set about heating up the leftover soup that Eluned had barely touched the previous night, she set off in search of a place in which to relieve herself. What she really wanted to do was cry. It was one thing to have suffered such a terrible wound, but would it never stop aching? She wasn't sure she could stand it much longer.

When she was far enough away from their picnic spot, she seated herself beneath a large fir tree at the edge of a tiny clearing and wept. She hadn't realized how much she'd taken her beauty for granted until she was no longer beautiful.

Maybe I'll just spend the rest of my life invisible, she sobbed, picturing herself wrapped in Gwrhyr's Mantle of Arthur. Her Treasure was awkward because it left her one handed, and that thought brought a fresh round of tears. Why, Omni, why? She railed silently against her God. Why would you do this to me?

The feeling of being watched caused the hairs on the back of her neck to prickle, and she looked up expecting Gwrhyr to have caught her crying in self-pity. Her cheeks colored in anticipation of the commiseration she would no doubt see in his eyes. But when she looked up, it wasn't Gwrhyr she saw but a woman of ethereal beauty. Her huge brown eyes were lined in kohl, and hair as black and shiny as onyx flowed over her shoulders, covering her breasts and ending at her waist. She wore nothing but jewelry—an elaborate necklace of gold and jewels encircled her throat, numerous bangles sparkled on her wrists, and gold shimmered at her ankles and on her toes. A gold filigree belt encrusted with gems sat low on her hips, and a giant ruby glowed from her navel. A crown of fresh flowers—bright pink roses and frangipani interspersed with delicate, virginal white baby's breath, rested upon her hair, and she held a golden trident in her right hand.

Eluned shivered under her cloak. How could she stand the chill, she wondered before realizing that her mouth was hanging open in awe. She snapped it shut, brushing away the tears on her right cheek as she stood. Without a word, the woman approached until they were standing only a couple of feet apart.

Touching her left cheek, the woman nodded at Eluned who swallowed hard and pulled back the bandage. She watched as the woman's eyes widened in understanding. Raising her trident, she gently pressed it to the wound. Eluned felt the pain and discomfort of the swollen flesh recede, and lifted her hand to her face to touch the wound.

The tear in her flesh was still there but it was now mending smoothly. It no longer felt bumpy and ragged, or even swollen. There would be a scar, of that there was no doubt, but it would not be the horrendous seam of bunched scar tissue that she had feared.

Eluned had been so focused on her wound that she'd almost forgotten the mysterious woman. She looked around her in order to give her thanks and discovered the woman had disappeared. Squinting into the gloom of the copse from whence the woman had materialized, she saw nothing, not even a glimmer of gold.

Patting the tear-soaked bandage back into place as she still intended to take good care of the wound until it was completely healed, Eluned returned to the brooklet where Gwrhyr was preparing their lunch.

He glanced up from the fire he'd started, and once again noted Eluned's swollen eyes. Considering her mood, he decided he wouldn't say anything. She sat down next to him, mouth parted in awe.

As Eluned pulled back the bandage, he saw that the scar that had been forming on her cheek was now a nearly healed, straight seam.

"I don't understand," he said.

"You know you could have told me just how bad it was."

Gwrhyr flushed. "I meant to. I was going to this morning. I just . . ."

"Fortunately, you no longer have to," she said, but her voice sounded reproachful.

"I can never apologize enough," he admitted.

She spent the remainder of their lunch break telling him what had happened. "At least you won't have to mince my food anymore," she said when she was finished telling her tale. She paused. It was her turn to blush. "And thank you for that. You really have gone out of your way for me since we were attacked."

He leaned forward and kissed her forehead. "I love you."

Toward midafternoon, Eluned reined in Ronan. "Doesn't it feel like we've been ascending for quite a while?"

"The terrain is definitely changing," Gwrhyr agreed. He looked over his shoulder and was surprised to see they had left the rolling hills behind. "I think we must be climbing up to a plateau or something."

The forest on either side of the road was mostly spruce now rather than pine, Eluned saw. She'd been so lost in her thoughts that she hadn't noticed the changing geography. "I've got a bad feeling," she said.

"In what way?"

"You know the geography of the Thirteen Kingdoms better than I do, but isn't there a sagebrush scrubland somewhere in Kamartha?"

Gwrhyr groaned. "The Empty Steppes. Damn, I'd forgotten about it."

"How long will we be on it?"

"It's bisected by the River Qyhr, which we should reach in a few days. I should warn you that the bridge that crosses it is about a mile above the river."

Eluned's eyes widened as her stomach sank. She was not fond of heights.

"It also means that we will have to camp in designated sites for the next week or so until we leave the steppes."

"Wonderful," Eluned rolled her eyes. "I should have remembered Chokhmah's advice this morning."

"How so?"

"She always made me say 'Omni willing'. I should have said, Omni willing, it looks like we'll have another night alone."

"It's still pretty early in the season, though. I imagine we won't run into a lot of travellers."

"I guess I need to come up with a story about why I have this bandage on my cheek," she said before clicking to Ronan to get him moving again. "Hey!" she brightened.

"You've already thought of something?"

"No, but I just realized that it will give me an excuse not to sing if I leave the bandage on."

"That's true," Gwrhyr said, inwardly releasing a sigh of relief. He actually knew a number of songs that he could entertain fellow travellers with if necessary. Eluned could only play a few songs on the harp—the one ballad she'd written, and a couple of other songs, one of them an ancient hymn called O Come, O Come Emmanuel.

"Speaking of my injury," she continued, "shouldn't the stitches be removed soon? It seems like it may have healed enough to do that? What do you think?"

"We'll take a look at it tonight, but you're right, we definitely don't want you to start forming scar tissue around the sutures."

As predicted, they reached the summit of the Empty Steppes toward the end of the day to discover an open landscape scattered with dwarf sagebrush. After the water-rich environment of the hills they'd just passed through, this new terrain was desert-like. They would have to camp in the designated site if for no other reason than a water supply.

Because of their early start, they reached the camping area a couple of hours before sunset. As they were the first arrivals, they quickly secured a site as far away as possible from the water, which came from a hand pump next to a three-sided shelter. That way, Gwrhyr reasoned, they avoided other campers constantly tramping past them on the way to get water.

Gwrhyr set up the tent with the entrance facing away from the camping area to give them an extra measure of privacy, but they were alone for another hour or so before anyone else arrived.

It was heading toward dusk when a family, travelling westward, pulled into the site in a cart drawn by two mules. The man jumped down from the cart and led the mules toward the shelter. Parking the cart alongside it, the remainder of his family, presumably his wife along with two adolescent children, exited the cart and set about gathering the gear they needed for the evening while the man unhitched the mules.

The woman looked up to see Gwrhyr watching them, and returned his wave before setting to work getting a fire started in the pit in front of the shelter.

"They're clearly Dzironese," Gwrhyr told Eluned, voice low, as she crawled out of the tent.

The girl who looked about twelve was busy spreading bedrolls in the shelter. Her thick, glossy black hair was pulled back in two long braids that were tied together at the bottom with a bright red ribbon. Her brother was busy pumping water into a couple of buckets. He, too, had thick black hair, and like his father, it was plaited into one long braid down his back.

"So we'll probably be camping with them until we descend the steppes, huh?"

"And anyone else who shows up tonight, assuming they're heading toward Dziron and not away from it."

"Well, they seem relatively harmless." She paused and then said. "Omni willing."

Gwrhyr chuckled. "Omni willing indeed."

Even the wound on her cheek couldn't mar her happiness. She sent an arrow prayer of thanks to Omni for sending her the mysterious woman during lunch. She didn't know who or what she was, but the gash on her face now itched mildly rather than throbbed, and it didn't hurt to talk or chew. Most importantly, she wouldn't be hideously scarred for life and that alone was something to be thankful for.

CRAWLING OUT OF THEIR TENT the next morning, Gwrhyr and Eluned found that no one else had arrived after they settled down for the night.

They quickly broke camp and headed out for the day in order to maintain some distance between themselves and the family of four. The couple had also agreed that it would be to their benefit to once again arrive at the designated camping area early so they could have some time alone before anyone else arrived.

The day promised to be sunny and cloudless, and secretly Eluned was glad that she might have the chance to expose her cheek to the air that day without being seen by other travellers. Gwrhyr had removed the stitches before they went to bed the previous evening, and she thought it would be good for the wound to feel a little sun and fresh air before she covered it up again.

18ᴛʜ Sᴀɪᴛʜᴇʜ

Njima knocked confidently on Purva's bright blue door. Yona stood behind her holding the reins of both their mounts, and prayed to Omni that the old woman was still there. Njima had insisted that the first and most important thing they needed to accomplish was to find somewhere affordable to stable their horses.

Yona had expressed her concern that returning to Purva's might put them at greater risk, but Njima had convinced her otherwise.

"I don't have gut feelings that often, my dove," she had said, "but I know in my heart this is the right thing to do."

Njima waited a minute and when there was no answer knocked more forcefully. A few seconds later the door opened and Purva peered out at them.

"Is your horse in pain?" she asked, looking past Njima to where Makeda stood patiently, though a little drowsily, next to Yona.

"Oh no, she's fine. She just needs some rest," Njima said. "But as you know, we are new to town, and were hoping you could recommend a reputable, if somewhat inexpensive, stable in which to board them."

"You're speech is rather sophisticated for a performer," Purva's eyes narrowed.

Njima had the grace to blush. "The truth is my father is a lord," Njima lied, "and I am doing this against the will of my family."

"And you?" Purva asked Yona, voice harsh.

Despite the cold, Yona felt sweat starting to tickle the skin in the pits of her arms. "Yes, ma'am," she responded politely. "We've been best friends since childhood, and have always dreamed of running away and coming to Kaumari. But I'm beginning to think my parents were right." She sniffed, willing the tears to rise in her eyes. Eluned would be proud of her. "Nothing seems to have gone right since we arrived."

Purva studied them for a moment. "Well come on inside," she offered, "where we can talk in private." After Yona had tied the horses to the hitching post outside Purva's door, the healer led them into the room in which she'd performed surgery on Eluned and Makeda.

"And I am guessing your names aren't Zenobia and Skaði?" Purva said without preamble.

Yona flushed as her heart began to race. Surely they wouldn't get caught the day they arrived, she thought trying not to panic. She bit her lip and looked at her feet, attempting to seem contrite. "You're right, ma'am. My name is Miryam."

"And I'm Libni," Njima said. "Zenobia and Skaði are our stage names."

"You said you've been friends since childhood, but you don't seem the same age," Purva said.

"I'm five years older," Njima lied. "Miryam came to stay with us when she was seven because her father wanted her to have the same tutor as me. To be completely honest, I was an only child and was happy to have someone to talk to even if she was younger."

"Well, I was pretty mature for my age," Yona said, and laughed.

Purva smiled. "You do seem very comfortable together. And I saw the way you were looking at each other earlier. I suspect you are more than just friends."

Yona blushed again, but Purva's smile was kind. "Do not worry, my dear. That is something that is not judged here in Kaumari." A shadow seemed to pass across her face. "Things are different at the palace. They don't condone this but neither do they forbid it as they do in the Kingdoms of Simoon and Annevwen. The theatre district draws many visitors. It is a boon to the economy of Kamartha so they turn a blind eye to the many performers who are not heterosexual."

"That was my understanding," Njima said, "which is why we felt comfortable coming here."

"Speaking of which," Purva said, "perhaps we should make ourselves a little more comfortable. Why don't you bring the horses in," she looked at Yona who glanced at Njima who nodded.

"I apologize," Yona said over her shoulder as she made her way to the door. "I'm still spooked from the attack this morning."

Once she'd brought the horses inside, Purva led them down the hallway toward the back of her building. "Through that door there," she told Yona, "you will find a small paddock. You can leave the horses there for the time being. They will be perfectly safe. Libni and I will be upstairs where I have my private living quarters."

After settling the horses in a grassy area surrounded by a fence, which Yona assumed was what Purva had meant by paddock, she studied the area around her. From the street they'd entered on, it appeared to be wall-to-wall buildings of three stories or more. But, the buildings either filled up their entire space or, like Purva's, only a third to a half with the remainder being fenced in.

Yona returned to the three-story building and climbed the

narrow staircase to the second floor. At the top of the staircase, a door opened to the right on a sitting room and to the left on a large kitchen. It was here that Njima and Purva were sitting at a round table painted a sunny yellow, waiting for the kettle on a four-burner oil stove to boil.

Njima had pulled a bright red stool from the corner of the kitchen and indicated Yona should sit on it as there were only two chairs, also cherry red with yellow cushions, at the table.

"You're the youngest," she smiled at her.

"The benefits of seniority?" Yona nodded at Njima's chair.

"Exactly, my dove."

"Do you live here alone?" Yona asked Purva as she took her seat.

"Only for the past couple of years," Purva said. "My partner of thirty years, Auriel, passed on then. She was a performer, too, an actress on The Masala."

"I'm sorry for your loss," Njima said. "I cannot imagine."

"She was older than me," Purva said, rising as the kettle started to bubble, "we always knew it was a likelihood, but I will never get used to her being gone."

The women were silent as Purva prepared the tea. Yona glanced around the kitchen, which was nearly sparkling it was so clean. White curtains with a pattern of yellow and pink flowers were pulled back from the two windows in the room that looked out over the street below. The walls were painted pale blue, but the cabinets were grass green. A large purple icebox sat against the far right wall.

Purva turned with a tray in her hands to see Yona taking it all in. "My Auriel did like lots of color," she laughed putting the tray down on the table.

"I like it," Yona couldn't help but smile. "It makes me happy."

"We have a sitting room," Purva said, "but when she was feeling down, Auriel liked to come and sit in here and drink tea. The sitting room was my refuge. After dealing with wounded animals all day, I needed somewhere quiet and dark, a place to soothe the senses."

"I can see needing that," Njima said, thinking there had been times after some of her more contentious council meetings that she would seek that sort of refuge. Her private apartments, which were bigger than the rooms her fellow Questers had stayed in, included a darkened den with a comfy chaise lounge on which she could recline. But, she also had a light and airy sitting room with lots of windows, which she could open to hear the wind chimes and birdsong in the courtyard below. It, too, was decorated in bright colors and featured fabrics in lots of different textures.

"I almost forgot to ask," Purva interrupted Njima's thoughts. "What happened to your friends?"

"Ivanhoe and Rowena?" Yona stalled for time as she tried to come up with a suitable lie.

Purva nodded, eyebrow lifted and one corner of her mouth raised in amusement.

Yona blushed. "Of course, I'm sorry. The word 'friends' threw me off. We hadn't been travelling together long."

"And though we all felt comfortable together right away," Njima added, "we didn't quite consider them friends yet."

"Anyway," Yona continued, "they are minstrels and had a performance scheduled here that they needed to go cancel because Rowena said it really hurts to move her jaw."

"And probably will continue to for the next few days to a week," Purva agreed. "That was a serious wound."

Yona winced. Serious was putting it mildly.

"I'm sorry," Purva patted her hand. "Auriel was always getting on to me for being so blunt. She said my bedside manners left much to be desired."

"Anyway," Njima hurried to change the subject, "We agreed that now we are here in Kaumari, it was time to go our separate ways."

"Yes," Yona agreed. "They were going to cancel the performance, and find somewhere to bunk down for awhile so Rowena can have a chance to heal."

Purva nodded, and asked, "Are you both actresses?"

"No, we have an unusual sort of act," Yona said. "It's very simple . . ."

"But scary," Njima quickly supplied.

"Yes, scary," Yona agreed. "For both of us. When we perfect it, we hope to add some more feats to our routine."

"And what is this talent?"

"I shoot a piece of fruit off of Zenobia's head with an arrow," Yona said.

Purva raised her eyebrows and nodded. "I'm not sure I've seen that performed by two women."

"Exactly," Njima said. "We were hoping it would add some tension to our performance to have a female archer."

"Our plan was to arrive here and see if there is a circus or something else of that nature that takes on this type of act," Yona said.

"I'm sure you will find numerous options," Purva said, and paused. "I have a thought. But first, is it possible for me to see you perform?"

"The answer is yes but," Yona said.

"But what?" Purva said.

"We still need to find somewhere to board our horses," Yona explained, "and we had hoped to do that before we found something to eat. I haven't eaten since dawn, and the truth is I'm a little shaky."

"Which means it's not a good time to shoot anything," Purva said.

Yona nodded, grimacing at the implications.

"And now that it's heading toward late afternoon," Njima said, "it would be nice to find our lodgings for the night. I think I will remain a little anxious until all these things are settled."

"I understand," Purva said. "And yet, you haven't asked me for anything but recommendations."

Yona's eyes widened. "We would never do something like that!"

"The presumption!" Njima exclaimed.

Purva smiled and patted both their hands. "It is rare to see this kind of concern for others in people of privilege. You have been raised well."

"My parents lived in fear of people taking advantage of them because of their position," Njima said. "When I was a teenager I vowed that I would never live in that kind of fear. And the best way to avoid it was by treating others as I would treat myself."

"Has it worked for you?" Purva asked.

Njima nodded. "Yes, for the most part. There are always exceptions, of course, but I think on the whole, it holds true." Njima picked up Yona's empty teacup and placed both of theirs on the tray.

"I have a proposition for you," Purva said, adding her cup to the tray.

The women looked at her expectantly.

"You and your horses may board here," she said.

"In exchange for?" Njima asked.

"Some help around the place," Purva said, "and, of course, you'll provide for your horses' feed and help out with the meals you eat here."

"What kind of help?" Yona asked.

"Cleaning up after your horses, yourselves, for example," Purva said. "Maybe some help in the surgery if you're around when I need it."

Yona was nodding. "That seems more than fair. Libni?"

Njima wanted to say it felt like an Omnincidence, but it was too early to be that open with Purva. "I would be eternally grateful," she said instead, standing and picking up the tray.

"And I can start by washing the tea things if you go get the things we need from Makeda and Aine, Miryam."

"Your room will be the one to the left on the third floor," Purva said, relaxing back in her chair. Njima smiled at her before turning toward the sink. Clearly Purva thought that it would be nice to have someone in the house again.

When Yona rejoined them in the kitchen, Njima suggested they make a quick run to pick up enough food for dinner. "I've already discussed it with Purva, and I know exactly where to go," she said.

"Sounds good to me," Yona said. With the anxiety having passed about what they were going to do with themselves and their horses, her shakiness and hunger pains had disappeared. It wasn't the first time she'd gone hungry during the Quest; she could now easily wait until dinner before she ate. As long as it was an early dinner.

THE FOLLOWING MORNING YONA AND NJIMA prepared to perform their act for the first time. The fact that Purva would be watching them increased Yona's anxiety.

Njima had to give her a pep talk as they dressed for the day because the young woman was suffering from pre-show jitters.

"I'm so terrified that I'll kill you," she confessed.

"You will kill me if you don't calm down and remember that you truly excel at this sweetheart," Njima attempted to soothe her. "I am completely confident in my ability to stand unflinchingly still, and if I can do that, then you can easily spear . . . what was it Purva said she had?"

"A pear."

"A pear then. You will not miss. I have every confidence in you," Njima said.

"If I can take a practice shot or two first, I'll feel a lot better about it."

"I don't see why you can't," Njima caressed her face. "Now

take some deep breaths and then let's go have some coffee and breakfast first."

"Coffee, maybe," Yona said, following her out of the room and down the stairs to the second floor. "I can't risk a caffeine headache, but I'm not sure I'll be able to eat until it's over with."

"Actually, it's going to be nice to get the 'first time' over with," Njima said. "First times are often the scariest."

Two practice shots and two pears neatly skewered later, the women finally prepared to perform the act for real. Njima stood about a foot or so in front of the fence at the end of Purva's lot and placed a pear on her head. They had debated whether or not to blindfold Njima, but decided it would increase the tension if the audience knew that she was watching her possible imminent death.

Taking several deep breaths, Yona carefully found her stance before nocking her arrow, setting her grip, and then drawing the arrow. A few more steps, each of which she maneuvered through with great care, and Yona was finally ready to take aim and release the bowstring. The arrow skimmed through the air as Njima and Purva held their breath in anticipation, and with a liquid thwock, pierced the pear perfectly. The arrow tip lodged briefly in the fence behind Njima's head, before the weight of the pear sent it tumbling to the ground.

Njima grabbed the arrow by its shaft and waved it in the air, whooping. "You did it! I knew you could!"

Yona threw herself into Njima's arms and hugged the woman she loved fiercely. "Thank you for believing in me. Thank you, thank you, thank you."

Smiling, Purva walked over to join the celebration. "Thank you for showing me," she said. "I had to make sure you were telling the truth before I could make my offer."

"What offer?" Njima asked. "You've already given us and our horses somewhere to stay."

"I intend to send you to Auriel's agent with a letter of recommendation," she explained. "I'm sure he will be able to guide you in the right direction."

Yona's eyes filled with tears, the stress of the morning and her gratitude for all that Purva had done for them finally making itself felt. "I don't know how to thank you," she hugged the older woman. "This all seems like so much more than we deserve."

"Don't be silly," Purva said. "I believe everyone deserves a chance to pursue their dreams."

Which made Yona feel even more guilty as the woman now seemed to trust them implicitly, and while it was true that the act was real, almost everything else was a fabrication. And yet they couldn't risk revealing any of the truth for fear that Purva might accidentally let something slip. Quite a difference, Yona thought, since their stay in Kuna. They had once erred on the side of revealing everything, but the stepped up aggression from the Awen Alliance and the attack the previous day meant that it was much wiser to be safe than sorry.

AFTER A BELATED BREAKFAST OF A POACHED EGG atop quinoa, avocado, soy beans and a grated hard cheese, the women headed off, Purva's recommendation letter in hand, to see when they could meet with Auriel's agent.

Following Purva's explicit directions through the labyrinthine streets of Kaumari, they found their way to Yoel's place of business. As he was meeting with someone, his assistant read the letter before asking them to take a seat.

"Yoel was very fond of Auriel," the assistant, who introduced himself as Symon, said. "I'm sure he'd like to see you even if just to find out how Purva is getting along."

A quarter of an hour later they were seated on a comfy sofa in Yoel's office waiting as he read Purva's letter. Putting it down on his desk, he looked up at them, his dark brown eyes curious.

"So, I take it that Purva is getting along okay," he said. "How did you chance meeting her?"

"My horse was wounded on our way into town," Njima said, trying to be as vague as possible, "and someone suggested I take her to Purva."

He nodded, running a hand through dark brown hair threaded with silver. "What is it you do?"

"Interesting," he said, scratching his goatee, after Yona had explained what they did in their act. "I think I know of a few places to contact that are always looking for the unusual. Fortunately, I still have Auriel's pigeon here. I just never could give Olive up so she's been taking up a space in my loft for two years now. Actually, the first year I would send her with a note to Purva just to check on her, but I have to confess to being lax this past year."

"Thank you," Yona said. "This means the world to us."

"I'd ask to see the act, but I imagine it takes some space?"

"Yes," Njima said. "We can set that up, if you like. Purva saw it this morning before she wrote the letter. I assume she said so?"

He nodded. "Highly complimentary."

Yona grinned. "We were so lucky to find her."

"Should I speak of you by your real names or would you prefer to stick with your stage names?"

"Stage names," Njima said quickly. "We need to get accustomed to hearing them."

"Can you write those down for me? I don't want to get the spelling wrong," he said, pushing a piece of paper across his desk.

"However you spell it is fine with us," Njima interjected as Yona began to reach for a pen.

"But I've been practicing," Yona flushed, realizing her near mistake. "Purva showed me how to make the letters after we showed her our act," she lied.

"You didn't say," Njima said, voice tinged with reproach.

"I wanted to surprise you."

Njima smiled. "But I am already so proud of you."

Yona glanced at Yoel who was now watching them with barely concealed amusement. "She's right," she told him. "It's best that you spell our names so that they are understandable to those who might read them."

"Zenobia and Skathee, correct?"

"Yes," Yona agreed. "Or Skaði and Zenobia, whichever makes the most sense to you. I'm Skaði, the archer."

"Got it." He stood, slender, effete, and impeccably attired, and Njima realized that he probably suspected they were other than as they represented themselves by the amused glint in his eye. Clearly he respected Purva's opinion, though, and was willing to take them at face value. Extending a well-manicured hand, Yoel said, "I will send Auriel's Olive as soon as I know something. Make sure her loft is clean and has fresh water and food just in case you don't notice her arrival right away."

"We will do that," Njima shook his hand.

"And you're going to do something with your hair?" he asked.

"As soon as we leave here," Yona said. "We intend to cut and bleach it again."

"What about costumes?" Yoel asked.

Yona's eyes widened and she raised a hand to her mouth. "I hadn't thought of that. I was so concerned with practicing the act that I didn't even think about the fact we should have costumes."

"Think about it," he said, "But you needn't do anything until you have to perform."

"I THINK HE SUSPECTS," Njima said after they had walked a few blocks in silence.

"Yes, but what?"

"Hopefully, nothing more than what Purva saw," Njima said.

"I can't imagine that Arawn's or Hamartia's or even Hevel's spies could get information on keeping a lookout for us to every agent in Kaumari," Yona said quietly, looking around to make sure no one was listening. "There must be dozens, even hundreds here."

"And that would be assuming they knew we were using the ruse of being performers as our cover," Njima lowered her voice. "It might be just as easy to conjecture that we travelled here incognito but intended to present ourselves to the palace as who we are."

"I keep forgetting how careful we need to be," Yona said. "We've been incredibly lucky so far, but what happened yesterday could happen again. I need to get into the mindset I was in when I stole the Hamper." She sighed. She had not enjoyed living in constant fear of being discovered during that time, yet she had been safer because she was constantly on the lookout for danger. But that had been nearly a year ago. Since then, in the company of her friends, or alone with Njima, she had been lured into a false sense of security.

Njima nodded and took her hand. "You're right. I'm fully invested in the Quest, but I also have a Kingdom to which I must return. I need to learn to be more casual in the way I talk and not let on the extent of my education."

"We can do it," Yona said, "but perhaps we should develop our 'disinherited children of lords' backstory."

"Much easier to pull off than the 'we're just commoners wanting a taste of fame and glory on The Masala' version," Njima agreed.

"That would give us another advantage," Yona stopped in front of a stall where fabric was being sold.

"What's that?" Njima ran her fingers across a bolt of deep purple velvet.

"We could afford nicer costumes."

They left the stall and began walking toward Purva's house. Suddenly Yona pulled Njima into an alley.

"What is it?" Njima's eyes were wide as she scanned the street ahead of them.

"It just occurred to me that despite the fact we say we are going to be ultra aware, we haven't been. We're not. Anyone on this street could be one of the men from yesterday as far as we know."

"What are you saying?" Njima frowned.

"Take a deep breath."

Njima complied.

"Now breathe again, deeply, but this time smell."

Njima did, and frowned again. "Damn. You're right. We've been so caught up in the our own drama that we haven't been paying attention."

"We've spent the past month in the country with nothing but the odors of the outdoors—trees and grass and water, fire at night and in the morning. The smells of Kaumari should have overwhelmed us."

Njima breathed deeply again, inhaling the aroma peculiar to cities: a perfume of fresh flowers, spices, herbs and roasting foods, burning wood and oil and charcoal with a base of body odor, horse urine, and decaying vegetables.

"Now listen," Yona instructed. They stood quietly for a moment as they picked out the different sounds—the clip clop of horse hooves on the cobbled streets, people laughing, talking, and hawking their wares, people coughing, spitting, and clearing their throats, the creak of cart wheels, and the cooing of pigeons.

"Now close your eyes and then look at the street again."

This time everything came into focus, and the women were able to place from whence all the sounds and smells emanated.

They scanned each face in their vicinity, and Yona gasped and pulled Njima further into the alley.

"What is it?" she whispered.

"It's one of the men who was holding Tancorin," Yona said, pressing a hand to her wildly thumping heart.

"Do you think he was following us?" Njima asked.

Yona edged her way closer to the alley entrance. The man was on the opposite side of the street purchasing some food from a vendor. He seemed completely oblivious to their proximity.

Turning back to Njima, she shook her head.

"That was close," Njima whispered when she returned.

"They're looking for us," Yona said. "I knew it."

"I agree. We're going to have to be very careful coming and going from Purva's."

Yona pulled the hood of her cloak over her head, and Njima followed suit. "We'll give him time to get ahead of us," Yona said, "but we're going to have to lose ourselves in the crowd as long as possible."

"We should also start running our errands solo," Njima said. "They'll be on the lookout for two to four people, probably not just one."

23ᴿᴰ Saitheh

More than two weeks had passed since they reached the beach, and Bonpo and Jabberwock were still marveling at how primeval the Devastation of Pelf seemed. Other than seabirds and sea creatures, they had seen neither hide nor hair of any animal life, human or otherwise.

One grey and foggy morning a few days earlier, Bonpo swore that he'd seen a ship on the horizon. But by the time he'd awakened Jabberwock from his doze, he could no longer find it.

They had developed the pattern of walking along the hard packed sand near the ocean's edge as it was easier for both Tikvah and Bonpo. The rounded pebbles that covered most of the beach up to the cliff face, tended to roll ankles and make them footsore by the end of the day.

On this late spring morning, they were plodding along, enjoying the mild breeze and the gentle roar of the waves hitting the shore, when Bonpo stopped abruptly in his tracks. Tikvah, who was trudging along behind him ran into his back, snorting in surprise as she was brought up short.

"Is dat?" Bonpo said.

Jabberwock who had been thrown forward in his basket was scrambling to his feet. "Is that what?" he asked, scanning the beach ahead of them.

"No, up dere," Bonpo pointed further up the beach to a spot next to the cliffs.

"A boat?" Jabberwock's voice sounded perplexed. Two weeks without a sign of a human or even an Aberration and suddenly a boat?

"Go rook?" Bonpo asked.

"It certainly hasn't been sitting there for centuries," Jabberwock mused as they detoured up the beach.

Once they were standing in front of the small vessel, it was clear that it was currently in use. Oars were neatly stored under the plank seats, and a rope secured the boat to an iron hook protruding from the cliff face about six feet from the ground.

"It seems to have been freshly tarred and painted," Jabberwock noted. They scoured the ground looking for footprints or some other sign of who might own the rowboat, but found nothing.

"Maybe lain rast night wash away footplints," Bonpo suggested.

"Very possible," Jabberwock admitted. The previous day they had lucked on a bigger than average cave as they watched the storm gathering over the Anoon Ocean. It had provided them enough room to be well out of the way as the rain lashed the cliffs and soaked the entrance to the cave. It meant they'd been required to stop early for the day, but it had given them enough time to gather some driftwood so they could have a fire while the storm raged around them. The campfire also provided steady light and they weren't forced to depend on the lightning flashes that occasionally illuminated the otherwise empty cave.

The storm had passed by the time they settled down for the night, and they'd started out on their walk that morning to a clear sky.

"I guess we keep on moving," Jabberwock said after contemplating the boat for a little while longer. He had become so accustomed to their being the only mammals in this strangely antediluvian world that seeing the vessel was like seeing a porpoise riding a horse. It made no sense.

Bonpo led Tikvah back down to the beach and he and Jabberwock were silent for the next half hour as they contemplated the new development. Jabberwock was just about to pose a question when Bonpo stopped again, this time more slowly.

"Wat dat?"

"What this time?" Jabberwock looked up the beach towards the cliffs before Bonpo corrected him.

"No, stlaight ahead," he said. "Rook rike it go arr way in wata."

"A wall?" Jabberwock guessed. A wall might mean they were nearing Buta, but he didn't remember the capitol having a barrier around it. Zhaleh Palace would have had fortifications, but it was located atop the plateau overlooking Buta's harbor.

The Bandersnatch squinted into the distance, perplexed, and finally heaved a sigh. "Boats and walls," he said. Clearly they were leaving behind the primal landscape for civilization. "I have no idea what they mean, and I have a bad feeling about this, but I don't see any other way than forward. I imagine all will be explained to us once we arrive there."

Continuing along the water's edge, the three of them moved closer and closer to the wall. As they drew within three hundred yards of the edifice, they began to realize that barrier wasn't just any wall. The height of the barricade was staggering, at least a hundred feet or more.

"That must have taken years to build," Jabberwock growled. "Clearly there was something someone wanted to keep out."

"Abelations, maybe?"

Was there a group of people like the Preternaturals, Jabberwock wondered, who had run off the Aberrations? Were they just Pelfans who had survived or maybe Aberrations that had evolved somewhat?

They had advanced perhaps another fifty yards, and Jabberwock was seriously considering retreating until they could figure out how to get around the wall, when an arrow struck the sand at Bonpo's feet.

Tikvah brayed in surprise and Bonpo jumped backwards, pulling the donkey with him as more arrows followed.

"Retreat!" Jabberwock barked scrambling to get as low as possible in his basket. Breaking into a trot, Tikvah and Bonpo hurried back the way they'd come, not stopping until they were well out of arrow range.

"Not vely fliendry, are dey?" Bonpo said when he could stop to catch his breath.

"I guess seeing a giant arrive unannounced was a little daunting," Jabberwock said. "At least, I hope their policy isn't to shoot first, ask questions later."

"Wat we gonna do?"

"I think we go back to the boat by way of the cliffs," Jabberwock said. "Maybe we missed a pathway up to the plateau. I feel certain whoever owns that rowboat hasn't anchored it too far from where they reside."

"An' it fal enuf flom da warr dat no one see it."

"Yes," Jabberwock agreed. "I'd say we walked a good half hour or so before the wall was visible. Let's just hope that whomever owns the boat is friendlier than whoever is behind the wall."

They followed the cliff face searching carefully for a path that might lead to the top of the plateau but except for the occasional cave, it seemed mostly solid. Just in case, though, they searched both of the caves they passed on the way back to the boat. But it was to no avail as one was too small for anyone but Jabberwock and the other had caved in not far from its entrance.

With the boat in sight, Jabberwock conjectured that the path might have been prior to their reaching the boat. They had walked diagonally up the beach to reach it but hadn't really paid attention to the cliffs except for within sight distance on either side of the vessel.

They passed the boat, which was in the same position they'd left it in, and there were no additional footprints to indicate that anyone else had been there since they'd returned to the sand. A few minutes later their eastward trek brought them to yet another cave.

It had a narrow but tall entrance, perhaps just a couple of feet higher than Bonpo's head, and the giant was forced to enter sideways. Once inside, the cave broadened by several feet before making a sharp right turn. About the length of Bonpo's shadow away, they could see light filtering in from what was clearly another turn, this one to the left.

Making the turn, they soon found themselves in another broad but shallow cave, which opened up on a narrow V-shaped valley blocked by a cliff to the south. On either side, the plateau fell steeply to the valley, which seemed to rise toward the plateau in the distance.

A well-worn path started at the cave and made its way north toward the head of the valley. Somewhere along this path, we'll find the owner of that boat, Jabberwock thought.

"Let's go," he said. "And may Omni be with us."

THEY HAD WALKED ABOUT TWENTY MINUTES, ascending a gentle rise covered in shrubs and short grass, when the path reached the crest of the ridge and began to descend. Here the trail wound downward through a small forest of deciduous trees—rowans, oaks, birches, ash, and hazel trees—whose new leaves provided the shade they had not had on the beach.

Reaching the floor of the hollow, they stepped out of woods and into a large clearing dominated by a log cabin and a small barn. Smoke wisped from the chimney, and Jabberwock could smell the scent of roasting meat.

"Polk?" Bonpo said as quietly as he could.

Pork, indeed, Jabberwock was thinking just as the door to the cabin swung open and a middle-aged woman carrying a basket of what looked like wet laundry stepped into the dooryard.

Seeing Bonpo, she dropped the basket and scurried backwards toward the doorway.

"No need be aflaid," Bonpo raised his hands to show they were empty. "We jus tlyin' to find da way to Buta."

"Who da beeg man, mama?" a teenaged male appeared behind the woman, eyes that slanted upwards were wide with curiosity. As he was mostly hidden behind his mother, Jabberwock couldn't see much more than his face, but the small nose and mouth and slightly protruding tongue confirmed that the woman had a child that was what they called untarnished in the Thirteen Kingdoms. That is, he amended himself, in the Triquetra Alliance. Omni only knew what they called children of that sort in the crueler Awen Alliance.

Unfortunately for Bonpo, the woman and her son were speaking Pelfan. He was going to have to speak for them. Clearing his throat, he said, "We come in peace."

The woman gave a little shriek and took another step backwards.

"Owee Mama! You step on me foot," the young man was still surveying the trio with interest. He'd never seen such—a talking dog and a giant. "Say someteeng else," he giggled.

"We were travelling along the beach to Buta, but had arrows shot at us as we approached," Jabberwock explained. "We have business in Buta and were hoping to find another way to get there. Please don't be afraid. We mean no harm."

The woman studied them for a while, and Jabberwock realized he was going to have to read her thoughts if he wanted to know what she really thought.

'The giant seems affable enough,' she was thinking as Jabberwock concentrated his telepathic powers on her. 'He's big but he has a pleasant look on his face. The fox-like creature seems capable of speech,' she thought, and Jabberwock sensed that somewhere in the back of her mind was the knowledge that he was a Janawar.

'It's small, though,' her study of them continued. 'Doesn't strike me as dangerous, though I'd feel a bit more comfortable if I had the fire poker in my hand.' The Bandersnatch continued to monitor her thoughts from his basket atop the large donkey that was nibbling placidly at the grass at its feet. He was trying to be patient as she weighed the merits of helping these strangers.

"We does not have thee room to provide thee weeth shelter," she said staring pointedly at Bonpo.

"We're not asking for lodging," Jabberwock said. "We want to know if there is another way to get into Buta?"

'There is a way,' she thought, as Jabberwock focused all his attention on her.

Her son, Samee, he learned, occasionally led travellers to Buta although it was both a rare and complicated process. It would be made simpler this time, she mused, as these travellers could be led straight there.

Jabberwock received an image of a pigeon leaving a guard post just west of what must be the entrance to their valley. He saw Samee bringing the bird to his mother, who read the message. Samee would then make the journey to that guard station and for a small fee lead the traveller or travellers, usually shipwrecked sailors, to the guard post just outside the city's walls.

'I suppose the money they give Samee is a small kindness,' her thoughts rambled. Jabberwock learned that the powers that be in the city had forced her to leave when she gave birth to a slow-witted child. And, despite the fact that there were enough soldiers to escort travellers to Buta, they had watched her beg for money too many times not to have devised a way to help them out.

'This trip could mean more coins for Samee,' she thought, and Jabberwock saw that the little that he made each year paid for small indulgences such as sweets for him and necessary items that she couldn't provide for herself.

The Bandersnatch felt her bitterness rise as she considered yet again, he felt, that it was all she could do to be as self-sufficient as possible. 'As a single mother,' she thought, 'I have neither the time nor the energy to grow additional crops, or raise more animals than necessary, or any of the other things I might could do for a little extra coin.'

Glancing at the sky, Jabberwock saw her realize that the sun was well past the meridian and lowering toward the western horizon, which in this case was the top of the plateau. It was called the Noontide Valley, he learned, because most of the light here was from mid morning until mid afternoon. 'Dusk is fast approaching,' she thought, 'and there isn't time to send Samee to the guard station at the top of the plateau and have him return before nightfall. The trip there and back takes an entire day.'

She sighed audibly. 'Sending them on their way was a possibility,' she considered, 'but the top of the plateau wasn't the safest place to camp as those who'd been exiled from Buta frequented it when things got tough in their refugee camp, which was most of the time. Not the most savory lot.'

The woman sighed again and returned to the dropped basket. "Yee might camp een our yard tonight or een thee barn, eef eet rains," she paused, "though that ees unlikely because of thee storm yestern evening." She picked up the basket, and headed toward the clothesline that was strung between two nearby poles. "I'm Zoya, and thees ees me son, Samee," she said over her shoulder. "Samee, show them where thee water ees."

Bonpo chose to set up their tent on the opposite side of the clearing from Zoya's home. The way she continually glanced over her shoulder at them while hanging her clothes, and scurried quickly into the house once they were hung led him to believe she was uncomfortable with their being there. He hoped distance would put her a little more at ease.

The giant also found it odd that she had washed and hung out the clothes so late in the day until he realized that all that was on the line were a pair of trousers, some small clothes, and a couple of towels. Perhaps Samee had spilled something on himself or had an accident, Bonpo mused as he scavenged the woods for downed limbs with which to build a cooking fire.

Aromas of roasting pork and freshly baked bread had set his stomach to growling, and tonight there would be no seafood. He had been looking forward to arriving in Buta so that he could replenish their supplies. Tonight's meal would be limited to rehydrated beans and vegetables. All the dried meat and sausage had long since disappeared.

While he puttered about setting up their camp, Jabberwock was patiently fielding Samee's questions, which ran the gamut from 'how can a dog talk?' to 'ees dat a real giant?' to 'does he eat kids?'. Zoya sticking her head out the front door, and calling for her son finally rescued him.

"Samee, yee get een here thees instant!"

"He's not bothering me," Jabberwock said as Samee wailed loudly that he wanted to talk to the "doggee". It might have been the first time in the past five centuries that the Janawar didn't mind being compared to a dog.

Zoya insisted even in the face of her son's tears. "We need to leave thees," she faltered for a second, searching for a word, "thees travellers in peace. Come now."

"I suppose she won't be convinced we're harmless until she awakens safe in her bed tomorrow morning," Jabberwock said once the door closed on the sniffling Samee.

"As rong as we get to Buta tamollow," Bonpo said. "We ar-mos' outta food."

Jabberwock eyed the cauldron Bonpo was dumping dried beans into and grimaced. "A slice or two of that pork would have been most welcome."

Settling down in front of the fire, Jabberwock mused on what the morrow might bring. He wasn't sure he liked the thought of entering a city in which they'd been attacked before they had even gotten near enough to speak to whoever was behind the wall. The Bandersnatch just hoped that they'd be al-lowed into the city once they talked with someone at the guard post on the plateau.

The following morning, Bonpo was cleaning the breakfast dishes when Samee stepped out of the cabin carrying a wicker basket.

"Mama made us lunch," he said to Jabberwock when he reached the far end of the clearing where they were camped.

"We're nearly packed," Jabberwock said. "Would you like Bonpo to attach the basket to the donkey so that you don't have to carry it?"

Samee nodded and handed the basket to Bonpo. When Jabberwock was settled in his basket, Samee led them back across the clearing to a path that started behind the barn. They ascended through the woods on the opposite side of the hollow until they once again reached the top of the shrub- and grass-covered ridge. From here the trail climbed slowly northward to the top of the plateau with occasional detours down into and back out of hollows and the fording of numerous small streams.

The sun was directly overhead when the quartet arrived atop the plateau although Jabberwock wasn't aware they had done so until they stepped out of a forest of tall pines. Looking southward, he saw that the tall trees blocked the view of Samee's valley. Interesting, he thought, wondering just how many strangers had found their way into the valley much less down to Zoya's cabin. Maybe that's why she found their appearance in her dooryard so shocking.

In front of them stretched a juniper-covered scrubland broken by a wide and sandy road. The path they followed angled westward toward the road and when they reached it, they were only a hundred yards or so from the guard post.

"Hail, Samee!" A guard stepped out and waved at the teen.

"Heello, Keer!" Samee called back. He pointed to a picnic table beneath a canopy that extended from the building. "Can we eat lunch dere?"

"Of course you can, Samee," he said, but he was looking at Bonpo. He touched the sword at his hip. "Let me grab me lunch and I'll eat weeth yee."

Kir disappeared into the guard post, and returned a minute later with his own basket. Samee had passed out cold pork sandwiches, and Bonpo was cutting Jabberwock's meat into smaller pieces.

"So what brings thee to Buta?" Kir asked Bonpo, who stared at him blankly.

"He don't speak thee langage," Samee said, "but thee doggee does."

Kir turned to Jabberwock, eyes narrowed. "You speak?"

"I'm afraid so," Jabberwock said, deeply regretting the need to do so.

"Yee're not, yee cannot be a Janawar," Kir said, frowning. "Thee were keeled off centuries ago."

Jabberwock returned his stare, glassy eyes reflecting the cobalt blue of Kir's uniform. "Apparently not all of us," he said, voice as dry as the sand that blew around their feet.

"And thees giant here? Ees he also from Dziron?"

"Yes," Jabberwock said. "He's a yeti."

"I thought yeti couldn't leave Dziron? I've never seen one," Kir turned to stare at Bonpo again.

"It is rare," Jabberwock agreed. He preferred not to reveal that Bonpo had been exiled.

"What beeseeness do yee have een Buta?" Kir asked.

"It is private," Jabberwock said, "but we were hoping to speak to whomever is in charge. Can that be arranged?"

"Not here," Kir said, "but at the guard post outside the walls of the town, we might be able to make that happen."

"We?" Jabberwock asked.

"Thees ees highly unusual," Kir said. "I think eet would be better for me to lead you to the next post." He turned to Samee, who was just finishing the last bite of his sandwich. "Sorry, Samee, but I think yee should return to yee're mama."

"But I 'posed to lead them to Buta," Samee said, visions of future sweets disappearing before his eyes. "My fee!" he cried, eyes tearing up.

"Don't yee worry about yee're fee, Samee boy," Kir said, standing and lifting the basket he'd never emptied. "I'll pay yee yee're fee. Hail, Jaspar!" he shouted.

Another guard stuck his head around the side of the door so quickly that he must have been standing there listening, Jabberwock thought.

"What do yee need, Keer?" he said.

"Can yee get Samee's coin?" Kir asked. "I'll be leading these Dzironese to Buta."

Jaspar disappeared back into the building, returning shortly with a handful of coins that he deposited in Samee's basket. "Geev mee love to yee're mama," he said. "Best yee get on back to her. Eet looks as eef there's another storm gathering." He pointed southward where they could all see massive banks of cloud building out over the Anoon Ocean.

Jabberwock felt the hackles rising on his neck. Something was seriously wrong, but he couldn't quite place his paw on what that might be.

4TH SAITHEH

The road that led out of Mwezi-barafu was straight and wide and crowded on either side with homes and shops. About a mile outside of town, the homes became more and more dilapidated the further east Chokhmah and Faolan travelled. They were sitting silently alongside the driver in a horse-drawn cart. As his grasp of the Common Tongue wasn't good enough to permit conversation, they studied the passing scenery instead.

When the dilapidated homes gave way to makeshift shacks and tents, Faolan tried to make himself understood with as few words as possible. Pointing to the tents with a quizzical expression, he simply asked, "What?"

"Refugees," the slender man answered. "Seemoon."

Chokhmah and Faolan looked at each other, eyes wide. If it was so bad that people were fleeing the kingdom, Chokhmah's eyes seemed to say, then crossing the border illegally was no longer a matter of playing it safe, but imperative.

A couple of miles from the border crossing, the driver slowed the horse down and began looking for the small sign that would indicate that he needed to turn the cart left. Soon thereafter, he guided the horse northward along a narrow track that wound through the tall pine trees to either side of it. Other than the creaking of the cart, they travelled silently for another hour before the young man reined in the horse pulling the cart.

"That ees path yous follow," he pointed to a barely discernible trail to their right.

Faolan nodded and jumped down from the cart before extending his hand to help Chokhmah to the ground. The driver handed Faolan the modest, brown leather bag that contained the bare minimum needed to supply his and Chokhmah's needs until they reached Sigwald, including the dark glasses that would hide her eyes.

Faolan helped the driver guide the horse so that the cart could be turned around, and the two of them watched as it disappeared back down the track toward Mwezi-barafu.

"Are you ready?" Faolan asked once it was no longer in sight.

"There is no time like the present, right, my love?" Chokhmah answered. "I think I am ready." She had used henna the previous day to make her dark hair redder. It was now pulled back in a bun and covered by a headscarf woven of dark green wool. The days were still chilly this far north so she also wore a long, loden-green dress of thick tweed covered by a brown woolen cloak.

Faolan was similarly outfitted in clothes of subdued earth tones, the better to camouflage themselves as they hiked through the forest. He would shift into a wolf at night and when necessary, but for Chokhmah's sake wanted to remain human as long as possible until they reached the outskirts of Sigwald. Because they were walking, they figured it might take them a week or more to get there.

The path they were about to take led to a chasm that was cut by a river that had long since disappeared. King Adeyemi had assured them that crossing the border there would not be a problem as it was far enough away from the main road that people seldom wandered that way. The trail also included a difficult climb, which made it a scarcely-used passage to Simoon.

"Besides," the king had said, "no one wants to sneak into the Kingdom of Simoon at this point. They are allowed to enter of their own free will if they approve of King Hamartia's, uh," he'd paused, "policies," he finished, diplomatically.

Once the couple ascended the opposite side of the chasm they would officially be in Simoon. From there, they would travel eastward, eventually reaching a road that would take them southeast to the capitol.

Because the trail was narrow, they would have to proceed single file. Faolan insisted on leading the way so that he would be the first to face any possible dangers.

THEY HIKED FOR THE REMAINDER OF THE DAY, stopping only for a quick lunch of cold chicken and fruit. Most of the time was spent making the perilous descent to the bottom of the chasm before climbing back out of it again.

When they'd first reached the precipice, Chokhmah had quailed before gritting her teeth. Resolutely, she had pulled the back of her dress through her legs and secured it behind the belted pouch she wore around her waist, but it still made for clumsy climbing.

"Don't look down," Faolan said, "it'll be less dizzying."

"I have to look down to see where to next put my foot," she frowned at him.

"I'm going first," Faolan said. "I won't take another step until I'm sure you're secure. Okay?"

She bit her lip and sighed. "Yes, let us do this." But it had been more difficult than she had been prepared for. Her dress would slip out of the belt and several times she found one or the other foot caught within it and her balance shaken.

When they finally reached the bottom, although it was significantly cooler and dustier than the trail they had left, she had begged for a break. "I know climbing up will be easier," she had said, "but I need to prepare myself." Looking around, she noticed that a few feet away, the ground became somewhat sandy where the river once flowed. True, there were boulders and pebbles in abundance, but the sand called to her.

Quickly removing her boots, she buried her feet in its coolness, and luxuriated for a while as her throbbing feet took a much-needed rest. When she felt sufficiently rested and calm again, she pulled her boots back on and stood, once again pulling her skirt through her legs. "I am ready," she had said. "I go first this time."

"I never want to do that again," Chokhmah said when they stopped to rest once they were safely in the Kingdom of Simoon.

"Never say never," Faolan warned.

Sighing, Chokhmah studied the woods around them. He was right, of course, because she did indeed want to be doing that very climb as soon as possible. "I did not mean so much the climb as doing a climb that dangerous in a dress," she murmured.

"I'm sorry, darling," He pulled her into his arms.

She leaned her head on his shoulder. At least they were alive, she thought. "My breeches would have made it easier," she said, "but I just could not risk bringing them."

Late afternoon light filtered down through the pine needles above them. "We'd better find water and a spot to camp before it gets too much darker," Faolan said, drawing away from her.

The trail on the Simoon side of the chasm was even more overgrown than the Sheban path, but it was still discernible. If this section of the border had ever been guarded, and Faolan thought it must have been at some point because another trail paralleled the chasm, then there ought to be water nearby.

"If I shift," he told Chokhmah, "then I will have a better chance of hearing any water. Do you mind?"

"Of course not," she said, smiling and reaching for the leather bag in his hand so that he could remove his clothes. A year ago, safe and sound in her vardo, she would never have guessed that watching a man shift from man to wolf and back again would become common place for her. Taking his clothes in her arms, she watched his transformation. It would never cease to amaze her—one minute human and then, in almost a blur of motion, a four-legged creature.

He trotted down the trail, nose twitching, and she followed, smiling to herself.

They had been walking eastward for about ten minutes or so when Faolan suddenly stopped, ears cocked to listen. He looked at Chokhmah to make sure she was following, and proceeded, nose to the ground. He thought he heard water, maybe a small stream, and following the scent of the other forest animals that frequented it would lead him there more quickly.

Shortly thereafter, he found a narrow path to their left, and turned down it. A few minutes later, the trail descended steeply down a boulder-strewn slope crowded with rhododendrons and mountain laurel to a brook that burbled quietly around the boulders and over smaller stones.

The slope was too steep for camping. They would have to carry their water back up to the ridge along which they were travelling. Faolan shifted back, dressing quickly, while Chokhmah removed a leather sack from their travel bag. She unrolled it, and handed it to Faolan who filled it with water from the brook.

Returning to the main trail, they found a spot between a few pine trees where they could bed down for the night. The water was for drinking only as Chokhmah couldn't carry all the camping gear needed if Faolan was forced to shift unexpectedly. Not only did this mean they had no pot in which to cook food, but also no tent, no blankets, and no dishes. They could roast meat on a spit when Faolan caught something, but other than that they were going to have to subsist on what they could find in the woods—fungi, greens, early berries, and any remaining nuts from autumn.

"I just think that if you're carrying a pack," Faolan had said, "it would look suspicious if someone stumbled upon us along the way."

"I guess if I am carrying only a leather bag," Chokhmah had mused, "I can say that I am out gathering herbs and the other things I need for healing."

Together they gathered enough wood to make a small campfire, and Chokhmah kept an eye out for anything edible or that could be used for her medicinal stores while she did so. She managed to scavenge a few mushrooms, but nothing else.

The couple ate the last of the chicken for dinner along with the mushrooms, which Chokhmah skewered on a long and slender branch and roasted over the fire. They were left with the last two apples, strips of dried meat, three hard boiled eggs, nuts, and hard biscuits should they be unable to find anything fresh. It wasn't much, but they could ration it, Faolan reasoned, and arrive in Sigwald starving if it was necessary for them to do so.

As night fell, the flames of the fire were the only thing they had available to push back the darkness. Chokhmah slept wrapped in her cloak, and Faolan's, while he slept as a wolf by her side providing additional heat.

THEY AWOKE AT FIRST LIGHT, consuming the eggs and pouring the remainder of the water on the fire to make sure it was out.

Faolan was quiet and clearly grumpy as they returned to the trail.

"My love?" Chokhmah said.

"What is it?"

"Give me your hand," she said.

Faolan extended his hand and Chokhmah pressed a handful of chocolate-coated beans into it.

"What is this?" he asked.

"Roasted coffee beans coated in dark chocolate. Try one."

He crunched one between his molars, and then quickly popped a few more in his mouth. "You never cease to amaze me," he smiled.

"I didn't think now was the time to go through caffeine withdrawals," she said, eyes glimmering with amusement.

"You're lucky you only drink herbal teas," he said. "Thank you, darling. Those headaches are no fun." He turned and started walking again, and Chokhmah smiled at his back.

This trip is stressful enough, she thought, and keeping Faolan happy would make it pass much more quickly. Besides, she admitted to herself, seeing that smile on his face brought her great joy, even more so when she was responsible for it.

Six days later the trail ended at the road that would take them south to Sigwald. As it was late afternoon when they reached it, Chokhmah and Faolan decided to backtrack into the woods and camp at a spot they had noticed about a half-mile back.

A mostly clear trail had led to a clearing just off the main path. Out of curiosity when they first passed it, Faolan had jogged down it just to see if it led to anything with possibilities for camping or water. He'd only jogged down the path for a couple of minutes. More than that wouldn't be worth wasting time over, he'd told Chokhmah as he disappeared down the trail.

"It's too early in the afternoon to stop," Faolan said when he returned, "but it led to a beautiful little glade with a spring."

"Were there any flowers or herbs?" Chokhmah had asked.

Faolan had shrugged. "I only noticed the rabbit droppings."

Now they returned to the glade, Chokhmah's stomach rumbling in anticipation of some fresh food that evening. The past two nights, Faolan had only managed to catch squirrels, and Chokhmah had sacrificed her share so that he might remain strong. That meant her fare for the past two days had been nuts and hard biscuits supplemented with the occasional mushrooms and wild onions she spotted while hiking.

"I will gather the wood for a fire," she said when they reached the glade, "if you can attempt to catch us some dinner."

Faolan quickly stripped and disappeared into the woods as Chokhmah began scrounging for firewood. He hadn't returned by the time she got the fire started, so in the late afternoon light, she began to check the clearing for any greens or fungi that they might be able to eat. She was delighted to find a patch of early arugula near the spring at the far side of the glade, and just under the trees, some fiddleheads.

As Chokhmah was dipping the leather pouch into the spring, she noticed something shimmering at the bottom, mostly covered by sand and pebbles. Pushing the sleeve of her dress up so that it wouldn't get wet, she reached into the spring to see if she could find out what it was. The water had just reached her elbow when her fingers finally skimmed the top of the object. Another inch, and she was able to push away enough of the dirt and small stones to reveal the edge of the object. It looked as if it might be a bowl or a pot.

Working it free from the bottom of the spring, she finally retrieved a tin pot. She rinsed the remainder of the sand from the pan and turned it over to discover the bottomed was blackened from fire although the sand had scrubbed some patches away to reveal the tin beneath. Chokhmah could not help but chuckle to herself before thanking Omni. Their last night in the woods, she thought shaking her head, and now she had a pot. Better late than never, though, as she could steam the greens she had found.

She gathered the water she needed in the pouch and returned to the fire just as Faolan entered the clearing, large hare dangling from his jaw. He laid it at her feet before shifting back to his human form.

"I'll dress . . . what's that?" he asked as he noticed the tin vessel next to the campfire.

"I found it in the spring," Chokhmah said. "Either someone was interrupted while washing it and then forgot about it or perhaps it was left there for a next time that never arrived."

"Too bad we didn't find that our first night out," he said, picking up his clothes.

"Omni has a sense of humor, does It not?" Chokhmah smiled.

"Hmpfff! If that's what you want to call it," he pulled on his pants and sweater before removing his dagger from its sheath. Picking up the hare, he headed back to the woods. "I want to bury the skin and innards away from camp," he explained as he left.

While he was gone, Chokhmah found two forked branches and a sturdy branch to use as a spit. It would be nice to arrive in Sigwald, and not have to worry about food first thing.

"This is it," Faolan said. He'd spent half an hour gathering as many large rocks as he could find. The previous evening he'd used his dagger to scrabble out a hole in the earth behind one of the pine trees that surrounded the clearing. He'd covered the bottom with pine needles and now he was laying his boots, followed by his sweater and pants and small clothes, into the depression. He spread more pine needles over his clothes before covering everything with the rocks he'd gathered. Only Omni knew when they'd be back and whether or not the clothes would still be wearable.

The morning was chilly so he was still wearing his cloak, but that would soon be folded into the leather bag along with his dagger. Chokhmah thought she could risk being caught with a wool cloak, but not with men's clothing.

When they reached the road they would need to be fully in character, which meant Faolan was about to shift. He couldn't risk being a man again until they were safely ensconced in whatever lodgings Chokhmah managed to find. This would be made more difficult by the fact that she was supposed to be blind, and he wouldn't be able to communicate. He had taught her as much Simoonese as possible, but her backstory was going to have to cover the fact she wasn't a native speaker.

Chokhmah glanced longingly at the clearing. It would be nice to spend yet another day in this spot—free of any worries. But, that would only prolong the inevitable. "I am ready, my love." She kissed him, and looked deeply into his grey blue eyes for a moment, praying to Omni that she would be holding him in her arms that night in Sigwald.

As they approached the gates to the city that mid-afternoon, the short line that had formed at the guard post in front of the town gate halted the blind woman and her wolf.

"Name?" a soldier who couldn't have been much more than eighteen asked her when she reached the front of the line, looking askance at the big wolf that stood placidly at her side.

"Magdala, widow of Hans of Beowulf."

"I'm not familiar with Beowulf," he said, writing the information down in a ledger.

"It is a sheep farm northeast of Sigwald, not far from the Terminus Mountains."

"What's your business in Sigwald?" the soldier asked

"I seek residence here," Chokhmah replied. "I lost my

sight, and I was forced to sell the farm. I hope to do business here as a healer."

"Is that possible when blind?" he asked.

"Yes, it is," she said. "I have been a healer for most of my life. I know the herbs by scent and touch, and can still make potions."

"You don't happen to have something for a toothache," he touched his jaw, tenderly, as if even that brought him pain.

"I do," she said, opening her leather bag, and feeling for the little pouch that contained the leaves she was seeking. "Put these between your gum and the tooth," she said, extending her palm with the leaves on it. "It should numb the pain."

The soldier did as she asked, and they waited in silence until the leaves did as promised. "Much better," the man sighed. "And the wolf. Is it completely tamed?"

"I have had him since he was a pup," Chokhmah said. "He would not hurt anyone unless they were hurting me."

The soldier glanced at the wolf to see it watching him, a look of expectation in its eyes, head slightly cocked as if waiting for an answer. "He seems very intelligent," the soldier said.

"He is," she said. "I trust him with my life."

"You don't sound as if you're from here," he said.

"I am not from here," Chokhmah admitted. "I met my husband when he was in Adamah for business. He was buying some sheep from my father that he hoped to crossbreed with his own."

The soldier nodded. "Do you know where you are boarding tonight?" he asked, pen poised above the ledger.

"I do not," Chokhmah said. "I have not been here in perhaps twenty years."

"I recommend Ebbe's," he said. "She will treat you well. Go straight for about five minutes," he paused, trying to decide how to give directions to a blind woman. "Just a minute. "Hesse!" He called to another soldier, sitting in the shade of the gate.

"What is it?"

"Grab Bölli for me."

A few minutes later, a little boy with white blond hair scampered up to the guard's side. "Yes, Mephi? What do you need?"

"Could you lead this woman to Ebbe's?" Mephi said.

The boy was staring, round-eyed, at Faolan, mouth hanging open. "Is that a wolf? I've only seen drawings."

"Yes," Chokhmah answered him. "We come from further north where we still have a few around, although very few now. I have had Dodi since he was a pup. Let him smell your hand."

Bölli extended his hand and Faolan sniffed it obligingly, and then licked it for good measure. The boy giggled. "Can I touch him?"

"Scratch him behind his ears," she said. "He likes that."

Bölli did so, and Faolan licked his face in appreciation. "I think he likes me!" The boy laughed, smiling broadly, pale blue eyes shining.

"Dodi likes anyone who likes him," Chokhmah said. "Lead the way, and he will follow you." She dropped her hand so that it rested on Faolan's back, and they began to move through the gate and into Sigwald.

To Chokhmah's surprise, the city was teeming with people hurrying about their business. *How can they abide to live here,* she thought, as her eyes behind the dark glasses took in the sights. *Everyone seemed so normal. It was as if they were blissfully unaware of the persecutions that were forcing hundreds to flee the kingdom,* she thought.

Hearing Faolan whine quietly, Chokhmah realized that she was frowning. She smiled down at him, hoping to reassure him that all was well.

"Is everything all right?" Bölli asked, hearing the wolf's whine.

"I think Dodi senses that I am overly tired," she lied. "Is it much farther?"

"We're almost there," he said, and pointed. "Just down that next street to the left, see." He paused, realizing his mistake. "I'm sorry, of course you can't see. But truly, it isn't too far."

A few minutes later, Bölli was ringing the little bell that hung on the front door of Ebbe's boarding house.

The door opened to reveal a short, squat woman with iron grey hair pulled back in a tight bun, and eyes as blue as forget-me-nots.

"Bölli!" she exclaimed, but her eyes were on Chokhmah, whose gaze fell somewhere just above her head, and the large wolf standing next to her that seemed to be studying her with its unusual grey blue eyes.

"Strange eyes for a wolf," Ebbe remarked.

"Yes," Chokhmah agreed. "We always thought there must be some dog in him."

"We?"

"My husband, Hans, and I."

"Where is he?"

"I am afraid he passed away a couple of years ago," Chokhmah explained. "I was already losing my sight at the time, and when I could no longer see, I was forced to sell our sheep farm and move to Sigwald."

"Please come in," she put her hand on Chokhmah's arm and led her inside, Faolan following closely behind.

"Till later, Ebbe!" Bölli said, retreating down the steps. "I need to get back to the gate."

"Give my love to Mephi!" she called after him, chuckling to herself. "That boy has more energy." She led Chokhmah to a sitting room ond helped her sit down on a sofa there. Faolan lay at her feet, as Ebbe settled herself into rocking chair. "Tell me what it is you see yourself doing here in Sigwald."

That's a loaded question, Faolan thought, forcing himself

not to glance over at Ebbe. Instead he shut his eyes and pretended to doze.

"It was my hope that I might find work here as a healer," she explained. "I have a little money from the sale of the farm, and I was hoping to find lodgings in which I could practice my trade."

Ebbe asked questions similar to those Mephi had asked, and was soon satisfied of Magdala's sincerity.

"I'm sure we could find you somewhere in which live and work," she said, "but to be completely honest, it would be a great boon to my boarding house to have a healer in residence. There are so few of them these days."

"Why is that?" Chokhmah asked.

Ebbe paused, and then said quietly after glancing around, "Because many of the healers in Simoon were the sort of people the king did not want living here."

"Ah," Chokhmah said, "such as gypsies and shamans and the like."

"So what with you being from a Kingdom in the Awen Alliance and having been married to a citizen of Simoon, well, I can't see any danger in your just staying here if you wish to do so."

"Can you afford the lost space?" Chokhmah asked.

"We can work this one of two ways," Ebbe said. "Room and board and I receive the payment from the services you provide. Or, you can pay for room and board and keep the payment you receive."

Chokhmah considered this. If things were as Ebbe intimated, then she would be receiving many people who needed help, and that would mean a good income. Yet, she thought, *I need someplace to be where I can see what is going on, and leaving here and trying to find someplace else . . . who knows what might happen. This might just be Omni giving me the support I need.* "Which would you prefer as they would both seem to work out well for me, assuming I get some of the income for new supplies and incidentals?"

Ebbe thought for a moment. "Hmmmm," she murmured, "to board you and your wolf will cost me more in the short run, but once word of mouth spreads, you'll more than likely see plenty of business." She paused as if she were trying to come to a decision, brow creased, lower lip pinched by her upper teeth. She nodded to herself and continued. "I hinted that there is a lack of healers in Sigwald, but I wasn't entirely honest."

"No?" Chokhmah said.

"I didn't want to scare you away by telling you, but you'll find out soon enough anyway. The situation here is dire. There are so few healers that even the castle has to make do with a woman who should have long since retired."

"I am not afraid of work," Chokhmah said.

"It would be of great benefit to me, financially," Ebbe admitted, to give you room and board and I can use what profit you bring in to make some long-needed repairs on this building."

"I assume by profit," Chokhmah said, "that you are agreeing that some of what I make can be used to refresh the herbs and other things I will need for healing among other things. For example, Dodi needs a lot of meat, some of which he can hunt for, but . . . ?"

"Of course! Of course," Ebbe assured her. "It would not be to our benefit for you to run out of supplies or to suffer because you couldn't live properly. Can you start right away?"

"I will need to make a trip to the market," she replied, "but if I can do that first thing in the morning, yes, I am willing to start right away."

"Then we need to get the word out," Ebbe stood. "I'll show you your room so you can rest while I set about doing that."

11ᴛʜ Eahth

Reining in their horses at the summit of the Phlux Pass, Eluned and Gwrhyr paused to take in their first glimpse of Dziron. The Qahept Heights towered above them to the north and south, snow-covered slopes sparkling in the noonday sun.

Below them they could discern the shimmer of the River Draq as it wound its way southward through Dziron's capitol, Jungnay. Just ahead of them sat a small guard post to the left, and another to the right, cattycornered to it—the entry and exit stations for Kamartha and Dziron.

"They must not get a lot of traffic," Gwrhyr said quietly to Eluned, who was sniffling into a handkerchief. The higher they ascended, the colder she became, and the colder she was, the more her nose ran. At this point in time, she felt as if someone had turned on a faucet.

"I'm not surprised," she grumbled. "Now I understand all the jokes about Dziron and cold. I can't imagine why anyone would want to visit, much less live here."

"I doubt many people live at this elevation," Gwrhyr said. She glared at him.

"I'm sure the weather in the valley is much more temperate," he said as a blast of wind hit their backs causing Eluned to moan, and the horses to duck their heads, ears twitching rapidly.

"Let's get a move on." Eluned nudged Ronan forward. "The sooner we're in the valley, the better. I just want to get out of this wind."

They passed by Kamartha's outpost, waving politely as they did so, before stopping at Dziron's. Having just spent two months on the road, they looked like the travelling minstrels they claimed to be.

Because he spoke Dzironese, Gwrhyr quickly gained their entry into the most isolated of the Thirteen Kingdoms. Bordered to the north by the Northern Waste, and the west and south by the Anoon Ocean, two thirds of Dziron's eastern border was protected by the Devastation of Pelf, the remainder bounded by Kamartha.

Eluned looked back over her shoulder at the road that led eastward toward the Kingdom they'd just left, and to the kingdoms beyond it. She had never felt so far from home. It was a long, long way back to Zion and she was beginning to have second thoughts of returning there through an unallied kingdom in which she'd already been attacked.

When they were far enough down the pass that she could risk speaking without being overheard, she spoke to Gwrhyr of her fears.

"So, I'm thinking that once we have the Treasure," she finished, "we should make our way to Dangjin on the coast, and see if we can find a boat that will take us to Tartessos, or Ponike if the Princess doesn't want to break her betrothal."

"That's a long voyage," Gwrhyr said.

"I know," Eluned sighed, "but the thought of getting stopped at the border with Kamartha or before we get to Naphtali really worries me."

"You've got a point," he agreed. "We could probably get to

Dangjin before it's realized that we went that way. Once they realize the Treasure is missing, it's a sure bet they'll send someone to the pass to intercept us, if possible."

"Or have someone chase us if we make it into Kamartha."

"In that case," Gwrhyr said, "we're going to want to find lodgings on the west side of the River Draq. That way we don't risk getting stopped on one of the bridges."

"The west side it is," Eluned agreed. "All I want tonight is a hot bath, a hot meal, and a warm bed. It doesn't even have to be luxurious. A hay mattress would feel like feathers after so many nights on the hard ground."

"I agree," Gwrhyr said, massaging the small of his back with his right hand. They'd been single minded in their pursuit of reaching Jungnay as soon as possible, he thought. Surely he could treat his bride to a couple of nights in an above average accommodation before they sought more modest lodgings. A delayed honeymoon, he'd tell the innkeeper.

As they descended, the temperature began to rise incrementally and so did Eluned's spirits. The eastern side of the River Draq was composed of small farms and homesteads. The closer they got to the river, the more luxurious the housing became and the bigger the farms. The land here was fed continually by the snowmelt from the Qahept Heights.

Tsering Palace was located on the western bank of the river. Crossing the bridge, they could see the castle complex with its six-storied main building towering over the town to the north.

"They say there are more than eighty buildings in the complex," Gwrhyr noted when he saw Eluned studying it.

Like all the palaces she'd seen since she began her journey, including her home, Castle Mykerinos, a great wall surrounded Tsering, and Eluned immediately began to fret about how they might get inside.

Noticing her furrowed brow, Gwrhyr put a hand on her arm and shook his head. "Save your worrying for another day," he said. "We deserve a day or two to do absolutely nothing. Wouldn't you like to hang out and read for an entire day or nap?"

Eluned smiled. "Or spend time in your arms or all three. It feels like a guilty pleasure, but I'd love nothing more."

PLACING HER GUILT IN A ROOM in the back of her mind, closing the door, and making sure it was locked securely, Eluned was able to enjoy the two days and three nights she and her husband spent doing absolutely nothing of import. Anytime she was tempted to open that door, she turned her back on it by opening a book, distracting herself in Gwrhyr's arms, or napping.

It was easy enough to do, as the view from their second floor window in the Hotel Phurba wasn't particularly exciting, she noted on arrival. It looked down into a back alley that seemed to have more litter on the ground than in the trashcans themselves. The room itself was sufficient for their needs as Gwrhyr had splurged on a private bathroom, but was devoid of any decoration on the walls except for one cut brass dragon in the shape of the Kingdom's sigil.

"I didn't realize how bone tired I was," she said on the second day while snuggled up in their bed, wrapped in her husband's arms, feeling drowsy and content. A fire crackled in the fireplace and for the first time in months, she felt warm again.

Tracing the scar that ran along her cheek, Gwrhyr agreed. "I think we needed the rest in more ways than one. The exhaustion alone might have made our attempts to secure the Treasure clumsy and put us at risk of being caught."

"I hadn't thought of that, either," Eluned said. "I was so frantic about getting the Treasure and escaping with it that I wasn't considering how cautious we're going to have to be."

"We also need to keep in mind that once we're among the residents of Jungnay, we're really going to stand out."

Eluned grimaced. "I hadn't thought of the that, either." While most of the Dzironese had coal black hair like her own, theirs was razor straight. They also had dark almond-shaped eyes and were a little broader of face than she was. "And you're so much taller than most of the men," she said. "Do you think we'll be watched?"

During the past two days, they had not left their room for anything other than meals, which were served in a dining room downstairs. They hadn't even been outdoors, and she had been so tired on their way into town that she hadn't noticed whether she'd drawn any attention.

"Oh, I imagine they'll be keeping an eye on us," he said, kissing her gently. As nice as it might be, Gwrhyr thought, they couldn't risk spending yet another day in this hotel without the staff beginning to wonder how two minstrels could afford it. "But, let's worry about that tomorrow and enjoy what little time we have left here."

Eluned closed her eyes, lips curved in a slight smile. "And right now I think I would enjoy a nap, or something else if you're up for it."

Arising early the next morning, Gwrhyr and Eluned gathered their horses from the stable, strapped on their gear, and began to make their way closer to the palace.

Gwrhyr had made inquiries the previous night during their evening meal.

"There's got to be an area of the city where entertainment is offered," he'd told Eluned before they went downstairs. "I have yet to visit a city that doesn't have one. I was here when I was eighteen, but it was only for a few days."

"Do you think someone will recognize you?"

"I couldn't even grow a beard at the time, and I was travelling with one of my lords, ostensibly to sell the Dzironese some wine from Aden."

"Wine?"

"I was really just spying out the land, seeing where the Kingdom's loyalties lay."

"And?"

"As you might have guessed, the people weren't really concerned with politics. On the other hand, anyone closely connected to the palace supported the Kingdom's connection to the Awen Alliance."

Eluned wasn't surprised but it didn't make her particularly happy. She would have to be very careful about what she said until she knew the extent of the Kingdom's conservative ideology.

No one had seemed dismayed when Gwrhyr had asked where he and his wife might find someone to employ their minstrel skills. He'd been told the theater district was located just north of where they were staying, near the southwest corner of Tsering Palace.

Not that we have any intention of finding a gig, Eluned thought. Hard travel had prevented her from composing any more ballads. But, they could still use the cover to secure cheap lodging. Her main concern was gaining access to the palace, and she had a sneaking suspicion she was going to have to use the cloak to do so.

Once they reached the theater district, Gwrhyr began to ask passersby about inexpensive lodging, and they were pointed in the direction of a hostel. Once there, they were able to secure a private room, but the rest of the accommodations were shared—bath, kitchen, dining room, and a common area.

Depositing their gear in their room, they took Ronan and Ruari around to the back of the hostel where they arranged to stable their mounts for a small fee. Eluned and Gwrhyr would be responsible for tending to them—feeding and grooming, and cleaning the stall that they shared. The two horses were used to each other's company and seemed happy to be housed together, and it was less expensive than renting two stalls.

That taken care of, the couple decided to explore the area around the palace. The far eastern side of the palace wall faced the river and was inaccessible, but they could wander around the remaining three sides.

FOOD TO PREPARE THEIR EVENING MEAL in hand, Eluned and Gwrhyr returned to the hostel at sunset having completely examined the area along the southern wall of the palace. They had been unable to find a single entrance along that side of the palace. They had also been forced to go out of their way as they explored it in order to avoid the notice of the guards as the southern wall was patrolled regularly.

This meant they'd had to walk along a portion of wall before turning southward for a couple of blocks, and then making their way back to the wall again. Scanning a block's worth of wall, they then repeated the process until they reached the end.

"Hopefully, we'll have better luck tomorrow," Eluned said as they stood in the kitchen chopping up chicken and vegetables for a stirfry.

"The main entrance is on the western side of the palace, if I remember correctly," Gwrhyr said. "And I'm willing to bet that because there wasn't an entrance on the southern wall, there won't be an entrance on the northern wall either."

"It's not so much that I worry about getting in," Eluned said. "The cloak will take care of that. It's more that I don't know how I'm going to go about finding the Treasure and contacting Princess Xiang once I'm in."

"The Treasure is the most important," Gwrhyr said, adding some soy sauce to the mixture. It was sitting on the counter along with assorted spices and oils. Clearly hostellers left behind the condiments they no longer needed, he thought.

"I know," Eluned sighed. "And I'll abandon that plan if it doesn't look like it will be easy to talk to her. Wouldn't it be nice, though, if she could tell me exactly where the Treasure is in return for me helping break her betrothal with Prince Aahil?"

Gwrhyr chuckled. "Fantasize much, Fy Drysor?"

Eluned sighed again. Her last fantasy, Prince Irirangi of Favonia, nearly destroyed the Quest. She glanced up at Gwrhyr who was intently stirring the vegetables and meat while she watched the rice. He'd pulled his dark brown hair back in a ponytail so that it wouldn't be in his face while he cooked, and she was able to admire the line of his jaw and strong profile. She smiled, silently thanking Omni for allowing her the chance to fall in love with the man she was betrothed to, and then shuddered, remembering the Favonian Prince. What had she ever seen in Prince Irirangi?

AFTER A HASTY BREAKFAST OF COFFEE AND TOAST with jam, Eluned and Gwrhyr hurried to the stable to see to the horses before setting off for the western wall. Because the main entrance to the palace was located toward the center of the mile-long wall, there was a lot of traffic—foot, horse and various horse- or mule-drawn conveyances—on the road that passed in front of it.

Gwrhyr and Eluned took their time walking the length of the wall on the opposite side of the road from the Tsering Palace pausing to study the main entrance before continuing northward.

As they suspected, the main gate was heavily guarded with soldiers stationed at ground level as well as atop the wall.

Eluned was flabbergasted. "Is Castle Bennu that heavily guarded?"

Gwrhyr shook his head.

Neither was Castle Mykerinos, Eluned thought, nor Seemu Palace in Favonia or Castle Indalo in Jazeel. Nor, apparently, had been Castle Lavieven in Stonehelm when Yona stole the Hamper. "Do you think this might be in reaction to the Treasures we stole from Annewven and Adamah?" she asked.

Gwrhyr grunted. "I think that's exactly what it is."

"Then Yona and Njima, and Chokhmah and Faolan, will be facing similar difficulties," Eluned said, worry for her friends creasing her brow.

"We'll just have to pray that they're especially cautious," Gwrhyr said, "particularly Yona and Njima because they're going to need an excuse to get into Lamaxana Palace."

They walked in silence until they reached the northern end of the wall, and Gwrhyr suggested they sit for a moment. He pointed to a café across the road that ran along the northern wall. "Let's have some tea. We don't want to be seen heading back too soon."

Once their tea had been served and they were munching on almond flavored biscuits, Gwrhyr noticed that the café seemed to be frequented by travellers as well as locals. There were some pedlars sitting at a nearby table who looked like they were from Kamartha. At another table, a man who could have been an entertainer like them, as he was dressed similarly, was enjoying a late breakfast of steamed dumplings, which he was dipping into a sauce. There was also a table of local women chatting over tea while their babies napped in baskets at their feet.

Eluned marveled at how peaceful it all seemed. Were they really unaware that Dziron was one of five kingdoms preparing to go to war with the Triquetra Alliance? Had they noticed the increased security around the palace? How could they not? "What reason do you think they were given for all the guards around the palace?" she asked Gwrhyr, voice low.

Gwrhyr leaned over and nuzzled her cheek, whispering in her ear, "Probably the truth but they don't seem to care."

"Why?"

"Because only those who will gain by it seek war."

Eluned nodded, and took a sip of her tea. It was true, she thought. People would fight if they thought their lives were being threatened. But they would have to be forced to battle to help their leaders gain whatever it was they wanted. For the sake of the people of the Thirteen Kingdoms, they really needed to put a stop to the three kings who were behind the rising hostilities.

After lingering over their tea and biscuits for nearly an hour, Eluned and Gwrhyr began the trek back to the southern end of the wall.

They had nearly reached the main gate when there was a sudden commotion, and the large gates swung outward to let a gilded carriage drawn by a pair of snow white horses pass through. The carriage turned northward and Eluned strained to see who was inside, but the curtains had been drawn.

She nodded to Gwrhyr and they turned around, following the carriage as it made its way back in the direction from which they had just walked. The carriage stopped in front of a bookstore Eluned had noted the first time they passed by. She was hoping they could return to it after they had lunch.

A footman jumped to the road from where he'd been standing on a small platform attached to the carriage, and lowered a step before opening the conveyance's door. Three teenage girls in brightly colored silk dresses were handed down from the carriage.

"I think that's Princess Xiang," Eluned grabbed Gwrhyr's arm and surreptitiously pointed to the young girl with jet-black hair arranged in an elaborate hairdo that was the first to step down. The royal blue silk in which she was clad highlighted the paleness of her skin and her dark, flashing eyes.

"Look at the girl behind her," Gwrhyr said.

Eluned's face drained of color. "Kussemak," she whispered. Long flowing hair the color of burnished copper framed a striking face with full lips and large bronze eyes. There could be no doubt as to whom her father was. "One of King Arawn's bastard children," Eluned murmured. The girl's face was softer than the king's, probably more like her mother's, she thought. Her turquoise silk dress was of a similar style to Princess Xiang's—high collared and form fitting.

Eluned looked at the third girl. Full lips, skin the color of heavily creamed coffee, dark brown hair curled around her head in intricate braids, and dark lashed caramel brown eyes. Her fuchsia pink dress was in a style common to Kamartha.

"Princess Chandra, no doubt," Gwrhyr whispered.

The princesses were escorted into the bookstore, and Gwrhyr and Eluned waited a few minutes before following them. Eluned pulled the hood of her cloak forward in an attempt to hide as much of her face as possible.

When they first entered the shop, Eluned and Gwrhyr headed in the opposite direction from the princesses. As they pretended to peruse the poetry books, Eluned whispered. "Arawn must have been young when she was born, right?"

"I'd say seventeen or eighteen," Gwrhyr agreed. "She's probably his oldest child." They casually moved closer to the girls until they were looking at the shelf of books in the row behind them.

"Buy that one, Morri," Princess Chandra was giggling. "I promise not to tell your father."

"Morrighan," Eluned mouthed to Gwrhyr.

He nodded, and she moved closer so that she could whisper, "Arawn's great grandmother was Morrighan."

Gwrhyr nodded again. Quite an honor, he thought, naming your first illegitimate child for an ancestor. He wondered if all Arawn's bastard children were as well taken care of.

"He wouldn't care," Morrighan was saying, "but I imagine King Zhang would be horrified to know that his daughter was dreading her upcoming marriage to Prince Aahil."

"Shhh!" Princess Xiang chided her. "I shouldn't have told you that. You promised not to say anything. Anyway, it isn't as if I have a choice."

"It's that lesbian queen's fault," Chandra said, "otherwise they might have chosen my brother, Chetan."

"He's two years younger than me," Xiang objected.

"Better than twenty-two years older," Chandra retorted.

"It was political," Xiang said. "My father hopes to woo the Kingdom of Tarshish into the Awen Alliance. Now, let's stop talking about this. There are too many people here."

The princesses returned to chattering over the latest romance novels until they had each chosen a few. These they handed to the lady's maid that had accompanied them before returning to the carriage where they waited for her to settle the transaction.

Once the lady's maid had left the bookstore, Eluned turned to Gwrhyr, eyes sparkling. "I have an idea. Let's go find some lunch and I'll tell you."

Sitting at small table in the back of a poorly lit restaurant, Eluned filled Gwrhyr in on her plan while waiting for the steamed dumplings. She'd been craving them since they had their tea at the café.

Gwrhyr frowned, eyes clouded with doubt when she finished. "I don't know, E, uh, Rowena," he glanced around making sure no one was listening. Eluned had spoken quietly but you couldn't take too many chances. He felt safer talking here than at the hostel, though, because there was no way of knowing who might be listening at your closed door.

"But I know it will work," she said. "I feel it in my gut the way I felt something was wrong the day we reached Kaumari."

Gwrhyr bit his lip. "What if she reacts poorly when you reveal who you are?"

"I'll dress like the queen I am," she said, "and I'll be ready to pull the cloak around me and run for my life, if necessary."

"What if they sound the alarm and keep the palace gate locked until you're found?"

Eluned rolled her eyes. "Eighty buildings can't be searched all at once for an invisible woman. Besides, I'll run directly for the gate, and slip out the first time it's opened."

"That could be days."

"Days but not weeks as they won't be prepared for a reverse siege of sorts. At some point they'll have to open the gates to bring in food. I can't imagine how many people live in there, but I'm sure they have a lot of mouths to feed."

Gwrhyr sighed. "Let me sleep on it. If I can't come up with another plan, we'll begin work on it tomorrow. The longer we're in Jungnay, the more likely it is that we'll blow our cover."

"If it works," Eluned said, "we may be sneaking back to the hostel either that night or the next, and we need to be prepared to leave for Dangjin immediately."

Gwrhyr opened his mouth to say something, but Eluned put a finger to her lips. Their food was arriving.

27ᴛʜ Saitheh

Njima was in the surgery helping Purva with a wounded donkey when Yona rushed in carrying a slip of paper in her hand.

"Olive just arrived!" she said, eyes wide with hope, and a little fear.

"What does it say?" Njima looked up from where she'd been cleaning an abscess on the donkey's neck.

"I don't know. I was so excited, I rushed straight inside after taking it off her leg."

"Read it aloud then," Purva, who was at the counter mixing an ointment for the animal, said, turning around to face Yona. "Perhaps Yoel sends good news."

"You have an audition," Yona read, "at nine o'clock tomorrow morning—Sirak's Circus Salmagundi, 2807 Masala Avenue. Make us proud. Yoel."

"The Masala," Purva nodded approvingly. "That's starting at the top."

Yona felt her knees weakening and leaned against the examination table for support. She pressed her forehead into the cool surface of the oft-bleached wood of the tabletop.

"Are you okay?" Njima placed a hand on top of Yona's white blond crew cut.

"I will be," she said. "The reality of all this made me feel faint." She emitted a strained laugh. "Guess I'll be putting the finishing touches on our costumes this afternoon, huh?"

While they had hired a seamstress to sew their basic outfits, Yona had taken it upon herself to add the flourishes.

Njima patted Yona's head. "And they are going to be stunning."

Yona righted herself. "Well, first it's back to the horses. I wasn't finished when Olive arrived," she said. "Speaking of which—what do I feed her?"

"Cracked corn," Purva said. "I have a bag of it in the store room. Just give her a scoop. Let her rest for an hour or so, and then we can send her back to Yoel with a note saying that you'll be at the audition tomorrow."

"Thanks," Yona said. "I'm so glad you know this stuff. I'd be lost. Oh, and I'm pretty sure that Makeda's stitches are ready to come out."

"I'll check on her after we finish with the donkey," Purva said, returning to mixing the ointment.

That evening, while sitting at the table in the kitchen eating their curried lentil soup, Purva told them that the royals occasionally made it to The Masala.

"The King and Queen prefer the theater," she said, "but I understand that Prince Chetan and Princess Divya are great devotees of the circus."

"What about the others?" Njima asked.

"The others?"

"Aren't there two other princes and three other princesses?"

"Well, the older siblings are married and busy with young children and the like," Purva said, "and I believe Princess Chandra, who is sixteen, is currently in Jungnay."

"Jungnay?" Yona asked. "Why is she there?"

Purva closed her eyes, as if trying to remember then shook her head. "One of the kings in the Awen Alliance, I can't remember which one, thought it would be a good idea if their children were sent to other kingdoms when they reached the age of fifteen or sixteen."

"Why?" Njima asked. "To strengthen the bonds within the Alliance?"

"Something like that," Purva agreed. "Seems like foolishness to me. That Princess Chandra is a spoiled and empty-headed brat. Personally, I think they sent her to Dziron to get her away from Vollmar."

Yona shook her head, expressing her ignorance.

"He's very popular with the young women," Purva explained. "Big blue eyes, hair the color of wheat, tall and muscular, and a voice like velvet. Princess Chandra was smitten and insisted on attending every one of his concerts."

"Ah," Njima said. "I am guessing that King Janak and Queen Lakshmi were less than thrilled."

Purva nodded. "So when King Zhang and Queen Ling invited Princess Chandra for an extended stay at Tsering Palace with Princess Xiang they jumped at the opportunity. I believe King Arawn of Annewven sent his oldest daughter, as well."

Yona shook her head in wonder. "How do you know so much?"

"My dear," Purva laughed. "This is Kaumari. Sometimes I think the residents of this city subsist on gossip alone. You can't go anywhere in this town without hearing something about what's going on in the Thirteen Kingdoms."

"I'm going to have to start listening," Njima said. "I feel like I know very little but the basics."

"Do you know about the Thirteen Treasures?"

Njima's eyes widened and she shook her head. "Other than the myth that if they are all gathered they will bring either peace or war to the Thirteen Kingdoms depending on who gathers them, I know very little," she lied.

"Perhaps it's not a myth," Purva said. "I have heard that the Princess Eluned of Zion, who is now Queen Eluned of Aden, is seeking all the Treasures and has managed to gather quite a few already."

"I thought she wasn't to get married until she turned twenty-one," Njima said.

"Perhaps, but it is said she and King Uriel had a private ceremony at Castle Mykerinos back in Neeon."

"I didn't realize how little I knew," Yona said, but her mind was racing. They'd been so caught up in their own little world since leaving Favonia. Fear of being recognized forcing them to take abnormal measures to keep away from other travellers. And since they'd seen one of their attackers on the street, they'd become even more cautious. It continued to be a surprise to her how dangerous this quest was becoming, and yet, here they were hoping to perform for the entire city. It was probably insane to do so, but they'd been unable to devise any other plan.

Njima lifted a spoonful of soup to her mouth, praying to Omni that Purva didn't suspect them, and if she did that she would keep it a secret. Barring the injuries to Eluned and Makeda, Omni had been gracious so far. But Jabberwock had hinted that every Divine endeavor demands a sacrifice of some sort. And while they had all sacrificed their comfortable, safe, and secure lives for this quest, would more than that be required? They had now suffered a significant injury, Eluned's disfiguring facial wound. Would death be next, Njima thought, and if so, for whom? She swallowed her soup, and changed the subject back to their audition.

The following morning, Yona and Njima set out for The Masala and Sirak's Circus Salmagundi with butterflies in their stomachs.

"It's funny," Njima said.

"What is?" Yona looked at her, brow creased in confusion, because she didn't find the situation in the least bit amusing.

Njima chuckled. "I'm more afraid that we won't get to work for this Sirak than I am of having a pear shot off my head."

Yona had continued to practice diligently every day since they'd spoken to Yoel, and was confident in her abilities to perform. "I guess you're right," she said. "It's fear of not impressing him with our act that's got my stomach flipping, not worrying about whether I'll be able to do it or not."

"If we fail here," Njima said, "it means we'll probably have to start our act off The Masala rather than on it. It could make all the difference in gaining the attention of the palace, don't you think?"

"It could," Yona agreed, remembering what Purva had said the previous evening. "If Princess Divya, or Prince Chetan, likes our act, we might be able to schedule a private performance at the palace."

"It's all so ephemeral at the moment," Njima agreed. "If, if, if. If we fail to get invited to the palace within the first few weeks of performing, then we don't have a hope of getting noticed for our act. If that happens, we're going to have to go back to Zion and wait for either Chokhmah or Eluned to return, if they haven't already, so that we can go back with something that will make one of us invisible. Unless, of course, one of us is suddenly struck with an even more brilliant idea."

"Omni have mercy that we don't have to resort to returning to Zion in defeat," Yona said. "I've finally reached the point that I just want this quest to be over with. A normal life seems incredibly appealing."

Njima stopped and pointed. The next road was The Masala. When they reached it, Purva had told them, they would turn left and within the second block they would find Sirak's.

As they turned left onto the theater district's main road,

Yona suddenly realized that they were turning a lot of heads, and she laughed out loud.

"What is it?" Njima asked.

"I was just wondering why people keep staring at us," she explained, "And then I realized it would be strange if they didn't."

Njima glanced at her and chuckled. "I guess there aren't a lot of women strutting down The Masala in tight leather pants with a bow slung over their shoulder."

They both wore close fitting black leather pants with a strip of red leather running down the outside leg seam from hip to foot. The pants laced up in the back and knee-high black leather boots covered their lower legs. Yona's top was a form fitting black leather jacket with a sweetheart neckline. The buttons that fastened it in front were made of heart-shaped pieces of onyx. The jacket had tight leather sleeves in order to protect her arms while prohibiting interference with the bowstring. Njima had a red leather bustier that laced up the front. Sewn onto the back of their respective tops, a red heart pierced by a golden arrow, and a similar heart of black for Njima. With their hair shaved close to their heads and dyed platinum, they made a conspicuous couple.

As BEFITTED A CIRCUS, the building that encompassed Sirak's would have been a wonder to behold if it hadn't been surrounded by other buildings similarly designed to draw the attention of potential customers. Even so, Yona found her breath catching in her throat as she stared up at the towering building of white marble inlaid with semiprecious stones. The entrance to the building featured a large arched doorway topped by an onion dome and finial. On each side of the main entrance, two stacked vaulted archways containing balconies looked over The Masala. Smaller domes and spires topped these archways.

"Quit gaping," Njima prodded her. "You'll lose your nerve."

The women walked up to the window next to the large doors that marked the entrance to the circus. Behind an elaborately carved grating, a young woman with henna red hair looked up from the trade daily she was reading and frowned at them.

"We have an audition with Sirak at nine o'clock," Njima said. The woman glanced at the clock on the wall behind her. The hands assured her that the women were ten minutes early.

"You are?"

"Zenobia and Skaði," Njima said, politely, though her fists were clenched. Were there really that many female archery acts scheduled to audition at nine o'clock?

Pointing to the entrance to their right, she said, "Go through those doors to the first room on the right. Have a seat there and someone will be with you shortly."

"Thank you," Yona gave the young woman her most brilliant smile, which was met with a yawn as the young woman returned to perusing the gossip in the daily.

Despite the fact the doors appeared to be very heavy, when Njima grasped the intricately carved handle of the portal to her left, it swung open both quietly and with ease on well-oiled hinges.

The lobby of the building was another work of art. A long counter at which refreshments were no doubt served was inlaid in delicate detail with semi-precious stones forming twining vines, fruits and flowers. The walls they passed were highly decorated with dado bas-relief, intricate lapidary inlay and refined calligraphy panels. Yona wanted to stop and study the artwork in detail, but Njima kept her moving with a gentle but firm pressure on the back of her arm.

Passing through the foyer to the short hallway straight ahead of them, they found the room they were looking for and took a seat on a low sofa covered in a patchwork of peach-toned silks.

Yona's heart was thudding in her chest and she tried to concentrate on taking deep breaths. If she displayed the least sign of nervousness, it could destroy their chances. She needed to be confident in her abilities. She had convincingly played a Sister of Holy Supplication. Now she needed to convincingly play the part of skilled archer. She chuckled.

"What is it?" Njima looked at her, brow creased with worry. "You're laughing."

"I was just telling myself that I needed to 'play the part of skilled archer.'"

Njima smiled in understanding. "My dove, you are a skilled archer."

A brief tap on the door interrupted them, and they looked up to see a little boy of about seven or eight peek around the doorframe.

"Sirak will see you now," he said, and bowed deeply. He was dressed in white silk pants that gathered at the ankles, an ornately embroidered vest, and silk shoes that curled at the ends. A small, round hat of red velvet sat atop his shining ebony hair.

Yona coughed into her hand to suppress a smile, and stood. "Thank you, kind sir. Will you lead us there?"

"It would be my deepest pleasure, madam," he said, dark brown eyes glowing with self-importance.

They followed the boy's straight back down the hallway and through another door, which took them to yet another hall. As they were led down the lengthy corridor, Yona guessed they were bypassing the circus performance area. At the end of the hallway, the youth opened a door, and led them down a tiled passageway to yet another door. This he opened, and indicated that they should enter. Passing through, Yona could see they were in a large open area clearly used for practice.

A short and rotund man, also dressed in white silk trousers and an embroidered vest, although he wore a voluminous shirt underneath, turned toward them when they entered. He was standing with a young woman who was gesticulating wildly, hands forming words in the air. He nodded and patted her on the shoulder, and she moved to leave the room. Smiling at Yona and Njima as she passed them, her big blue eyes widened as she took in their striking appearance. She gave the young boy a quick hug before exiting the room.

"Very nice," Sirak said, indicating their costumes. "It is always good to stand out before you have even begun your act."

"Thank you," Njima said. "Skaði worked hard on them."

Yona blushed. "I only created the embellishments," she said.

"Ah," Sirak said, "but that is the best part otherwise all the black would be boring. So, how much space do you need for this?"

"No more than one hundred and fifty feet," Yona said. "I'm not comfortable with any further than that."

"Fair enough," Sirak said. "Come this way."

"May I come Papi?" The little boy who had led them to the practice area was still standing beside them.

"Of course, my son," Sirak said. "If it is okay with Zenobia and Skaði?"

"It's fine with me," Yona said. "I need to get accustomed to being watched."

"If I may, why Zenobia and Skaði?" Sirak asked.

"Because we thought they sounded more enticing than Miryam and Libni," Njima said. "If you can think of something better, we are more than willing to entertain your suggestions."

Sirak chuckled. "Yoel said you were educated."

"It is true that our fathers are lords in Tarshish," Njima said. They had agreed on Tarshish as their home Kingdom because of its neutrality—the Kingdoms in the Awen Alliance being too risky a choice as their lords might be a known quantity. Similarly, they did not want to risk being tied to the Triquetra Alliance.

"And if you fail here?" he asked.

"At this point," Yona said, "we won't be welcome back."

"So there is much at stake."

Yona nodded, eyes solemn. "Yes, there is." More than you can ever know, she thought.

"It has taken much courage, then, for you to leave your home and venture here against your families' wishes," Sirak said. "I pray that you will be successful. Yoel spoke highly of you." Leading them to an area in which Yona could shoot freely without fear of striking anyone, the women set up to perform for Sirak.

Sirak's son, whom he called Raki, stood quietly by his father's side, eyes wide in anticipation.

As she had done at Purva's, Yona drew out the tension of the act for as long as possible. She felt that she could probably do it more quickly, but taking her time not only heightened the suspense, but also allowed her to be as careful as possible. She hoped to perform this act as few times as possible.

"Splendid!" Sirak chortled when Njima held up the perfectly speared pear. "And I have just the name for your act—The Brave Hearts."

Njima laughed. "I like it."

"Come," Sirak said, "let us go to my office where my secretary can draw up the papers for a contract. We can come to terms on the way there. Raki run ahead and inform Ajit that we will be there shortly, and to begin the paperwork."

"Doesn't Yoel have some say in this?" Njima asked.

"I have had many performers over the years represented by Yoel," Sirak said, "and I know what he expects. Don't worry. Neither The Brave Hearts nor Yoel will be cheated of what they are owed."

Yona blushed as Njima thanked him. This was all so new to her, she realized. It was the first time in her life that she had to negotiate for services rendered.

A large mahogany desk, behind which the owner of the Circus Salmagundi seated himself in an overstuffed armchair, dominated Sirak's office. Yona and Njima settled into the two straight back chairs in front of the desk, and the three of them made small talk until Ajit brought in the contract papers he had written up.

Sirak's Circus Salmagundi was open nightly except for Deethseel, which meant that The Brave Hearts would perform twice a day—once at the matinee and once at the evening show. They could choose another two days in which they wouldn't perform, giving them a total of three days a week off. This would continue until their act no longer drew crowds.

"That could mean years or months," Sirak said.

"I understand," Njima said. "We always knew that we would have a limited amount of time to perform, and hoped that we might come up with a new act along the way."

"Good," Sirak nodded. "As long as you understand."

With the papers signed and in hand, Yona and Njima returned to Purva's. They were scheduled to begin performing a week later on the 6th of Eahth in order for Sirak to have time to advertise his new act.

24TH SAITHEH

"How far is it to the next post?" Jabberwock asked Kir once Samee disappeared into the pine forest at the edge of the plateau.

"Not but three miles," Kir said, glancing at the other guard, Jaspar, who nodded.

Jabberwock had the feeling his nod was answering an unasked question. "Pigeon?" the Janawar said, catching the word from Kir's thoughts. The man was clearly trying to keep his mind empty.

Kir stared at him blankly for a moment, and Jabberwock could only pick up the fact the soldier was repeating a nonsense rhyme over and over in his head. Another bad sign. Clearly he knew enough about the Janawar, even if Kir had learned it as legend, to know they were telepathic.

Had Jaspar sent a pigeon to the post outside Buta while Kir distracted them during their lunch? Were they to be taken prisoner?

"When do we leave?" Jabberwock asked as Jaspar reentered the building.

Kir sighed, shifting from foot to foot a few times before answering. "We have to wait unteel thee pigeon returns."

"I don't understand," Jabberwock said. "Why did you send a pigeon?"

"Eet ees necessary to confeerm we have accommodations for you before we take you to Buta," Kir said.

Jabberwock had the distinct impression he was lying and silently debated the wisdom of fleeing for the hidden valley before the reinforcements arrived.

Bonpo was watching the exchange, a troubled expression on his face. He couldn't understand what was being said but Jabberwock's tail and ears were standing at alert and Kir's face was sullen as if he were answering Jabberwock's questions reluctantly.

A flutter of wings distracted the three of them and they turned to watch a pigeon enter the guard station via an open window.

"There's your answer," Jabberwock said.

"Wait here," Kir ordered them and stepped inside the building.

"Wat goin' on?" Bonpo asked as soon as Kir was inside.

"I don't know," Jabberwock said, "but I suspect it's not good."

"'Ow not good?"

"I don't think they have any intention of taking us to Buta unless it's as prisoners."

"Dey seem vely suspicious of us," Bonpo agreed.

"I'm just remembering the reception we got when we approached from the sea," Jabberwock frowned.

Bonpo nodded, mouth flattening as he, too, remembered. He'd nearly been skewered.

"They've been isolated for five hundred years," Jabberwock continued. "We don't know how xenophobic they may have become." The Bandersnatch bared his crooked teeth in a grimace as a thought occurred to him.

"Wat is it?" Bonpo asked.

"What if they don't take prisoners?" Jabberwock said.

"What if they execute anyone who tries to gain access to Buta?"

If that was the case, Bonpo's mind raced, then at least one of them needed to make it back to Zion to let the others know about the situation here. He was big, but he wasn't armed. Could they run away quickly enough to escape? Glancing over his shoulder at the flat landscape on top of the plateau, he determined that it was unlikely. But, it might be worth a try.

Bonpo scooped the Janawar up and placed him in the basket atop Tikvah just as Kir and Jasper stepped out of the door to the guard station.

"Den I tink it's time we make our exit," he said, as they heard the thunder of hooves that marked the approach of the soldiers from the guard post closest to Buta.

"What are yee doing?" Kir asked when he noticed Jabberwock in the basket.

"We are taking our leave," Jabberwock said. "Clearly, we aren't welcome here."

"Eet is too late for that," Jaspar said, reaching into the building and retrieving a bow and quiver of arrows that must have been placed next to the door. He quickly nocked an arrow and aimed it at Bonpo as the giant took a step backwards, pulling the donkey with him.

While Bonpo couldn't understand what was being said, the implication was clear. If they ran, they would be shot at—both by Jaspar and the soldiers who were nearly at the guard post.

This was his chance, he thought. He could save the life of the Janawar who had already faced persecution in his lifetime, and he could finally atone for having taken a man's life.

Bonpo would do this for Eluned, who had been like a daughter to him. He would do this for the curmudgeonly Hiurau, who had been a most faithful companion. But mostly he would do this for the daughter he had loved and disappointed. Dalha's face, as he had last seen it more than twenty years ago, seemed to float before him, eyes shining with adoration for her beloved daddy. His one regret was that she would never know that he had lamented the split second decision that had destroyed the remainder of his life from that day forward. But this time he could save two lives with a quick determination.

"Den I tink dere is onry one sorution," Bonpo said in the Common Tongue.

"What's that?" Jabberwock asked as Bonpo began to raise his arms. Jabberwock assumed it was in surrender until the yeti bellowed, "Lun!" and slapped Tikvah's flank forcefully.

The donkey brayed and took off in the direction from which they'd come, and Jabberwock was tossed against the side of the basket. As soon as he regained his feet, he checked to see that Bonpo was following them, but the giant was staggering toward the guards, the arrow that Jaspar had loosed protruding from his back.

"Bonpo!" He screamed with his mind.

"Get away!" Bonpo thought. "Get back to 'Leened. Ret dem know wat," his thoughts were interrupted by a roar of outrage as an arrow from an approaching horseman pierced his abdomen.

Jabberwock watched in horror as arrows filled the air. He and Tikvah were being ignored for the moment as the half dozen soldiers concentrated on subduing the giant. He ducked down into his basket, praying to Omni that one of the arrows would provide the mortal blow that would relieve Shangsung of the pain he was enduring so that his friend might escape.

As Tikvah entered the woods at the edge of the plateau, Jabberwock risked a look back toward the guard station. Bonpo now lay stretched out next to the picnic area, the six soldiers prodding him with bows and feet to make sure he was dead.

Kir glanced over his shoulder at the retreating Janawar, and Jabberwock telegraphed his thought loudly enough in Pelfan so that Kir might receive it. "Queen Parisa will hear of this."

Jabberwock felt a flash of shock and bewilderment from Kir before he and Tikvah disappeared from view.

As Tikvah plodded her way down the path that would take them to the little valley in which Samee and his mother, Zoya, resided, he had plenty of time to ruminate over what had just happened.

As he and Bonpo had journeyed closer and closer to Buta, he had felt the yeti's sadness and discontent increase incrementally each day. In truth, he was feeling the pressure of drawing nearer and nearer to Dziron himself although he had dealt with the very same depression years before when he'd become a mentor to the future Queen Fuchsia in the Wilds of Discord south of Kamartha.

Hiurau, as he was still known at that time, did not know why Omni had chosen him to help carry out Its plans, but he had followed the god and Its calling, albeit half-heartedly at first, without question.

When Jabberwock had been called to travel to the Kingdom of Kamartha, he had done so with much trepidation. It bordered the Devastation of Pelf and he had not returned to that area since he had fled Dziron and lost his beloved Kamali in its poisoned sands—nearly five centuries previously. The Wilds of Discord were very close to the border of Pelf and had he known that he would have to once again face an Aberration, he might have disobeyed his God as other prophets had done from time to time.

It wasn't just the The Wilds and The Devastation that gave him pause, it was the fact that he would be one Kingdom away from his home of how long? Millennia, perhaps? He had no idea how much time he had spent in the Vale Vixen. The time he'd spent with Kamali, alone, had seemed an eternity.

And yet he had obeyed. But as he travelled there, he had felt the pull of Dziron and the Peaks of Vulpecula, and had nearly been overwhelmed by an insatiable curiosity. Had any other Janawar survived? He wanted to travel there and discover whether or not it was true. It was only the fact that discovery would mean certain death that stopped him.

When he felt the mounting melancholy in Bonpo, he had known it was not Buta but the proximity of the Kingdom of Dziron that was causing the transition in his normally jocund disposition. Not just the Peaks of Vulpecula, Jabberwock corrected himself, but the family he'd left behind, the family he could never return to.

He and Bonpo had fled their homes and their Kingdom because they were forced to do so. And while they had both suffered great loss, it was only the yeti that had been compelled to reckon with the fact he had brought his circumstances upon himself.

Upon reflection, Jabberwock understood the sacrifice his friend had just made. Logically, even emotionally, it made sense. Despite that, his heart cried out at the unfairness of it all. They had simply wanted to gain access to a city that had been closed off to the rest of the Thirteen Kingdoms for five hundred or so years. They had even been willing to talk with whomever was in charge, and explain the situation.

Jabberwock surmised that he was still in shock that Buta was inhabited. He had fled Dziron so soon after the Apocalypse that his mind balked at the thought of anyone but Aberrations inhabiting this waste. But it wasn't a waste any longer, and clearly Pelfans had survived. The Pelfans at Kuna in Naphtali made sense—they had fled The Devastation. The fact that others had hidden and survived and once again inhabited what he'd always believed was uninhabitable—that boggled his mind.

But I've survived for however long I've survived, Jabberwock thought, and it never once occurred to me that this was possible. And on the other hand, I was willing to work with it. So yes, damn you Omni, he felt the tears welling in his eyes, this was unfair to Shangsung. Murderer or not, he only meant well, Jabberwock thought as he wept, and his life is a harsh punishment for someone who made himself so indispensable to the Quest that You ordained.

The Janawar continued to weep quietly for his friend for a while before it slowly occurred to him that he would be travelling back to Zion without the Knife of Llawfrodded the Horseman. Would Omni understand? Would twelve Treasures be enough, assuming the others could retrieve theirs?

Jabberwock no longer had a choice. Despite his size, he doubted he could sneak into Buta, search out the ruins of the palace, assuming it was still in ruins, and find the Knife without being discovered. He had no idea what the city looked like now but he did know that Pelfans afraid of outsiders resided there.

Besides, he thought, looking down at the loyal donkey carrying him away from this terrible circumstance, he had Tikvah to think about. It was going to be horrible enough to deliver the news of Bonpo's death, but he couldn't also come back with the news of Tikvah's, as well. Yes, he knew some might think the death of a donkey trivial, but Eluned wouldn't. And the price of Tikvah added to the reckoning of Bonpo, would be more than she could bear. He would just have to pray that they returned safely to Zion.

As Tikvah continued to trod the path toward Zoya's small farm, Jabberwock found himself dozing off in spite of himself. Or, perhaps, it was in self-defense from the shock he'd just suffered. When he was cognizant, he debated whether or not to continue on past Zoya's. Would their staying there put the mother and son at risk? Both he and Tikvah could bed down for the night just about anywhere.

On the other hand, did he not owe it to the woman to let her know what happened to the travellers her son led toward Buta? Wouldn't Zoya and Samee be better off if he suggested that they return to the beach with him, and seek safety in Naphtali? Surely the little money they received from Samee's engagements wasn't worth the price of countless lives?

Jabberwock's breath caught in his throat as the solution to his problem struck him like a bolt of lightning. Neither Eluned or Uriel or Njima, all of whom had access to money, would allow a poor woman and her untarnished son to suffer.

So, now the choice—should he request that they travel with him? He could leave them in Kuna until things were settled. Nahid would probably give them shelter and incorporate them into the community. They were Pelfans after all. And if they didn't fit in there, they could move on to Jazeel. Yes, Jabberwock decided, despite the fact that it would be easier to travel alone, it made perfect sense to bring the disavowed family with him. They needed some place to call home where they wouldn't be Other and have to barely survive. In Kuna, Jazeel, Goshen, or Ponike, something would be arranged for them.

JABBERWOCK AND TIKVAH ARRIVED in Zoya's clearing just as dark was descending. Samee was leaving the barn just as they entered.

"Dogee!" he giggled. "What you doing here?"

"Where is your mother, Samee?" Jabberwock demanded, deep voice rising an octave at the thought of what he must tell her.

"Mama!" Samee bellowed, and the door to the cabin opened.

"What is eet Samee?" a weary voice asked before Zoya realized that a donkey was standing in the middle of the clearing. Then she realized they were alone, and unconsciously raised a hand to her heart. "Where ees thee giant?"

"I have bad news," Jabberwock said. "Is it possible for you to remove me from this basket so we can talk?"

Zoya nodded to Samee, and he lumbered over and gently picked up The Bandersnatch and set him on the ground.

"Thank you, Samee," Jabberwock said. "Could you tether Tikvah and make her comfortable?"

"Yes, dogee, I happy to," he said, and picked up Tikvah's much abraded lead and led her toward the barn.

Jabberwock trotted toward Zoya and passing her, entered the house. When they were settled in front of the fire, the Bandersnatch related what had happened after Samee had left them.

ZOYA STARED INTO THE FLAMES of the fire for a minute or so after Jabberwock stopped speaking, and then she heaved a big sigh. "I always knew eet was too good to be true. Why would they run us out of Buta but accept strangers?"

Jabberwock was silent as he let it continue to sink in.

"So what becomes of us? Weel they let us stay here?"

"Do you want to take that risk?" Jabberwock asked.

Zoya shook her head. "But what are our choices?"

"Come with us," Jabberwock said. "We will travel to the Kingdom of Naphtali. There is a Pelfan community located there in which I think you can find refuge; at least to begin with. They speak Pelfan."

Zoya's eyebrows raised. "There are Pelfans outside of Pelf?"

"Yes," Jabberwock said. "In Kuna, and in the current capitol of Jazeel."

He ducked his head to lick his flank when he saw the tears rise in Zoya's eyes. When she had hurriedly dashed them away, he continued. "I am familiar with the Queen of Naphtali as well as the Queen of Pelf. We will take care of you."

"Queen of Pelf?" Zoya stuttered.

"Yes, we have found that the royalty of Pelf is still alive," he said. "Granted Chokhmah, or Parisa, which is her real name, was never aware of this nor did she know that she had a Kingdom she might govern, but she is, nonetheless, alive, and she feels a duty towards her, um, people."

"I don't know what to say."

"And even if she didn't," Jabberwock continued, "I know that the Queen of Naphtali and the King and Queen of Aden would not let you and Samee suffer."

At this point, Zoya broke down in tears, sobbing. "Never," she sniffed, "never deed I see thees happening."

"All that being said," Jabberwock replied, trying to remain sober in the midst of all the emotion, "I would suggest that you and Samee accompany us westward tomorrow. You might be left alone for a day or two, but I suspect at some point . . ."

"Keer and hees friends will be here to eenterrogate us," Zoya spat while snuffling into a handkerchief.

"I'm afraid so," Jabberwock said. "Can we leave first thing in the morning?"

Zoya stared into the flames for a minute.

"What is it?" Jabberwock asked as he watched her forehead wrinkle in consternation.

"What am I to do weeth thee livestock?"

"How much livestock do you have?" he asked.

"I have a sow, boar, and several peeglets along weeth a rooster and several chickens." She paused. "I also have a ram, a ewe, and a few lambs."

"That's a lot of animals to take with us."

"I have a cart," she said. "Would that help?"

Jabberwock pondered this for a moment. "While I imagine Tikvah could carry some of the livestock in the cart, you will also need to bring along those possessions that are important to you as well as cooking gear, blankets, and any food you might have already prepared."

Zoya's mouth thinned and Jabberwock could see that she was nonplussed.

"I'm sorry," he said, "but we'll be travelling along the beach, which will make the cart more difficult for Tikvah to pull. Also, once we reach Naphtali, we'll have to travel through the forest on top of the plateau to avoid the Aberrations."

The color drained from Zoya's face. "What would yee suggest?"

"Bring the pigs," Jabberwock said. "They might entice prey on the plateau, but if we can get them to Kuna, they will be happy to add them to their livestock as they have only sheep, goats, and chickens." And horses, he thought, but didn't say.

Zoya nodded, and he continued. "It would also do well to bring the chickens as we can slaughter them on days we can't scrounge enough food. I imagine Samee consumes a lot at his age?'

She nodded again, and he continued, "And it's hard to keep well fed when travelling unless we've prepared enough dried meat, vegetables, and fruit to take with us."

"And wee do not have thee time to do that," Zoya was shaking her head, imagining her son complaining of hunger pains, something he already did on a constant basis. She pondered. "Thee lambs are too young to kill, still at their mother's teats. We can slaughter thee ram. That weell geeve us enough meat for a day or two before eet goes off." And at least Samee could eat his fill for a couple of days for a change, Jabberwock heard her think.

Zoya told Jabberwock that she'd prop the barn door open so the sheep would have shelter if they needed it and they could graze freely. If the soldiers did show up within the next few days, she said, they were more than welcome to them.

"All I know for certain ees that Samee and I can't remain een thee Noontide Valley and hope to remain alive," she said. "They are now aware that I know Buta's secret.

"And the city that exiled you is very unlikely to want you to remain a threat to revealing that knowledge," Jabberwock said.

"Yes," Zoya agreed, looking into Jabberwock's glassy eyes. "We weell be ready to go een the morning."

DESPITE THE STRESSES OF THE DAY and their accompanying exhaustion as well as the storm that lashed the hollow around midnight, Jabberwock and Zoya worked through the night to make sure they were ready to leave before first light. They left in the dark knowing that once they ascended out of the valley, the grey light of dawn would greet them.

Jabberwock was once again ensconced in his basket atop Tikvah's back, and Zoya had managed to bring only the truly bare necessities to get them to Kuna. The cart was piled with the things they needed along with the clucking hens, an angry rooster, and several piglets.

The sow and boar were tied to the back of the cart, which was moving slowly enough up the trail to allow them to walk easily behind it. Samee had been allowed to sleep so that he wouldn't be too grumpy when they set out, and he was in high spirits as they hiked southward toward the beach.

"Can we bring thee boat, Mama?" he asked at one point.

"No, I'm sorry son," she said, "we are going to have to leave eet behind. But we won't need eet where we are going. Eet weel be more like our leetle valley."

Samee nodded. Jabberwock sensed that Samee understood that something terrible had happened to the beeg man, that he was not coming back anymore, and that the dogee and his Mama were sad about this. "Will they like us at dees new place?" Samee asked.

"Absolutely!" Jabberwock said. "They are very good people."

WHEN THEY REACHED THE CAVE, they were forced to remove everything from the cart, turn it on its side, and slowly push and carry it through to the beach. Samee was forced to do most of the work as he was stronger than his mother.

Once they had carried or guided everything through, and reloaded the cart, Jabberwock suggested they were long overdue for a lunch break.

As they munched on the mutton Zoya had roasted the previous night, Jabberwock contemplated the next two weeks, which he amended to himself, might take as long as three considering how they were now forced to travel. It would probably mean that more nights would be spent on the beach than in caves although they could bed down in the empty cart.

He glanced with a wince at Tikvah. Eluned would be so angry if she knew what he was forcing the animal to do. But they had no choice. He had no choice. It was escape or death for all of them.

Once they finished their rather hurried lunch, Jabberwock directed them down to the hard-packed sand. He had debated whether or not they should travel over the small stones or on the smoother sand silently during lunch. The Bandersnatch had opted for the mode of travel that would be easier for them all in the long run. The cartwheels might roll more smoothly over the pebbles, but they were much harder to walk on. If necessary, Samee could push the cart if it ever dragged or got stuck in the sand.

Fortunately, Jabberwock thought, this early spring day was overcast, which made the walking easier—no sun beating down on their heads. But, it would clear with or without raining first. However long it took them to reach Naphtali—hopefully between five and six weeks total—they would definitely face a variety of weather. It was something to which he had grown accustomed, but he doubted very much that Samee and his mother would enjoy hiking in the rain. At the moment they were determined to put Buta and the travails they'd suffered behind them.

Jabberwock calculated that it wouldn't take long experiencing the hardships of travel to make Zoya start to rethink her decision.

7TH EAHTH

After more than three weeks at Ebbe's, Chokhmah and Faolan had long since settled into a routine. First thing in the morning, Bölli, often still blinking the sleep from his pale blue eyes led her to the market. She had grown quite fond of the little boy. For the first few days, Faolan had led her, quite successfully Chokhmah might add, but Ebbe had been dubious and enlisted Bölli's help.

As it turned out this was a boon. While Chokhmah, otherwise known as Magdala, gathered the herbs she needed from the market, Faolan would take a quick run through the capitol to the woods on its outskirts.

For some of the time he was there, he would change into his human form knowing that he would be a wolf again until nightfall, and he was safely situated in Chokhmah's room. Then he could be Faolan again, and not Dodi, and he and his beloved could talk to each other about the day.

Occasionally, Chokhmah would have Faolan lead her into the woods where she would gather roots and fungi and other things she might not be able to find in the marketplace. She explained to Ebbe that as she was losing her sight, she had trained Dodi to help her smell out the things she might need. This was something, she'd said, that Bölli could not do for her.

As Ebbe had predicted, Magdala's services were greatly needed. Once she returned from the market, she would spend the remainder of the day offering what help she could.

Mistress Magdala was much sought after as she provided a wide range of concoctions from an anti-colic tea comprised of anise, fennel, caraway, and coriander seeds to her tincture for rheumatism that involved a concoction of pine needles and the oils of rosemary, spruce, mountain pine and camphor, among other things. From infants to those in their waning years, she offered them some relief from their sufferings.

AND ON THIS DEETHSADOORN NIGHT, Chokhmah looked forward to more than a day of rest before the week began again. She had insisted to Ebbe that except for emergencies, she must have at least one day to relax and refresh herself, and she preferred it to be on a day she could also attend worship in the local chapel. It had been far too long since she had seen the inside of a church—not since her time in Castle Mykerinos.

On her first visit to the Church of Saint Kakukilla, Chokhmah was shocked to find the sanctuary stripped of all the usual items one would find in a church dedicated to Omni. The heavy oak pews still remained, a reminder of earlier times, but the gold candlesticks had been replaced with pewter, and the only art remaining was an icon of the saint, which was badly in need of restoration.

Even the altar was bare of the richly embroidered cloths that usually covered them. She was also disappointed to discover the congregation numbered less than a dozen. The elderly priest, Father Walafrid, had informed her that although King Hamartia frowned on the worship of Omni, he still allowed it to occur, but had relinquished them of the finer trappings of worship, including a gem-studded chalice.

"Unfortunately," he'd said, "that means most people have

just drifted away from the faith altogether, whether it be Omni or the King's Sacred Three."

Chokhmah unconsciously flashed the sign against evil, and Father Walafrid had raised his eyebrows. When Chokhmah did not respond because being blind, she would not have seen him, he said, "I haven't seen that gesture in a long time."

Chokhmah had chuckled. "As you can probably tell from my accent, I am not originally from the Kingdom of Simoon. My family is from Adamah, but I married a man from Simoon, a sheep farmer."

"Are they particularly superstitious in Adamah?"

"My mother was a gypsy," she said. "I learned my healing skills from her, but I also picked up some of those mannerisms, as well."

"Interesting," Father Walafrid said. "It's my understanding that it's unusual for Roma to marry outside the tribe."

"It is," Chokhmah agreed, "but it does happen occasionally."

"I suppose you must be the new healer at Ebbe's. Those whom have sought your services are saying good things about you."

"I must admit that I have been surprised by the response," she said. "I thought it would take me a while to find enough work to support myself. But Omni provides." She chuckled. "Although, I think that Ebbe has made the better end of the bargain."

Father Walafrid had laughed. "She always does. She always does."

Now she was looking forward to her visit to Saint Kakukil-la's on the morrow. She enjoyed her weekly conversations with Father Walafrid, and the liturgy of the service helped her get through the week.

"I am not sure how much longer I can do this," she said to Faolan that evening as they settled down for the night.

Chokhmah always spoke to him quietly. She would prefer that they not get caught although she doubted anyone would begrudge her a lover.

"Why is that?" he asked, reaching for Chokhmah's hand and pulling her into his lap. He was sitting in the room's only armchair watching her prepare for bed. "I thought you enjoyed working with the folk that need your help."

"It is not that," she said, leaning her head against his shoulder. "I do enjoy that aspect of being here, and I think that is what I would like to do once we return to Bogaine."

"Then what is it?" he kissed the top of her head.

"We have not figured out a way to gain access to the palace," she tried to explain, "and I begin to despair that we will be here for months. I am so tired of pretending to be blind, and I hate hiding you. I want things to be the way they were."

"You may just have to put on the ring and start snooping around."

"But I stay so busy here," she sighed. "And Bölli is with me in the morning. The only free time I have is Deethseel, and by then I need the rest not to mention the extra time with you. But," she sighed again, "I suppose I am going to have to take that time and begin exploring. There does not seem to be any other option."

"I'm sorry, my love. You know that if I could, I would do anything to help you."

She kissed him. "I know that. I do. And it is time for me to stop procrastinating."

When she left Saint Kakukilla's the following morning, she found Bölli waiting for her. He was standing next to Faolan who had "lead" her to the church.

"You are to come with me," he said, taking her hand after he announced his presence.

"What about Dodi?" Faolan was now at her side, his furry shoulder pressed firmly against her thigh. She placed a hand on his head and scratched the velvet smooth hair behind his ears.

Bölli studied the large mammal for a moment. The wolf seemed placid enough, he thought, its dark blue eyes stared into his as if waiting for a decision. The boy shrugged then remembered that Magdala couldn't see.

"I guess he can come along," Bölli said, giving the wolf a sidelong glance, "though they might make him wait outside the castle."

We will see about that, Chokhmah thought as she allowed herself to be guided by Bölli and Dodi, but said, "We are going to the castle?"

"Yes," he said, "but I don't know anything other than that I'm to take you there."

Why might she be needed at Castle Rodolph, she wondered, as people stepped aside to allow the healer and her wolf to pass, often with a murmured 'good morning, Mistress Magdala.' She had already gained quite a reputation, and Faolan as wolf had been on perfect behavior since they arrived in Sigwald. Despite the looks of fear he had often received, he had been nothing but friendly even going so far as to lick the hand or face of anyone courageous enough to approach him.

Dodi could not be the reason, which meant it could only be one of two things—they required her healing skills or someone had discovered that her tale of being the widow of a sheep farmer in northeast Simoon was false.

She prayed to Omni that it was the former, and if that were the case that she might cure whatever ailed the one who needed her help. If she could develop a good reputation with the royals, she might be allowed freer access at Castle Rodolph. It also did not escape her notice that they had known where to find her, and whom to send. Had Bölli been tasked with keeping tabs on her?

IF POSSIBLE, CASTLE RODOLF was even more heavily guarded than Salama Palace. Chokhmah was able to get Dodi through every checkpoint by insisting that while he would definitely remain well behaved while by her side, she could not guarantee his behavior were they to be separated.

"I have had him since he was a cub," she explained each time, "and he is very protective. He might fret if he does not know where I am."

Finally, she and Faolan were within the walls of the castle, and Chokhmah found herself musing upon the fact that this was her sixth Kingdom to have been presented with an opportunity reserved only for the privileged—being inside a castle, often as an equal of sorts. Her aunt's palace in Favonia being the exception to that rule as she was family, she smiled to herself.

They were led to a small sitting room and asked to wait. "Prince Bemot will be with you in a moment," the servant bowed slightly, then caught himself, and hurried from the room.

"Prince Bemot," Chokhmah whispered once the door shut behind him. "What do you suppose?" Faolan could only return her gaze, brow furrowed and ears twitching in frustration. What he wouldn't give to be able to speak.

Glancing around the room, Chokhmah noted the severity of the decorations, mouth thinning in anger when she noted the large wolf's head mounted over the fireplace. The wolf was the Kingdom of Simoon's sigil, but she hated to think of any wolf being hunted. Faolan bared his fangs and growled quietly when he saw what she was looking at.

She seated herself on a sofa upholstered in dark green leather, which was flanked by two armchairs in charcoal grey velvet. A sturdy oak coffee table sat between the sofa and fireplace. On either side of the fireplace, two tall thin windows with a diamond pattern of leaded latticework emitted a soft grey light. It was an overcast day, and the greyness set a pall over the entire city.

Other than a few oil paintings—a couple of unremarkable landscapes and one of Castle Rodolf—there was little else in the room.

After making a circuit of the room, Faolan padded back over to the sofa and settled himself at Chokhmah's feet. They had only waited a few minutes when Faolan's ears pricked up and he scrambled to his feet.

A brief knock, and a servant opened the door, saying, "His Royal Highness, Prince Bemot."

A tall and skeletally thin young man entered the room. His dark hair was cropped close and nearly black eyes took in the standing wolf before sliding to the woman who had stood as he was announced and was now turning toward the door. Dark glasses covered her eyes, but couldn't hide the smooth skin of her face nor the full lips.

"You are the healer, Magdala?" Bemot asked.

Chokhmah dipped in a brief curtsy before admitting that she was.

"It's my son," Bemot said, voice wary as he approached the sofa keeping a watchful eye on the wolf.

"Do not worry about Dodi," Chokhmah said. "He would not attack anyone unless they were threatening me, or unless directed to do so. What is wrong with your child?"

"He cannot seem to keep any milk down," Bemot said, and Chokhmah did not have to see his face to realize how anxious he was. "He either vomits it up or has severe diarrhea."

"How old is your son?" Chokhmah used the tone of voice that helped her calm people down.

"He is only three months old," he said, "and this has been going on for days now. My wife and I are at our wit's end."

"May I ask what you have tried so far?"

Bemot took a deep breath, remembering. He had been

coached by his wife, Lioba. "She says she's tried both raspberry and blackberry leaf teas as well as chamomile tea."

"Who made these teas?"

"Our healer, Hulda."

Chokhmah nodded. She had assumed the castle had its own healer, she just needed to confirm that.

"So you have not tried tormentil tea?"

"Tormentil?" Bemot said. "I have never even heard of it."

"I have some of the root back at Ebbe's," Chokhmah said. "Would you like me to bring some back? I have always had great success with tormentil."

"At this point," Bemot said, "I am willing to try most anything. If he doesn't eat soon, he will die."

"I will be back as soon as possible," she said.

"I will order you a trap," Bemot said. "It will get you there and back much more quickly."

He left the room only to return a moment later. "To save time, make sure you have what you need to spend several days here. And bring whatever you might try if the tormentil doesn't work."

Chokhmah curtsied, but inside her heart was hammering, and she was praying fervently to Omni. If she could not cure the child, there would be a mark on her that might never be removed. Whatever happened, she would have to find the Whetstone while she was here in Castle Rodolf.

WHEN THEY RETURNED, they were set up in a small room adjacent to the chambers belonging to Prince Bemot and his wife. Chokhmah asked for some water to be heated as she entered the castle. The most important thing was to get some tormentil tea into the infant as soon as possible.

While the water was being heated, she diced enough of the root to make two cups of tea, and put it into her tea strainer. After steeping it for ten minutes, she was led to the couple's infant son, Grini.

He didn't look good. His tiny face was pinched and wan, and he whimpered constantly. Speaking softly and in her most soothing voice, Chokhmah held out her arms, and asked that Grini be placed in them. Holding him securely against her chest, she picked up the syringe she had created for this purpose. She gently pried open his mouth and squirted a teaspoon of the tea down his throat.

Then she waited. Five minutes passed and the tea was not regurgitated. She repeated the process. Once he'd ingested half a cup, she placed him back in his mother's arms.

"If he holds this down for half an hour, then I will begin the process again," she explained. "It would be best, considering Grini is low on fluids, to get at least two cups of the tea into him today."

Lioba had tears in her eyes. "I'm just thankful that he's managed to keep down what you've given him so far."

"Well," Chokhmah continued in her soothing voice, "let us pray that he continues to do so. But let Grini nap for a while and we will see if the tormentil does its work." She did a half-curtsy, half-bow, and said, "I will return in half an hour."

While she waited in her chamber, a servant arrived with a bowl of mutton stew and some freshly baked bread for her lunch along with a plate of meaty bones for the wolf.

Half an hour later, Grini was still responding well to the tea so Chokhmah began administering the tormentil again. A half cup later, the color had begun to creep back into his cheeks.

"I would suggest," she told the Prince and his wife, "that this time we wait an hour. If he has not had diarrhea or vomited in that time, I think it might be a good idea to try to nurse him again."

"And if that goes well?" Lioba said.

"I will give him another half cup of tea to be on the safe side," she said. "Because he has not really eaten in so long, and if the tormentil is working, it may be as long as twenty-four hours before he has a solid bowel movement."

She turned to leave the room, then turned back. "If there is any change, particularly if it is for the worse, please let me know as soon as possible. Do not take any chances. We do not want to risk his life."

The couple nodded, eyes wide with hope. Lioba held up crossed fingers.

Chokhmah returned to her room to wait once more. Faolan looked up when she entered, and she said quietly, "So far, so good."

While she had a nearly overwhelming urge to slip on Eluned's ring and search the castle for the Whetstone, she held it in check. She could not risk being found absent from her room should Grini suffer a setback. But should evening arrive without incident, Chokhmah decided she would take the chance to scout out the castle as quickly as possible. She did not know where the Treasure was kept much less if it were easily retrievable. On top of that, she was not sure about the layout of the castle.

A servant had led her and Faolan straight to the chamber near the Prince's quarters, and because she had to pretend to be blind she could only peripherally look at what she was passing along the way. If she could only speak with Faolan, Chokhmah thought, but they could not risk his being caught in human form.

His storm blue eyes followed her as she paced the room, and he whined in frustration. Here they were, finally in the castle, and neither of them could roam it. But when it got dark, he thought, he could try. Castles tended to have lots of shadows and dark corners. He might be able to do a quick run through before she went searching for the Treasure. Perhaps while she was occupied with the infant.

Faolan stood and whined again. Chokhmah walked toward him and he led her into the small bathroom hidden only by a heavy curtain. As soon as the drape closed behind them, he shifted into his human form.

"I know we shouldn't take this chance," he whispered as soon as he could speak, "but we have to have a plan for looking for the Treasure."

"I cannot risk leaving this room until I know Grini is settled for the night," she said, voice barely above a murmur. "Once it gets dark, and the castle seems to be asleep, then I can chance leaving for a little while."

"I have an idea," Faolan whispered, pulling her into his arms. Speaking quietly into her ear, he outlined what he thought they might do.

Chokhmah was smiling as Faolan shifted back into a wolf. Why had she not thought of this? She had been so preoccupied with the child, but of course it would be a reasonable request to ask to be led somewhere so that her wolf could relieve himself. Dodi could not be expected to use a toilet.

"I will ring for a servant right away," she said, exiting the room. But she did not have to. A servant, a young boy of about eight or nine, was sitting on a padded stool between the Prince's quarters and her small chamber, and he jumped up as soon as he spotted Chokhmah.

"Is someone here?" she asked, turning her head from side to side as if trying to locate the direction of the approaching footsteps.

"Yes, Mistress Magdala," a voice said. "I'm here in case you or the Prince need anything."

"Praise Omni!" Chokhmah exclaimed. "I do need something."

"What can I get you?" the boy's face shone with eagerness, cheeks flushed red, eyes shining.

"I really need to take my wolf out for a short walk. He has been cooped up in this room for hours. He needs a place to relieve himself."

The boy's eyes widened in understanding, and he bit his lip in hesitation.

"Is something wrong?" Chokhmah asked as he paused.

"It's just that . . . well, what if Prince Bemot needs you?"

"I promise I will not be gone long enough for that to be a problem," she said. "But, if you would prefer to take him. I promise he will behave."

The color drained from the boy's cheeks, but the smile quickly returned to his face. Chokhmah guessed that he was relieved that the healer couldn't see his fear. "I think it might be better for me to remain here so that I can say where you are should they need you."

Chokhmah smiled to herself. "I am sure Dodi can lead me. I know how to direct him left and right, if you can give me directions."

"There's a yard for the palace dogs just down the stairs and to the right," the boy said. "It's where we let them out before turning in for the night. It's an inner courtyard, and it's the first door to your left."

"So I go down the stairs, turn right, and find the first door to the left?"

"Yes."

"Thank you," Chokhmah said and reentered her room. "We have the opportunity to do a little exploring," she told Faolan after she closed the door. "But we will have to be quick. If we are gone too long I am sure the boy will come looking for us."

Hand resting upon the wolf's back, she left the room. "If you can direct me to the stairs, we can handle the rest ourselves," she said in the general direction of the boy, who once again was sitting on the stool.

Launching himself to his feet, the servant hurried over to Chokhmah and took the hand that wasn't resting on Faolan's back. "Follow me, Mistress Magdala," he said, tugging her toward the left. At the top of the stairs, he placed her hand on the bannister. "Be careful," he warned as her right foot descended toward the first step. "The stairs are kind of steep."

"Do not worry," she assured him. "Between the bannister and my Dodi, I shall be just fine." She continued down the stairs at a slow pace despite the fact her body was begging her to move as quickly as possible because they did not have much time.

Once they had turned right at the bottom of the stairs, Chokhmah hurried to the first door on the right. She tried the handle and the door opened onto a sitting room in which half a dozen women sat in armchairs or on sofas doing needlework.

"Yes?" A woman who looked to be about sixty or so asked.

"My apologies," Chokhmah said. "I must have gotten my directions confused."

"What are you looking for?" A younger woman of perhaps twenty asked.

"I am looking for the courtyard where I can take my wolf for a quick walk," she said, careful not to look at anyone directly.

"Other side of the hallway," the young woman said. "First door on the left."

"Thank you," Chokhmah said, beginning to ease the door shut.

"Wait," the older woman said. "You must be the healer that Prince Bemot sent for."

"Yes, I am," Chokhmah replied.

"How is Grini doing?" the young woman asked.

"So far, so good," Chokhmah said. "Omni willing, he will continue to improve."

"I am so glad to hear that," the older woman said. "Our Hulda is getting on in years, and it would be a great blow to her if she were responsible for the death of the child."

The younger woman grunted in agreement as if to intimate that the blow might be more than emotional. Knowing what she did of King Hamartia, Chokhmah would not be surprised if the healer was punished for being unable to cure Grini.

"I am so glad I have been of some help," she said, "but I had better get Dodi walked so that I can get back upstairs." She quickly shut the door, wondering if the women in the room were ladies in waiting or part of the royal family.

She and Faolan crossed the hallway, and Chokhmah opened the door onto the outer courtyard, glancing longingly down what she could see of the rest of hallway before it disappeared in the shadows. Having been informed once again of the location of the dog run, she could not risk further exploration.

One door down, she thought as Faolan took a quick run around the outskirts of the courtyard just to expend some energy, and Omni only knew how many more to go.

"Come on!" she called to the loping wolf after he finished his fourth circuit around the perimeter. "Time to get back upstairs before they send out a search party for us."

17ᵗ ͪ Eahth

As the sun moved closer to the western horizon, Eluned began her preparations for gaining entrance to Tsering Palace. She pulled on the long sleeved gown of shimmering sea green silk accented with bands of gold brocade along the hems of the gown and sleeves that she would wear to meet the Princess Xiang.

The deep V-neck descended to just below her breasts to another band of gold brocade. A panel of pale pink gossamer covered her cleavage, and another band of gold brocade encircled her waist. The sleeves and skirt of the gown were embellished with embroidered pale pink orchids.

Her curly black locks gleamed after being washed, and she'd managed, with Gwrhyr's help, to pull them into a purposefully messy bun with corkscrews escaping around her face. An ornate hairpin of mother of pearl in the shape of an orchid completed the hairdo.

"You look very regal," Gwrhyr said.

"My crown or even a tiara would have been a nice touch," she said, "but this will have to do."

As she couldn't wear her worn leather boots, Eluned had

also been forced to purchase a pair of shoes. She would have liked something a little more eye-catching, but had opted for a pair of plain silk flats of sea green, remembering how she'd lost her pearl- and diamond-studded slipper in Annewven while trying to escape King Arawn's Lord High Steward, Hywel.

The Queen took a deep breath and shuddered.

"Nervous?" Gwrhyr asked.

"Very, but I don't have a choice," she said. "We have to get into the palace, and I think this is a better way than sneaking in and never having contact with anyone."

Gwrhyr chuckled. "What you mean is that this will let you kill seven flies with one blow."

Eluned had the grace to blush. "You know me too well. It worked out for us but we're close in age. I know she's marrying him because her parents made the match. I want to give her the option for something different."

The plan was that Gwrhyr would have everything ready to leave for Dangjin on a moment's notice—whether it be Eluned fleeing with the Treasure or Eluned fleeing with the Treasure and Princess Xiang.

As soon as it got dark enough, Eluned would don the cloak, and walk, invisible, over to the palace gate with Gwrhyr. Once there, they would wait for a chance to enter, and as soon as she was safely inside, he would return to the hostel to wait. Gwrhyr would know it was time to begin his wait because she'd loose his hand. He would wait five minutes, and if she hadn't returned to him within that time frame, he would have to assume that she had made it inside safely.

Gwrhyr watched the gathering gloom with a growing sense of dread. He should be the one using the cloak to scout out the palace grounds for the Treasure. And yet he knew instinctively that if he didn't give his wife the opportunity to talk with Princess Xiang, she would forever resent not being given that chance. Gwrhyr hated he wouldn't be there to help, whatever that might mean. He hadn't felt this impotent since his father, King Gavreel, had died when he was still a boy.

When it was full dark, he gathered Eluned in his arms. "I can only pray to Omni that this all goes well," he said. "But I beg you, Fy Drysor, not to take any chances. If Xiang seems interested, fine, but if she seems spooked, run."

"Don't worry," she said, looking deeply into his eyes. "I understand that the Treasure is all important, and I will not leave the palace without it."

It didn't take long for darkness to overtake the city and they set out for Tsering Palace, both with their hearts in their throats. Eluned realized having insisted that she speak with the Princess might jeopardize the Quest, but there was a part of herself that knew she would forever regret not doing so. She had to take the chance.

As Eluned waited, heart thumping painfully against her ribs, she recalled the previous afternoon. After having spent the morning cleaning up to the best of her ability, she dressed in the one skirt she had packed. It had been badly wrinkled from being in her saddlebag for months, which meant she had to take it to a laundry and have it pressed before she could wear it.

They had to be very careful, and not risk raising any eyebrows. Eluned couldn't set out to purchase an expensive dress looking like a poor minstrel. Her cover story when she went shopping was that she had lost her clothes in a river crossing while travelling and had to scrounge together something to wear.

"So when I arrived in Jungnay," she'd explained to the shopkeeper, "I had nothing appropriate to dress in."

Fortunately, their wait wasn't long. Within a quarter of an hour the gates opened to release a late merchant and his donkey cart. Squeezing her husband's hand, wrapped in the voluminous Mantle of Arthur, she sped across the street and slipped in through the gates just as they were closing.

Gwrhyr waited five minutes or was it fifteen? Then, heart heavy, he trod back to the hostel to await the outcome.

Inside, Eluned quickly scurried along the wall until she was well away from the gate. Now she just had to figure out where the family of King Zhang and Queen Ling resided. Was it in the main building, the one that towered above the wall and looked the most palatial to her? She hoped so because that was where she would try first.

Once again she had to wait, because here, just like the outside gate, it was guarded. Well that's promising, she thought. Why guard a building unless what was inside it was valuable?

It also meant, she admitted to herself, she might be spending the night outside. But wait, her thoughts continued to race, surely servants and others exited from somewhere other than the main door. Maybe she should search the side of the palace and see if there was another entryway. It was a risk, certainly, she thought, but it might gain her access to the building sooner.

Pulling the Mantle more closely to her, Eluned began to make her way around the palace. And Omni was with her. She had just skirted past a side door when it was opened and a servant came out carrying a large kettle of kitchen scraps.

This was it, she thought. Gain entrance through the kitchens. The servant had propped the door open so he could dump his refuse in a large pile near the castle wall to the right of the entrance. While he was preoccupied, Eluned hurried to the door and slid in through the crack he'd left.

Definitely the kitchens, she thought as she waded through the hot, steamy air redolent with a mélange of scents—onion, garlic, ginger, soy, and even a tinge of cinnamon. She scanned the room looking for a way to the main palace. Although she was invisible, everyone seemed so intent on what they were doing, mostly clean up at this point, that she doubted they would see her if she were not.

If Tsering Palace were like most castles, the bedrooms would be on the upper floors. The trick would be discovering which belonged to Princess Xiang. And hopefully, Eluned thought, she would have a room to herself.

Eluned found her way to a main corridor, and stopped for a moment, listening. The clink of cutlery against china and the chatter of numerous voices speaking at once could be heard to the left of the door near which she was standing.

Omni was with her! The family was still at dinner. She tiptoed in that direction hoping to muffle the tap of her shoes on the golden bricks that paved the hallway. The dark crimson walls glimmered with murals depicting the history of the Kingdom. A wide and arched doorway gave entrance to the dining room where nearly a dozen people sat around a large round table. The dining room was also painted red and heavy drapes of gold brocade covered the numerous windows on the back wall. Golden chandeliers provided plentiful light, and fires crackled in the marble hearths at both ends of the room.

Eluned recognized most of those sitting there—King Zhang and Queen Ling were obvious because they were much older than the others. Three young men ranging in age from early twenties to late teens were no doubt the couple's sons—Qiang, Chao, and Huang. There were a couple of young women and two toddlers Eluned didn't recognize, but she knew that both Qiang and Chao were married, and that Qiang had children of his own. The three princesses—Xiang, Chandra, and Morrighan—she recognized from the bookstore.

The diners looked to be nearly finished with their meal with the remains of dessert on the plates in front of them. If Eluned waited outside the dining room, she could follow the princesses when they left. She hoped they would retire to their rooms, but it was more likely they would head to a parlor or some other room where they would find some form of entertainment until it was time to ready themselves for bed.

Preparing herself to wait, Eluned stationed herself against the wall to the left of the door. She assumed the parlors, library, or wherever they would take themselves, would be toward the back of the palace rather than the front. She only had the chance to go over her prepared speech once before she heard chairs being pushed back as everyone stood to leave.

Once everyone left the dining room, with only King Zhang turning toward the front of the palace, Eluned followed at a discreet distance behind the others. She said a brief prayer of thanks to Omni that the King hadn't run into her as he walked past her. But she had felt the rush of air, and his right hand had come awfully close to brushing the Mantle.

As she'd suspected, the girls broke away from the remainder of the family, turning into a room that was clearly a library. It was not as impressive as the library at King Arawn's castle in Prythew, but it was all Eluned could do not to peruse the shelves. Tucking herself away in a corner that contained books on economics and statistics, subjects in which she currently had little interest, she made herself comfortable on the floor. She glanced at the books again, wincing. Once she was sitting on the throne in Aden, she might be reading books very similar to these.

Xiang collapsed into an armchair of gold-flocked crimson velvet while Chandra found her way over to a shelf containing board games and decks of cards. Morrighan cleared off the small table in front of the sofa as Chandra returned with a box of small tiles with different patterns on their faces.

Groaning and placing a hand on her forehead, Xiang said, "I'm just not sure I am up to playing that game tonight."

"Why? What's wrong?" Chandra asked.

"I've got a slight headache," Xiang said, "and I'm not sure I can concentrate enough."

"You can watch," Morrighan said.

Xiang rolled her eyes. Watching Chandra and Morrighan

play a game was not the way she wanted to spend her evening. "Actually, I think I'll just go to my room and get ready for bed. I'd rather this headache not get any worse. I'd hate missing the concert tomorrow."

"Vollmar," Chandra sighed, eyes lighting up. "I hope he remembers me."

"He'll remember you," Xiang said. "How could he not?"

"Really!" Morrighan exclaimed. "I can't count the number of times you've regaled us about meeting him."

"Backstage at one of his concerts," Xiang rolled her eyes.

"And the passionate kiss," Morrighan teased.

"Until your bodyguard interrupted you." Yawning, Xiang stood, and said her goodnights. Eluned, in her corner, scrambled to her feet. She had settled in for a long wait, and was surprised to see the Princess exiting the room so early.

"I think a full night's sleep will do me a lot of good," she said as she left the room with Eluned scurrying, as quietly as possible, behind her.

"See you at breakfast," Morrighan called after her.

"Sweet dreams, Princess," Chandra giggled.

Xiang rolled her eyes again, and when she was out of earshot began to grumble to herself.

Eluned couldn't quite make it out but it seemed to be something to the effect of wondering how much longer she could stand the company of the other two princesses.

When they reached Xiang's room, Eluned allowed her a couple of minutes before removing the Mantle. The moth eaten wool cloak was dirty and stained and contrasted starkly with the opulence of her dress. She folded it as small as she could and quietly knocked on the door. She didn't want to scare her by having arrived too quickly as Xiang hadn't seemed to realize she was being followed. Too caught up in her own thoughts, Eluned mused.

The door opened and Xiang stared at Eluned for a moment before speaking. "Who are you?"

"May I come in?" Eluned asked. "I'll explain everything, I promise, but I really don't wish to be seen."

Xiang pondered this for a second. "Or I could scream for help."

"Yes," agreed Eluned, "but I would prefer that you hear me out first."

Studying the young woman in front of her for a moment, Xiang considered Eluned's request. The dress she was wearing was exquisite and expensive, and except for the scar, which ran like a fine etched line from her ear and down across her cheek, she was very beautiful. Something about her rang a bell—those raven curls and pale green eyes.

Eluned waited patiently, and Xiang finally relented, opening the door wider and beckoning the woman into her room.

After Xiang shut the door, she turned to Eluned. "I'll ask again. Who are you?"

"I'm Princess Eluned of Zion," she paused. "Actually, no. I'm not. I'm Queen Eluned of Aden. I'm not quite accustomed to the name change that comes with marriage. And marriage is what has brought me here."

"I don't understand," Xiang said.

"May we sit?"

The Princess led her over to a loveseat upholstered in royal purple velvet that sat in front of the fireplace where a small fire crackled.

"For most of my childhood," Eluned began, "I was betrothed to a man I had never met. A year ago, I was so opposed to marrying him that I set out to see if I could find true love before I was forced into a marriage I didn't want."

"But weren't you engaged to the King of Aden?"

Eluned chuckled. "Ironic, isn't it, that the man I fell in love with was my betrothed?"

Xiang nodded.

"But Uriel is just a few years older than me," Eluned said. "Not twenty-two."

"I'm supposed to marry Prince Aahil in two years." Eluned could hear the despair in Xiang's voice. "He'll be forty! That's so old." She sighed. "I know some girls like older men, but I'm not one of them. I want to be with someone closer to my own age, someone of my own choosing. I hate politics."

"And Chandra and Morrighan don't seem particularly sympathetic," Eluned said.

"How do you know about Chandra and Morri?" Xiang gasped.

"I saw you in the bookstore a couple of days ago."

"And you overheard us?" Xiang said, brow furrowing.

"I'm afraid so," Eluned said.

"I told them to be quiet," Xiang said. "There's no telling who else might have heard."

"Probably no one," Eluned said. "We were trying to listen."

"We?"

"Uriel and I."

"King Uriel is here in Dziron?"

"It's very important that I know whether or not you wish to break your engagement to Prince Aahil," Eluned said, ignoring her question.

"Of course I want to break it," Xiang said, "but there is no way my father will allow me to do that."

"What if he doesn't have a say in it?"

"I don't understand."

"What if you travelled with Uriel and me to Tartessos, and we negotiated breaking the betrothal with Aahil and his parents?"

"How do you know Aahil will want to do that?" Xiang asked.

"I have a very strong feeling," Eluned said, "and my instincts are usually correct."

"Why do I have to go?"

"Because we need your word," Eluned explained. "It's highly unlikely that we would be believed. It could be seen as some sort of political move aimed at getting Tarshish to join the Triquetra Alliance."

"I guess that makes sense," Xiang said, "but I don't see how my father is going to let me go."

Eluned didn't speak so that the Princess could consider the offer for a moment. She'd experienced so much in the past year or so that she had forgotten just how young a sixteen-year-old could be.

Xiang's eyes widened and her mouth dropped open for a second before she snapped it closed. "Oh! You mean that he wouldn't have a say in it because I would leave without permission."

"It's only an offer," Eluned said. "If you feel it is too risky, you are more than welcome to say no."

A light began to burn in Xiang's eyes, and Eluned thought the Princess was probably finally envisaging what freedom from a marriage to Prince Aahil might mean for her.

"You do understand that at forty," Eluned continued to press her, "he will expect you to bear him children as soon as possible."

"I'm not an idiot," Xiang said. "I wanted a chance to live life—maybe not as exciting a life as yours, but not stuck in some palace far from home with a man old enough to be my father."

Eluned nodded and Xiang smiled.

"Besides," Xiang said, "I know my betrothal to Aahil isn't the only reason you and Uriel are in Dziron. You're gathering all the Treasures."

"This is true," Eluned said.

Xiang giggled, the sixteen-year-old again.

"What is it?" Eluned asked.

"I just find it funny that the entire Awen Alliance is on the look out for you and your friends, and here you are sitting in my bedroom."

Eluned fingered her scar. "Being part of the Quest requires taking chances."

"That happened on the Quest?" Xiang asked.

After explaining what had happened, and reflecting briefly that Gwrhyr probably wouldn't be too pleased that she was already revealing so much, she said, "It is true that we desire the Treasure and peace for the Thirteen Kingdoms. We would really like to avoid war, but . . ."

"War?" Xiang interrupted her. "Who said we are going to war?"

"The Kingdoms of Simoon, Annewven, and Adamah have already started making raids into the Kingdom of Sheba. Had you not heard?"

Frowning, Xiang shook her head. That explained the sudden silences when she and the other two princesses had suddenly entered a drawing room, parlor, or dining room when her father was talking to her brothers. Did he not trust them or did he just want to protect her?

"So," Xiang asked, still frowning, "is taking me to Tarshish a way to prevent aligning that Kingdom with the Awen Alliance?"

Eluned smiled. "It would look like that wouldn't it? But no. Uriel would kill me for saying, but what we really hope is that we can talk King Dodi and Queen Chahindra into allowing representatives from the Thirteen Kingdoms to meet in Tartessos once the Treasures are gathered."

"I guess that makes sense," Xiang allowed. "I understand that Naphtali is now aligned with the Triquetra Alliance. At least, that's the rumor."

"Yes, it is," Eluned said, "which means Tarshish is the only the neutral Kingdom remaining. And we don't really know anything about Pelf other than it's rumored to be populated by Aberrations." She would keep Queen Parisa a secret, for now.

Xiang chuckled. "I said I hated politics and I do, but I also hate war. It's great if you win, but you could be imprisoned or worse if you don't. I find it amusing that I am talking to you about this because the Queen who made the Triquetra Alliance stronger is also the reason I am bound to Prince Aahil."

"Omni has a sense of humor," Eluned smiled. "If it's any consolation, Njima is madly in love with King Hevel's former fiancée. And don't you want that—to find the man you love, not the one you're stuck with? I did."

"What if I fall madly in love with Prince Aahil when I meet him?" Xiang giggled, reminding Eluned once again that she was only sixteen.

"Stranger things have happened." Eluned smiled back.

"What's the plan?" Xiang returned to being serious. "Do I even get to leave a note?"

"Only if it's misleading," Eluned said. "We'll need a head start or we'll be caught immediately. We can be creative."

"How so?"

"I don't know," she said. "You could say that if you have to marry Aahil then you need some time to be with the man you actually love, and you're going to be with him, but you'll be back before the wedding or some such."

Xiang smiled almost wickedly. "Vollmar," she said.

"Vollmar?"

"I was supposed to go to his concert tomorrow," Xiang said. "I'm assuming we need to leave as soon as possible?"

"Time is of the essence," Eluned said.

"Anyway, Chandra has a crush on him and I am so tired of hearing about him. What if I intimate that he's the one I'm running away with?"

Eluned laughed while musing that she was glad she had never had to deal with teenage machinations.

"Why don't you write the note while I look through your things and see what you'll need. You can't take much. Do you have one preferred nice outfit?"

Xiang stood and walked over to her armoire and pulled out an exquisite gown of royal purple silk embroidered with gold dragons.

"Perfect," Eluned said joining her. "Do you have shoes to go with it and something in which to pack your belongings?"

"I have to ask one last time," Eluned said. "Are you fully committed to this?"

They had packed Xiang's bag with the barest necessities. Gwrhyr had arranged travelling clothes just in case, and she had explained that she couldn't give her any details because, at this point, the less she knew the better the chance they would get away.

The note she had written, now sitting on her desk, was extremely vague, but her father would probably waste some time questioning poor Vollmar, who would be completely clueless as to what was going on. Although he would remember Chandra, the experience would chase him away from royalty forever.

"Yes," Xiang said, eyes flaring. "I want to have the chance to live the life I want to live. I hadn't realized until now just how desperately I need a taste of adventure in my life."

Eluned imagined that Xiang, like herself, had probably been confined to the palace, and most definitely to Jungnay and its environs for her entire life. This might be her one chance to experience life outside the Kingdom of Dziron before being stuck in Tarshish for the remainder of her life. "It won't always be comfortable or easy," Eluned warned.

"I don't care," Xiang said. "I do this now. Or never."

Waiting until the palace settled down for the night, Eluned and Xiang crept out of her room and found their way back to the kitchens.

"My parents decided that no one would suspect that we

might hide one of the Treasures outside," Xiang had said. "I wasn't supposed to know, but I overheard them talking."

The fly on the wall, Eluned had thought. Gwrhyr would be proud. He had done something similar himself as a young, soon-to-be king.

Xiang opened the door from which Eluned had entered, and there to the left of the door sat a homely iron cauldron planted with basil and thyme. She hadn't even noticed it when she was entering. Eluned almost laughed out loud. Why hadn't she become accustomed to the fact that the Treasures didn't necessarily look particularly valuable?

But she couldn't carry it full of herbs. It would be too heavy. She carried it over to the refuse pile to the right of the door and dumped it out. Nose wrinkled and with a bit of regret, she pushed some of the garbage over the very live herbs so they wouldn't be noticed immediately.

She was still holding the Mantle, but she didn't want to use it until they cleared the walls of the palace. But, when they reached the southernmost corner, she paused. She was essentially kidnapping the Princess of Dziron. If they were caught, Omni only knew what would become of them.

This was going to be difficult but she prayed to Omni that it would work. If Xiang held on to her waist with one hand, and she held onto the Cauldron of Dyrnwch the Giant, she paused again at a sudden stab of pain at the thought of her giant, Bonpo, and the other Questers—were they all right? She prayed so, but she couldn't consider that now. If the cloak concealed her and Xiang, they might make it through the gates.

"Wait," she whispered to Xiang. "We need to wrap the Mantle around us."

Xiang's dark brown eyes widened. "The Mantle of Arthur?"

"Exactly," Eluned said, unfolding the greyish wool. "It may be our only chance of getting out of here without getting caught."

Xiang smothered an excited shriek. This was even more thrilling than she'd imagined. "It's not very eye-catching, is it?"

"It's been around a long time," Eluned said. "Let's just pray it covers both of us."

It did. Shuffling across the outer courtyard, they made it to the gate unseen. And Omni was with them once again as barely a quarter of an hour later, they opened to admit a change of guard.

As the guards maneuvered through the change over, Eluned and Xiang slipped through the gate and made their way to the hostel, doffing the Mantle when they were out of sight of the palace.

13th EAHTH

Relaxing in their dressing room following their fifth day of performing at Sirak's Circus Salmagundi, Njima and Yona sipped the sparkling wine that was the nightly reward for a show well done.

"Compliments of the house!" Yona toasted, dipping her glass toward Njima as her still frayed nerves sought some soothing. Five days, ten performances, and she still wasn't accustomed to shooting a pear off Njima's head. On the other hand, she mused, perhaps it was better to hope that she never would be.

A solid rap on their door startled Yona out of her reverie enough to cause her wine to nearly slosh over the sides of her glass. "Does he have to do that every time?" she grumbled.

"Enter," Njima commanded. "It's open."

Yona smiled. Sometimes the woman she loved couldn't help but sound like the queen she was.

The door opened to reveal a large man and a wide-eyed girl, lanky and boyish. "Her Highness, Princess Divya of Kamartha," the man announced.

The girl rolled her eyes and stepping into the dressing

room, shut the door on the burly bodyguard who'd escorted her there.

"Sometimes I get so tired of him," she whispered, "but he's probably popping a cork over the fact that Chetan didn't want to come with me this time." The Princess and her brother had visited the Brave Hearts the previous four times they'd performed.

"Popping a cork?" Yona asked.

"Like the wine you're drinking," Divya nodded at the glass in her hand. "Under a lot of pressure to keep tabs on him, but he had to bring me here, first, and Chetan's skipped off to Laxmi's dressing room, I guarantee it. She is igneous."

Yona paused trying to remember Laxmi. Ah, she thought, the magician's assistant. Yes, she is volcanic, she smiled to herself, remembering. What fourteen-year-old male wouldn't want to be near her?

"An why are we graced with your presence tonight, your Highness?" Njima asked, eyebrow raised. The first two visits had seemed almost obligatory, but it was getting clearer that there was a greater purpose to her post performance stopovers.

"Well," the girl began, "I really enjoy your show, and I .. . " she trailed off. "But, I, um," she no longer seemed as confident, "was just wondering about the way you look. I mean," her voice rose again, almost in anger, "what I wouldn't give to wear my hair cut short like yours. I hate this," she grabbed her long braid of nearly black hair and gave it a tug. "I've begged my mother to let me cut it, but she won't let me. And to be able to wear men's clothing," she pointed at their costumes. "I hate wearing dresses. I hate looking like a girl."

Njima regarded her solemnly. This seemed to go deeper than wanting to eschew girlish things. "So, you wish you were a male and not a female?"

"Yes, I guess so," she looked up at them to see how they were taking it. Neither of them appeared to be nonplussed. "I guess I've always felt like a boy trapped in a girl's body."

Njima nodded. "And naturally that is anathema to your parents."

"They would die if they knew," Divya said. Her eyes widened, and the color in her cheeks receded. "You won't tell them, right? I'd die or they'd kill me. I'd be dead either way."

"Of course not," Yona assured her. "You don't have to be Divya with us, you can be?"

Divya smiled broadly. "Dev."

"Dev, then," Yona said.

"But that's only a temporary solution," Njima said.

Dev deflated. "Yeah. I don't want to spend the rest of my life as Divya, and only be Dev in secret. But mostly I don't want to be forced to marry a man." Her jaw clenched and she shook her head. "That's disgusting."

"I understand what it's like to be betrothed to someone you don't want to be with," Yona said. "Is this something that will happen to you or has it already?"

"Has. They've already signed the contract. I'm to marry one of King Arawn's sons."

Illegitimate sons, Yona thought, and grimaced. A fate worse than death, in her opinion. "Both of us escaped being engaged to men we didn't want," she said.

"Perhaps," Njima hurried to say, "there is a way we can help you escape that same fate."

"I don't see how," Dev said. "I'm only twelve."

"It doesn't matter how old you are," Njima said. "It matters only that you want the chance to live another life desperately enough."

Dev regarded them, large brown eyes sad, her young mouth stretched thin at the thought of a future she abhorred. "I don't understand. How do you think you can help me?"

"I can't tell you right now." Njima took Dev's hand and pulled her closer so that she could look into her eyes. She had seen Chokhmah use this trick. "You will have to trust us. At this point all you need to know is that we both come from families that did not approve of who we are."

"We both did things to escape futures we didn't want that ended up alienating our families," Yona said.

"Was it worth it?" Dev asked.

"Absolutely!" Njima and Yona agreed simultaneously and laughed.

"We both realized," Njima said, "that we wanted to live our lives the way we wanted to live them, and not how someone else wanted us to live them. Too many people get trapped into living lives they later regret."

"And that wasn't going to happen to me," Yona said. "Not once I realized that there were other options."

"So, what do you think?" Njima asked.

"Yes," Dev said. "Yes. If you think you can help me, then yes."

"Well, first of all," Njima took control, "we can't tie it to this performance or this meeting. You need to return home, and perhaps, what can we do, my dove?" she turned to Yona. "Have her come to another performance in a week? Meet her somewhere?"

"We need time to think," Yona stalled. They could come up with a plan on the spot, but that might scare Dev, particularly as the Treasure was what they were really after. They needed her to think about and really want this. If she changed her mind, they would have to be okay with it. "It would be best to go home and act like everything is normal for a week, and maybe request to see the show again next weekend?"

"Yes," Njima agreed. "We can have a fully formulated plan by then. Do you think you can do that?"

Dev was grinning, nearly bouncing on her toes. "I can do it but it's going to seem like an eternity."

DESPITE THE FACT THAT PURVA kept her busy during her free time, Yona felt as if the following week would never end. Each performance was torture, and the days off even more so. Yona thought she would burst her skin, it felt so tight.

The plan they configured was to take Dev with them, but they had to bring the Horn of Bran as well. Fortunately, Dev, in her twelve-year-old innocence, had trusted them enough to impart her secret, and couldn't risk that being exposed.

Ah, the trust of youth, Yona mused. She remembered when she had trusted unthinkingly. Of course, all that had changed when she turned sixteen. Now they would have to count on Dev trusting them. That, and the fact that the young were more likely to take risks.

Njima had already reached that stage of trust with her, Yona thought. It was a testament to her trust in Yona that she allowed herself to be shot at twice a day, four days a week. Yona, on the other hand, was still willing to take bigger risks. She thought betting on kidnapping, in a sense, a Princess of Kamartha, was a pretty huge gamble.

They both agreed that Dev would gladly flee Kamartha with them, but would she bring the Treasure as the price for her escape? As it was, they would have to flee in the dark of night, which would mean what, Yona wondered. Dev stealing away from her bodyguard? Dev sneaking out of Lamaxana Palace with the stolen Horn of Bran? There were so many variables.

To add to the complexity, they couldn't use the main trade route. They would have to take back roads, forge their own paths, if necessary, Njima had insisted. By taking that route they would be getting dangerously close to the Devastation of Pelf and the Sea of Blood. But, she'd reasoned, Bonpo and Jabberwock were doing it, so why couldn't they?

THE DAY THEY'D ARRANGED TO MEET DEV again arrived unceremoniously with Yona helping with the birth of a donkey foal first thing in the morning—a doe-eyed jennet that Yona thought of as Dear Heart, enjoying the play on words.

After cleaning up, she gathered her bow, arrows and the other things she needed. They left their costumes in their dressing room, but she wouldn't leave her precious equipment there. She also liked the extra protection her weapon offered as they travelled to and from the circus.

As they were walking to that day's performance, Yona stopped so suddenly that Njima had continued to walk a few steps before she realized Yona wasn't beside her.

"What? What is it?" she asked as Yona hurried to catch up.

"I just had a fantabulous idea!"

"Yes?"

"We need to get Laxmi to do a favor for us," she said. "If we can get her to delay Chetan for a while somewhere not in her dressing room, keep the body guard distracted looking for him . . ."

"Then we can slink away with Dev."

"Unfortunately," Yona said, "I don't see how we're going to do all of this without letting Purva know."

Njima was silent a moment. "You're right. We'll need our horses, and I hate to sneak away in the middle of the night."

"I'm not even sure it's possible to leave without her hearing," Njima said. "She's a light sleeper, and we have no excuse to pack and take the horses when we leave for the show . . ."

"As we always walk," Yona agreed, "there's no precedent."

"Then there's no way around it," Njima said. "We leave everything packed in our rooms, and tell her when we return. We'll make the plans tonight if Dev is still in, and plan on yet another visit to the circus."

"Which will mean yet another week."

Njima groaned in response, but she couldn't see a way around it without raising suspicions.

A moment later, it was Njima's turn to come to a sudden halt. "By Omni, look at that, Yuh, uh, Miryam."

Njima had stopped in front of one of the many stands along The Masala that sold souvenirs and other trinkets for tourists.

Yona turned to her, wide-eyed, "I, I just don't believe it." She threw back her head and laughed. "I think Omni is definitely in our corner."

Among the many objects on the stand was a bin full of replicas of the Horn of Bran. Yona felt sure they probably barely resembled the actual Treasure, but it might make it easier for Dev to steal the original if she had something with which to replace it.

Njima was already picking through the bin, searching for one that most matched the shape she remembered from the drawing in a book she had in her library back at Castle Indalo.

While she did that, Yona scrabbled through the leather pouch in which she carried her arm protector, gloves and other necessary items, searching for enough coins to purchase the horn.

Once bought, she tucked it into the bag and they continued to the Circus Salmagundi.

It seemed as if the day would never pass before evening finally arrived and they finished their final performance for the day. Sitting in their dressing room, Yona and Njima awaited the sharp rap on the door that would alert them to the arrival of Dev. As soon as she was safely ensconced in the room, and the bodyguard had wandered off to look for Chetan, who once again was fawning over Laxmi in her dressing room, Yona asked the question.

"So, what's the answer, Dev? Do you want to come with us or would you prefer to remain here in Kaumari until you're married off to, who did you say was your intended?"

"I didn't," she said. "It's King Arawn's thirteen-year-old son, Cadeyrn."

"I believe I've seen him," Yona said. "It's hard to miss Arawn's children running around Prythew. That hair makes them stand out a mile."

"He has red hair?" Dev wrinkled her nose as if the color of his hair somehow made him even less appealing than he already was to her. "My dream woman has blonde hair and blue eyes," she explained. "Just like Vollmar's. My sister, Chandra, drooled over him so much that she insisted her bodyguard get her backstage. When my parents found out they forbid her from going to any more of his concerts. But, I have to admit that his hair was amazing. It reminded me of the straw woven into gold in that faery tale my nanny used to tell me."

"Dev?" Njima said, interrupting her chatter.

Dev blushed and apologized. "The answer is still yes, but what happens once we get out of Kamartha? Where will you take me? If it's another Awen Alliance Kingdom then I might as well stay here."

"It won't be in the Awen Alliance," Yona promised. "It could be Naphtali, Zion, Dyfed, Aden, or even Favonia. We have connections in all those places."

"We won't abandon you, if that's what you're worried about," Njima said. "We, or one of our friends, if you prefer, will take care of you until you're an adult and then you can make your own decisions."

"I want to stay with you," Dev's voice shook, and she said in a smaller voice, "I'll be leaving Kamartha forever, won't I?"

"Not necessarily," Njima tried to reassure her.

"Are you sure you want to do this?" Yona asked. "Because once Libni and I leave here, we won't be welcome back. You might be able to come back on your own someday, but we can't."

Biting her lip, Dev regarded the two women standing before her. "You're everything I want to be," she said, "or at least as close as I'll ever get to it. If I stay in Kamartha, in six years I'll wind up far away from my family in the Kingdom of Annewven married to a man I can't possibly love. My oldest sister, Amala, will be next door in the Kingdom of Simoon because she's married to King Hamartia's son, Jarvis. But we're ten years apart, and we barely know each other."

"And King Hamartia isn't known to think favorably about people like us," Njima frowned.

"If I go with you, if I stay with you," Dev said. "Where will we go?"

"Eventually Naphtali," Njima said. "Unfortunately, we have one stipulation if you intend to leave with us." Because, Njima thought, if she says no, we will be leaving tonight. They would have to retreat to Jazeel and come up with a new plan.

Dev paled. "Of course there's a catch," she sighed. "What is it?"

Yona took a deep breath. "We need you to bring the Horn of Bran with you."

Dev's knees weakened, and she sat down hard on one of the stools in front of the dressing table. Yona and Njima watched the young girl's face betray her as she realized who was standing before her.

"I knew there were more people than just Princess, um, Queen Eluned searching for the Thirteen Treasures," she said. "It's such a fantastic tale! I've heard Chetan talk about it so many times. First King Arawn's Treasures were stolen, and then King Hevel's. And there were rumors that even more have been found." She paused to take a breath. "By Omni," her voice was little more than a whisper as she stared at the shorter of the two women, "are you King Hevel's fiancée?"

"I am," Yona admitted.

"Where's the Hamper?"

"In a safe place," she said.

"And if I go with you, you'll tell me everything?"

"As soon as we are safely out of Kamartha," Njima said, "or at the least, well on our way, yes. The less you know now, the better."

Dev's eyes shone with excitement. "This is more than I ever dared dream of! Where's the giant? Isn't there supposed to be a giant and a what's it called, a Janawar? And two others?" She studied Njima. "You don't look like a gypsy."

"The others are elsewhere," Njima said, "and our numbers have grown."

"Who are you?"

"Just call me Libni," Njima said. "Once again, the less you know the better."

"Count me in," Dev said, face serious as she extended her hand for a shake. Before Njima could take her hand, the trio jumped at a sharp rap on the door. Her bodyguard was back. "Tell me what to do," she whispered.

"Just a second," Yona called, and pulled the faux horn out of her pouch. "Here," she whispered back, "you can use this as a decoy. Be back here next Friday with anything you absolutely can't part with. Don't worry about clothes, we'll arrange that. Just remember, we can carry very little with us."

Opening the door, Yona ushered Divya out, handing the Princess over to her bodyguard. "It was so good seeing you again, Princess Divya," Yona called after them as they retreated down the hallway. "Look forward to seeing you again next week!" Go ahead and plant the seed, she thought, as she returned to the dressing room and shut the door.

THEY SPENT THEIR FINAL WEEK in Kaumari in an agony of suspense—waiting for the knock on the door at Purva's, or their dressing room at the circus, that informed them that they had been caught. Of course, Njima reasoned, they could always plead innocence and blame a young girl's imagination if Dev let slip that she wasn't long for the Kingdom of Kamartha, but they would still have to disappear.

Other than that, the week passed as usual although Njima found a map of the Kingdom so that she might plan out their escape route as they would be forced to take back roads.

Yona hatched a plan to transform Divya into Dev before they left their dressing room—cutting off her long locks and cladding her in boy's clothing. Dressed as a boy in peasant garb, they would garner less attention while hurrying back to Purva's after their final show on Deethgwener.

She had also used all her charm to get Laxmi to detour Chetan somewhere away from her dressing room using the excuse that the Princess Divya seemed to need some extra time with them, hinting at sexual issues that Laxmi picked up on immediately and with sympathy.

"Of course, the poor little girl," she'd said. "It must be so difficult to be so inclined and be a Princess, especially a Princess of Kamartha."

Purva's possible reaction also caused Yona's anxiety to ratchet upwards. She hated that they had deceived the woman who had done so much for them. Njima could offer her sanctuary in Naphtali, but Yona felt sure she would refuse to leave the home she had shared with Auriel. Perhaps her safety would lie in not knowing, Yona thought. What if they said nothing except that they were forced to leave, and let Purva figure out later what had happened.

Because, she realized, it would not take the Royal Family long to figure out that the Brave Hearts had kidnapped the Princess. She didn't know how long it would take them to figure out that the Horn of Bran was also gone, but she was sure it wouldn't be much longer. If they were lucky, they would think that they would hold the Princess ransom and not focus on the Treasure. Still, it was only a matter of time.

THE 27TH OF EAHTH FINALLY ARRIVED. They had packed everything they intended to carry with them and stowed the bundles in the paddock with Makeda, whose injury no longer prevented her from travelling, and Aine.

Walking to the Circus Salmagundi that day, Yona couldn't help continually glancing over her shoulder or jumping at any sudden movement.

"My dove, you must calm down," Njima finally stopped her in the middle of the street. "Either Omni is with us or It is not. Either way, we must do this. I will not fail without a fight."

Yona took a deep breath and let it out slowly, nodding. "You're right. Why would Omni desert us when It hasn't yet." She recalled fleeing with the Hamper and the fear she had felt then, and yet, had that not worked out beautifully? "All right, I can do this," she said, and started walking again. "Bless us, Omni," she said under her breath. "I really don't want to hurt either Purva or Dev."

FOR THE SEVENTH TIME, a sharp rap on the door signaled the arrival of the Princess Divya. As soon as her burly body-guard, whose name Yona had neglected to ask, disappeared toward Laxmi's dressing room, Dev turned to the women, eyes shining.

Pulling the Horn of Bran from the intricately embroidered leather bag, she grimaced. "I would prefer plain leather," she indicated the bag, "but my mother insists I have a fancy one." She handed the Horn to Yona. "Paid in full," she said.

Yona took it from her and tucked it into her leather pouch. "Time to get out of that ridiculous outfit," she said, holding up some leather breeches and a long woolen tunic.

Njima held up a pair of scissors. "And time to shear the lamb."

THEY TRANSFORMED DEV CAREFULLY, but quickly, and hurried out of Sirak's Circus Salmagundi without a backward glance. Yona had her archery gear but the flashy costumes had been left behind. On the other hand, everything that Dev had carried into the dressing room, including her shorn locks, were carried with them, to be dumped in an alley on the way back to Purva's.

Wrapped in their cloaks, they could have been a family hurrying home after a late night of entertainment.

They reached Purva's, and as quietly as possible they hurried out back to saddle the horses. If they could leave without alerting Purva, the healer would be much safer.

BUT PURVA WAS STANDING at the bottom of the staircase when they led the travel-ready horses back into the building.

"I suspected as much," Purva said.

Yona regarded her, cheeks flaming. "When did you figure it out?"

"Let's just say it didn't take me long," Purva said. "I knew something was up when the four of you showed up in my surgery."

Yona was staring at her, face continuing to blaze. She'd been so sure they'd pulled it off. "How? Why didn't you say anything?" she stuttered.

"It was the savagery of the attack, for one," Purva said, a sparkle in her eye. "And if they'd been after your horses they wouldn't have hit Makeda."

Yona groaned, cheeks flushing again.

"And then there was the way you spoke—both to each other and in general. Very genteel."

It was Njima's turn to blush. She knew she'd been more guilty of this transgression than the others.

"And then the silly stage names. Sorry, darlings, but most people who come to Kaumari seeking fame and fortune want to be who they are, prove themselves."

Yona's eyes were moist with tears of embarrassment. "And I felt so guilty these past five weeks because we were hiding it from you."

"Finally, your appearance," Purva said. "Beautiful, all of you. Not unusual for Kaumari, but despite the fact you said you'd been travelling for weeks and were clearly worse for the wear, and even though you professed to be Common, you still looked like you'd been well taken care of during your lives."

"And yet you didn't alert the Palace of our whereabouts," Njima said.

"No!" Purva exclaimed. "Believe me, most of the people in Kamartha just want to live their lives. We don't want war. If I had been avaricious, maybe. But I'm not nor was Auriel. You see where we live. We could have had a much grander home had we wanted."

"Thank you," Yona said, "and I mean it from the bottom of my heart. We really just want to do what's right for the Thirteen Kingdoms."

"I do have one question before you go," Purva said, "and you must go soon just in case the Princess Divya's . . ."

"Dev," the Princess corrected her. "From now on, I'm Dev."

Purva smiled at the Princess. "Dev. I like it." Turning to Yona, she asked, "Who are you really?"

"I'm Yona."

"Ah, King Hevel's former fiancée."

"And I'm Queen Njima of Naphtali," she admitted.

Purva's and Dev's eyes widened. "I've been sharing my home with a Queen? All the things I've asked you to do . . ."

Njima chuckled. "Believe me, since I've joined the Quest, I've seen a lot worse."

"The Aberrations," Yona muttered.

"Among other things," Njima said.

"And the other two with you? That was Queen Eluned, wasn't it?"

"Yes," Yona said, "and her husband, King Uriel."

"King Uriel," Purva breathed. "Now it makes sense. But they weren't the only ones on the Quest. Weren't there . . ."

"A Janawar, a yeti and a gypsy," Dev interrupted.

"They have travelled elsewhere to retrieve Treasures," Njima said. "And as we are about to leave, and I don't want you to find out later, the gypsy, Chokhmah, is actually the last surviving member of the royal family of Pelf."

"What?" tears rose to Purva's eyes. "The Queen of Pelf? You mean," she stopped for a moment calculating. "There are now more Kingdoms in the Triquetra Alliance than the Awen?"

"In that case," Dev piped up, "it's a good thing I'm leaving with you. It might prevent the Kingdom of Kamartha from engaging in war if their youngest child is held captive in the Triquetra Alliance."

"You're not a captive," Yona objected.

Dev smirked. "Yeah, but they don't know that."

"In that case," Njima said, "we might want to be heading out. We don't want this to end before we've even left here."

It wasn't even an hour later that Princess Divya's bodyguard showed up at Purva's. And this time his knock wasn't a sharp rap but rather a pounding fist.

Purva opened the door, pulling on her surgery smock as if she were opening the door to a medical emergency.

"What is it?" she asked, pretending to wipe the sleep from her eyes.

"I'd have a word with the Brave Hearts," the bodyguard said.

"I'm not sure they're back yet," she said. "Let me go check. I've been asleep for an hour or more."

She turned around and slowly trudged back up the stairs, buying the trio as much time as possible.

"No," she said when she'd returned, shaking her head

in dismay, "they don't seem to be back yet. Unusual, but not unheard of. There's a club they go to sometimes. What's its name?" She thought for a moment. She smiled, suddenly. "The Treasure Chest," she said. "That's it. They go there occasionally. It's a tavern that caters to a certain female clientele. Do you know it?"

The man shook his head, and she offered him directions.

"There," she murmured, as she closed the door, smiling, "that should buy them some more time."

10TH DEER

Jabberwock beheld the entrance to the Kuna community compound with great relief. Having never travelled with a bitter middle-aged woman and her untarnished son, the Bandersnatch found his patience being tested on a daily basis. Some days it took all of his self-control not to abandon the two of them. But, he would have had to leave Tikvah with them. He only had to imagine staring into the accusing green eyes of Eluned after she discovered that he'd sacrificed Tikvah for his own peace of mind to prevent himself from doing so.

Prior to the yeti's death, at least he and Bonpo had fallen into an easy camaraderie born of a shared homeland and the tragedies that had forced them to leave. Now, he was looking forward to time spent completely alone. He had prayed continually to Omni that the Kuna community would gladly welcome Zoya and Samee into their midst along with their pigs. Surely the two of them could find some way to make themselves useful to the people that lived there.

The Bandersnatch had to admit that despite Zoya's constant complaining and the need to prod Samee continually, the two of them had more than pulled their weight on the tedious and sometimes dangerous trip back to the Kingdom of Naphtali and the relative safety of Kuna.

They'd bypassed Kamea completely, but the pigs had been a beacon to other predators—both wolves and the same wild cats that had killed the donkey, Derry, the first time they'd quartered themselves in the area. Fortunately, in order to keep their livestock alive and have something to offer to the Kunans, Samee and Zoya were willing to take shifts, along with Jabberwock, during the nights they travelled, so that they could keep their campfire burning and the beastees, as Samee called them, away from their campsite. The youth had also turned the cart on its side each night to act as an additional barrier in front of the tent.

Jabberwock was able to catch glimpses, during his stint at the fire in the wee hours of the mornings, of the glint of eyes watching their campsite from the edge of whatever clearing they were camped in. Fortunately, no animal had ventured closer. To add another level of safety to their nights, the pigs slept in the tent with whoever was not fueling the fire. Tikvah was too big to fit in the tent, and had to be kept tied up right outside the door.

As they approached the gate to Kuna, Jabberwock recognized the teenager who had received the first horse produced by the Halter of Clydno Eiddyn the previous winter. He watched the boy's eyes widen as he spotted the large and unusual looking donkey.

"Firuz!" Jabberwock called from his basket atop Tikvah, as the stocky lad approached them, puzzlement in his amber eyes.

"Jabberwock," he said, glancing at Zoya and Samee. "Where is Bonpo?"

"Please let me talk to the Imperator about this first," Jabberwock said, his voice huskier than usual as yet another wave of grief washed over him. "I don't have it in me to tell the story more than once."

Firuz nodded and looked pointedly at the woman and boy in the cart that Tikvah had pulled all the way from the Noontide Valley.

"This is Zoya and her son, Samee," Jabberwock introduced them. "Zoya, Samee, this is Firuz. Zoya and Samee helped me escape from the Devastation of Pelf, and I promised them I would help them seek asylum here."

"Do you want me to go find Nahid?" Firuz asked.

"Yes," Jabberwock started to speak further, but before he could continue the Kunan Imperator, a stocky and curvier version of Chokhmah, was calling out a greeting as she hurried down to the gate. As she took in the tableau, Jabberwock could see her face lose color.

"That bad?" she said.

Jabberwock nodded.

With most of the community gathered at dinner that night, Jabberwock took some time to tell them about what had happened after they left Kuna on the 18th of Feharn. It had only been just under three months ago, but as far as Jabberwock was concerned, it had been a lifetime.

The Bandersnatch joined Nahid at her table for dinner afterwards, as Zoya and Samee were made comfortable with the family that would host them until a small home could be built for the two of them.

"I should be shocked that my fellow Pelfans would do such a thing," Nahid said, "but I have no personal knowledge of what those times were like; just the journalings of our ancestors."

"That was a very terrifying time," Jabberwock said. "At least, the aftermath was horrifying. Protected as I was in the Vale Vixen, I had no knowledge of what was going on in the outside world. Although the genocide of the Janawar was part of the fear induced by all the things that happened as civilization was collapsing."

"And yet the survivors apparently pulled themselves together and tried again," Nahid said.

"They did," Jabberwock agreed, "and once again we're not getting it right. It's so difficult to achieve that balance—who should be granted what knowledge, who should be allowed the power to rule people, or whether or not the leaders should be chosen. No system is foolproof."

"What's the old saying?" Nahid asked.

"One bad apple?" Jabberwock said.

"I believe it was 'date' in Pelfan," she smiled, "but yes."

"King Arawn and King Hamartia," Jabberwock said, "so two bad apples, in this case. But the point holds." He sat staring into space for a moment. "I should have trusted my instincts," he admitted. "When they shot at us on the beach, I should have known it wouldn't get better. I just hoped I would find someone rational, and the need to find the Knife of Llawfrodded was all consuming . . ."

"Clearly a Kingdom in which fear of the stranger is promulgated," Nahid said. "I would imagine that even if we, as former and still pure Pelfans, approached them, we would be greeted the same way."

Jabberwock nodded sadly. The wall. The wall had been the giveaway. "Xenophobia. I should have known. Now I must return to my friends and explain why we are now," he choked up for a second, "now without the one of us no one ever quarreled with." Even when I was grouchy, he thought, Shangsung had only laughed, knowing it was who I am and loving me despite it.

And then he gave his life for me. And yet, Jabberwock also knew that in doing so the yeti was trying to redeem himself and what he had forced upon his family. He could not take that away from him.

Nahid let him silently reflect for a while before asking, "How long will you be with us?"

"I'll leave tomorrow," he said. "Without Tikvah. It will be easier for me to travel alone, and we can return to get her if Eluned," whom he hoped was still alive, "feels the need to do so. Feel free to use her as needed." It seemed a fair trade for taking care of her.

"Are you sure? Can you not stay even one day?"

"Not without being anxious," Jabberwock said. "I need to get to Jazeel, see if there has been any word. If not, I will travel on to Zion and wait there. Hopefully, Chokhmah and Faolan will be back by that point as they had the least distance to travel."

AND LEAVE HE DID. The next morning at the break of dawn—carrying nothing. For the first time in ages, since before he'd met Eluned's great-grandmother, Queen Fuchsia, he felt almost free. If it weren't for the reality that Bonpo's death goaded him as it did, and the fact they might be short one Treasure, he would have rejoiced. Two more burdens to carry on top of the loss of his mate, Kamali, he thought as he left the compound behind. Would he ever be shed of them?

He left the community with a mix of emotions, as well—both sad and relieved to be rid of the responsibility of Zoya and Samee, glad that he was once again on his own, and feeling a bit guilty that he was leaving people who'd offered him and his friends so much hospitality so soon after dumping two new residents on them. Although, they had been happy about the pigs, there was that.

But the need to return to Zion, even if by way of Castle Indalo in Jazeel, was making him fretful. There were still weeks of travel ahead of him, and he needed to keep moving forward. He was ready to put an end to all of this. Omni only knew what had happened in Simoon, or other places, since he and Bonpo had left Jazeel.

THREE DAYS LATER on the 13th of Deer, Jabberwock reached the castle gates. Requesting the ear of either Eremias or Kess, he waited somewhat impatiently for someone to arrive. It was Eremias who guided him into the castle and ordered that Jabberwock's previous room be prepared.

"I just need to know," Jabberwock said as he was ushered into a parlor to wait for his room, "have you heard anything?"

"Not since you left," Eremias admitted. "Not even rumors," he paused. "Well, except that there are people looking for you."

Jabberwock chuckled, but the way his jaw was clenched it was clear that it was bitter. "Well, the Awen Alliance didn't find us," he said, "but the Kingdom of Pelf didn't even want to know why we were there."

Eremias looked taken aback. "You mean, the giant isn't with you because . . ."

"Because they killed him," Jabberwock stated, voice cold. He was tired, and he just wanted this all to be over with.

"I'm sorry to hear that," Eremias said. "He was such a sweet man."

That made Jabberwock grin, though it was lopsided. "Yes," he agreed, "yes, he was."

There was a knock at the door and Eremias called, "Enter."

A servant came into the room and bowed. "The braziers have been started, my Lord," she said. "The room is ready."

"Well, I won't keep you," Jabberwock said. "I could use a good night's sleep," though that isn't likely, he thought before continuing, "before I start out again tomorrow."

"Tomorrow!" Eremias exclaimed. "Surely you'll spend several days with us?"

"I'm afraid not," Jabberwock said. "I've been out of touch for so long. I need to get back to Zion and see what, if anything, has happened in my absence." He paused. "I appreciate the offer, I really do, but my anxiety levels are escalating. I've heard from no one. You've heard from no one. I just worry that it's going as bad for others as it did for me."

Eremias nodded. "I understand that. I would love to know that Queen Njima is all right. It has been a while since this Kingdom has had a ruler as fair-minded as she. I pray daily to Omni that she and Yona are doing well."

"Thank you," Jabberwock said. "Will I see you in the morning before I leave?"

"I will have an early breakfast prepared for you in the dining room. You remember where it is?" Eremias said.

Jabberwock nodded. They'd spent a lot of time there both prior to and after their time in Kamea.

"I will see you there," continued Eremias. "Break of dawn, you say?"

"Yes," Jabberwock said. "You don't have to go to that trouble."

"Why would I not be willing to go to trouble for those who are trying to prevent war?" Eremias asked. "Only fools want war."

"I couldn't agree with you more," Jabberwock said as they left the parlor. He said his goodnights to Eremias before trotting up the stairs to the room he once shared with Bonpo. The others had slept alone, for the most part, although he'd had to do his duty as guardian more than once with Uriel and Eluned, he smiled. That was one small victory he could relish.

But Bonpo. It wasn't that he missed the giant's snoring, but it was nice to have someone there to grouse to. Sometimes, he mused, they'd seemed like an old married couple—he would grumble about the day and Bonpo would listen and commiserate. He had yet to grow accustomed to that missing, but important, aspect of his life.

MUCH TO HIS SURPRISE, Jabberwock had to be awakened the following morning. He guessed the stress had finally taken its toll, and being completely safe for the first time in months allowed him to sleep more than usual. He had had, as he did most every night, the nightmares that had plagued him for centuries. But, in the darkest of those predawn hours he had finally sunk into a deep and dreamless sleep.

Just as well, he thought, submerging his head into the bowl of now cold water near his bedside. He'd requested hot water the previous night because he didn't want to bother with the bath as he didn't want a servant hovering over him as he washed the travel grime off himself. But, now the water was room temperature, which was on the chilly side at this point, a benefit as it woke him up more quickly.

He trotted downstairs to join Eremias in the dining room.

"Good morning," Eremias said as Jabberwock entered. "I see that you are set on this."

"I'm afraid so."

"In that case," Njima's Lord High Steward said, "I've taken the liberty of ordering a light carriage to take you to the city gates more quickly."

Jabberwock looked up at him, teeth bared in a lopsided grin. "Thank you, Eremias. That will definitely save me more time." And keep early risers from wondering about a strange little mammal wandering the streets of their city, he thought, nibbling at the sausage on his plate.

THERE WEREN'T MANY PEOPLE ABOUT when he and the carriage driver pulled away from Castle Indalo, and none of them paid particular attention to the little "dog" curled up at the driver's feet.

The sun was turning the horizon a misty gold when he passed through the gates. Good, he thought, the weather should be nice on this early summer day. He was walking, but he was doing it on four legs, so he calculated he would reach Goshen in about a month.

Omni only knew what would happen in that amount of time, but they had decided long ago that instant knowledge was detrimental. It taught people to react too quickly rather than respond to a problem. Too much communication, they'd discovered, had been the downfall of their world.

It was addictive, so he'd read, and polarized people in ways they had never seen in history. So back to not knowing, back to knowing at the speed of a pigeon or horseman. But, he reasoned, he would discover all when he reached Castle Mykerinos and until then, he couldn't actually do anything about it anyway.

8ᴛʜ Єᴀʜᴛʜ

Once back in the chamber adjacent to Prince Bemot's rooms, Chokhmah tried to come to terms with what she was going to have to do that night while the castle, hopefully, slept. If the poor little infant slept through the night, there was no doubt that his parents would do so as well. They were exhausted.

Her knowledge of the remainder of Castle Rodolph was nonexistent. How many guards, who stayed up when, where the Treasure was kept, were all a mystery to her.

She was just going to have to roam around, invisible, until she found what she was looking for. But, she worried, the Kingdom was so security conscious that surely the Whetstone was well-protected? Or maybe not. Maybe they felt their outer security measures were so secure that no one without cause could gain entrance to the castle. She collapsed on the sofa, face in her hands.

Whining, Faolan came up to her and buried his nose in her neck. He was right, she thought. Why worry about something that she had absolutely no control over? And yet, and yet, it was difficult not to do so. This was their mission and she wanted to complete it successfully, especially after what had transpired while they were in Kamea.

They were interrupted by a knock on the door. An hour had passed and it was time to administer more tea to the baby. Chokhmah let the servant lead her to the nursery. She would give Grini the tea, assuming there had been no complications, and then suggest that they let him sleep and waken naturally to be fed. If he made it through the night, they were well on their way to his healing.

The scary part, she thought, as she squirted more tea down the baby's throat, was that they were definitely being guarded, even if it was by a youth. She knew she could slip by him or someone else if she were invisible. The question was whether or not she would be needed while she was searching the castle, as they would find only a wolf when they opened her door.

And yet in her heart she knew that tonight was the night to try—it was a now or never situation. Getting back in Castle Rodolf once they had returned to Ebbe's was nigh on impossible. No, she decided, she had to take the risk.

Grini was still too thin, gaining the weight back would take time, but his color had definitely returned and his eyes no longer looked quite as sunken. Thank you, Omni, she prayed silently, please be with me tonight if You think we must have all the Treasures to bring about peace.

When Grini had finished the last, she hoped, of the tea, Chokhmah instructed his parents and returned to her room to wait. She ate the dinner she was brought mechanically, each bite tasting like chalk and sticking in her throat. She wanted to wash it down with the wine in the decanter they had brought her, but she knew that would be a mistake. Instead, she mixed a little of the wine heavily with water and drank that. The remainder she poured into another container to avoid suspicion. Besides, she thought, I will probably need it when I return whether or not I am successful.

She placed the tray outside her door and informed her

new guard, a girl of no more than twelve, she thought, that she was exhausted and was going to try and sleep, but to wake her if Grini's parents felt something had gone awry. She was almost certain that this would not happen.

With Faolan at her side, velvet muzzle pressed firmly against her throat, she dozed fitfully for a few hours, waking shortly after a clock somewhere in the castle tolled midnight.

She sat up after gently shaking Faolan awake. "I need to start preparing myself," she told him. "I wish I had some of your coffee beans."

There was nothing she could use with which to stimulate herself. She had been caught off guard at the church, and had been so flustered when she returned to Ebbe's for the tormentil root that she would need that she had not even thought about any other possibilities.

For example, she chided herself, why did you not bring a sleeping aid? If not for myself, for whomever might be guarding her. She could have said it was a stimulant tea. And why had she not brought a stimulant! Her anger at her own thoughtlessness made her blood boil and the next thing she knew she was as alert as if she had had several cups of coffee.

She stood up and paced the room as quietly as possible for a few minutes as Faolan watched her, distress in his eyes, ears and head cocked.

"I know, my love," she went over to him and whispered in his ear. "I know that you would give anything to be doing this instead of me, but it has to be done and I have to be the one to do it."

After retrieving the moonstone from the leather pouch at her waist, the ring had been easy to pass off as her wedding band, she slipped her dark glasses into the bag just in case she was somehow caught. Blindness covered a world of sins.

Clutching the stone in the palm of her left hand, she exited the room. Thank Omni they make sure to oil the hinges on the door, she thought as she closed it softly behind her.

Chokhmah tread as lightly as possible down the hallway, past the dozing girl, and down the staircase. She already knew that the first doors on the right and left were out, so her plan was to start checking every door after that. It was like finding gold in a mountain of pyrite. It could be anywhere. Did she waste her time by checking every room thoroughly? Where would King Hamartia, for surely he would decide, put something like that?

Pausing a moment before the second door on the right, Chokhmah considered her last question to herself. Hamartia was clearly an egomaniac—everything Eluned had told her, everything she had heard while at Ebbe's, and at church, proved that. He would not hide it away, she thought. He would have to display it somewhere that people could see it.

Did Hamartia, like King Hevel, have it displayed in the entrance hall? No, she was sure she had not seen it when she was hurried through there three times already. Where else? Who would he want to see it? Other leaders, she answered her question. He would want leaders to see the Treasure, whether they be from Sigwald, the Kingdom of Simoon, or other kingdoms in the Awen Alliance. A dining room was a possibility but what made more sense was a meeting room, or rather the parlor that was the reception area for the meetings because depending on the attendance the space in which they met might vary.

So where would that be? Not far into the castle, she felt sure. He would not want people to see any private spaces. She needed to make her way to the entrance hall. Chokhmah turned around and headed in the opposite direction.

Once in the foyer, she stopped to consider which way to try first. It was human to want to turn to the right so if she was approaching the foyer from the opposite direction, she should turn left. The room would probably be close to the entrance.

The first door on the right was not a door at all but rather a large arched entranceway that led into a room in which sofas and chairs were scattered around the open space and in front of the fireplace on the wall to her right. In the center of the room stood a large, glass display case. Not so different from Castle Lavieven after all, she thought. But that did not surprise her. From what she had heard over the years, King Hevel's father, and his father before him, had liked to bow and scrape to the other kings in the Awen Alliance, particularly those of Annewven and Simoon. Naturally, they would have tried to imitate the Kings of Simoon by displaying their Treasure similarly.

Yona had said that the Hamper had been in its case for more than a century, according to King Hevel. Somehow she suspected that King Hamartia kept a tighter grip on his Treasure than the Kingdom of Adamah did.

Chokhmah walked over to the display case and studied the whetstone within. No, she decided, it was wrong somehow. It was too new, too little used. Her experience with the Treasures, with the rare exceptions like the Chessboard and the sword, Dyrnwyn, were that they were common looking articles. Even the gold band she wore around her left ring finger had been a circle of plain gold until King Seraphim had had it engraved for his daughter.

This was not the real Treasure, she was sure of it. So where was the actual Treasure? She could not believe it was tucked under Hamartia's pillow or hidden away in a lock box. There would be some people to whom he would have to brandish the real Whetstone of Tudwal Tudglyd. He would share the joke of the ersatz treasure and pull out the real one. Where? Was there a secret drawer in this display case, she wondered?

Running her fingers over and around the case carved out of dark wood, she searched for a hidden button like the one they had found in the tunnel between the labyrinth and the opposite side of the River Duir in Annewven. She found nothing.

Stepping back and surveying the cabinet from a distance, she looked for something that seemed normal but might not be. The only light came from a half moon that shimmered through the slits of the numerous narrow windows that were set high in the wall of the room. The lower windows, three of them, were covered by nearly opaque curtains.

The upper windows were still closed but they would later be opened in order to release any midsummer heat that might have collected in this reception room. Chokhmah closed her eyes and took a deep breath before looking again.

There, at the bottom of the cabinet, was that not a drawer? There were no knobs to open it so perhaps it needed to be . . . she pushed the drawer inward and it bounced back toward her. There was an ornately carved box sitting in the drawer. She couldn't make out the wood because it was too dark, but she retrieved it and was relieved to see it was not a puzzle box.

A slight notch on one side fitted her thumb nicely and she pushed it away from her and the box opened. Inside, was a bag of thick velvet. She pulled it out and loosened the silken drawstring. She pulled a plain yellow stone, just a slim rectangle, slightly concave in the center, from the bag. She recognized the rock—coticule—her brother had a whetstone not unlike this one.

"I knew it," she breathed. This stone had been used and it was hardly pretty. This was the Whetstone. Removing the dark glasses from her waist pouch, she inserted the Whetstone before hurrying back to her room. She paused near the top of the stairs to place the glasses on her face. The dim light made it difficult to see with them on, but as she passed Bemot's rooms she did not wish to take any chances.

As she tiptoed past the girl who was acting as guard, she paused. Her poor head was cocked at an uncomfortable angle. She was deeply asleep. Chokhmah debated adjusting her neck, and just as quickly found herself wondering whether or not she and Faolan should flee that very night. What if it was discovered that the Whetstone was missing before they left in the morning?

She fretted for a moment before realizing that they could not possibly leave Castle Rodolf that night. Faolan could not become invisible. Please Omni, she prayed, let us leave unmolested first thing in the morning. Dropping the moonstone back in her bag and returning to visibility, she took a deep breath. She would take her chances.

As she adjusted the girl's head, the child awoke.

"I was just checking to hear if Grini was awake or sleeping," Chokhmah said, "and I stumbled on you. I forgot you were here. Were you asleep?"

The child blushed furiously in the low light of the lantern that flickered next to her chair. "I, I, I," she stuttered. "What time is it?"

"The clock has not yet tolled one o'clock," Chokhmah said. "What time is your shift over?"

"Three o'clock," the girl said.

"Then drift off again, my dear," Chokhmah said. "I was just anxious about Grini but I see that all is quiet out here and that is a good thing."

"But . . ."

"Do not worry," Chokhmah smiled. "I will not tell. They should not have set you so difficult a task."

"Thank you," the girl said.

"Thank you for your service," Chokhmah said. "I am hoping that I will not see you again," she paused as the girl gasped in surprise. "Do not misunderstand me. It is because I pray that Grini is healed, and that I will leave first thing in the morning, and it is also because I wish you good health."

The girl smiled up at her even though she knew the healer couldn't see it. "Thank you, Mistress Magdala. I hope we meet again in a better situation."

"As do I," Chokhmah said, extending her hand, but deliberately missing the girl's hand as she proffered it. The girl found Chokhmah's palm, clasped it, and shook it, face serious. "Goodnight," Chokhmah continued. "I pray to sleep through the remainder of the night. And I hope that you will sleep well when your shift is over," she smiled.

"I'm definitely going to be awake when the shift changes," she said, standing, "even if it means pacing for the next," she paused as the clock tolled one o'clock, "two hours," she giggled.

CHOKHMAH ENTERED HER CHAMBER and made a beeline for the wine, gulping down half of it to steady her nerves before whispering to Faolan, "I need you to be a man for a minute." She waited while Faolan shifted back into human form.

"Did you find it?" he whispered once he could speak again.

She pointed to the bathroom. As soon as they were tucked away behind its curtain, Chokhmah pulled the Whetstone from her bag.

Faolan pulled her into his arms. "If only we could leave right now," he murmured into her ear.

"I know," she said, voice low. "But, it will look less suspicious if we do not. The only problem I foresee is returning to Ebbe's. By the time we arrive, there are sure to be people lined up needing my help."

True, he thought. They'd only taken Deethseel off, but there were always people needing help. "So we won't actually be able to leave until tomorrow night."

"No," she agreed, "but we'll have to be ready. I will have to leave invisibly through the city gate."

"And I will have to go through the forest."

"Yes," she agreed. "I hate that we have to leave separately, but I do not see any other way."

"No," he said. "It's what we have to do." He pulled her closer. "But we can celebrate now," he whispered in her ear.

She smiled. "Yes, but very quietly."

THEY WERE AWAKENED THE FOLLOWING DAY by the grey, dull light of early morning pushing away the dark shadows of night.

"Thank Omni," Chokhmah murmured. They had slept, undisturbed, the remainder of the night. Grini must be healing, she thought.

Faolan whined.

"Yes, my love, let us leave this place as soon as possible," she said. "We can claim that people will be waiting on me to heal them."

When they left the room, there was yet another young child sitting outside of the door to Prince Bemot's chambers.

Faolan yipped, waking the drowsing boy, and Chokhmah said to the air. "Are they awake?"

"Not yet, Mistress Magdala," he said. "At least, I haven't heard them stirring."

"I need to return to Ebbe's, she said. "People will be expecting me. Please tell them that I hope Grini continues to heal, and to come and get me should there be a relapse."

"I will do that, Mistress Magdala," the child said, and bowed slightly.

Chokhmah smiled and thanked the child, and continued down the stairs, hand resting on Faolan's back.

They weren't stopped, and as she passed through the Castle gates, she informed the guards that they need only come to Ebbe's if they were alerted that Grini seemed to be regressing in his health.

"If so, I will hasten to the castle immediately," she promised them.

Stopping at the market, she replenished what had been depleted on Deethsadoorn. When Chokhmah returned to Ebbe's, Faolan departed for a quick run in the forest as she found herself to be correct, there were already patients lining up to be seen on the day after Deethseel. It was as if the threat of imminent war made the people feel every pain their body had to offer.

For the next ten or so hours Chokmah's work was unremitting. She finally had to claim exhaustion and ask the folks still standing in line to return the following morning despite the fact she knew she would not be there to see them.

When the gypsy finally stumbled into her room, she seemed completely drained to Faolan—dark circles under her eyes, skin pale, it was as if each step cost her twice the energy it usually did. More than ever, he wished he could shift into human form and take her into his arms.

Yet, he knew that would be a huge risk at this point. They needed to leave this boarding house before first light. They needed Ebbe, when she arose, usually an hour later than they did, to assume that he was hunting and she was in the marketplace. He only prayed that Bölli would still assume she was at Castle Rodolf when she wasn't waiting by the door.

Because he knew beyond a shadow of a doubt that once Ebbe realized they were gone, she would sound the alarm.

RISING THE NEXT MORNING when it was still dark, Chokhmah prepared her things for travel. The previous day it was not only herbs that she purchased at the market. She also stocked up on food that could travel—dried fruit, meats, cheese, nuts, hard biscuits, and she even managed to find some hardboiled eggs. As it was late spring, there would be more greens available, but she remembered how difficult those eight days had been when they were making their way to Sigwald.

They would not be able to travel any faster back to Sheba, she thought as she packed. She and Faolan had pushed themselves hard. This time they might even be pursued. Chokhmah shook her head. No, she did not even want to think about it. She would just push forward.

Because she would have to leave invisibly, she needed a way to carry the leather bag on her back so that it could be covered by a cloak and therefore not seen. Chokhmah had not forgotten Eluned's demonstration and the teacup floating in the air.

Faolan shifted long enough to help her attach the leather bag now laced to her back by a slender rope. In addition to the food and the leather bag for water, she also carried Faolan's cloak. Omni how she wished she was not doing this alone. She hated the fact that he would be meeting her at the clearing. He always made her feel so protected.

They left Ebbe's as silently as possible and Faolan, after an intense hug from Chokhmah, slipped away toward the forest north of Sigwald. He had avoided the section of forest near the main road their entire time in the capital city as it was frequented by hunters, lovers, and the occasional teenagers wanting to intoxicate themselves in private. It had only taken one foray into that area for him steer clear. People in Sigwald, it seemed, weren't overly fond of wolves despite the fact a wolf marked their sigil.

As soon as Chokhmah was out of sight of Ebbe's, she ducked into an alley, and removed her dark glasses. Looking around, she found a rubbish bin in which to toss them. But, just before she dropped them, she quickly slid them back over her eyes. It was too soon, and she was not yet safely out of the city. Instead, she ducked behind the bin, and pulling the moonstone from the leather pouch at her waist, she clutched it in her left palm and disappeared to sight.

Her plan was to go hover by the city gates until they were opened for the day, which she assumed would be at first light. Then, the first chance she had, she would slip through and walk as fast as she could to the clearing where, hopefully, Faolan would be waiting for her. She would remain invisible until she reached the clearing in the event they were chased more quickly than they accounted for.

That is, she thought, jaw clamped, they hoped that when Chokhmah did not return by the time the doors were opened for service Ebbe would assume she had been called back to the castle.

The real question was—how long would Ebbe wait before she checked on Chokhmah's whereabouts? They could not take any chances. As a wolf, Faolan could slink off into the woods and hide himself. Chokhmah would have to become invisible. The key would be remaining alert enough to be able to hear any possible approach.

She made it to the city gates where the guards, Mephi and Hesse, were preparing for the day—getting out the log sheets, preparing pitchers of water to quench their thirst, and, most importantly, preparing the morning coffee.

As soon as the gates were opened, Hesse took a seat at the table while Mephi wandered away with his mug of coffee. He was back up for Hesse at this time of day, but there was no one in line to enter the city. Chokhmah slipped through the gate treading as quietly as possible.

When she was out of hearing distance, she began walking normally again. She felt the tension begin to release in her shoulders as the cramping muscles in her calves gasped for oxygen. *I cannot wait to be back in the Triquetra Alliance,* she thought, hurrying down the road. *I am so tired of watching my every word, every step,* the tears rose to her eyes. *No, I will not cry,* she nearly sniffed. *I will not cry.*

By late afternoon, Chokhmah had reached the clearing. Faolan was not there. It had taken her longer than she planned because she was more tired than she had realized. She had not slept well while at Castle Rodolf, and she had not slept well the previous night. Afraid to wait in plain sight, she wandered into the woods and found a tree wide enough to support her back. She would doze while she waited.

CHOKHMAH WAS AWAKENED by the sound of approaching hooves, and was startled to discover that night had descended. Reaching into her bag, she searched frantically for the moonstone before finding it at the very bottom lodged against the seam. She pulled it out and grasped it tightly for her life depended on her being invisible.

A few minutes later, she heard horses arrive in the clearing. She had eaten sparingly and had chosen not to start a fire as she needed it to appear as if the clearing had not been used in some time. She watched as the torches they carried flashed around the glade.

"No one here, Sir," she heard a soldier shout.

"We better push on," another voice said. And Chokhmah waited while they rode out of the clearing and back down the trail, heart beating furiously despite the fact she knew she was invisible. The bag, on the other hand, lay on the ground next to her. She had forgotten it, but it must have been hidden by the shadow of the tree.

Chokhmah had absolutely no idea of the time. It was pitch black and the half moon was high in the sky so it could be anywhere between nine at night and three o'clock in the morning. And there was no Faolan. She knew because his sensitive nose would have sniffed her out. Where was he? What had detained him?

With the soldiers gone, she fell back into an exhausted, but troubled sleep.

18TH EAHTH

It was shortly after midnight before Gwrhyr and Eluned, along with Xiang, managed to leave the hostel. They were all tired, but Gwrhyr felt they needed to get as far away from the town as possible before daybreak. They maneuvered their horses down the dark streets until they reached the road that would take them to Dangjin.

"Last chance," Gwrhyr said. "Are you sure you want to do this Princess Xiang?"

"I have to try," she said, face hard with determination.

Princess Xiang had left her door in the palace locked as a precaution when she and Eluned left. She knew that if anyone knocked on it late, and she didn't answer, they would assume she was asleep. "Hopefully, they won't notice my absence until breakfast tomorrow," she had murmured as she and Eluned had made their way quietly downstairs.

Now Xiang was dressed in the ubiquitous Dzironese breeches of thick felt along with a wool sweater covered by a hooded fur jacket that Gwrhyr had purchased at the market. He'd also bought her sturdy leather boots, guessing her size to be near that of Eluned, and thick socks. It might be late spring but this far north it was still cold, especially at dawn and after the sun set for the evening.

Xiang rode behind Eluned on Ronan, while Gwrhyr took on the burden of the Cauldron, which they would use instead of their own cooking gear. He prayed to Omni that they were considered brave enough to allow the Giant's Cauldron to boil for them.

Travelling southwest from Jungnay, Gwrhyr figured they'd reach Dangjin in about two weeks. During that time, the three of them would be crowded into the tent usually shared by just himself and Eluned. He sighed inwardly. He could sacrifice two weeks, but he would be sure to get them a private cabin when they sailed to Tartessos.

Travelling through the night and keeping a steady pace until early evening, Gwrhyr thought they were probably enough ahead of any possible pursuit to set up camp for the night. The landscape was mostly exposed, but they were able to find a dry wash, which they followed a quarter of a mile as it curved out of sight of the road, and then climbed to the top and set up camp.

"We can't be in the wash," Gwrhyr explained when Xiang wondered aloud why they couldn't camp at the bottom, "in case it rains and floods."

They scavenged as much of the dead branches from the short shrubs that abounded on the tundra, and started them burning using some of the dry grasses and sedges as fire start-er.

"It looks like it hasn't rained in weeks," Eluned said.

"It is true," Xiang agreed. "It is the dry time of year."

There was no water to be found so they were forced to use their drinking water to make something warm to drink as the temperature began to fall quickly as the sun set. They watched the Cauldron anxiously, Eluned praying to Omni that it would boil, and collectively released a sigh of relief when bubbles began to rise from the bottom.

"Tomorrow," Gwrhyr said, "we need to make sure we stock up on water every time it's possible. We have pork dumplings for tonight, but tomorrow we'll have to start rehydrating our food."

Observing Xiang when she could, Eluned noticed that for the first few days, the Princess travelled still high on the prospect of adventure. But it did not take her long to grow tired of the burdens imposed by the journey—the cold; the meager, plain meals; and having to bathe and attend to her private necessities in the chilly temperatures and barren landscape through which they were passing. But, Xiang also seemed to consider herself an outsider.

Eluned was aware that she and Gwrhyr were closer than most married couples she knew, including her parents. They had travelled extensively together, and Xiang had barely travelled. Clearly, the Princess hadn't realized the complications when she'd accepted Eluned's offer. Xiang continued to insist the journey to Tarshish was something she wanted more than anything else. So, Eluned watched her try to tough it out and pretend she was fine.

Eluned found herself apologizing constantly for the burdensome conditions. She talked Gwrhyr into spending one night in a hotel or some other lodging the next time they passed through a town large enough to have something semi-luxurious.

A little over half way into their trip to Dangjin, they passed through a town that boasted a decent hotel, and Gwrhyr reined in Ruari. "We need a break," he said. "A bath, a decent meal, and a comfortable bed. Shall I see if they have rooms available?"

COMPARED TO THE PRIOR WEEK OF CAMPING, their night at the Hotel Hkhorlo, (Eluned couldn't remember the name of the town they were in and she wasn't sure she wanted to) was paradise even if the view from her window was not exactly thrilling. The only thing to recommend it was the mother dog and the six puppies that gamboled about her in the alley behind the hotel.

They took hot baths, ate their fill of a decent potato- and meat-filled stew that satiated their ever-present hunger, and spent the evening playing tarok once Eluned had taught it to the Princess. The promise of a decent night's sleep prompted them to retire to their separate rooms on the early side. It was only the one night, but it made it worth the effort to go on. And Xiang seemed more than happy to give the couple some time alone and spend the night in a room across the hall from them.

The only precaution they took while other people were around was to use their assumed names—Gwrhyr and Eluned were still Ivanhoe and Rowena, and Xiang chose to be called Lin.

Despite the fact he was eager to get back on the road, Gwrhyr agreed that giving them all a chance to sleep in the following morning would go a long way to improving morale. After a substantial breakfast, they finally retrieved their horses from the stable and were on the road again. Another week or less and they would finally be in Dangjin.

JUST UNDER TWO WEEKS AFTER THEIR FLIGHT from Jungnay, they rode into Dangjin and found their way to the harbor. Other than the occasional traveller or workman, they hadn't run into anyone suspicious. It was always possible, Gwrhyr reminded them continually, that they could be passed or overtaken during the night and awaken to someone entering the tent. But that had never happened.

"Omni is still with us," Eluned said every morning when they woke once again unmolested.

Now that they had reached their destination, Gwrhyr needed to know when the next ship was heading out to the Kingdom of Tarshish before booking rooms for the night. It could be days or weeks.

Fortunately, it was only a matter of a few days before The Black Cobra would leave the harbor at Dangjin for the capital of Tarshish, Tartessos.

Omni again? Gwrhyr wondered as he quickly went about securing accommodations on the ship. Which, unfortunately, as far as he was concerned, meant they would once again be sharing space. Everything else was booked—the three of them would have to share a cabin—he and Eluned would take one bunk and Xiang would get the other. It was all that was available, and yet it was better than nothing. They needed to keep moving.

Gwrhyr was starting to feel frantic because he didn't know what was going on with any of the other Questers. Yet, he understood why his wife felt the need to work things out with Prince Aahil, and more importantly, why it would be beneficial to have a Neutral Kingdom in which to work things out with the two Alliances once they'd gathered all the Treasures.

He brought himself back to the present. Now they had to find someplace to stay for the next few days. When he asked the first mate, who was handling his booking, the man took him aside and delivered the bad news.

"I mus' tell you, dey're searchin' all da ships," he said.

"Searching the ships?" Gwrhyr repeated.

"You were spotted in Yewenjie," the man said. "Someone recognize da Princess."

Gwrhyr groaned. "Why are you helping us?"

"Because like mos' da people in da Tirteen Kingdom, I no want war."

"What do you suggest we do?" Gwrhyr asked.

"I tink safes' to stay at Dà Guō," the first mate said. "It

bawdy house, but I tink dey no look dere. Ask for BingBing, say Shin sent you."

The first mate went on to explain to Gwrhyr that the three of them should leave Dangjin at the break of dawn, heading south to the smaller port town of Wangmiao where The Black Cobra would pick them up. Shin said he would explain their predicament to the captain, who felt the same as Shin about the prospect of war.

"If you mus' stay someplace in Wangmiao, try da Máo. It own by friend of mine. Tell him . . ."

"Shin sent me," Gwrhyr finished for him.

AT THE BORDELLO, BingBing met with them in a small parlor decorated in tones of pale pink and deep crimson. As she had only one spare room at the moment, she graciously invited Princess Xiang to take her room.

"I will share with one of my girls if I must though I rarely go to bed before dawn," she said. "You are more than welcome to use my bath."

Eluned and Gwrhyr, on the other hand, would have to use the communal bath shared by the women who worked for BingBing.

Once in their room, Eluned ran to one of the two windows on the far side and parted the thick navy blue curtains. She breathed a sigh of relief and tugged the curtains to the side while it was still light. "What a great view of the harbor," she said. "I can see The Black Cobra."

Gwrhyr joined her at the window. Clearly preparations were being made to make sail soon. Longshoremen carried cargo aboard as sailors mended and cleaned where needed.

Eluned turned, "I'm going to check on the bath and see if someone has already claimed it. I need something to warm my bones."

"Sounds good," Gwrhyr agreed. "It would be nice to wash

a week's worth of grime off our bodies before enjoying some time beneath the covers."

Grinning at him broadly and tossing him a quick wink, she retrieved her few toiletries and left the room.

When they met Princess Xiang for dinner, they all looked as if they had scrubbed their bodies clean with a pumice stone as even their cheeks boasted a rosy glow. Although it was possible that the couple might have had even more reasons for their flush.

Because they were being searched for in the town, Bing-Bing had instructed her cook to serve the trio in her private dining room. After eating their fill of sautéed vegetables and chicken in a spicy sauce served over rice noodles, they returned to their rooms to retire early in order to leave town at first light.

After two days of hard riding across the peninsula that separated Dangjin from Wangmiao, they arrived in the port village just after noon on their third day of travel.

Rather than risk the three of them being seen asking for directions to Máo, Gwrhyr left the two women sheltered in a small clearing just off the main road, and went into town on his own.

"It's all taken care of," he said when he returned a little over half an hour later. "Shin sent a pigeon to his friend, and he was expecting us."

"That's a relief," Eluned said, remounting Ruari, and helping Xiang up onto the horse.

"It's not the best lodgings in town," Gwrhyr said, "but we have our own rooms. The only drawback is that he doesn't serve food. We're going to have to go out if we want to eat, but Cheng assured me that he hadn't seen anyone suspicious wandering around."

After they'd settled in their rooms, which were as Spartan as Gwrhyr had promised with only narrow slits for windows high in the walls offering no views but the sky, they'd taken quick baths in the common bathroom. They met to search out dinner just after sunset when they would be less visible on the narrow, sandy streets of the town.

"Cheng told me that there's a tavern not far from here," Gwrhyr said, "which serves a dish called 'Eight Treasures'. How can we resist?"

Eluned laughed. "I'll bite. What's in it?"

"It's basically stuffed chicken in a milk soup," Xiang said.

"Is it any good?" Eluned asked as they began to walk in the direction of the restaurant.

"Obviously it depends on who makes it," Xiang said, "but I would presume to think that food here is going to be the real thing. This town seems so . . ."

"Prosaic," Eluned said.

"Plebeian," Gwrhyr countered.

"I was going to say 'common', but yes. I think we'll taste the real thing."

"Is that bad?" Eluned asked.

"Not necessarily," Xiang said. "On the bright side, no matter what, it's bound to be better than what we were eating while camping."

Both Gwrhyr and Eluned groaned. That had to be true. Trail food tended to be substandard. You were subsisting on what you could carry with you. The only thing that spiced it was hunger.

Eight Treasures turned out to be quite palatable, and thanks to the clear alcoholic beverage they consumed with their meal, neither Eluned nor Gwrhyr could remember its name, they incautiously stumbled back to the hotel singing the Vollmar songs Xiang was teaching them. It was probably just as well they agreed to sleep in the following morning. It was also probably providential that they had a couple of days to relax and enjoy themselves before they began their voyage.

The next two days were spent sleeping, enjoying the local cuisine albeit with a lot more caution, and wasting time by enjoying the luxuries of reading, playing cards, and listening to Cheng and his friends playing the traditional music of Dziron.

Gwrhyr knew that they would be doing much the same aboard The Black Cobra—only so much for passengers to do on a cargo ship—but allowed Eluned and Xiang to enjoy time with the ground solid beneath their feet. He realized that the trip they had taken from Seemu in the Favonian Islands to Thírnagall in Dyfed had been highly unusual. Smooth sailing was an idiom for a reason, but it was because it was out of the ordinary.

It was the evening of the 9th of Deer when they boarded The Black Cobra and made themselves ready for the four- to six-week trip to Tartessos. It really all depended on whether the wind was at their back or against them.

"Do you prefer the bottom or top bunk?" Eluned was solicitous enough to ask before they settled into their cabin.

"Bottom," Xiang said. "If you do not mind?"

Eluned glanced at Gwrhyr. This was new for them.

"I'm fine with the top bunk," he said, stashing his and Eluned's gear in one of the cupboards. It wasn't like they were going to be getting up to any shenanigans up there. Probably just as well, he thought, if they'd been on the bottom bunk he might have been tempted.

Xiang quietly packed away her meager belongings in the cabin's dresser, as Eluned smirked at her husband. Sometimes she could read him so well.

THEY HAD BEEN ON BOARD The Black Cobra for a little more than two weeks when black clouds began building ominously in front of them. Little of incidence had occurred up to that point. A northern wind had pushed them southward at a decent clip, but now they were turning eastward along the coasts of Dziron and Pelf. It was the last day of the month of Deer, and it looked as if they were in for an early summer storm.

"Now we find out who the sea survivors are," Gwrhyr said to Eluned.

Brow creased, she turned to him from where she was surveying the growing cloudbank at the prow of the ship. "What do you mean?"

"I mean, so far it has been light sailing," Gwrhyr said. "Storms can turn the stoutest sailor into a quivering jellyfish."

Eluned's eyes widened. "That bad?"

"Worse," Gwrhyr's jaw clenched, and he shook his head. "Bring out the buckets."

"What?" Eluned still looked confused.

"Believe me, you won't be able to hold anything down," he said. "It's the worst part of sailing."

So he says, Eluned thought, but I've been fine with sea travel so far . . .

GWRHYR'S DIRE PREDICTION proved itself true less than a day later as the ship, lashed by the storm, tossed and turned so much that Eluned prayed to die. All of them—Gwrhyr, she, and Xiang had lost their lunches into the buckets that Gwrhyr had insisted they have on hand.

Xiang seemed to be taking it the worst, and while Eluned held the Princess' head over the bucket, smoothing back the dark hair that wanted to fall in her face, she had a sudden remembrance.

Eluned carried in the leather pouch around her neck the pearl of Namaka that she'd been given on the island of Paliaina in Favonia when they were seeking a place to hide the Chariot and the Chessboard. The ship lurched again as she reached for it, and she clenched her teeth against the nausea. She had to try. Pulling the black pearl from the bag, and clutching it in the palm of her hand, Eluned prayed fervently to Namaka and Omni to calm the storm.

At first, the lurching of the The Black Cobra grew worse and Xiang retched though she had nothing left to give. Eluned began to fear for their lives, but within ten minutes the horrendous waves seemed to subside and they were soon sailing on a nearly dead calm. There was a pleasant although not overly strong breeze at their backs, completely at odds with the state of the waves.

Eluned pressed cold cloths to Xiang's face and forehead, and eventually the Princess returned to herself.

"I don't want to do that again," she muttered. "I mean it. Ever."

"That means a land trip back to Dziron," Eluned joked.

Xiang grimaced and swallowed hard. "I'm not sure I want to go back to Dziron," she sighed before slipping into an exhausted sleep.

Eluned stood, palm massaging the small of her back. "She needs that," she told Gwrhyr who had been watching them from the top bunk where he'd been busy with his own bucket, face pale and covered with a thin sheen of perspiration.

"You astound me," he said. "I've never seen someone put aside their own misery like that. Caring for Xiang," he shook his head. "You are going to be an amazing mother, and I can't tell you how proud I am that I will be their father because of that. You are something else Queen Eluned."

Eluned blushed. "I was only doing what I had to do," she said, "and besides I had Namaka's pearl to help me end the storm."

Gwrhyr chuckled. He still found it hard to believe that this was the same woman he'd met in Mjijangwa more than a year ago. A lot had happened since then, but what she'd become was more than that. It was as if she'd needed the chance to prove herself, something she would never have had a chance to do confined to Castle Mykerinos.

THE FOLLOWING MORNING the three of them woke to the smooth sailing to which they'd become accustomed, and Gwrhyr hurried into the hold to check on the condition of their horses. They would have also suffered from the storm even if it had just been the tossing of the ship. He hoped they had prostrated themselves.

The pen Ronan and Ruari shared seemed to have some soured hay, which indicated a bit of sickness, but they looked to have righted themselves. Both horses were standing waiting for their morning oats and hay.

While they munched, he cleaned out the small mess they had made and thanked Omni for keeping Faolan's horses safe.

Next time clouds started building, he mused as he returned to the main deck, he would remind his wife to get out the pearl and start praying. For now it was back to meals in the dining room with the few other travellers, and days spent trying to figure out how to amuse themselves for hours on end.

A LITTLE OVER TWO WEEKS LATER, on the nineteenth of Teeneh, the coast of Tarshish finally appeared.

Please Omni, let Prince Aahil receive us, Eluned prayed as she watched the city loom closer and closer. We need this so much, she thought, glancing up at her husband who had humored her in this pursuit. She realized that he thought gaining support for a neutral meeting place for the Triquetra and Awen Alliances was of primary importance, but she couldn't help but have Xiang's best interests at heart.

The white plastered walls of the buildings that lined the

harbor sparkled in the morning sun. On a hill, high above the harbor, the soaring towers of Iqbal Palace, also blindingly white, loomed over the city of Tartessos. With arched windows placed near the top of each watchtower, Eluned was reminded of the cobras they had faced while searching for the Treasure in the ruins of Shamash Palace. She chuckled.

"What is it?" Gwrhyr asked.

"The towers remind me of the cobras in Kamea," she said.

Gwrhyr shook his head. "Except these cobras are not blind."

"I'm sure they've long since spotted the ship," she agreed. "Hopefully, we can disembark and lose ourselves in the city without too much notice."

"It would be nice to find lodgings and get cleaned up before we have to make ourselves known to the Prince," he said. And while both Eluned and Xiang had clothing suitable for such a visit, Gwrhyr still needed to shop for something cleaner than what he had with him.

When they had stayed in Ponike while enroute to Naphtali late the previous summer, the King had not been questioned when he ordered rooms for the group of filthy travellers.

If they wanted to stay in a hotel considered respectable for royalty in Tartessos, they would have to find somewhere in which they could clean up first. After more than a month on board a ship in which a bath meant a bowl of lukewarm water and a hand cloth, it would take some effort to wash away the grime and stink of the trip.

Eluned glanced down at the skirt she had worn to shop for a gown in Jungnay. This time she hadn't been able to take it to a laundry and it was very wrinkled, and now dirty because she'd traded her leather breeches for it as the mid summer temperatures began to soar. But, she didn't have a top, and she had fashioned her headscarf into a shirt of sorts when she couldn't bear wearing her wool sweater any longer. She looked like a vagabond, and Xiang wasn't much better.

The Princess wore Eluned's nicest pair of leather trousers as the heavy felt trousers, her only travelling pants, had become unbearably warm. One of the crewmembers had lent her a cotton shirt that was much too large and badly stained by the man's sweat, yet better than her wool sweater.

No female sailors on this ship, Eluned thought, frowning, a testament to the misogynistic tendencies of King Dodi. And that was another reason why it was all-important to contact Prince Aahil first. He was rumored to be significantly more liberal than his father. She had no doubt that King Dodi would insist that Princess Xiang uphold her end of the bargain if for no other reason than she had no right, as a female, to dispute the betrothal.

Glancing at her husband, who was looking pretty ratty himself, Eluned realized they would all need something clean to change into before they found better lodgings than the hostel the captain had suggested.

"They be used to sailors," he'd said. "And ye're not even half as deerty."

Eluned had tried hard not to smile. If he only knew, she'd thought, lip twitching.

Fortunately, leaving the ship and entering the city went easier than Eluned had prayed for. With the two horses in tow, the three of them had passed through the customs portal with barely a glance as they carried so little with them.

"Look!" Eluned said as they passed several storefronts selling clothing on their way to the hostel. She handed Ronan's halter lead to Gwrhyr. "Xiang and I will go get what we need, then we'll hold the horses while you get what you need."

Gwrhyr's eyes glimmered with amusement. "Yes, Your Highness," he said so only the two of them could hear him.

Xiang giggled and Eluned laughed and said, "And don't you forget it!" Arching an eyebrow at him and raising her chin, she led Xiang into the store. A half an hour later they re-emerged, arms filled with packages.

"Did you buy out the store?" Gwrhyr asked.

"Very funny," Eluned mock scowled at him. "We each got a skirt, blouse, and small clothes as well as a pair of shoes for Xiang because we decided her boots would look decidedly funny with the outfit."

"And nightgowns," Xiang added.

Gwrhyr nodded. Good thought. Following the storm, they'd sacrificed the fresh water for their morning ablutions in order to rinse out their sweat- and sea-sick-stained nightwear. But, the clothes still brought back bad memories, and he'd be glad for new.

"My turn," he said, handing the leads to Eluned.

It only took Gwrhyr a quarter of an hour to reemerge from the store.

"Less to choose from," he explained as he strapped his packages onto Ruari.

They found the hostel not long after they departed the store, and as Eluned held their horses, Gwrhyr went inside to make arrangements.

"He speaks the language of Tarshish as well as Dziron?" Xiang was amazed.

"I think the only language of the Thirteen Kingdoms he doesn't speak is Pelfan," she said. "But I imagine he'll start learning it, as well."

"Why would there be a need to speak Pelfan?" Xiang asked.

"There's a community of Pelfan refugees in Naphtali that still speak the language," Eluned explained. "He was already starting to learn it when we were there. It's important to him that he be able to communicate with every one, not just those that know the Common Tongue."

Gwrhyr returned a few minutes later. "We can stable our

horses there," he pointed to a barn to their right. "And we have two rooms for the night. It is a public bath, though, so I suggest that you, Xiang," he handed her her key, "go ahead and make use of it while we settle Ruari and Ronan."

"Thank you," she said, eyes shining, and taking her bag and newly acquired clothing, she moved toward the hostel.

14ᵗʜ Deer

Taking the smaller roads and trails that ran somewhat parallel to the main trade route, Yona, Njima, and Dev were able to make it to the border with Naphtali in a little over two weeks.

Njima had wished they could travel by night, but some of the roads brought them closer than she preferred to the Sea of Blood. While prepared to fight off Aberrations in the light of day, she didn't want to risk doing so at night. Both Njima and Yona took the burden of caring for the young Princess very seriously, and it would not help their cause should something happen to her.

Dev, on the other hand, was anxious to take on an Aberration should they run into one. While Yona and Njima set up camp each night, Dev would practice with the short sword she'd filched from Chetan's room before she'd left Lamaxana Palace. She'd hidden it beneath her cloak, which she then had to leave on for the entire performance, sitting with her legs straight out in front of her, but it had been worth the effort. Now she wanted to use her weapon on an Aberration.

Be careful what you wish for Dev, Yona had thought one

evening when they were about a week distant from Kaumari, and drawing nearer and nearer to the Sea of Blood. Wishing to be companions with Eluned and her friends had certainly changed Yona's life in wonderful ways, but it had brought dangers as well.

A year previously she had been so scared she thought she might vomit on Eli, the Lord Mayor's assistant, when she was stopped at the gate in Hagafen. She was sure she'd been caught stealing the Hamper. If she had been told how much more she would still have to do, would she have continued the Quest? Perhaps it was fortunate that she had to live it moment by moment—almost every day was just trying to survive until the next.

She smiled as she watched the Princess slash at her imaginary foe, and had to admit to herself that it wasn't a bad idea to get accustomed to the heft of a sword. It would help her build the muscles she'd need if she had to use it.

Two days later, they'd been sitting around the campfire, eating their rehydrated beans and salt pork, when Aine had whickered.

Yona glanced at the horse and following the direction of its eyes, saw what it had seen. A lone Aberration.

"Ssshhh!" she whispered loudly, hand reaching for the bow and arrows she always kept handy.

"What is it?" Njima said. She might be the Queen, but Yona was always the first to think, hear, smell, and see things. Her overactive mind was constantly processing what was around her.

She pointed to the opposite side of the clearing they were camped in. Dev gasped and jumped to her feet, hand on the hilt of the sword always scabbarded at her side.

"Kussemak," Njima breathed. Yona had said it enough that she'd finally incorporated the pirate word into her vocabulary. How ironic, she had time to think while jumping to her feet, and pulling the throwing ax from her belt.

Whether it was because they were armed or because there were three of them, they didn't know, but the Aberration had grunted, ducked beneath the branch of a fir tree, and retreated into the woods.

Yona and Njima had taken turns standing guard over the horses that night, but neither of them did much more than doze when it was their turn to sleep. Would the creature return? Had it gone to fetch reinforcements? Even Dev tossed and turned in the blankets she was wrapped in.

The pearly grey light of dawn barely illuminated the sky when they broke camp and hurried on their way, breathing a sigh of relief as the trail turned slightly northward until Njima had reminded them that the Sea of Blood also extended northward to where it bordered with the Kingdoms of Kamartha and Naphtali.

It was Yona's hope that once they crossed the border they might be able to seek out one of the gnomes that had helped them, or one of their friends. They would be taking the northern roads across Naphtali to Goshen in the Kingdom of Zion rather than turning southward to Jazeel. Even a little help was better than none at all, she thought, and as no one was aware of their whereabouts, it was doubtful another gnome had been kidnapped.

Njima felt as if a great weight had been lifted from her shoulders when they finally reached the Whispering River, which formed the border with Kamartha and Naphtali. They were on a little used deer trail to the north of the main trade route when they reached the river.

"They should have called it the Thundering River," Dev yelled. "I can barely hear myself think."

The trail they were on ended at a rapids before turning northward along the river. Presumably, Njima thought, there would be a place to ford the river upstream as there was not a similar trail running southward along the river's bank.

About ten minutes later, the river widened and became shallower in depth. Njima pointed to the opposite side where a small, sandy beach beckoned them. A trail leading away from it clearly saw a lot of use but whether by animals or humans, Njima couldn't tell.

"I'll go first," she said, urging Makeda into the river. Dev was riding with Yona, and the two of them waited until Njima had made if safely halfway across before they began to make their way.

The beach was sunny and dry and wide enough for them to sit comfortably for a quick snack break before heading on. Because they'd been in such a hurry to break camp that morning in their eagerness to cross the border, breakfast had been limited to the hard biscuits they ate while riding. Now they enjoyed a handful of dried fruit and nuts while basking in the sun for a quarter of an hour.

Despite her relief at finally being back in her own Kingdom, Njima was aware that they still needed to be on the lookout for spies and Aberrations. Fortunately, the latter would become less and less of a threat the further east they travelled. Once they were far enough away from the Sea of Blood, Njima wanted to stop early every few days or so because it would be nice for Yona to have some time to try to hunt for their dinner. Or they could fish.

The meager rations they were feeding Dev were really not what a growing girl needed, Njima thought. She could use a lot more protein and fresh vegetables, among other things. And as they'd been pushing themselves so hard since they'd left Kaumari, they'd barely had time to scavenge firewood, much less fresh greens, berries or mushrooms when they set up camp each night.

"I wish Eluned was with us," Yona said as they remounted their horses and began to ride eastward along the trail that turned out to be a bit wider on the Naphtali side of the Whispering River.

"Why is that?" Njima asked.

"Because she seems to draw magical creatures to her like cream draws a kitten," Yona replied.

Njima grunted. It was true. If she didn't know better, she'd say Eluned was part fae herself.

A FEW DAYS LATER Njima felt as if they had put enough space between themselves and the Sea of Blood that they could stop early for the night. They were now riding down a narrow track that meandered through the hills north of the main trade route to Goshen.

It was a beautiful summer's day and they were enjoying the rare warmth. Following a stream around a hill, they found a likely spot to camp and began to set up for the night.

"Would you gather some firewood, Dev," Njima asked, "so that Yona can try to catch us something to prepare for supper?"

"Sure!"

"Just don't wander too far into the woods," Yona warned her. "We don't want you getting lost."

Dev nodded, patting the sword at her side. "I don't want to get lost either," she assured them, "but at least I have this in case something happens."

Omni forbid it does, Yona thought, hefting the quiver of arrows on to her back and grabbing her bow. Setting off northwards along the stream, it wasn't far before she spotted a trail curving into the woods. She trod it as quietly as possible hoping to spot a hare or even a deer with which to supplement their rations.

The trail ended in a small clearing lush with early summer grass and ripening blueberries, still too green to pick, but they would surely be a draw for small mammals and birds later in the summer.

Opting to sit with her back at the edge of the clearing, partly obscured by one of the berry bushes, Yona waited to see if the grass and other greens that carpeted the floor of the glade might bring animals as well. Seems like a deer would love that grass, she mused.

Yona was beginning to nod off in the dozy heat of late afternoon when she heard the crunch of leaves in the forest. A mother deer with two fawns soon appeared, stepping cautiously into the clearing.

And she couldn't do it. Had it been just one deer or an entire herd, maybe. She just couldn't bring herself to kill a mother and her children. Instead, Yona sat quietly and watched them nibble at the grass. Maybe a rabbit, feeling safe, would soon join them, and rabbits, after all, bred like rabbits, she thought. Or maybe even a head of pheasants or covey of partridges or grouse would find their way into the glade.

As the sun sank lower and lower in the sky, Yona watched the two fawns frolic around their mother. She seemed oblivious to their antics as she munched contentedly on the grasses and herbaceous plants that carpeted the glade.

Yona was just about to admit defeat when a large hare bounded into the clearing and began nibbling at some clover. Pulling an arrow quietly from the quiver, she nocked it behind the blueberry bush before leaning away from the plant and sighting on the small mammal.

A minute later she was making her way back to camp. The startled deer had bounded back into the woods but at least they were alive, she thought.

CAMPED ATOP A BLUFF overlooking the Pegasus River a few days later, Yona and Njima were trying to decide the best way to go about fording it. The river was a lot narrower this far north of Jazeel, but after nearly losing Jabberwock the last time she crossed it, Yona was loathe to make a second attempt without being assured of its safety.

"We could travel north along the river for a mile or two and see if there is somewhere that looks more likely," Yona said, surveying the water whose current seemed too fast for her taste.

"One pint eight mile, ter be exac'" a deep voice said from behind her.

Yona squealed and jumped simultaneously, spinning to face the voice.

"A gnome," Njima smiled, returning her throwing axe to her belt.

"Junbist at yer service," the little man bowed. "We be sorry about wot happened wit Tancorin."

"I'm sure he had nothing to do with the attack," Njima said. "I pray that he made it through alive."

"They were so busy chasin' after yer'uns that he managed ter escape," Junbist said. "Yer did a mighty fine job of hidin' yerselves. We never heard a peep."

"That's good news," Yona said. "We were really worried we'd be discovered."

"Princess Divya, I presume?" Junbist eyed the girl who looked like a lad.

"Dev," she said, extending her hand. "I've never seen a gnome before. This is glacial."

"Glacial?" Junbist asked.

"You know," Dev said. "Zero cool."

The wrinkles in Junbist's already much weathered face deepened.

"I think what she is trying to say," Yona said. "Is that she's pleased to meet you."

Dev nodded. "Exactly."

Junbist grunted. "Anyways, when we heard that Princess, er, Dev, were missin' along wit the Horn of Bran, we started keepin' an eye out."

"So, we've managed to hide ourselves pretty well so far?" Njima asked.

"If'n I hadn't been gatherin' mushrooms in ther forest," he

said, pulling on his long chestnut brown beard, "I would'na 'av heard yer."

"So," Yona nearly interrupted, returning to the original subject. "If we ride upriver, we'll find a better ford?"

"A bridge, in fact," Junbist said. "It berlong to a farmer who be a good friend to ther gnomes. He's got some long'n fancy name but we jus' call him Drezzar."

"Do you think Drezzar would be willing to help us?" Njima asked. As Queen, she could order him to do so, but she didn't want to put them at risk.

"Wot d'yer 'ave in mind?"

"I think we'd be less conspicuous and could travel more quickly if we could hitch our horses to a cart and travel along a bigger road," Njima said. "We could disguise ourselves as a couple travelling with their son."

"And we could also use a decent meal for a change," Yona added. "Our rations have been pretty meager since we left Kaumari."

Junbist studied them for a moment before he nodded. "It could work although yer might want'a dye yer hair black, first."

After nearly a month on the road, the roots of their hair contrasted sharply with the platinum they'd colored it for their Brave Hearts act.

"I agree," Njima said, "and Yona can cover her hair with a scarf, as well."

"Then let me go talk to Drezzar," Junbist said, "and I'll be back firs' thing in ther mornin' with an answer."

THE FOLLOWING MORNING, Junbist led them upriver to Drezzar's bridge; Yona breathing a sigh of relief when they reached the other side. From the eastern bank of the Pegasus River, it was another ten minutes or so to Drezzar's farm.

Passing beneath an arched gateway, which proclaimed they had reached Ravensfield Farms, they followed the road up to a sprawling single level home sitting atop a small rise overlooking the road.

Drezzar, a tall man with coarse black hair pulled back in a ponytail, waited on the porch while they hitched their horses to a post in front of a water trough.

"So this be the Queen of Naphtali," he laughed, his teeth made whiter against the ebony of his beard. "I never dreamed I'd meet you, but I am most definitely at your service."

"Thank you," Njima said, extending a slender hand, which was immediately engulfed by Drezzar's much larger, calloused one and pumped enthusiastically. "I understand that things are still going poorly in the Kingdom of Sheba? The aggressions by the Awen Alliance haven't stopped?"

"That's right," Drezzar said, "and into Zion, Aden, and Dyfed, as well. That be why it's so important these Treasures be collected. How be that going?"

"Unfortunately," Yona spoke up, "we haven't heard from anyone since we split up. I know we secured the Treasure we were sent for, but as for the others . . ."

Drezzar shook his head. "We've only heard rumors, but supposedly Princess Divya be not the only Princess to have disappeared."

Yona's smile split her face. "She did it!" She hugged Njima. "I can't believe she did it!"

"Did what?" Dev asked.

"It was Eluned's plan to help Princess Xiang break her betrothal to Prince Aahil of Tarshish," Yona explained. "She must have convinced the Princess to leave with her and Gwrhyr."

"Gwrhyr?" Dev said.

"King Uriel," Njima said.

"Well I hope they're not travelling through Kamartha," Dev said, "because everyone is going to be on the lookout for me. I'm sure they're questioning every traveller they find."

"I've got a strong feeling," Yona said, "that Eluned would not be willing to risk passing back through Kamartha."

"If they intend to break the betrothal with Prince Aahil," Drezzar said, "Then they probably headed to the coast and found a ship to take them to Tartessos."

Njima nodded. "That's what I'd do."

"Junbist tells me you need help finding new disguises for yourself?" Drezzar said.

"Taking the back roads is really slowing us down," Njima said. "It just seems that as we are now in Naphtali and heading to Zion, we should be able to travel a little more freely although we still need to be careful."

"What would really help is finding someone else to travel with us," Yona said. "Spies will be looking for three people not four."

Drezzar's brow wrinkled in thought. "I could probably spare one of my children," he said, and paused as if mentally perusing his brood. "He's usually a great help with the cattle," he finally said, "but Boaz has spent more time amongst the stars than on the ground lately. A little adventure might do him some good."

"Perfect," Njima said. "He can travel with us to Zion then accompany me back to Jazeel. From there, I can find someone to escort him back home."

Yona was staring at Njima, mouth open. "What about me and Dev? Will we not be returning with you?"

"I assumed you'd want to wait for Eluned and Gwrhyr to reach Castle Mykerinos," Njima said.

"If they're going to Tartessos first," Yona said, "it could be months. I think I'd rather be in Jazeel with you and wait for a pigeon to let us know they've returned, and what we are supposed to do next."

"In that case," Njima said. "Once we reach Castle Mykerinos, it might be best if Boaz and I leave separately for Jazeel, and you and Dev follow within a week. That way we continue to throw off any spies."

"I don't like it," Yona said, "but it makes sense. First we have to get to Goshen."

"And Drezzar's wife, Keilah, and my wife, Lokwin, intend ter help wit yer transformation," Junbist piped in. "They be waitin' in ther house fer yer."

"And probably wondering what's keeping them," Drezzar said. "I'll go talk with Boaz while you all get started." Bounding down the steps to the porch, he strode off in search of his son.

Following Junbist into the house, they were introduced to Keilah and Lokwin. Drezzar's wife could have passed for Dev's mother with her big brown eyes and dark brown hair. Lokwin was Keilah's opposite—birch thin with silver blonde hair and ice blue eyes.

Keilah returned to the large table in the center of the kitchen where she'd been working on the dye she would use on Njima's and Yona's hair. She checked on the mixture of crushed black walnut shells, before glancing up.

"It should soak for about three days," she told Yona, who was standing next to her, "but I assume we don't have that long?"

"We could wait to leave until tomorrow morning," Njima answered, "but we really can't spare any longer than that."

Lokwin had returned to the chair where she was mending a dress of homespun linen. The color reminded Yona of heavily creamed coffee flecked with bits of dark chocolate. "Yer intendin' ter be a fam'ly, right?"

Yona nodded. "Playing the part of Dev's mother will be Yona of Seagirt."

"At least yer both have dark brown eyes," Lokwin said. "Yer'll prob'ly pass."

"I won't pass as her father," Njima said. "But, if Boaz looks anything like his mother, he might do. I don't even know . . ."

"What's this about Boaz?" Keilah asked.

"We thought we'd look less suspicious if there were four of us travelling together instead of three," Njima explained.

"Drezzar said he thought it would be okay for Boaz to accompany us to Goshen, and then travel with me back to Jazeel before coming home. Can you spare him?"

"Won't it be dangerous?" Keilah's brow furrowed with worry.

"A lot less dangerous if he's with us and we're disguised," Njima said.

"We can make it even less dangerous," Yona said. "If you have a cart or small carriage we can borrow, Njima can be our chaperone. I'm thinking we're going to have to play siblings—I can be the eldest, but I'll be travelling with my two brothers. How old is Boaz?"

"Sixteen," Keilah said.

"We'll still be camping," Yona said, "though Boaz will need a tent."

"And if we stick to established campsites and act like everything's normal," Njima said, "I doubt we'll receive a second glance. I'm sure we can come up with a backstory in case anyone asks."

"Easy!" Yona laughed. "I'll just say we've been orphaned and we're travelling to our grandparents house in Goshen."

"Better say Roodspire," Njima said.

"Right, then it won't tie us to Goshen," Yona agreed.

"Well," Keilah chuckled, "it sounds like you know how to think on your feet, and Boaz could really use some time away from Ravensfield. He's the eldest and his siblings are driving him crazy."

"How many children do you have?" Yona asked.

"Seven," Keilah chuckled, "and they can be quite a handful."

"Dev probably understands," Yona said, "she's also one of seven, but Njima and I are only children."

Dev nodded vigorously. "I'm the youngest, though, so mostly I get ignored."

"What can we do to help?" Njima said.

Keilah's eyes widened in shock, "I couldn't ask you to do anything, Your Majesty."

"Of course you can," Queen Njima said. "I've done all manner of things since I began this quest."

A QUARTER OF AN HOUR LATER while in the kitchen preparing lunch for twelve people and two gnomes, Boaz entered the house bursting with excitement. And his enthusiasm increased as his mother introduced him to Queen Njima, Princess Dev, and Yona.

"I can't believe I'm actually going to play a small part in this quest," he grinned, brown eyes bright. "Will I get to meet any of the others?"

"That will depend on whether or not anyone else has made it back to Zion," Njima said.

"Thank you for doing this," Yona added. "You'll never know how much we appreciate it. Do you think you'll be able to act the part?"

"What's the part?" he asked.

"We're playing grieving siblings who've just lost their parents," she explained, "and we're being sent to our grandparents."

"I can do that if you and Dev can," Boaz said. "I'd love to have the chance to do something different." He slid a glance at his mother, but she didn't appear to have heard him.

Turning to Dev, Yona asked, "Can you help Boaz pack for the journey to Goshen? I think you can help him figure out what he needs to bring."

"Sure." Dev turned to Boaz, who reminded her somewhat of her brother, Chetan. "Lead the way!"

BECAUSE THE KITCHEN TABLE wasn't large enough to squeeze five extra people around it, Boaz and Dev joined the remainder of the children at it while the four adults and two gnomes carried their plates to a smaller table on the back porch.

It was a balmy summer day, and Yona enjoyed the chance to relax as well as the hospitality and entertainment provided by Drezzar, Keilah, Junbist, and Lokwin. She was looking forward to the remainder of the day—it would be a nice respite from the past month spent constantly on the move.

THE FOLLOWING MORNING at the break of dawn, Yona and Njima with their hair freshly dyed sipped coffee with Drezzar as Keilah went to awaken Dev and Boaz.

Yona chuckled suddenly and Drezzar grunted.

"She does that all the time," Njima explained. "What is it?"

"I just realized we have an interesting dilemma," she said.

"What be that?" Drezzar asked.

"With the addition of Boaz," Yona explained, "I am now ostensibly the only female on this journey. Will that seem odd?"

Njima reflected on that for a moment before sighing. "I suppose if you share a tent with Dev, it won't seem as odd as sharing a tent with you're sixteen-year-old brother."

Yona nodded, "And you'll share a tent with Boaz?"

"Yes," Njima said. "It's the only way to make sense of our backstory."

"Did you hear that?" Yona asked as Boaz and Dev wandered into the kitchen rubbing their eyes.

"What?" Dev asked, sitting down next to her and leaning her head against Yona's shoulder.

"As I'll be the only female on the trip to Goshen," she said, "you'll be sharing a tent with me, and Boaz will share with Njima. Is that okay with both of you?"

"Mmmhmmm," Dev yawned. "That works."

"Fine by me," Boaz said, blowing on his mug of coffee. "It should look natural to anyone who's paying attention."

"Good," Yona said, standing. "I'm going to finish packing. We should be on the road, in what, Njima? Half an hour?"

"Yes, half an hour guys," she said. "Can you do that?"

"Of course!" Dev looked offended. "Haven't I been doing that for weeks?"

"She means me," Boaz said. "Yes, I'll be ready. I could leave now if you needed me to."

FOLLOWING DREZZAR'S DIRECTIONS to the main road, the travellers fell into a simple pattern for the next few weeks—sharing the chores involved in setting up and breaking camp, caring for the horses, and preparing meals.

They were a little over a week into the journey, having crossed the Yarden River, which formed the border with Naphtali and Zion, that morning. Camp had been set up and the horses munched quietly at their oats while the quartet gathered around the campfire to share the lentil stew Boaz had prepared.

"Who knew that learning how to cook would come in so handy," Dev said to him, and sniffed, playing the part of orphaned child should any passerby happen to hear them. The camp was bustling with other travellers making their way to and from the water pump, setting up their own tents, beginning their evening meals, and taking care of their livestock.

"I would have learned a lot more if I had known our parents would be gone so soon," Boaz replied.

Yona was just opening her mouth to say something when a trio of armed men thundered into the camp.

"Everybody stay just where you are," he yelled in the Common Tongue as the other two nocked arrows and scanned the campers.

"Act like you don't speak the Common Tongue," Njima whispered as the men rode around the large clearing questioning its occupants. "We're from Naphtali. Boaz can speak if he needs to in that tongue as can I. Pretend not to understand what they're saying."

"We're in trouble if they speak Naphtalian," Yona hissed.

"We have to take our chances," Njima said.

A couple of minutes later the riders reached their camp. "Where yer from?" the rider without a bow asked in the Common Tongue. Yona, Boaz, and Dev stared at him blankly and waited for Njima to reply.

"Who's askin'?" She growled, glaring at them.

"We be on official bisness," he glared back.

"What kind o' bisness?" she replied. If this were official, she'd eat her boot.

"None o' yer bisness," he shifted in his saddle. "Jes' tell me where yer from."

"We be from Naphtali," she said. "I be transportin' these orphans to ther granfolk in Roodspire."

The man studied the other three. "What're yer names?"

"They don' speak ther Common Tongue," Njima said.

"Then yer can tell me," he said. "What's all yer names."

Kussemak, Njima thought. I can't use Libni, Dev, or Miryam. It could be known. "I'm Matt, and these are Elsie and her brothers, Boaz and Gav."

"Ask 'em what happened to ther parents," the man demanded.

Njima turned to Boaz and said in Naphtalian, "Tell him what happened to your parents."

Boaz launched into a story in Naphtalian about how his mother and father were taking cattle to market in Jazeel, and how they were set upon by thieves, while Yona and Dev hugged each other and pretended to cry. Midway through his story the man said, "enough," before turning his horse toward the next site.

They ate the rest of the meal in silence, watching as the men completed their loop around the camp and disappeared back down the road, before speaking again.

"That was close," Yona broke the silence.

"They believed I was a boy!" Dev grinned. "I never have to be a girl again."

Boaz punched Dev lightly in the bicep. "I never doubted for a second.

"And you played your part convincingly, as well," Yona squeezed Njima's hand. "Thank you."

THE REMAINDER OF THE TRIP passed with little of incidence occurring although every time they made camp, they were on edge until they finally crawled into their tents for the night. On the 17th of Teeneh, they finally reached the outskirts of Goshen. In the midmorning light, the white limestone battlements of Castle Mykerinos gleamed from atop the plateau overlooking the River Musk. By noon, Yona thought, they should be within its walls.

11ᵀᴴ EAHTH

When Chokhmah awakened that late spring morning, sore from sleeping propped up against a tree all night, there was still no sign of Faolan. She wanted nothing more than to prepare herself a mug of hot tea and dawdle hoping he might still show up, but starting a fire and delaying her departure did not seem like a wise idea.

Instead, Chokhmah drank some of the clear, cold water from the spring and listened intently for a couple of minutes—nothing but the usual sounds heard at dawn—birds beginning their morning symphony, squirrels rustling among the leaves on the forest floor, and the buzz and chirps of various insects. Regardless, she intended to keep the moonstone handy, tucked into the pocket in her cloak, in the event she heard the sound of human approach.

Faolan knew the way back to Mwezi-barafu, and remaining in Simoon now that she had the Treasure wasn't even an option. Her heart was heavy as she strapped the leather bag to her back and began to make her way back to the main trail. She prayed to Omni that Faolan wasn't lying somewhere wounded, unable to help himself, or worse, dead.

He cannot be dead, she thought, tears springing unbidden to her eyes. Surely Omni would not deprive her of yet another love?

Around noon, Chokhmah forced herself to stop and eat something. She would need her energy if she wanted to make it back to Salama Palace. The hard-boiled egg she retrieved from the bag seemed to stick in her throat, and she feared she might choke before she could wash it down with water. The egg was all she could manage, she realized, when looking at the dried fruit she had planned to nibble on turned her stomach. I'll just have to do better when I stop for the night, she thought, repacking the bag and settling it onto her back.

"Just keep putting one foot in front of the other, my dear," she murmured to herself, "and within the week you will be back in Sheba."

Chokhmah imagined she would reach the climb down into the gorge sooner than if she had been travelling with Faolan. She was too fearful of being caught to stay still for very long, and she dreaded her first night out without Faolan by her side. The previous night, she had been expecting the arrival of the man she loved at any moment, and so it had been easier for her to drift off to sleep.

Tonight, and until she reached Mwezi-barafu, she would be completely alone barring the chance that Faolan managed to catch up with her. Her intuition told her that was not likely to happen. Only capture, a severe wound, or death would have kept him from meeting her. Capture meant certain death, and she did not want to entertain that thought nor did she want to think he had died another way.

No, she thought, he must be wounded. I cannot bear it otherwise. Mind racing, she hurried down the trail planning ways to optimize her time so that she might make it to the border more quickly.

Chokhmah knew from their previous trek along this path that she would occasionally cross streams—to that effect, she kept her jug filled constantly so that she would not have to wander off the trail to search for water.

In addition, she put her recently honed gypsy skills to work by gathering trailside greens, herbs, roots, and fungi. She also ate on the trail rather than finding a clearing within the woods. Now that she had Faolan's rations, as well, Chokhmah would have no problem making it to the border although she did eat of them sparingly, just in case.

That left the nights. Only when it was finally growing dark, would she begin searching for a spot, just off the trail, in which to sleep. Chokhmah doubted that any of the woodland creatures would try to harm her, but she kept the moonstone at hand just in case. And, as uncomfortable as it was, she continued her practice of propping herself against a tree at night. Not only did it protect her back, but it helped her to sleep more lightly in case something should happen.

It was nearly noon on her sixth day out of Sigwald when Chokhmah finally reached the gorge that formed the border with the Kingdom of Sheba. She removed the leather bag from her shoulders and debated leaving it behind. The Whetstone was tucked away in the leather pouch at her waist, and the bag would be an extra burden on her back, making her balance a little more precarious.

Yet, she waffled, if she should fall or otherwise injure herself on the way down or ascending the other side, the first aid items that she carried in the pack might come in handy.

It pained her to do so, but she unloaded everything that she would not need in order to make the bag lighter, and that included Faolan's cloak. She consoled herself by realizing that if the soldiers checked this way again and found the discarded items, along with his cloak, they might think that he had escaped, as well. Assuming, of course, she grimaced, that he was not already their prisoner.

By the time she reached the other side, it would be nearly time to bed down for the night. Keeping that in mind, she discarded any food she would not need following the time she broke her fast in the morning.

Chokhmah was certain that if she made it to the opposite side of the gorge unharmed, that she could reach the road that led to Mwezi-barafu well before noon the following day. And she hoped that once on it, she might catch a ride on a cart or carriage.

Packing her cloak into the bag, she pulled out the rope and set about securing her dress in such a fashion that it would not trip her up as it had done the previous time.

Climbing in and out of the gorge took Chokhmah longer than anticipated. Despite how frightened she had been the first time, the second time was even more terrifying because there was no one to fall back on for reassurance and help should something happen to her. She had forgotten just how many times Faolan had steadied her on the climb down and encouraged her on the trip up.

It was rapidly approaching dusk by the time she pulled herself over the final boulder and onto the edge of the chasm, exhausted. But she was back in Sheba and that thought alone seemed to lift a huge weight from her shoulders. Yes, there was still the problem of Faolan's fate, Chokhmah thought, but she would trust in Omni to do what was best for her. First, she would see this quest through, and if there were still no sign of the man she loved, she would find out what happened to him even if it took the remainder of her life.

Now, she just wanted to find a sturdy tree near a patch of grass to lean against while she hurriedly consumed her rations for the evening. Then all I want to do is sleep, she thought, as she unbound the rope holding her skirt, and made her way away from the gorge. "I just want to go to sleep," she murmured. She could not remember the last time she had felt this tired.

Chokhmah was just nodding off when a thought startled her awake, staring blindly into the darkness of the forest. The Knife! No one but she knew that it was in the new Buta. If none of the other Questers had reached Castle Mykerinos by the time she reached the castle to drop off the Whetstone, it would be up to her to search for it. She shook her head and swallowed the lump that was rising in her throat. No point feeling sorry for herself. The choice to be a part of the Quest had been hers.

IT WAS LATE AFTERNOON on the following day when Chokhmah finally reached the gates of Salama Palace, just as tired and hungry as she had been the previous day. She had been forced to walk the entire way as there had been very few carts on the road from whom she could beg a ride. Communication was also a problem. Her Sheban was poor and those driving the carts did not speak the Common Tongue.

Chokhmah cursed herself for having never learned. Despite the fact she had wintered in Sheba for years, she had always left conversing with the natives to her brother, and later, her husband. She needed to start schooling herself in it immediately.

Her intention was to spend a couple of days at the palace resting, and giving Faolan a chance to catch up with her. If he did not arrive within a few days, she would request an escort for her return to Zion. It was one thing to travel alone through the woods and quite another to do so as a lone female on a main trade route.

Moshe and Daniel had said they would remain at the camp by the River Spruce until she and Faolan returned from Simoon. She hoped they were still there. If they had moved on, she would return to Castle Mykerinos before sending back her escort.

ONCE ENSCONCED IN THE ROOM she had shared with Faolan back in early Saitheh, Chokhmah finally allowed herself the luxury of a good cry. She wept until her throat ached and her eyes were swollen and puffy. And just when she thought she did not have another tear to expend, she broke down once more.

They had not even known each other for a full year, she thought as she cried, and while their romance had progressed rapidly, it felt far from finished. At this point, she could not imagine life without him, and absolutely refused to give up hope until she knew for sure what had happened to him. If that meant returning to Simoon following the Quest then so be it.

Dragging herself off the couch, Chokhmah headed toward the bathroom to fill a hot tub in which to soak her aching body. She had just reached the entrance when there was a forceful knock on the guest chamber's door.

Sighing at the delay, and wiping the tears from her cheeks, she hurried to the door and opened it to find Prince Uwem and Princess Prisce standing before her. She had met them the night she and Faolan had dined with King Adeyemi and Queen Yobachi.

"Your Highnesses," she smiled, hoping that her face did not betray her recent break down. "To what do I owe this honor?" The look of pity on Prisce's face told her otherwise.

"I am so sorry to hear about Faolan," Prisce said. "I pray that he reaches Mwezi-barafu before you must leave."

"As," Chokhmah's voice was still hoarse from crying, and she cleared her throat and tried again, "as do I." Realizing they were still standing outside her room, she ushered them over to the loveseat, which was once again in the corner. Pulling the chair away from the desk, she seated herself before them.

"What can I do for you?" Chokhmah asked again.

"It's just that . . ." Prisce started.

"It is the fact," Uwem interrupted his younger sister, "that even though the Kingdom of Sheba is a part of the Triquetra Alliance, we feel ourselves very distant from the Quest."

"I did not know there was interest in the Kingdom of Sheba being involved," Chokhmah said. "Certainly your parents did not lead me to believe so when we were last here. I got the feeling King Adeyemi was more concerned with the attacks on the Kingdom's borders."

"It is true," Prisce said. "Father has too much to worry about, and Mother, of course, feels it's too dangerous."

"But you do not?"

Uwem stood up and began to pace. "It's not that. I just feel that it is only fair that we have some stake in this especially as Sheba is the main Kingdom that is being attacked."

Chokhmah nodded. The youth had a point. "And what would that stake look like?"

"Perhaps it will seem like nothing," Uwem said, "but if we could at least travel with you back to Zion, assure King Seraphim that Sheba supports the Quest fully? That we hope to be a part of whatever the resolution is?"

Chokhmah worried her lower lip with her teeth. Travelling with her back to Zion seemed essentially inconsequential. Would they want to continue with her to New Buta if they discovered she was going there to retrieve the Knife? They seemed so young. "How old are you?"

"I am sixteen, and Prisce is fourteen."

"I have to think about this," Chokhmah said. "Can we meet again tomorrow after I have rested and had a night to sleep on it?"

"That seems more than fair," Prisce said.

Chokhmah stood. "We will discuss this more tomorrow. I am exhausted from my journey and want nothing more than a hot bath, a glass of wine, a full belly, and a good night's sleep."

"Then we will see you on the morrow?" Uwem said.

"Name the time," Chokhmah walked them to the door. "We can meet here or somewhere else, if you prefer."

"Here," Prisce hurried to say. "It is probably the most private place we can meet."

Uwem nodded. "At noon? We have lunch and a break from our studies then."

"That sounds fine," Chokhmah said. "I will ask them to prepare lunch for three."

Having someone from the royal house of Sheba with her when she travelled to New Buta might make retrieving the Knife of Llawfrodded the Horseman considerably easier, she mused, returning to the bathroom.

UWEM AND PRISCE STARED AT HER, absorbing what Chokhmah had just told them.

"You had a dream that told you the Knife was there?" Uwem was shaking his head. "Of course, I would like to make the journey with you to retrieve it, but how will we convince my parents that the dream is real? Why are you so sure?"

"Because not only was I raised a Roma and have experience with dreams such as this one, which I have had twice," Chokhmah said, "but I am also Queen Parisa of Pelf."

"But I thought all the Pelfans were killed when New Buta was attacked more than forty years ago," Prisce said, eyes wide.

"All but two," Chokhmah said. "Myself and my great aunt. She escaped with me and left me to be raised by the Roma."

"How long have you known this?" Uwem asked.

"Jabberwock figured it out when we were in Naphtali this past year," Chokhmah explained, "because the Treasure, the Coat of Padarn Red-Coat, fit me and it only fits the well born."

"You know this for a fact?" Uwem said.

"We know that all the Treasures perform as promised," she said, "but we also tested the Coat by trying it on both Queen Eluned and Yona, who is not royal. It did not fit Yona."

Uwem's eyes were glowing. "This is very exciting," he said. "I would love to help retrieve one of the Thirteen Hallowed Treasures."

"So would I!" Prisce said.

"Then I would suggest you arrange for me to meet with your parents," Chokhmah said. "I should do the talking as I will need to explain to them who I really am and why I feel it is important for you to accompany me to the new Buta."

As they left the room, murmuring to each other about the possibility of travelling with her to Zion and New Buta, Chokhmah knew the chance of Prisce being given permission to travel with them was very slim. With the attacks along Sheba's borders as well as the ordinary dangers associated with being on the road, she would be very surprised if Queen Yobachi would allow her youngest child that much freedom.

A couple of hours later, Chokhmah was startled from her nap by a sharp rap on the door. She recognized it immediately—Prince Uwem.

"Just a moment," she called, rubbing the sleep from her eyes, and sliding out of bed. Pulling her boots on over her sock-clad feet, she straightened her clothes and moved to the door. "Your Highnesses," she smiled when she opened it. "It is good to see you again."

"Queen Parisa," Uwem's teeth shone pearly white in a wide grin. "We have good news. Our parents have agreed to meet with you at six o'clock for drinks in the Desert of Serket Parlor."

"Desert of," Chokhmah began before remembering the room decorated in tones of the high desert. "Ah, yes, the parlor in which Faolan and I met with them on our previous visit." She looked down at the badly wrinkled and travel-stained dress she had been wearing non-stop for more than a week. The heavy tweed had been exchanged for a lighter dress of lavender flax in Sigwald, but it had not held up as well to travelling. Looking at Prisce she said, "I am afraid that I have nothing appropriate in which to dress myself."

The Princess studied her for a moment. "It is true you want to make the best impression," she said. "My sister, Nala, might have something you can borrow. She is about your size, perhaps a little heavier."

Uwem snorted, but looked chastened after the glance his sister shot him.

"It will not matter if the dress hangs on her a little," Prisce said. "At least it will be clean."

THE NEXT FEW HOURS WERE SPENT bathing once again as she still felt the grime of travel like a second skin. To continue her disguise while in Simoon, Chokhmah had expected to dye her roots with henna while there. That time had not arrived but looking in the mirror, she noted that her roots were now significantly more silver than before she travelled to the Kingdom of Simoon. She had not realized just how stressful their time there would be. Chokhmah did not have time to remove the henna before her meeting with the King and Queen of Sheba as it was a long process—several nights spent with oil-coated hair—but she would begin that process that evening. She wanted to be herself again.

Chokhmah had had a difficult time hiding her amusement when Prisce arrived at her room an hour or so later with a dress that was clearly too big for her. Although the brightly embroidered ribbon of fabric that ran down the center of the loosely flowing dress was to her liking. The dress, itself, was of a rough spun grey cotton with a slight V-neck and flowing three-quarter length sleeves. Fortunately a belt of the same grey fabric and tipped by more embroidery would help her cinch the dress around her too-thin frame. She had lost weight during the trip to Sheba; even forcing herself to eat had not replaced the calories she was burning each day.

Now, clad in Princess Nala's dress and, humorously, she thought, her walking boots, she made her way down to the desert parlor to meet King Adeyemi and Queen Yobachi.

When she was ushered into the room, both the King and Queen stood and bowed slightly, and inwardly Chokhmah shook her head. Apparently Prince Uwem had needed to tell them more than she had hoped he would for them to take her request for an audience seriously.

"Queen Parisa," King Adeyemi said, but it sounded more like a question. "Let us seet."

A servant offered her a glass of the too-sweet wine on a tray of hammered brass, and she picked it up gratefully and took a sip because she needed it. "Let me explain."

"I SEE," ADEYEMI SAID when she finished speaking. "I believe that I can allow Uwem to travel with you, but I cannot allow Prisce to go. It is much too dangerous."

"I agree," Yobachi said. "She is so young, and I simply cannot take that risk."

"So, I would travel alone with Prince Uwem?" Chokhmah's brow creased in confusion.

"Oh no!" the king said. "We would send along at least a couple of my best soldiers as well as a lady's maid for you. It would be inappropriate to travel otherwise."

Chokhmah released a breath she did not know she had been holding. "Thank you. That would be wonderful, but I will not need a lady's maid. I am accustomed to caring for my self."

"No," King Adeyemi said, frowning. "You do not understand. It would not be appropriate for a Queen and a woman to travel unattended by another woman. You know this."

Chokhmah nodded. Of course she did. Had she not noticed that Eluned had been travelling alone with Gwrhyr, Bonpo, and Jabberwock? One of the reasons she had joined the Quest in the first place was so that she could act as the Princess Eluned's maidservant. "You are right, of course," she demurred. "I will gladly accept your offer of a lady's maid."

Besides, she thought, a royal party of five or six should reach the River Spruce without trouble. She must stop there and speak with her brother, let him know all that had transpired and what she was doing, before she travelled on to Castle Mykerinos to deliver the Whetstone. From there, unless any of the other Questers had arrived before her, they would travel on to New Buta.

THREE DAYS LATER, on the 20th of Eahth, Chokhmah set out at dawn with Prince Uwem, two soldiers, and a lady's maid with a mule carrying their gear. The intent was to spend the night in hostels, travel shelters, and the occasional inn along the way.

Once again Chokhmah sat astride Halelu. She had left Faolan's big black horse, Fiachdubh, behind because she hoped he would eventually reach Mwezi-barafu. She could not quite put into words how deeply her heart yearned for his presence. It was a physical ache that occasionally brought tears to her eyes, which she would blink back furiously as crying would not return him to her.

Princess Prisce had cried and begged, but her parents had been unrelenting. Privately, Chokhmah had promised her, assuming all the Treasures had been gathered and peace returned to the Thirteen Kingdoms, that she would return to Mwezi-barafu when the Princess turned sixteen, or eighteen if her parents insisted the latter was too young. From there, they would set out on a journey to wherever Chokhmah's brother was camped, and she could experience life with the Roma, if she liked.

The Princess had grumbled that it wasn't as good as going on the Quest, but that it was better than being locked in Salama Palace until she was married off to one of the sons of King Adeyemi's lords.

On the morning they left the capitol, Chokhmah hugged Prisce farewell, and repeated her promise, before passing out of the city gates, and turning westward towards Zion. One soldier led the way while the other brought up the rear, flirting with the lady's maid. Prince Uwem rode in front of her, head held high, clearly feeling the importance of this mission.

"Your Highness?" Chokhmah called to him.

"Yes, your Highness?" he responded, grinning at her over his shoulder.

"I would like to learn how to speak Sheban."

20ᵗʰ Teeneh

Gwrhyr left Eluned and Xiang at the hostel to do laundry while he wandered off to see if he could suss out any information on Prince Aahil. His first order of business, though, was to find them a respectable hotel for the next few days.

It didn't take him long to discover that the lodging of choice for the gentry was the Anfa House, which was only a couple of blocks distant from Iqbal Palace. Gwrhyr decided to hurry straight there and book them rooms, if possible.

After securing suites for himself and his queen, as well as another for Princess Xiang, he began the slow and tedious process of getting people to spill what they knew about Prince Aahil. That meant he spent most of the remainder of the day in cafés, marketplaces, various public houses, and gambling dens.

"I was beginning to get worried," Eluned said when he finally made it back to the hostel late that afternoon.

"Obtaining information isn't easy," he said. "Are you and Xiang ready to go? We have rooms at Anfa House."

It wasn't long before they were handing off their horses to the hotel grooms, and settling into their rooms. Eluned hurried over to the window to check out the view. Anfa House was snuggled into the side of the plateau on which Iqbal Palace stood. From their bedroom window on the second floor of the hotel, she could see over the gleaming white buildings of the city all the way to the harbor and the Anoon Ocean beyond it. The sun was a blazing ball of orange hovering over the western horizon. Within the hour, darkness would fall, bringing with it the cooler temperatures of evening.

The room was still warm from the heat of the day. Pulling the gauzy curtains aside, Eluned opened the windows for the breeze it provided, before collapsing on the azure silk sofa that faced it. A round table of pale wood sat in front of the window, and she poured herself some wine from a terracotta pitcher that sat on a tray of hammered pewter, which also held a ewer of water.

Eluned sipped on the cool and citrusy white wine while waiting for Xiang to join them.

"I've had quite enough, thank you," Gwrhyr said, grimacing, when she offered him a glass, and opted instead for a tumbler full of chilled water.

"Nice room," she observed, looking back over her shoulder. Their large bed was canopied with netting, no doubt to be used as protection against mosquitos during the capitol's monsoon season. She eyed the bed with near lust—it had been a very long time since she had slept on a soft mattress, more than six weeks. The bunks on board The Black Cobra had been bare wood, and the cots at the hostel the previous night, not much better.

She glanced at her husband. It had been impossible to be alone on the ship, and the hostel had not been conducive to romance. But, the stresses of the day revealed itself in the drawn expression of his face and the pale purple smudges below his eyes. She put her hand over his and squeezed it. "I love you."

"I love you too, Fy Drysor," he leaned over to kiss her just as a knock sounded on their door. "Maybe later," he said, pulling away.

Putting down her glass, Eluned jumped up and hurried to the door so Gwrhyr wouldn't have to go to the trouble. She opened it to find the Princess standing there. "Come in! You can sit with us over by the window," she said, leading the way to the small sofa. "It's much cooler over here."

Gwrhyr stood and retrieved the chair from the writing desk that stood in the corner of the room, allowing Xiang to take his seat on the sofa. He set it down facing the sofa, and sat, wincing a little as he did so. It had been quite a while since he'd been on his feet that much. "So," he said, scratching his beard before scrubbing his face with his hand, "where to begin?"

"Why?" Eluned's eyes widened. "What did you find out?"

"Is it good or bad?" Xiang asked.

"As far as you're concerned," he said, "probably good. It turns out that Prince Aahil has a mistress."

Xiang rolled her eyes. "That's not surprising."

"For a single man who is thirty-eight," Gwrhyr said, "you're probably right. What's more surprising is that he has the full support of the King and Queen, and the couple even has a home together. Outside the palace, of course."

Eluned frowned. "That doesn't bode well for the future if he is to marry Xiang."

Gwrhyr shook his head. "Nor does the fact that they have two children."

It was Xiang's turn to frown. "I'm supposed to marry a man twenty-two years older than me that has a mistress and two children! How long have they been together?"

"From what I gather," Gwrhyr said, "Prince Aahil met her, Merieme, when he was twenty and she was eighteen. She was a courtesan in training for the Palace harem."

Xiang's face screwed up in disgust. "Iqbal Palace has a harem? A mistress is one thing, but a harem!"

"They've been together eighteen years," Eluned marveled. "By Omni, poor, what did you say her name is? Merieme?"

"Why?" Xiang's forehead creased in puzzlement.

"Because he has been with one woman for nearly half his life, and definitely half hers," Eluned explained. "Can you imagine knowing that the man you love and have children with is betrothed to someone else? How can she bear it?"

"Exactly," Gwrhyr said. "Especially knowing that in less than two years, she'll be relegated to second position, and that the new and royally-approved spouse will no doubt have children to compete with Aahil's love of hers."

"I wonder how he feels about this," Eluned said.

"That's what we need to find out," Gwrhyr said. "I say we make our way to their home first thing in the morning, unannounced. I think it would be advantageous for us to see him in his usual situation, particularly knowing that King Dodi and Queen Chahindra are unaware of our presence here. It might allow him to speak more freely."

"Fortunately tomorrow is Deethsadoorn," Eluned said, "so it's even more likely that he will be around."

"But," Gwrhyr said, standing up and carrying the chair back over to the desk, "that's tomorrow. Tonight, we eat in the Anfa House dining room, and I'm told their food is excellent. I hope you two don't mind eating before sunset. It's going to be an early night for me." He yawned, as if for emphasis.

"Not at all," Eluned assured him. "I don't know about Xiang, but we only had the remainder of what was left from last night's dinner . . ."

"Which wasn't much," Xiang interrupted. "I'm starving."

GWRHYR HADN'T BEEN MISLED. Almost as soon as they were seated, a servant appeared with a tray of various dips and salads, which they scooped up with pieces of flat bread. Eluned tried them all—green peppers and tomatoes, a purée of sweet carrots with a dish of local olives alongside, and a smoked eggplant dip, seasoned with garlic, paprika, cumin, and a little chili powder.

This was followed by fish marinated in herbs and spices before being grilled over hot coals along with a stew of lamb and vegetables served over a grain-like wheat pasta.

All of this was washed down with heavily sweetened mint tea.

Despite all the food, Eluned tried to eat sparingly. She didn't want to be too full to sleep, and more importantly, she didn't want to be so gorged by her meal that she had to beg off any physical activity. Because, she thought, smiling to herself as they returned to their rooms, if she knew her husband, he would have to be on his deathbed to forgo being intimate with her after so long.

THEY WERE BOTH IN MUCH HIGHER SPIRITS when they awoke the following morning.

"I'd almost forgotten what it felt like to feel your naked body against mine," Gwrhyr admitted, pulling her close.

"It was a long trip to Tartessos, wasn't it?" Eluned almost sighed, enjoying the sensation of his lips on her throat. The early days of exploring each other leading up to their marriage now seemed a distant memory. The Quest has certainly taken its toll, she thought, before Gwrhyr distracted her by kissing his way down her body.

About a quarter of an hour later they were interrupted by a knock on the door and someone saying loudly, "Your breakfast, Sir."

Fortunately, they'd been snuggling, contented in each other's arms, when the servant arrived. Gwrhyr rolled out of bed, pulling on the pajama pants he'd never put on the previous night. Eluned waited until he'd retrieved the tray bearing their coffee and an assortment of breakfast foods, including a rich soup of beans sprinkled with cumin and fresh bread that was a local favorite, before hurrying into the bathroom to freshen up and don her nightgown.

Gwrhyr had a mug of heavily creamed coffee awaiting her when she joined him on the sofa. He'd also opened the curtains so they might enjoy the view of Tartessos in the early morning light.

Leaning against him, eyes partly closed, she sipped on her coffee until she was awake enough to consider breakfast.

"Would you like to try the soup?" he asked, ladling some into a small bowl for her. "It's very good."

"Mmmm," Eluned agreed after taking a sip, and reaching for a slice of the fresh bread. After a second mug of coffee, Eluned was ready to prepare herself for their meeting with Prince Aahil, Merieme, and their two children.

"Do you know how old their children are?" she asked while brushing the tangles from her curls.

"I didn't ask," he said. "The question seemed too probing, but I got the impression they weren't toddlers. Young teenagers perhaps? Between ten and fourteen, maybe? They have been together a long time."

Nodding as she braided her hair into a long ponytail, Eluned glanced at the armoire. "I assume as this is a casual visit, the skirt and blouse I wore yesterday will be fine?"

"Yes," Gwrhyr said. "We'll save the formal wear for our visit to the palace."

"Hopefully, there will be a visit to the palace."

"I am certain there will be," he said. "Once Prince Aahil finds out there is royalty here from three of the Thirteen Kingdoms, he'll have a duty to inform his parents."

"Especially if he wants to break the betrothal."

When she was dressed, Eluned hurried to Princess Xiang's room to see how ready she was toward leaving.

"It looks as if you're prepared to go," Eluned said when Xiang opened the door.

"I am," Xiang said. "I was so nervous that I couldn't fall back asleep when I woke up before dawn."

"I'm sorry," Eluned said. "I don't blame you. Do you still want to do this?"

"What? Of course! Now more than ever."

"Then let's go," Eluned said, turning toward her room where Gwrhyr was waiting for them. It would definitely have made a difference to her if she had discovered that Gwrhyr had a mistress and children before she married him. She wasn't sure she could countenance that.

BECAUSE PRINCE AAHIL'S HOME was within half a mile of Anfa House, they decided to walk. The morning air was still cool against their skin, but the mood was subdued.

"What if," Eluned thought, glancing over at Xiang whose clenched jaw revealed her tension. "What if he refuses to break the betrothal? Can Xiang refuse to honor it? How would the Kings and Queens of Kamartha and Tarshish respond to that?" Eluned felt the butterflies take flight in her belly. She sent an arrow prayer to Omni, begging It to free Xiang from this horrible situation.

As a prince of Tarshish, Aahil's home was provided with a sentry at the gate, which blocked access to his home. But, Gwrhyr was prepared for this. While Eluned was fetching Xiang, he'd been writing a note. This he handed to the guard and asked him to take it to the Prince. If after reading the note, Aahil didn't want to see them, they would have their answer.

Less than a couple of minutes later, the gate swung open and the trio made the trip up the wide carriageway toward the house—a rambling structure painted the ubiquitous white surrounded by white washed walls bordered by gardens profuse with bougainvillea, prickly pear cacti, poppies, and agave.

A man of medium height, dark hair beginning to grey at his temples, hurried toward them. His tanned face reflected his concern—heavy brows nearly meeting in the middle as his forehead furrowed at the sight of them.

"Your Majesties," he said, bowing slightly when he reached them. "Princess Xiang?"

Xiang curtseyed politely, and smiled.

"Please," Aahil gestured towards the front door, "please come in. We were just finishing breakfast."

They followed him into his house and down a tiled hallway into a sitting room where several small couches circled a large round table. A number of books were scattered on the table and Eluned tried to see what they were, but most of them looked to be in the language of Tarshish, although there were a few in the Common Tongue.

Taking a seat with Gwrhyr on a couch covered in tan leather, Eluned waited for Xiang and Aahil to seat themselves. She had just opened her mouth to speak when she noticed movement by the door to the room. "Who's there?" she called. "Merieme is that you?"

Merieme peeked her head around the corner of the door.

"Please join us," Eluned said, indicating the couch where Prince Aahil sat looking very uncomfortable.

Hurrying over to the sofa, dark eyes wide with fear, Merieme settled herself next to the man she had known for nearly twenty years. At thirty-six, she was still an attractive woman. Her figure was voluptuous but not flabby, her thick black hair shone in the light that filtered through the translucent curtains. She was biting her full lower lip in anxiety, and her skin was probably paler than normal, Eluned thought, but she could definitely see what had attracted the young prince all those years ago.

"Where are the children?" Eluned asked, and Merieme blushed.

"I sent them to their rooms," she stuttered.

Eluned nodded, and immediately addressed the business

at hand. "We have a request to make of you," she paused. "Actually Princess Xiang has a request."

Xiang cleared her throat, and stood. She bowed slightly before saying, "Your Highness, I respectfully ask that we break our betrothal."

Merieme gasped as Aahil's eyes widened.

"I know that this is the second time that this has happened to you," Xiang hurried to say, "but clearly you have built something with Merieme that would be a shame to destroy. And I, I would like the chance to marry someone of my own choosing. This betrothal system may have served its purpose centuries ago, but the Thirteen Kingdoms are changing, and I think we should change with them." She paused again, nodded once, and sat.

Prince Aahil swallowed visibly, and Merieme took his hand and squeezed it. "It is true," he said, "that I would prefer to remain with Merieme, but what would happen should my brother, Boutros, die?"

"Personally," Eluned frowned, "I'd be happy to get rid of the whole patriarchal system, as well. Why couldn't Huda rule as Queen? And doesn't Boutros have a son?"

Aahil sighed, and nodded. "Yes, and he is well within age."

"I think it's time you stop making excuses," Merieme said quietly. "Your children would appreciate it as would I."

"But would my parents allow this marriage?" he wondered aloud.

"Does it matter?" Gwrhyr said.

"We might lose everything," he said to Merieme.

"We still have each other," she said. "Besides, do you really think your parents will allow Hicham and Shatha to suffer? Your mother adores them."

Aahil heaved a great sigh, and raised his hands before laughing. "All right, all right, I surrender. We will talk with my parents as soon as I can arrange an audience. It would help if we all were there."

"Besides," Gwrhyr said, "I have a special request to make of them."

"What is that?" Aahil asked.

"We would like to request that Tarshish host a meeting of the rulers of the Thirteen Kingdoms once all the Treasures are gathered. It is the only neutral Kingdom remaining."

"Other than Pelf," Aahil chuckled as if that Kingdom were a possibility.

"No," Gwrhyr said. "Just Tarshish."

THE AUDIENCE WITH THE KING AND QUEEN of Tarshish took place two nights later during a formal dinner at Iqbal Palace. Eluned and Xiang had their travel-crumpled formal wear freshly washed and pressed, and Gwrhyr had spent their free day with a tailor having clothing fit for a king made for him.

They may not have been wearing crowns, but the trio looked like royalty as they were escorted into the palace. Eluned was once again in her sea green silk dress embroidered with pale pink orchids, the mother of pearl orchid pinned in her hair. Xiang wore her silk gown of royal purple on which golden dragons danced across the fabric. An elaborate hair net of gold thread glittered with amethyst and pearls against her gleaming black hair.

Uriel's doublet of royal blue samite was interwoven with silver rampant lions. It fit snugly to just below his waist, and Eluned thought she'd never seen his eyes look so blue. Eluned found her breath catching in her throat at the way his black leather trousers clung to his muscular legs. She was still amazed at herself for it having taken so long to become aware of how attractive he was. It was probably just as well, she thought, because it had given her the chance to get to know him better first.

Eluned could hear the notes of a harpsichord tinkling from somewhere down the hallway along which they were walking. They were led into a music room in which Prince Aahil's sister, Huda, abruptly stopped playing the instrument and stood as a page announced their arrival.

Huda, whom Eluned knew to be forty, was a tall woman with large brown eyes, thin lips, and an aquiline nose. Her hands, Eluned noted immediately, were slender with long, thin fingers. Eluned smiled at her, and nodded, and she nodded back as King Dodi and Queen Chahindra stepped forward to greet them.

The King's silver hair swept back from his high forehead and revealed a deep widow's peak. Queen Chahindra's hair had been colored with henna, which meant hers had probably gone grey, as well. With children ranging from thirty-eight to forty-two that wasn't surprising.

"Eluned plays the harpsichord," Gwrhyr said, explaining why his wife had greeted the Princess before her parents.

"It has been a long time since I've heard harpsichord music," Eluned said. "You play beautifully, Princess Huda."

"Thank you, Queen Eluned."

Prince Boutros, his wife, and Huda's husband were introduced as was Princess Xiang, and then the grandchildren, before everyone took seats on the chairs and sofas that formed a makeshift circle on the left side of the room.

"Aahil assured us that we needed to make this meeting as casual as possible," King Dodi said.

"We could do this formally," Gwrhyr agreed, "but we would prefer this to be a friendly meeting. I think you and Princess Xiang should begin this," he said, looking at Aahil.

"Are you sure this is something you both want?" Queen Chahindra said when they were through explaining.

"Yes," Xiang said, "especially after seeing Prince Aahil with Merieme and their children. I want that, too, but not yet. And I want someone who will grow old with me and not likely to leave me a young widow."

"And King Zhang and Queen Ling approve of this?" King Dodi asked.

"They're going to be furious!" Xiang laughed. "But at me, not at you or Aahil. I understand that I am their only daughter and they wanted to do well by me, but I did not have a choice in this. I think Eluned is right. Things are changing, and it is time for the rulers of the Thirteen Kingdoms to begin to make changes as well."

"What will you do now?" Huda asked.

"I would like to travel with Eluned and Gwr, I mean Uriel, back to Zion, and then . . ." she trailed off, as they had yet to speak of the future meeting.

"Yes?" Boutros said.

"She stopped because we have a tremendous favor to request of you," Gwrhyr said.

"And what is that?" King Dodi asked.

"You are probably aware that we are gathering the Thirteen Hallowed Treasures?" Gwrhyr said.

Everyone murmured in assent.

"And that the Awen Alliance has already started terrorizing the Kingdom of Sheba? And, from what I've heard here in Tartessos, forays have been made into Zion, Aden, and Dyfed, as well?"

"Yes," he frowned, "and quickly stamped out by those kingdoms' armies, no doubt because Hevel was behind them."

"Hevel isn't known for his, uh, fortitude," Gwrhyr said, "when it comes to war. He probably did as little as he had to do just to convince Arawn and Hamartia he was still a part of their plan."

"Which is why Sheba still suffers," Boutros said.

"It is prophesied," Eluned continued, "that if all Thirteen Treasures are gathered, peace can once again be established."

"Yes?" Queen Chahindra said.

"We would like to ask your permission," Gwrhyr said, "as

Tarshish is still neutral, to have the rulers of the Thirteen King-doms meet here once all the Treasures are obtained."

"And you think Kings Arawn and Hamartia will agree to this?" King Dodi asked.

"We think that if King Arawn is challenged to a game of chess using the Chessboard of Gwenddolau," Gwrhyr said, "he won't be able to turn it down."

"And who would play him?" Boutros asked.

"Jabberwock," Eluned said. "We have every reason to be-lieve that he will defeat King Arawn."

"Why is that?" Huda asked.

"Because when we were in his Kingdom this past year," Eluned said, "he practiced his moves with Jabberwock."

King Dodi chuckled. "Ah, the legendary Janawar. And this Jabberwock no doubt allowed him to think he was the better player?"

Eluned smiled. "Exactly."

"This Kingdom still intends to remain neutral," King Dodi said, "But it does make sense for the game to take place here. We will make arrangements as soon as the Treasures are all obtained."

"In the meantime," Huda spoke up, "perhaps Queen Eluned will treat us to some music on the harpsichord."

19ᵀᴴ Teeneh

Chokhmah, along with her escort, reached the coastal seaport of Baharimto late on a sweltering midsummer day. Located at the eastern edge of Sheba at the River Mab's delta with the Anoon Ocean, it was to be the group's starting point for their journey westward to find the new Buta, or what remained of it.

Even though it was only midafternoon, Chokhmah told the group that she would prefer to find lodgings for the evening and begin the remainder of their journey in the morning. The truth was that she was already exhausted and the thought of riding another mile under the blazing summer sun made her want to break down in tears.

Daniel and Avigail were now among the number that had made the trek, first to Castle Mykerinos to drop off the Whetstone, then southward to Baharimto. They had insisted on joining the envoy heading to the coast when Chokhmah, Prince Uwem, and the others had arrived at the camp on the River Spruce.

Chokhmah felt sure her brother, Moshe, was behind the offer. The look on his usually grumpy face when she had informed him that Faolan had never made it to their rendezvous point in Simoon revealed everything—he had not been able to keep the pity from his eyes.

Fortunately, Daniel had been eager to be a part of the Quest from the beginning, and it was a chance for him to share in the adventure. As they were the first of the Questers to arrive back in Zion with a Treasure, they had only spent a few days regrouping before setting out for New Buta.

"Should Faolan arrive here while we are gone, please insist that he remain here until we return," she had requested of King Seraphim. "I will not be able to live with myself if he risks his life again following after us."

It was her worry over Faolan, and the stress of returning to the site of the slaughter of her family, that had left her feeling continually exhausted, weepy, and nauseated, Chokhmah reasoned. A cool bath and a good night's sleep on a decent mattress would do her a world of good, she thought, before asking Daniel if he could secure them rooms for the night.

While they waited beneath the shade of the spreading boughs of a giant oak tree on the outskirts of down, Daniel went in search of an inn.

"I found an inn at the crossroad with the road we will be taking out of town," he said when he returned an hour later.

"Perfect," Chokhmah said, stifling a yawn. "I can already feel the pillow beneath my head. A half hour later they were settling into their rooms at the Seaside Inn, which was actually a quarter mile from the Anoon Ocean.

Chokhmah closed the blinds on the room's one window that overlooked a sandy courtyard in which chickens clucked beneath the shade of a lone fir tree. She was interrupted by a tap at the door and opened it to find Avigail standing outside, biting her lip.

"Is something wrong, my dear?" Chokhmah asked.

"Actually, I came to ask the same of you," Avigail said.

"Me?"

"You have seemed so tired lately," Avigail said. "On my way here, I passed Bibi in the hall, and she said she was hurrying to the market to get you more ginger."

Chokhmah nodded. "The worry of not knowing whether or not Faolan is alive, along with the stress of whether or not we will find the Knife, is taking its toll."

"Ginger tea is for nausea," Avigail frowned. "Would not rosemary, lavender, or chamomile serve your nerves better?"

"I think, perhaps, that bouncing around on a horse all day has made me feel queasy," Chokhmah said. "Once we have the Knife, a major burden will be lifted, and I am sure that the nausea will subside then."

"If you are sure it is nothing more?" Avigail raised her eyebrows.

"My dear, what else could it be?"

"Then I will leave you to get your rest," Avigail said. "You know your body better than I do. We were just worried, but what you say makes sense."

"I will see you in the morning," Chokhmah said as she began to shut the door. "I have asked them to bring a tray to my room for dinner in case I am still sleeping at dinnertime."

"Rest well, Aunt Chokhmah," Avigail said before turning away from the door. Chokhmah could not see that she was frowning.

BECAUSE CHOKHMAH HAD BEEN UNSURE of the exact location of the former village of Buta, other than the fact it was more than twenty miles from Baharimto, they followed the coastline westward, stopping at each village to enquire whether it was or had once been Buta.

The sun reflecting off the Anoon Ocean was blinding when they reached yet another small fishing village shortly after middday, but they could make out several small huts tucked away in the shade provided by the oaks and firs atop the small rise that overlooked the ocean.

They were now more than twenty miles inland, and although she had yet to ask, Chokhmah felt in her bones that the cottages she saw before her had been built over the remains of her birthplace.

"May I help you?" a voice called in Sheban, and she turned to survey the beach where a man sat in the shade of a lean-to repairing a net.

Chokhmah dismounted, handed her reins to her maid, and nodded at Prince Uwem. She had understood the man, but her grasp of Sheban was still limited.

She and Uwem walked down to the beach where the man stood to greet them. He was tall, broad-shouldered, and shirtless. His arms and chest bulged with muscles, and his dark skin glistened like polished obsidian in the midday sun. He must spend many hours on the water hauling in nets filled with seafood, Chokhmah thought.

"I am Prince Uwem of Sheba," the Prince bowed slightly, "and this is Her Majesty, Queen Parisa of Pelf."

The man's eyes widened as sweat beaded his forehead. Bowing deeply, he said, "I thought . . ."

"You thought we had all been killed," Chokhmah said in the Common Tongue.

Swallowing hard, the man nodded.

Good, Chokhmah thought, he speaks the Common Tongue. That helps. "All but myself and my great aunt," she said. "Am I correct in assuming this is where Buta was located?"

"Yes, we call it Mjipya now."

Uwem glanced at Chokhmah, and back at the man. "Queen Parisa was nineteen months old when the massacre occurred," he said. "You seem at least ten years younger than her if not more."

"I was not around for the massacre," the man admitted, "I am the son of my father's last wife. I am only twenty-eight."

"Why is that significant?" Chokhmah said, brow creasing in consternation. "That you are the son of your father's last wife?"

The man shuffled his feet and cleared his throat, clearly embarrassed. "I am Zuberi," he finally spoke. "I am the youngest son of Khalfani."

"Ah," Chokhmah said. The man responsible for destroying Buta. "Is he still alive?"

"Yes he is," Zuberi said, "but he is very old, and his memory is not so good as it once was. Also, he is feeble. He must use a cane to walk."

"Is it possible for us to speak with him?" Uwem said.

"May I ask to what purpose?" Zuberi said. "To demand an apology from him? Have him make restorations?"

"No," Chokhmah said, caught off guard as she was focused only on the Treasure. "Nothing can change what happened then. What I am interested in is a family relic. It would be nice to have that returned, if possible."

"A relic?" Zuberi asked.

"Something that has been handed down in our family for centuries, a knife," Chokhmah said.

"Do you know what it looks like?"

"Sadly, no."

Zuberi frowned in thought. "I do not recall a knife. We must ask my father. Perhaps he will remember such a knife." He glanced up to where the rest of the party waited at the top of the slope.

"Do not worry," Chokhmah said, voice soothing. "We do not need lodging. We have our own tents and food."

Zuberi nodded, and pointed to the huts beneath the trees. "My father does not live here. He still lives on his cattle farm in Mifugo. Let me tell my wife that I am leading you there."

ZUBERI APPEARED ABOUT A QUARTER OF AN HOUR later clad in a clean pair of trousers and a rough spun shirt of bleached white cotton although he was still barefoot. One of the soldiers offered to let Zuberi ride with him but Zuberi said he preferred walking. Mifugo was a couple of miles inland from the ocean, and a little under an hour later, the group arrived in the village.

"Now Mifugo is mostly inhabited by my father's children, grandchildren, and great-grandchildren," Zuberi said. "At the time of the massacre, there were more families here, but many of the men involved have since died or moved away. The attack has left a pall, a curse, over this village ever since."

"Is that why you moved to Mjipya?" Chokhmah asked.

"In part," Zuberi said. "Also, I was not interested in herding cattle. I have always loved the sea." The fisherman led them to an open shelter with a thatched roof, underneath which were a number of tables and benches.

"You may wait here," he said, "and I will go see if my father is in a condition to meet with you."

While the soldiers secured their mounts to a hitching post, Bibi set about making them all tea. Chokhmah, Uwem, Daniel, and Avigail settled at one of the tables.

"Do you think he will meet with us?" Daniel asked.

Uwem snorted, sounding more like a teenager than a prince. "He has no choice."

"What do you mean?" Avigail asked, readjusting the scarf that kept the sun from scorching the top of her head.

"I was always surprised that my grandfather never imposed any sort of penalty on Khalfani or the other men involved in the massacre," Uwem mused. "And I think my father has seen a certain irony in the attacks on our people by the Awen Alliance. Did our failure to allow such an atrocity to go unpunished make us seem a weaker kingdom to that Alliance?"

"Perhaps," Chokhmah agreed. "Had the Kingdom of Sheba stood up for its own citizens at the time, then King Arawn may have thought twice about ordering the attacks he and the other kings have been making."

"I agree," Uwem said, "and that is why Khalfani must now answer for what he did, even if it is only to relinquish anything he stole from the Pelfans."

Bibi had just served their tea when Zuberi reappeared. "He would like to speak with Queen Parisa alone if that is permitted."

Chokhmah looked longingly at her tea, she could really use it, she thought, gritting her teeth against the nausea. She glanced up to see Avigail staring at her intently. "Does he speak the Common Tongue?" she asked Zuberi, wondering why her niece was studying her.

"I am afraid not," Zuberi admitted.

"Then I will need Prince Uwem as a translator," she said, "but I think he also needs to see that I have the support of the royal family."

"He knows," Zuberi's voice was somber. "When I told him who was here, he broke down. 'I always knew this day would come,' he told me."

"Is he all right?" Chokhmah asked.

"I assured him that you were only searching for a relic although I did not tell him what it is," Zuberi said. "I assumed that you preferred to speak to him about that?"

"Yes, thank you," Chokhmah said. "I may not know what it looks like, but I am sure that I will know it when I see it." The truth was she still was not sure that she could trust this man who had had her entire family murdered. He might be repentant or he might not.

But when she and Prince Uwem were taken inside the small hut Khalfani shared with whichever wife was caring for him at the time—he had four wives, one of whom had predeceased him—she realized she had no reason to doubt his sincerity.

Zuberi had said his father was feeble, but the man was nearly insubstantial. Skeletally thin, his clothes hung on his body. What little hair remaining on his head glowed white in the semi-darkness of the hut. His face was deeply wrinkled although Chokhmah could see that Zuberi shared his facial structure, and the same broad, flat nose.

Even his skin looked more ashy than the nearly black it must once have been.

"I would stand up," he said in Sheban, his voice dry and creaky with age, "but I can no longer stand on my own."

Prince Uwem translated for Chokhmah before asking, "May we sit?"

Khalfani chuckled and coughed before answering. "You do not need my permission for anything."

Chokhmah and Uwem seated themselves on a low sofa on the opposite side a long narrow table in front of Khalfani's rocking chair.

"Zuberi says you are looking for a relic?" he asked once they were settled on the sofa. Uwem was just repeating this in the Common Tongue when Khalfani's youngest wife, clearly Zuberi's mother, entered with a tray of heavily milked and sweetened tea.

Chokhmah had learned enough Sheban that she was able to graciously thank the woman for the tea, but was lost when she spoke to her rapidly in return. Chokhmah looked at Uwem, eyes wide, and the Prince laughed and explained that Hema, as she was called, had called for the village to prepare a celebratory dinner in their honor for that evening.

And while she did not feel particularly like celebrating, Faolan's fate still weighing heavily on her mind, Chokhmah did understand that it would be considered rude not to accept the hospitality being offered. Once more she thanked Hema, who bowed to Chokhmah and Uwem now that her tray was empty, before leaving the room.

"So, this relic," Chokhmah began, "is actually a knife that has been in our family for centuries."

As Uwem translated what the Queen had said, Khalfani's face seemed to turn even more ashen. His voice was shaky as he replied. "I have not thought of that knife in more than forty years."

"Do you still have it?" Chokhmah asked, heart beginning to thud against her ribs. What if he had discarded it?

"I almost buried it," Khalfani said, "and then I considered burning it. I felt it was cursed."

"Why?" Prince Uwem asked.

"One of my sons scratched himself with it and died a few weeks later from poisoned blood," Khalfani explained. "After that, whenever I tried to use it something bad would happen—people and animals would get sick or die. Even food seemed to rot beneath its touch."

Because it was obtained through evil means, perhaps, Chokhmah thought, but said in Sheban, "Is it still in your possession?"

"Hema!" Khalfani called, his voice more of a croak than a shout.

"Yes, my husband?" she asked, entering the room drying her hands on a dishtowel.

"You know where my chest is, yes?"

"It is beneath the bed," she said, and turned to Chokhmah. "I must dust around it as it is too heavy for me to move."

After Uwem translated for Chokhmah, Khalfani asked him, "Could you help Hema retrieve it?"

A few minutes later they returned, Uwem carrying a chest covered in cracked leather that looked to be a few feet long and a third as high. Uwem lowered it onto the table with a grunt.

"He was not kidding," he said under his breath to Chokhmah, "it is very heavy."

Khalfani looked at Chokhmah, "Can you open it?"

A large brass padlock prevented her from accessing the chest. "Do you have a," she paused trying to remember the word in Sheban, "key? Is that right?"

"Ah, yes, I am forgetting the key." He fished a chain out of his pocket upon which several keys were hanging. Khalfani selected one and handed it to Chokhmah.

The tumblers turned easily and the lock popped open.

"Hema keeps the lock oiled for me," he explained, "although I have not opened the chest in many years."

Chokhmah removed the padlock and pushed back the top of the chest. It was filled to the brim.

"My share of the plunder," Khalfani said, his voice barely a whisper.

Staring at the silverware, jewelry, and other items that filled the chest, Chokhmah felt her eyes begin to sting with tears. This, and what the other men had kept, was all that remained of her family's possessions. She choked back a sob. So little, too little, to account for the lives that had been lost. These objects and Chokhmah, herself, were all that remained of the royal line of Pelf.

Perhaps that is a good thing, she mused, finally pulling her eyes away and looking up to see Khalfani watching her, tears sliding down his cheeks and into his sparse white beard. Her father, and the generations before him, had insisted on keeping the bloodline of the royal family of Pelf as pure as possible. To do this, they had been forced to keep themselves separated from the other residents of Sheba, to intermarry among themselves.

Segregation was not the answer, Chokhmah thought. Perhaps if her father, the final King Alborz, had agreed with Khalfani and become a part of, and intermingled with, the Kingdom of Sheba, things would be much different today.

"What you did was wrong," she said. "But, what my father did was wrong, as well."

"Please take it all," Khalfani said, pointing to the chest. "After my son died, the loot became anathema to me. I kept it as a reminder that I carry the weight of a terrible transgression. My only prayer is that Omni will forgive me. I pray you will forgive me as well."

Uwem translated and waited for Chokhmah's response.

"That Omni will forgive you, I have no doubt," Chokhmah said. "It always forgives the repentant, and Omni loves you despite what you did. That I believe with all my heart. As for me, I only learned about my heritage within the past year, and never had any real grief to associate with my past. It is sad, of course, but I did not grow up hating the person who did this to my family and cannot bring myself to do so now."

Khalfani began to weep even harder after Uwem translated what Chokhmah had said. "I do not deserve your forgiveness," he said, "but I thank you for your compassion."

Chokhmah nodded, and turning to the Prince, said, "And now I must see if the knife is in here. It is the most important thing." She began removing what was in the chest, placing the items on the floor. At the very bottom of the box, she found a knife with a forged steel blade and a handle of ebony wood, and her heart skipped a beat as she withdrew it from the chest.

The wood had once, no doubt, been polished and oiled to glossiness. But, after years in the box, the dark wood was dusty and dry and cracking in several places. It was the design that was inset into the wood on either side of the handle that assured her she had found the Knife of Llawfrodded the Horseman. Set into the handle was an embellishment that clearly some past ancestor had added to the otherwise plain knife. An oval of red enamel gleamed through the dust. Chokhmah rubbed the dirt away with her thumb to reveal the black kraken that swam upon its surface—the sigil of the Kingdom of Pelf.

"Is that it?" Khalfani's voice interrupted her study of the knife.

Chokhmah released a breath she had not realized she had been holding. "Yes," she said. "Eleven of the Thirteen Treasures." Her gaze returned to the knife. And if Eluned and Gwrhyr had obtained the Cauldron, and Yona and Njima, the Horn of Bran, she thought, the Quest would be over and they could return to their normal lives. What that would mean for her, she did not know. Would Faolan be a part of it? She wanted to jump up and head back to Castle Mykerinos immediately. What if he were there?

"Do you have any children, Queen Parisa?" Khalfani asked, once again intruding on her thoughts.

"Children? No, I am afraid not," she looked up, and smiled sadly. It had been a little more than nine weeks since she last menstruated, she realized.

Chokhmah stared at the knife in her hand, mind racing. She had thought the nausea she had been experiencing was caused by the stress of not knowing the fate of the man she loved, of the journey back to her birthplace and the site of the slaughter of her people. She had blamed her easy tears on those things as well.

It took every ounce of her strength not to place a hand over her belly. *Avigail had figured it out. It cannot be, can it? I thought I was too old. I thought I was barren.* She took a deep breath and smiled at Khalfani. "Let us part as friends rather than enemies," Chokhmah said. "This Quest is an effort to bring peace back to the Thirteen Kingdoms. I believe the best place to begin that process is here. Do you not agree, Prince Uwem?"

"I do," Uwem stood, and extended his hand to Khalfani. "May we live in peace."

"Amen," Khalfani said, as Chokhmah rose and walked over to his rocking chair to give him a kiss on his grizzled cheek.

THE FOLLOWING DAY, Chokhmah was among the first to arise. Unlike the others, she had grown tired early and wandered off to her tent to get some sleep, but not until after she had a heart to heart talk with Avigail.

"Do you think it is possible?" Chokhmah had asked her after pulling her aside.

"You are acting just like my sister-in-law during the first few months of her pregnancy," Avigail had said. "I cannot tell you how many mugs of ginger tea she drank and was still sick as a dog. Have you been vomiting?"

Chokhmah had shaken her head. "Just really nauseated. And so tired."

"And weepy?"

"And nothing smells or tastes right."

Avigail had laughed. "You are pregnant. Take my word for it. Surely you know the signs as well as I do?"

"I truly thought I was barren." But if I am not, she had thought, standing and giving Avigail a hug, then I have the right to pamper myself. Saying her goodnights, she wandered back to her tent. She could blame the exhaustion on the pregnancy and her age, but what she really wanted was some time alone to think about this revelation. She prayed to Omni that Faolan was still alive as the chance to be a father would make him so happy. But if he was not there when she returned, at least she would have his child. A wolf child, she smiled to herself, because, as Faolan would say, the 'curse' was patrilineal.

Chokhmah was happily sipping her tea, having pulled a bench out of the shelter so she could feel the warmth of the rising sun before it became too hot to bear, when Daniel and Avigail joined her.

"The water is still hot," she pointed to the kettle sitting at the edge of the fire pit, "it should not take long to return to a boil."

"Ginger tea?" Avigail sat down next to her as Daniel returned the kettle to the fire.

"Ginger tea," Chokhmah replied.

"It has really helped with the nausea," Chokhmah told Daniel who was looking at her, eyebrows raised. "I have yet to be sick. What is it Eluned says? Omni willing and the moon doth rise, I will remain well."

"Are you happy?" Daniel asked, sitting down on the other side of his aunt.

"Happy but terrified," Chokhmah answered. "It is still early and I am forty-six. There is much that can go wrong."

"Well," Avigail said, "Omni willing and the moon doth rise, nothing will go wrong and what? Seven months from now?"

"About that," Chokhmah agreed.

"You will give birth to a healthy child," Avigail finished.

"Do you have a preference?" Daniel asked, standing and removing the teapot from the fire.

"I cannot honestly say that I do," Chokhmah said. "I think either a boy or a girl would be wonderful as long as the child is healthy."

"Well, you are to take it easy for the next two days as we prepare for the return trip," Daniel said, filling his and his wife's mugs with boiling water. "From now on you are to do as little as necessary. I do not want to answer to Faolan should something go wrong."

"Let us just pray he is there when we return," Chokhmah said.

"Oh, he will be." Daniel returned to the bench. "I am sure of it."

16ᵀᴴ Teeneh

After reading the paragraph for a third time, and realizing he still hadn't paid attention to a word he'd read, Faolan tossed the novel on the table next to the couch he reclined on. He had never been one to read for entertainment, he would prefer to be physically active. But as the only Quester at Castle Mykerinos, not to mention the state of his leg, he had nothing to do but waste time. Alone.

King Seraphim and Queen Ceridwen stayed busy though they made time to check on him at least once a day. And they had even invited him to dine with them, but he felt awkward and took his meals in the sitting room, instead. Faolan tried to read to make time pass, but mostly he found himself fretting about Chokhmah and how she was doing and where she might be.

There was a double rap on the door. Bryn. He'd had two weeks to grow accustomed to the young page's knock. "Come in," he shouted managing to make it sound more like a threat than an invitation.

The door opened and the clatter of nails on tile could be heard as a familiar sonorous voice said over the sound of Bryn shutting the door behind him, "What are you so grumpy . . . Oh." Jabberwock caught sight of Faolan's right leg, splinted, wrapped in bandages and elevated on the arm of the sofa. Beyond that his head, face gaunt, the lines around his eyes and mouth deeper, frowned at him from where it was propped on the arm at the other end.

"Where's Bonpo?" Faolan asked. Had the yeti gone back to his inn? Abandoned the Quest? Taken a chance and returned to Dziron?

"Where's Chokhmah?" Jabberwock countered. Seeing the Shapeshifter's condition, he expected the worst. "What happened?"

The door opened and King Seraphim and Queen Ceridwen entered.

"Jabberwock," Seraphim said. "You made it back?"

"Where is Bonpo?" Ceridwen asked. It was impossible to miss the giant's presence in the small sitting room.

"Where's Chokhmah?" Jabberwock persisted. He wasn't ready to talk about the fate of Shangshung.

"She seems convinced the Knife of Llawfrodded is in the former Buta in the Kingdom of Sheba," Seraphim said.

Jabberwock's brow creased in confusion.

"She had a dream," Seraphim explained. "So she, along with her nephew and his wife, Prince Uwem of Sheba, and some soldiers, are travelling there to see if they can find it."

"I missed her by less than four days." Faolan groused.

"It's not as if you could have travelled with them," Ceridwen admonished him.

"I know," Faolan sighed, "but at least she'd know I'm alive. That's what galls me. By my calculations, they should be arriving there by this weekend. They've been gone more than three weeks."

"Jabberwock?" Seraphim asked. The little creature looked stricken—eyes wide and glazed, mouth pulled tight in a grimace exposing his sharp and crooked teeth.

Shaking his head rapidly as if he were ridding it of water, Jabberwock returned his attention to the group before him. "Of course," he choked, cleared his throat and tried again. "But of course King Alborz would have sent the Knife with his wife and children. Why had that not occurred to me?"

"What happened to Bonpo?" Faolan asked again. It couldn't have been good, he thought, there had been a note of deep sadness in Jabberwock's voice.

"You might want to sit down," he told the King and Queen before jumping onto an armchair and settling down.

FAOLAN WAS BLINKING BACK THE TEARS from his eyes, finger-nails slicing crescent moons into his palms they were clenched so hard, when Jabberwock finished his story. He had vowed to himself since the incident in Kamea that he wouldn't cry in front of his friends again. But Bonpo dead? He just couldn't fathom it.

King Seraphim was pacing the room, eyes blazing, "Something has to be done about this," he raged. "We cannot have a Kingdom assassinating every one who approaches their city. It's unconscionable."

"Perhaps once we've united all the Treasures," Jabberwock sighed, "we can figure out a way to sort this out. It's my hope we can do away with Alliances and once again unite as the Thirteen Kingdoms."

"I should hope so," Seraphim said, "as the death toll has risen to nearly a thousand since the attacks began last spring."

"At this point," Faolan said, voice subdued as he tried to take in what had happened to Bonpo, "we are still missing the Knife, the Horn, and the Cauldron."

"And no word from Eluned or the others?" Jabberwock asked.

Silence.

Queen Ceridwen stood. "I still have some things that I need to see done," she said. "I must leave you now. I'm sure

Faolan has yet to tell you how he ended up in his condition." She nodded a question at Faolan who curtly nodded back.

"Would you care to join us for dinner tonight?" King Seraphim asked, heading toward the door.

Jabberwock glanced over at Faolan. Clearly the man was spending most of his time in this room—it had the look and scent of being lived in. Jabberwock guessed that getting upstairs would be difficult. But what he mostly sensed was that Faolan was lonely and could use some company. "I think I'll share dinner with Faolan tonight, if you don't mind."

"I'll have Bryn let the kitchen know," Ceridwen said, and left the room, followed by her husband.

"Well," Jabberwock said, making himself more comfortable in the armchair, "let's hear how you and Chokhmah managed to get the Whetstone."

"And so we left Ebbe's separately," Faolan continued his tale, "me in my wolf form and Chokhmah made invisible by the ring. It was supposed to be so simple. I was going to run north through the forest until I was well away from Sigwald. When I felt I was far enough from the city, I was going to head west toward the main road, cross it when no one was around, and meet her at the clearing. I thought I would get there before her."

"What happened?" Jabberwock asked.

"I was so intent on getting to the clearing," Faolan said, "that I wasn't paying enough attention to the ground I was running over." He paused. "It was a trap. Probably a bear trap as there are few wolves left in Simoon. Anyway, when I had recovered from the shock enough to think logically, I realized I was going to have to shift into my human form in order to remove the trap from my leg."

"The pain must have been intense," Jabberwock said, baring his teeth at the thought of it.

"You have no idea," Faolan said, "and worse, I had nothing with which to splint or bandage it. I had to shift back into a wolf and limp to the clearing. It took me twice as long as it should have."

"It must have taken a great deal of willpower," Jabberwock murmured in sympathy.

"I reached the road that night just as Hamartia's soldiers were entering the woods," he continued. "I had to wait until they returned before I could get back on the path. By then, it was after dawn. I don't know how far they rode down the trail before they turned back but it must have been miles."

A knock on the door interrupted them.

"Come in, Bryn," Faolan called.

The boy entered with a tray.

Jabberwock wrinkled his nose. "Is that?"

"Garlic," Faolan said. "The castle's healer, whom I'm positive isn't as good as Chokhmah, insists that this will prevent the infection I arrived here with from returning."

Bryn placed the tray, which also held an empty bowl along with pitchers of water and wine, on the table.

"Thanks, Bryn," Faolan said, and the boy bobbed his head, and retreated from the room.

Faolan spooned a mouthful of the mixture of chopped meat and garlic into his mouth and chewed, grimacing a bit as he did so. After swallowing, he said. "Actually, I didn't mean that about the healer. Both she and the healer I had in Mwezibarafu were excellent at what they did. It's just they both seemed to lack Chokhmah's gift for, I don't know, empathy?"

Jabberwock nodded as Faolan choked down the rest of his garlic mash and then washed it down with several long swallows of wine.

"Needless to say," Faolan finally continued, "by the time I got to the clearing, she was gone, and I was faced with a serious problem."

"Whether to continue as a man and splint the break or as a wolf and limp?" Jabberwock asked.

"It really needed splinting," Faolan said, "and yet I travelled faster as a wolf."

"I would imagine it's also easier to hide as a wolf."

"But difficult to hunt with three legs," he said.

"So?"

"I remained a wolf," Faolan said. "When I reached the gorge that divides Simoon from Sheba, I realized there wasn't anyway I was going to be able to manage it so I had to follow the chasm southward until it was shallow enough for me to cross before I reached the main road."

"I'm going to guess that you were not only starving, but an infection had taken hold by that point. I don't see how you could've avoided it."

"I did get lucky at the gorge," Faolan said. "Chokhmah apparently dumped all the food and other things she wouldn't need, so I ate what was still edible. Then I shifted into my human form for a moment so I could fold my cloak in such a way that I could carry it in wolf form. It was annoying, but I knew I'd need it when I got to the main road in Sheba." Faolan stopped and refilled his mug with wine.

"Pain killer," he mock toasted and took another long swallow. "Yes, I was really sick by the time I got to the main road. Fortunately, I was able to get a ride on a cart all the way to the palace. I don't even remember what was in it or even getting there. The next thing I knew I was in a bed with my leg in a splint. I was in and out of consciousness for a few days, but once the fever passed, I soon felt well enough to get back on the road. I left a week after I got there."

He paused staring into the distance for a little while before continuing. "Unfortunately," he sighed, "the bone had begun to heal without being set back together perfectly. I'm going to have a limp for the rest of my life."

"But you're alive," Jabberwock said.

"I'd rather not be if Chokhmah doesn't make it back," his voice cracked. "It was easier getting back to Castle Mykerinos on Fiachdubh, but it took a lot out of me and I pretty much had to start the healing process all over again once I got here. But as far as I'm concerned it will all have been for nothing if I don't see her again."

"How long before the cast comes off?"

"Another four to six weeks," Faolan frowned at his leg.

"So likely before Chokhmah gets back."

Faolan finally smiled. "It would be nice to be able to greet her standing."

Jabberwock snorted. "In my experience, you two won't be standing for long."

THE FOLLOWING DAY, as Faolan had made it two weeks without a relapse, the healer announced that he was well down the road to healing, and not only did he no longer need the garlic mash anymore, but suggested he spend some time getting some fresh air in one of the castle's numerous courtyards.

"What I'd really like," Faolan told Jabberwock as he settled into a reclining chair in front of a small pool fed by water gushing from the mouth of a marble fish, "is to be able to shift back into a wolf again." He studied the fish darting amongst the water lilies for a moment. "Two months is really pushing it for me. I may not be able to wait that long."

"I take it that can't happen until the cast is removed?"

"Yes," he grunted as Bryn helped him hoist his leg onto a couple of pillows. "Thanks, Bryn."

"Your welcome, Sir. Be there anything else you need?"

"No, we're fine for now. I'll ring the bell if I need something."

Faolan and Jabberwock were dozing in the morning sunshine, when Bryn rushed back into the courtyard, eyes wide with excitement, less than an hour later.

"Sir! Sir!" he shouted, startling Faolan into knocking the bell from the small table at his side. The bell crashed to the tiles with a loud clang.

"By Omni, what was that?" a familiar voice said.

"Yona?" Faolan turned to look at the entrance. Jabberwock jumped from his perch on the ledge of the fountain and trotted over to meet them.

"Praise be to Omni! You've returned!" he said, as Yona crouched to give him a hug.

"And Njima!" Faolan laughed as the Queen stepped into the courtyard. Yona hurried over to embrace him.

"Where's Chokhmah?" Yona stepped back to take in his broken leg and his emaciated frame. "Is she . . .?"

"She's fine," Faolan assured her. "At least, as far as we know."

"As far as you know?" Njima repeated, but Faolan was scowling at the two boys standing behind her.

Njima glanced over her shoulder, and Yona quickly said, "I'm so sorry. Faolan, Jabberwock, let me introduce Princess Dev of Kamartha and Boaz of Ravensfield."

"Princess?" Faolan was still scowling.

"Prince, if you prefer," Dev stepped forward and extended her hand.

Faolan smiled, transforming his face into something more approachable. Taking her hand, he said, "Pleased to make your acquaintance, Your Highness."

"This so exciting!" Dev exclaimed. Turning to Jabberwock, she asked, "Where's the giant?"

"You tell them," Jabberwock said, heading back into the castle. "I'll go get Seraphim and Ceridwen."

"I'm going to have to leave for Jazeel in a few days," Queen Njima informed King Seraphim when they were at dinner that evening. He was sitting to her right at the head of the table.

"So soon?" Queen Ceridwen, who was sitting across the table from her, asked.

"I'm afraid so," Njima said. "I've been away from my Kingdom for far too long, and we don't know when Eluned will be back, and if Faolan is correct, it will be another month before Chokhmah returns."

"I'm sorry to hear it," Seraphim said, "but I understand. I imagine Uriel is feeling disconnected, as well. He's been gone from his Kingdom for more than six months."

Njima winced. "I pray that all is going well there."

"It is," King Seraphim said. "I've been keeping in touch with his Lord Chancellor by pigeon. But, as you know, it is preferable to be there."

"I will leave this weekend with Boaz," Njima said. "We feel it will be safer to split up as we know spies are on the lookout for us. Yona will leave a few days later with Dev."

Faolan, who had been relegated to the other end of the table because he needed an extra chair to support his leg, was pouting. "So, it will be just me and Jabberwock again?"

"We haven't even had a full day together yet!" Jabberwock protested. "Is my company that abhorrent?"

All eyes turned to Faolan and he found himself blushing. "I didn't mean it the way it sounded. I was worried that Jabberwock would feel himself burdened with me since I'm pretty much useless until this cast comes off."

"I was talking to the healer today," Jabberwock said, "and when pressed, he told me he thought you might be able to start walking a little more each day starting next week."

Faolan forced a smile. The least he could do was try. Raising his wine glass, he toasted, "To working legs!"

YONA AND BOAZ, NJIMA AND DEV were on their way back to Jazeel, and the castle was once again settling into its normal routine. Faolan, using the crutches that had been made for him, and Jabberwock found a courtyard in which they could avoid the direct rays of the midsummer sun by sitting beneath the branches of a red maple tree.

"I can't wait until this weekend," Faolan sighed as he settled his cast on the now ubiquitous pillow.

"I don't blame you," Jabberwock said. "It'll be nice to trade that heavy cast for something lighter."

"It'll be even nicer to be able to shift into a wolf," Faolan said, "Even if it's only for a little while."

They were silent for a moment, enjoying the light breeze that made the leaves of the tree dance above them.

"It's Queen Fuchsia's birthday today," Jabberwock mused, "which means that it's my birthday, as well. I'm sure Eluned had planned to celebrate it with me."

"She does love to make merry, doesn't she?"

"Just like her great-grandmother. I wish we'd hear from them. I'm starting to get worried."

"They have been gone longer than any of us," Faolan agreed.

King Seraphim appeared in the courtyard and hurried over to where they were sitting, face beaming joy.

"What is it?" Jabberwock scrabbled to his feet.

"A pigeon!" he exclaimed. "From Eluned!"

"What?" Jabberwock's voice rose an octave. "Are they are all right?"

"They're fine. They're in Tartessos."

"Tartessos?" Faolan frowned, remembering his time there. "Why are they in Tartessos?"

"The note doesn't say much," King Seraphim said, "as you can only fit so much on a pigeon's leg. It says: In Tartessos with Princess Xiang. Treasure in hand. Leaving 26 Teeneh for Zion. All our love, Eluned."

"That's tomorrow," Faolan said.

"Leave it to Eluned to be cryptic," Jabberwock said. "Princess Xiang, huh? They must be there to break the betrothal. Now, we'll have to wait a little more than a month before finding out what happened."

"That should be early Meen," Faolan said. "Chokhmah should be back by then. If I know her, she's going to want to wait until they arrive before returning to Bogaine."

King Seraphim was shaking his head, and chuckling. "Two kings," he said. "There are two kings in the Awen Alliance who have daughters with ties to the Triquetra Alliance. That may also work in our favor."

"I spent a lot of time talking to Dev," Faolan said. "She, or maybe I should say he, didn't seem the least bit interested in returning to Kamartha."

"Oh, Dev is definitely comfortable in her new life," Jabberwock agreed, then laughed, "and that wasn't even Eluned's doing."

"If it had been her instead of Yona and Njima," Seraphim said.

"The same result," Faolan finished for him.

THREE MORE WEEKS PASSED and Castle Mykerinos practically shimmered in the late summer heat. They had received a note by pigeon a couple of days earlier that Queen Njima and Boaz had arrived safely in Jazeel, and Chokhmah and her party were expected at any moment.

Faolan's cast had finally been removed the previous weekend, and he was now in the outer courtyard forcing himself to walk and re-strengthen the muscles that had lost their tone after so many weeks of disuse.

Just keep putting one foot in front of the other, he thought. But, it was really more of a drag than a step—step with the left leg, drag the right leg forward. But he had to do this, he thought, because he couldn't go for a run outside of Goshen until his 'fourth' leg was strong enough.

He had just made it back to the castle's main entrance when there was a commotion at the barbican. He turned around to see what was going on, and saw that a party of at least half a dozen horsemen were entering the courtyard.

No, he stopped, frozen in place. He'd recognize that horse anywhere. He looked up to see Chokhmah on Halelu's back. She hadn't seen him yet.

"My soul!" he cried out. He had convinced himself he'd never see her again. That truth must have been the same for her, he saw, because first she went pale and then she was sliding off her horse and hurrying across the courtyard towards him.

He limped toward her and soon they were in each other's arms.

"Oh my love," Chokhmah was weeping, "I was so afraid I would never see you again."

Faolan was now too choked up to do anything but hold her tightly against him, face buried in her neck. The embrace lasted long enough that Prince Uwem, Daniel, and Avigail, having handed off their horses to the castle's groomsmen, smiled at each other as they passed the couple.

Finally, Chokhmah pulled back and cradling Faolan's face in her hands, said, "I have news."

Later, when they were alone in their room, and Chokhmah had washed the grime of the road off her travel-weary body, she asked Faolan to join her on the small sofa in front of the fireplace, empty now in late summer.

"Remember I said I had news?" she asked, taking his hands in hers.

He nodded, staring into the amber eyes he thought he might never see again.

Chokhmah took a deep breath and released it. "I spent the entire trip back trying to think of a clever way to say this, but now that I am here . . ."

"You're scaring me," Faolan said, his heart beginning to race. "Just tell me."

Chokhmah bit her lip, praying he would take this as well as she hoped. "You are going to be a father."

Faolan stared at her for a moment, jaw slack and eyes wide with incomprehension. "I, uh, you're pregnant?"

"Yes, my love. I am more than three months along."

"And it's safe? You can do this?"

"I believe so," she said. "So far, everything seems to be normal."

Faolan pulled her into his arms. "I never dreamed that I would be allowed to be this happy. I'm almost afraid to believe it."

Chokhmah chuckled. "Well believe it my love. You are going to have a little wolf cub of your own."

More than two weeks had passed, and Faolan was still so happy about being reunited with Chokhmah and the impending birth of their child, that he walked with a spring in his step albeit an odd little jigged spring because of his limp. He wanted to return to Bogaine so desperately it nearly took his breath away. If they waited too long, then Chokhmah wouldn't be able to travel back to their home, Rose Cottage, to give birth. And for her to give birth on the farm that had been in their family for centuries meant the world to him.

But, as he suspected, Chokhmah insisted on waiting until she knew that Eluned had arrived back safely. And so they waited. Because of the travelling she had already done, and because she was about to have to travel again, Faolan spent a lot of time making sure Chokhmah rested as much as possible.

A more doting father, you could not ask for, she thought, as he checked on her for the perhaps billionth time that day. And the child was not even born yet! It was late afternoon and the heat was nearly unbearable. Of course she would be suffering through the early months of pregnancy during the hottest time of year. On the bright side, she smiled to herself, *I will have a little furnace in my belly in the winter.*

Her thoughts were disrupted by the sound of excited voices downstairs. A disruption, she thought. I can use that. The days seem to pass so slowly.

Chokhmah gratefully stood and made her way to the main stairwell. From her perch above them, it was difficult to determine who was the most excited to see Eluned's return. King Uriel and the Princess Xiang seemed to stand there forgotten as Faolan, Jabberwock, King Seraphim, and Queen Ceridwen all vied for a hug.

But it was Chokhmah Eluned locked eyes with as she scanned the room.

"Praise be to Omni," she and Eluned mouthed to each other and laughed. Chokhmah touched her belly and nodded, and Eluned's eyes widened before she broke into a huge grin upon understanding.

"By Omni, Faolan," her voice rang out, joyfully, "you're going to be a father! We have to celebrate!"

It was a more chastened Eluned that appeared in the dining room that night. "Yes, I know we need to be celebrating, but we also need to remember Bonpo—Shangsung—tonight." She stopped as her voice faltered, and took several deep breaths to regain her composure.

"All the Treasures are finally together," she said, "but at cost." She fingered her scar, looked pointedly at Faolan. "We all loved Bonpo. I have no words, but I can only say that we will never forget him or the way he touched our lives."

"May he ever remain in our memories," Gwrhyr said, lifting his glass.

The following morning they were all gathered in the sitting room first thing after breakfast.

"We need a plan," Eluned said. "Now. Gwrhyr, Xiang, and I are about to return to Ponike, Faolan and Chokhmah to Bogaine. What are we going to do now that we have all the Treasures?"

"Jabberwock and I have been discussing this," King Seraphim said. "It's perfect that you've managed to secure a meeting place in a neutral kingdom. But, despite the heat now, winter is fast approaching in the more northern Kingdoms."

"And travel may be impossible if we met this year," Eluned said, nodding. "That's why we put off our Quest last year until spring."

"Or should have," Faolan said. "We were held up until the Snow of Misery cleared enough for us to pass over the Mountains of Misericord."

"And we spent a lot of time miserably cold," Gwrhyr said.

"I think we should set the meeting early in Eahth next year," Jabberwock chimed in. "Giving everyone eight weeks of travel time after the Vernal Equinox."

"Fine," Gwrhyr said, calculating, "what's that, the 5th of Eahth?"

"Yes, the absolute soonest we could do it," Jabberwock agreed.

"Sounds good," Eluned said. "We should do this as soon as we can. Chokhmah's baby will have been born although," she glanced at the Queen of Pelf, "you don't have to be there."

"Oh, my dear, we will be there," Chokhmah said. "It is a short trip for us and I would not miss this for anything."

Faolan nodded. "Me either."

"So we will send out pigeons to the rulers of all the Kingdoms informing them that we have the Treasures and that Jabberwock is challenging King Arawn to a duel on the Chessboard of Gwenddolau. The outcome will determine whether or not we go to war, and we would like everyone to meet in Tartessos on the 5th of Eahth?"

Silence then, "Yes," King Seraphim said.

"Yes," King Uriel agreed, "but we need to send an additional message to Kings Arawn, Hamartia, and Hevel asking them to cease all hostilities until after the meeting."

Nodding, Queen Parisa also agreed. The three kings had joined forces and were now making incursions into the Kingdoms of Dyfed, Zion, and Aden. Those Kingdom's armies were now constantly patrolling their borders with Adamah to prevent further deaths.

"It's time to put an end to this," Jabberwock said.

Part Seven

"The peace which you proclaim with words must
dwell even more abundantly in your hearts.
Do not provoke others to anger or give scandal.
Rather, let your gentleness draw them
to peace, goodness, and concord.
This is our vocation: to heal wounds,
to bind what is broken,
to bring home those who are lost."
-Saint Francis of Assisi

"I object to violence because when it appears to do good,
the good is only temporary; the evil it does is permanent."
-Mohandas Gandhi

5ᵀᴴ ЄЛНTH

Surveying the meeting room at Iqbal Palace in Tartessos, Eluned wondered when the leaders of all Thirteen Kingdoms had last been together in one place. Centuries? There were more than thirty people attending the historic meeting, and nearly half of the delegations were staying at Anfa House as there weren't enough rooms in the palace to accommodate everyone.

With the chess game scheduled to start within the hour, Eluned was scanning the gathering crowd to make sure everyone was in attendance. She stood with her husband and Princess Xiang at the far end of the room. Xiang had decided to accompany Eluned and Gwrhyr back to Aden rather than be escorted to Dziron.

The Princess had sent a pigeon to inform her parents that she was well, and then a courier with a letter explaining that she had broken her betrothal to Prince Aahil, and she would be staying with King Uriel and Queen Eluned in Ponike until the meeting in Tarshish. "I am learning so much about the Thirteen Kingdoms," she said in the letter, "Now in addition to Kamartha, I have seen five other Kingdoms and travelled by sea."

She didn't tell them that she was excited about helping Eluned start a school for those at Castle Bennu who were interested in learning the basics of reading and arithmetic because she wasn't sure they'd approve. If the castle school went well, Eluned had told her, they would start more schools in the capitol city before extending throughout the Kingdom. Education would not be required but open to those eager to learn, and Xiang thought this a commendable goal as she had felt guilt on more than one occasion for being better educated than most of the citizens in her parents' kingdom.

As her eyes returned to the door, King Zhang and Queen Ling made their entrance. Eluned was about to say something to Xiang, but the Princess had already noticed their arrival. Xiang grabbed Eluned's right hand and squeezed it convulsively.

"Don't worry," Eluned murmured, releasing her hand. "Gwrhyr and I are here for you."

Xiang's parents were making their way directly down the room toward their daughter.

"King Uriel," King Zhang said, bowing, before turning to Eluned. "Queen." He stopped, eyes riveted on her mostly bare arm. "Where did you get that?"

Eluned had chosen to wear the dragon torque to the meeting for a couple of reasons—because she knew it would irritate King Arawn and because it looked lovely with the gown of layered lavender and blush lace she was wearing. The slender braid of white, yellow and rose gold wound its way up her left arm ending in a dragon's head with ruby eyes on one end and an amber tail on the other. It also went well with the golden tiara adorned with amethyst, diamonds, and pale pink enameled flowers that perched atop her glossy black curls. And despite the fact it looked a little odd with the lacy dress, she had her sword, Dyrnwyn, scabbarded at her left side—an additional warning to King Arawn.

"I bought it from a jewelry vendor when I was staying at

Castle Emrys in Arberth," she said. A vendor that had been killed after she'd purchased it, she thought. "Why?"

King Zhang slid a glance toward King Arawn who was at the far end of the room with King Hevel, King Hamartia, and Queen Foehn. They seemed to want to keep as much distance between themselves and Queen Eluned as possible. No doubt Dyrnwyn, which she now clasped casually in her gloved left hand to prevent the blue light from dancing along her arm, gave them some pause. Thanks to Eluned, King Arawn now sported an empty gauntlet where his right hand used to be. A dragon embroidered with gold and crimson thread decorated the glove hanging from his right wrist.

When he noticed the rulers of Dziron and Aden studying him, he cradled the missing hand, as if to protect it, with his left hand, and turned his back on them.

Facing Eluned again, King Zhang said quietly, "It belonged to my mother. The last time we saw it was more than fifteen years ago when Arawn and his parents came to Jungnay to arrange his marriage to my sister. We always assumed my mother misplaced it or a servant stole it."

Eluned quickly removed the torque from her arm, "Then you must take it back."

"I couldn't do that," Zhang said, and looked pointedly at her left hip. "And I assume that is the sword that took King Arawn's hand? Are you expecting violence today?"

"Honestly with Arawn you never know," Eluned said. "But, the reminder doesn't hurt. As for the torque, it's a family heirloom, and belongs in Dziron. Here Xiang," she handed the bracelet to the Princess, "this really belongs to you."

Xiang took it with a smile of thanks, and turned to her father and asked, "What happened with my aunt?"

"She refused the match," Zhang frowned at her.

Xiang blushed, and her father continued. "A family tradition, it seems."

"But Morrighan?" Xiang said. "Why did King Arawn allow her to come to Jungnay?"

The King glanced Arawn's way again. "I am guessing that our loyalty to the Awen Alliance was more important to him than the previous snub."

Eluned's mind was racing. Arawn would have been her age or younger at the time. Did he take the bracelet as some sort of payback or did he just take the things he wanted? She supposed he had later given it to a lover, one of the many who would go on to be a sacrifice to his Sacred Three. How many women had he killed over the years? She didn't even want to guess, but the torque had ended up with the same man who sold the earrings Yona bought for her.

"The more I learn of him," Eluned said, voice quiet, "the more evil I see."   "May I ask why you've aligned with him?" Gwrhyr asked.

"I am beginning to ask myself that question as well," Zhang said.

IN ANOTHER CORNER, Yona and Njima found themselves confronted by Dev's angry parents. Njima had sent a pigeon to Lamaxana Palace as soon as she and Dev had arrived safely in Jazeel to inform the King and Queen of their daughter's whereabouts, and that for the foreseeable future, she would be residing with the queen in Castle Indalo. That same day a courier set out with a letter from Dev explaining the reasoning behind what she had done.

They, naturally, had sent another pigeon demanding to see her, but Njima had put them off with a reply that she was waiting on certain information before she could arrange a visit, and that a courier was on the way with a letter from their daughter.

Once the pigeon had arrived informing her of the meeting in Tartessos on the 5th of Eahth, she sent another pigeon telling them that she would bring the Princess Divya with her to the meeting in Tartessos.

King Janak and his wife were not pleased, but agreed to wait until the courier arrived before pursuing it further.

"But I don't understand," her mother, Queen Lakshmi, was saying to Dev, who looked resplendent in her uniform, which was modeled on those worn by Queen Njima's army officers.

Dev fingered the short sword scabbarded at her side, and stood her ground. "I was miserable being a girl, Mama. I always felt like I was a boy trapped in a girl's body. Yona and Njima let me live like me."

"And in that case," King Janak said, "what will the future hold for you?"

"Queen Njima has already allowed me to start training to be an officer in her army," Dev said.

Queen Lakshmi gasped. "The army? Is that what you want? You could die!"

"Dev has at least another five years before he must make that decision," Yona said.

"Dev? He?" King Janak grimaced.

"I prefer the name, Dev, and I wish to be called 'he'," Dev explained. "I refuse to return to pretending I'm a girl. I know you don't like it, but I am going to be me."

"Dev is more than welcome to remain with us in Naphtali," Queen Njima said, "and we will arrange regular visits, if that is what you would like."

"I will never understand," Lakshmi said, "but you are my child and I want you to be happy. Don't you think you could be happy in Kaumari?"

Shaking her head, Dev explained, "I think Father would find it embarrassing. Wouldn't you?"

King Janak fidgeted with his crown before answering. "Divya is right. It would be easier to claim that she is being fostered in Naphtali than to have her traipsing about my kingdom acting like a boy. I assume this means you won't marry Arawn's son."

It was Dev's turn to grimace. "No!"

"Yet another reason," King Janak said. "Fine, stay in Naphtali, but I want the Horn of Bran back."

Yona shook her head. "I'm sorry, at this point it's not even a possibility." She pointed to the wall on the left side of the room where the heavily guarded Chariot of Morgan contained all the Treasures but Eluned's ring, which she was wearing, and the sword she was holding. Soldiers from Naphtali, Aden, Zion, Sheba, Favonia, Dyfed, and Tarshish surrounded the phaeton, whose back edge pressed against the stone wall of the room.

More soldiers waited in the corridor in case they were needed.

"We are not taking any chances," Njima said. She glanced at the clock that sat on the mantel over the fireplace. "In ten minutes, King Dodi and Prince Aahil will set up the Chessboard on the table in the center of the room, also under guard."

"So, you have joined the Triquetra Alliance." King Janak said.

"Yes," Queen Njima agreed, "as has the Kingdom of Pelf."

"Pelf is a wasteland," Janak frowned.

"Yes, I believe most of it still is," Njima agreed, "but Buta has been rebuilt and is inhabited, and there is a surviving member of the royal family."

Janak's eyes widened, "This is news to me."

"It will be news to most of the Awen Alliance," Njima said, "but Queen Parisa intends to make contact with her Kingdom at some point."

"Is she here?" Queen Lakshmi asked.

Yona pointed. To the left of the Chariot, a group of people gathered around a woman holding an infant. "Queen Miryam of Favonia with her granddaughters, Leleua and Talei. And I believe that's Prince Uwem of Sheba. Queen Parisa is holding her daughter, also Parisa, and Faolan, the man standing next to her, is her husband."

As Yona was speaking, she noticed King Adeyemi and Queen Yobachi heading their way. According to Faolan, Yobachi was very interested in reacquainting herself with her niece. Yona assumed she must have finally convinced her husband it was necessary.

She turned to say something to Njima, and saw that the Queen had already noticed her aunt approaching.

"King Adeyemi, Queen Yobachi," Njima greeted them as they walked up. "This is King Janak and Queen Lakshmi of Kamartha. Have you met?"

"No, we have not," King Adeyemi said, voice neutral.

"Have you heard that there is a Queen of Pelf?" Janak asked.

Adeyemi smiled. "I am proud to say that my son, Uwem," he pointed to the Prince who was now holding the three-month-old infant, "helped her retrieve the last Treasure, the Knife of, what was it? The Horseman?"

"Other than Annewven and Simoon," Njima said, "gathering the Treasures was a united effort on the part of all the Kingdoms."

Yona chuckled. "I hadn't really thought of that, but it's true."

"Depending on the outcome of the chess match," Njima said to Janak, "you may want to keep that in mind. If the Triquetra Alliance wins, there might be repercussions for those who bind themselves too strongly to the Awen Alliance."

Glancing at the three kings still huddled in the far corner of the room, Janak shuddered slightly.

"They almost emanate evil, don't they?" Yona said.

Janak nodded, and laying his hand on Lakshmi's arm, said, "Let us go meet the Queen of Pelf."

Lakshmi smiled. "Will you join us Div, I mean, Dev? Have you met her?"

"I met her last night, Mama," Dev said. "We were already

on our way to Naphtali when she got back from New Buta. But she looks just like the Pelfans who live in Kaumari," she chattered as she walked with them to the other side of the room.

As Njima talked with her aunt and uncle, Yona wandered over to Gwrhyr and Eluned who were now standing alone, surveying the room.

"How's Princess Xiang? Did the meeting with her parents go well?" Yona asked, and Eluned pointed to the far side of the Chariot where the Princess talked with her father and mother, mostly hidden by the guard around the Phaeton.

"I think Xiang has enjoyed, for the most part," Eluned qualified, "the adventure of the past, goodness, nearly a year, but I imagine she's ready to go back to Dziron."

"Even though her parents arrived by ship?" Gwrhyr said.

Eluned chuckled. "I guess we'll see how much sway she holds over them."

"She's not only their baby," Gwrhyr said, "she's also their only daughter. We may have another ally before the match begins."

"Omni I hope so," Eluned murmured watching the King and Queen of Kamartha introduce themselves to Queen Miryam and the others gathered around the Queen of Pelf. "Kamartha would be wise to do so as well." Please let Jabberwock win the chess game, Omni, she prayed silently. If Arawn won, she couldn't imagine what would happen in the Thirteen Kingdoms. What would he demand? Would he and Hamartia divide Sheba? And what about King Hevel?

"Stop worrying," Yona and Gwrhyr said simultaneously as Eluned's brow puckered and her frown deepened.

"I can't help it," she said. "I feel strongly that Omni had us gather the Treasures for a reason—to return peace to the Thirteen Kingdoms. But I also have a bad feeling about this."

Gwrhyr glanced over at Jabberwock who was watching

King Dodi and Prince Aahil set up the Chessboard and shook his head. "We no longer have a choice. We have to have faith that we are doing the right thing."

A long line of servants entered the room carrying padded chairs and placed them around the central table so that everyone else could sit and watch the game.

Eluned's parents, along with King Cian and Queen Chelli of Dyfed, were making their way toward them.

"It looks as if things are about to begin," King Seraphim said as he walked up. "How will it be decided who goes first?"

"We're tossing a coin," King Uriel said, "but we are going to let King Hamartia pull one from a chest so there is no question as to whether it's weighted or not, and we are going to let King Arawn call heads or tails first."

King Cian, who had raven black curls and azure eyes like his sister, Ceridwen, nodded. "We don't want to give them any reason to feel conspired against. I imagine the fact that Kings Zhang and Janak are avoiding them has set them on edge."

"I believe you're right, Uncle," Eluned said. "They remind me of dogs who've been banished to the pen while all the others are frolicking on the outside."

"Tails between their legs," Uriel said, "but that makes them even more dangerous."

"Hopefully the Chessboard doesn't take as long as humans to make its next move," Yona said.

"Let's just hope this Treasure works as well as all the others have," Ceridwen said. "It just seems so fantastic—a chessboard that makes its own moves."

"You've seen the ring work, Mother," Eluned said.

"I believe other than the Knife and Whetstone," Uriel said, "we've either seen them work or heard that they do. I'm thinking of the Horn of Bran, Yona. Did you use it?"

Yona nodded. "I have to admit there were several nights after we left Kaumari, that we needed wine and the Horn provided. Good wine, too."

"Several?" Eluned raised an eyebrow.

"You know me too well," Yona laughed and hugged her. "Almost every."

"Let's go get seats close to the table," Eluned said, removing the glove from her left hand and taking Yona's arm. "I'll save one for you, Gwrhyr."

"Thanks, Fy Drysor," he kissed her cheek before walking over to join King Dodi.

"Fy Drysor?" Queen Chelli asked.

"It means "My Treasure," Eluned smiled. "May Omni bless us," she said before leading Yona toward the far side of the chess table, stopping only to check that Jabberwock was still feeling confident about the outcome.

"I am going to win," he told her. "I know this beyond a shadow of a doubt. What I don't know is how King Arawn and the others will react to losing."

"My prayers are with you," Eluned said, crouching to pull him into a hug before kissing the top of his rounded skull. "I love you and I trust you."

"Thanks Princess," he said. "That means the world to me."

Eluned didn't have the heart to correct him because in his mind she would always be his Princess, and she liked that.

"Good luck," Yona said as Eluned lead her away.

"Thanks, Yona," Jabberwock grinned his lopsided and toothy grin. In some ways he was dreading the game that would end the Quest because after more than five hundred years, he was acutely aware of how easy it was to let life take over and lose track of those you were separated from by distance and busy lives of their own.

Prince Aahil returned with the chest full of coins, and King Dodi rang the chime a servant handed him to garner everyone's attention.

"It is time to be seated," he raised his voice. "If King Arawn and King Hamartia would join us?"

King Hevel and Queen Foehn moved toward the chairs as

the Kings walked over to where Dodi, Gwrhyr, Aahil, and Jabberwock were standing next to the table with the Chessboard.

Hamartia pulled a coin from the chest and dropped it in Gwrhyr's palm, eyelids narrowed. "King Uriel," he acknowledged.

"King Hamartia," Gwrhyr said.

Hamartia nodded, curtly, and took a couple of steps backwards before turning and retreating to the back of the room where his wife and King Hevel were seated.

Gwrhyr turned to King Arawn who glared at him. "King Arawn."

"King Uriel," he said, voice caustic, "I choose heads."

It took a great effort for Gwrhyr to maintain his composure. You would, he thought, before tossing the coin high in the air, catching it, and pressing it to his opposite palm. He removed his hand to reveal the coin. "Tails," he said. "Jabberwock is silver and goes first. You play gold."

"Jabberwock will play silver and make the first move," Dodi announced. "Jabberwock and King Arawn will make three moves each before the Chessboard takes over and determines the winner."

Jabberwock pattered over to the table, claws loud on the granite tile floor now that the room was silent. He jumped up into the chair and surveyed the board. He would ponder his first move, but he had been thinking about this for months. He would do something unexpected. Perhaps it would throw Arawn off enough to make it easier for the board to win. Of course, he thought, whiskers and ears twitching, Omni would do whatever It saw fit.

Arawn seated himself and glowered at the Bandersnatch, who watched as the King glanced quickly to the right. Jabberwock noted that Eluned was watching Arawn, jaw set and eyes cold.

"Shall we begin?" Jabberwock said.

Arawn nodded curtly, and frowned as Jabberwock used his right paw to push the King's Pawn two spaces forward.

A minute or two passed before Arawn finally advanced the Pawn in front of the Knight on the Queen's side forward one space.

He's being careful, Jabberwock thought, before he moved his Queen's Pawn forward two spaces.

Arawn's scowl deepened as Jabberwock watched him ponder for a few more minutes before pushing the Bishop on the Queen's side to the space vacated by his Pawn.

Jabberwock contemplated the tableau for a minute before prodding the Bishop on his King's side behind the Queen's Pawn.

The King looked confused and studied the board for a while before moving his King's Pawn forward one space.

Now it was time for the magic Chessboard to take over. Arawn sat back with a barely suppressed sigh.

Jabberwock tried not to smirk. He had caught a fragment of the King's thoughts as he was settling back into his chair. Apparently the King trusted in his Sacred Three enough to believe he would win the match. He glanced over at Eluned to see that her gaze was still watching Arawn's every move.

As the chessboard progressed through the game, Jabberwock sensed Arawn's tension mounting as the moves continued in Jabberwock's favor. They locked eyes for a moment when the King glanced up, and Arawn's thoughts were quickly reduced to static in the Jabberwock's head as he blocked them from the Janawar.

Jabberwock snorted quietly and returned his gaze to the board. He wasn't surprised.

Nineteen moves after the board took over, Eluned was distracted by Gwrhyr chuckling. "He's going to smother that mate," he said under his breath.

"Is that Pelfan?" Eluned asked, forehead puckered in confusion.

Gwrhyr smiled, and whispered. "No, Fy Drysor, that means that Arawn's King can't move because it's surrounded by its own pieces."

Sure enough, the Knight moved into a position in which Arawn's King was locked in place.

"Check mate," Jabberwock said, voice sober.

Eluned had been watching the color rising in Arawn's cheeks ever since his King had been mated. She shifted in her seat, watching the sweat bead up on the King's forehead as the board trapped his King in the corner of the board.

Her eyes followed Arawn's movements as his left hand dropped to his waistline, and she felt her left hand moving to Dyrnwyn's hilt of its own accord. As Eluned lunged to her feet, Arawn pulled the dagger from where he'd hidden it in the pocket on the inside of his jacket and plunged it into Jabberwock's heart.

Eluned screamed as she recognized the knife that had nearly taken her life and jumped forward, drawing Dyrnwyn from her scabbard. A second later, the blade was across Arawn's throat and it was taking all her willpower not to slice through it.

She glanced back at Jabberwock whose glassy eyes were already filming over as the blood seeped from the wound in his chest.

"No!" Jabberwock thought at her with the last of his strength, and then a little more weakly, "You don't want to be that person."

Pressing the sword more firmly against Arawn's throat, the blue light racing up her arm like lightning, Eluned stared into the dying eyes of her mentor, and struggled with herself. She wanted nothing more in the world than to slash his throat the way she had been forced to cut Hywel's back in Prythew, but as

Dyrnwyn's sharp edge raised a fine line of blood where it was pressed against the Crimson King's throat, she pondered Jabberwock's request.

"Please," the Bandersnatch's thought was barely a whisper. "Do this for me."

A line from her favorite hymn rang in her ears. "Disperse the gloomy clouds of night, and death's dark shadows put to flight." No, Jabberwock was right, she could not be that person. She could not fight evil with evil.

The soldiers converged on Arawn, pulling his arms behind him and constraining him with a heavy rope. Releasing the breath she'd been holding, Eluned stepped back, removing the sword from the King's throat. Hamartia and Foehn were in custody and now she could hear Hevel's sobs as he begged for mercy. She turned around, and rushed to Jabberwock—Gwrhyr, Yona, Njima, Chokhmah, Faolan, and Parisa were already at his side—as Seraphim and Ceridwen hurried over from their seats farther down.

"No!" Eluned sobbed as her mentor struggled for breath. "No, this isn't what was supposed to happen." Her sobs choked her last words. "Oh, Jabberwock. I . . ."

Kings Arawn, Hamartia, and Hevel, along with Queen Foehn, were stowed in separate cells in King Dodi's dungeons until what was to be done with them could be decided.

Kings Janak and Zhang had quickly pledged their allegiance to the Thirteen Kingdoms and were given latitude for that decision.

The following morning, the remaining Kings and Queens, along with the Questers, Princess Huda, and Prince Aahil, met in another room around a long table.

"Because that is what we will now be," King Seraphim said after the Kings and Queens of Dziron, Kamartha, and Tarshish confirmed their loyalty. "We are the Thirteen Kingdoms, united. We will each have a Treasure to protect, we will meet every five years with regular communication via pigeon. And there will be other decisions, yet to be determined, but they will be decided by us all."

"Meanwhile," King Uriel said, "we have to resolve the fates of the three Kings who opposed a peaceful Thirteen Kingdoms. Having spoken ahead of time with Kings Seraphim and Dodi, and Queens Njima and Parisa, I offer this," Uriel said. "King Hevel seems repentant. We think he should have to work in his Kingdom's vineyards for five years while Chancellor Chazak monitors the Kingdom with Princess Huda of Tarshish overseeing. At the end of five years we can decide what happens next when we meet again. What say you?"

Uriel waited as it was discussed while simultaneously worrying about Eluned who sat pale and silent at his side. The death of Jabberwock had cut her to her core, and she had spent most of the night either weeping or staring forlornly into the darkness.

"He was a curmudgeon, I admit it," she had wailed the previous evening once they were ensconced in their room, "but he only ever had everyone's best interests at heart." And she had broken down in tears again.

Gwrhyr couldn't blame her. The Bandersnatch had been as much a part of his life as hers. It was going to be a long time before he forgot, no never, he thought, he would never forget Jabberwock. It had been extremely difficult for him to say goodbye to the lifeless body, but he had made himself watch as they carried his friend away as it was the last time he would ever see him.

"And King Hamartia and Queen Foehn," Seraphim was saying, "are to be imprisoned on the island of Paliaina in the Kingdom of Favonia for the remainder of their lives to work as fishermen or whatever the islanders see fit to have them do."

A round of here, heres, and the King continued, "King Adeyemi and Prince Daud will oversee the Kingdom until Prince Kaiser is made sure. Otherwise, we will find someone else to rule Simoon."

That was approved and Seraphim continued. "Finally, King Arawn, who has committed the most grievous of offenses. He will remain in the dungeon here in the Kingdom of Tarshish. We had considered sending him both to Pelf and Dziron to get him as far away as possible from his Kingdom, but that would also put him closer to his daughter, who is being fostered by King Zhang and Queen Ling."

"You're going to continue to foster her?" King Janak asked.

"Yes," Zhang said. "She is Arawn's bastard daughter and is not in line for the throne of Annewven. We think it would be in her best interests to remain with us for the time being as she is only seventeen."

"Meanwhile," Seraphim continued, "the Kingdom of Annewven will be ruled by Prince Aahil and his family."

"That's fine," King Janak's said, "but what about the Treasures?"

"Yes," other voices responded, "what about the Treasures?"

"That's a good point," King Uriel said, "and we've thought about this and which Treasures should be assigned to which Kingdom."

Queen Eluned finally spoke, "This it how it will be. I will keep the sword," she patted Dyrnwyn at her side as always. "Adamah will retain the Hamper, Kamartha the Horn of Bran, Dziron the Cauldron, Simoon the Whetstone, and Pelf the Knife."

When she paused, Uriel continued. "Favonia will keep the Chariot, Dyfed the Halter, Sheba the Crock and Dish, and Tarshish the Chessboard."

"Finally," Eluned said, her voice just audible, "Zion will retain the Ring and Stone, Naphtali the Mantle of Arthur, and Annewven the Red Coat. Any questions?"

"No?" Gwrhyr said after a few seconds of silence, "then I suggest we adjourn until Eahth five years from now. King Seraphim has graciously accepted to host us at Castle Mykerinos. We are going to need to remain vigilant about what's happening in Annewven, Simoon, and Adamah."

6ᵗʰ Eahth

Eluned studied the alabaster jar that seemed to glow in the light of the candles on the high altar in the chapel at Iqbal Palace. Jabberowock's ashes now resided in the ornately carved, snow white, jar. He'd probably hate it, Eluned thought, but she had felt it suited his sacrifice.

"O Omni, whose mercies cannot be numbered," the priest began the Collect, and Eluned surreptitiously glanced behind her. She was deeply mollified to see that everyone, barring those monarchs still in the dungeons, had chosen to attend the memorial service for Jabberwock. From the infant Parisa to King Dodi, the oldest ruler in the Thirteen Kingdoms, they had all come to pay their respects to the last known Janawar.

". . . and may Yeshua grant Hiurau an entrance into the land of light and joy," the priest was saying as Eluned returned her attention to the service. She sighed, numb from a night of weeping, and glanced at her husband. He must have asked the priest to use Jabberwock's given name. Gwrhyr took her hand and squeezed it, and she leaned her head against his shoulder. She heard her father, sitting at her other side, swallow hard.

Seraphim had also spent much time with Jabberwock while Eluned was growing up. She felt sure he was mourning the Bandersnatch as much as she and Gwrhyr.

When her parents left for Castle Mykerinos a couple of days later, they promised Eluned that they would carry his ashes with them and bury her mentor in front of the boulder in their favorite glade. Despite the extravagant urn, Eluned would ensure that Jabberwock's grave marker was kept simple, and that his wife's name would be on it, as well. She also felt they needed to do something to commemorate Bonpo's sacrifice to the Quest, and she intended to speak with King Zhang about that later.

Following further negotiations and planning at Iqbal Palace, people began making their way back to their respective Kingdoms, carrying the Treasure they would be responsible for protecting.

The Questers, minus Princess Xiang who was returning to Jungnay with her parents, decided they needed a little more time together before they said their farewells. Travelling by ship to Thírnagall in Dyfed, for old time's sake they spent the night at the Lion and the Unicorn where they had lodged two years previously enroute to Bogaine, the horse farm belonging to Faolan and his brother, Olcan.

How much has changed since we were last at this inn, Eluned thought as she watched Faolan nuzzle his daughter. They were sitting around the largest table again enjoying a dinner of seafood stew, freshly baked brown bread with creamy butter, and strong dark beer.

Faolan caught her looking and blushed.

"Don't," Eluned said. "You cannot imagine how happy I am for you."

"I never dreamed I'd be a father," he smiled, "and now I can't imagine not being one."

"I feel the same way," Chokhmah said, "and I am so glad that I can raise her in a time of peace."

The following morning, Faolan, Chokhmah, and Parisa rode ahead for Bogaine on Fiachdubh and Halelu, whom they'd left stabled in Thírnagall while they were in Tartessos. They wanted to arrive ahead of their friends in order to arrange for everyone to stay for a night or two while the others followed behind on foot.

Just two years ago they'd travelled this same road caught up in their own thoughts, musing on the enormity of resuming the Quest, Eluned thought. She smiled as she watched Dev bouncing along beside Yona and Njima who were walking ahead of her and Gwrhyr.

Two years, two deaths, two people added to their party, and a child born, she thought, slipping her hand into Gwrhyr's. And she had married the man to whom she was betrothed, the man she had thought she wanted nothing to do with.

"I wonder if we can talk to, what was that goat farmer's name?" Yona interrupted her thoughts. "Jar something?"

"I think it was Jarlath," Gwrhyr said.

"Jarlath! Yes!" Yona agreed. "I wonder if we can talk him into another pitcher of goat's milk. I still dream about it."

Not only a pitcher of goat's milk as it turned out. Faolan had stopped and warned Jarlath of their approach and they were also greeted with cool cheese, mutton sandwiches, and crispy red apples.

They arrived at Bogaine in the late afternoon. There they split up to get things done. Dev and Njima happy to accompany Faolan, and his brother, Olcan, and his son, Conall, now nearly thirteen, to round up some horses for them to ride to Ponike, and later to Naphtali.

Eluned, Gwrhyr, and Yona insisted on helping Olcan's wife, Beibhinn, and her daughter, Fianna, now fifteen, prepare dinner. Chokhmah, they insisted, should relax from the travels, and tend to Parisa.

After dinner, Dev joined Conall and Fianna in the kitchen to help with clean up while the adults retired to the living area. While Olcan got a fire going on the hearth, Eluned bounced the sleepy Parisa on her knee.

"I've been assuming that all your time will be committed to Parisa for the foreseeable future," Eluned said, glancing at Chokhmah, "but it occurs to me that once she's weaned, you'll have more time to do what you want to do. Do you have any plans?"

"I plan to start an herb garden this spring," Chokhmah said. "Faolan plowed a space for me before we left for Tartessos. I enjoyed the work I did as a healer in Sigwald, and I hope to carry that on here."

"With five years of guaranteed peace," Faolan said, "there is no reason not to start right away."

"Both Beibhinn and Fianna have offered their assistance with Parisa," Chokhmah said.

"It has been a long time since I've had a baby to dote on," Beibhinn said. "I'm looking forward to it."

"And I'm looking forward to settling down and doing nothing but work on our farm for a while," Faolan said.

"It will be nice not to have to be gone six months out of every year," Olcan said.

Faolan nodded. "As soon as we returned from the Quest, Olcan left for Stonehelm."

"To spy on Hevel?" Yona asked.

"We had to keep an eye on what he was up to," Olcan said.

"And you think the peace will put an end to the spying?" Njima asked.

Olcan sighed. "I can't imagine it will completely, but I think it will be a lot less dangerous. My services won't be needed, anyway, and that's what's most important."

"I guess we do need to make sure everyone is sticking to their end of the bargain," Eluned said.

"I'm not sure spy is such a good word," Gwrhyr said. "Maybe ambassadors in residence? Make it official."

"Do you mean like someone from say, Dziron and Sheba, living at Castle Bennu?" Eluned asked.

"Something along those lines," Gwrhyr said.

"Now there's something Dev would excel at," Njima said. "I can see him as an ambassador for Naphtali."

"Did you say my name?" Dev poked his head around the door to the kitchen.

"See what I mean?" Njima said as the others laughed.

A couple of days later, after many tearful farewells, Eluned and Gwrhyr, Njima, Yona, and Dev took the main trade route north toward the Kingdom of Aden.

Glancing over her shoulder one last time before the road turned away from Bogaine, Eluned sighed.

"What is it?" Gwrhyr asked.

"They seem like they are going to have no trouble settling back into a normal life," Eluned said. "Do you think we will?"

"I don't see why not," Gwrhyr said. "I've been derelict at my duties for far too long, and your education program is still in its infancy."

Eluned nodded. Taking the main road would allow them to skip the treacherous Seven Sisters and stay on the eastern side of the mountain range, but Eluned wondered if she would chance upon the faery, Ziza, again, or even the sionnach síth, Rua, the beautiful faery fox that had spoken to them. To increase their chances that it might happen, she insisted they camp at the edge of the pine forest before it opened up onto the rocky plain beneath the Seven Sisters.

Gathered around the campfire that night, Eluned kept her ears and eyes peeled for any sound that might indicate the presence of some magical creature. They had just begun discussing turning in for the night when they were startled by a deep and resonant prruk, prruk, prruk, followed by a "well met travellers!"

Eluned jumped to her feet and spun around calling out, "Mérimée!"

The raven fluttered from the branch of the pine where it was perched down to Eluned's outstretched arm. A moment later, a flickering light indicated that Ziza was present, and she landed on Eluned's right shoulder.

"Where's Rua?" Eluned had asked.

"Hard it be, for Rua to fly in the woods," Mérimée croaked. "Walk he must."

Dev gasped, eyes wide with wonder, when the faery fox padded into the clearing, iridescent wings folded against his back.

"He's speechless!" Njima laughed.

"Probably the first time," Yona smiled, and ruffled Dev's short dark hair.

"With neither Faolan nor Jabberwock here," Gwrhyr said, "Mérimée will have to translate if Rua speaks."

"Where be the rest of ye?" Mérimée asked.

Eluned explained their reduced numbers.

Rua yipped, and Mérimée said, "Sacrifice and suffering oft be the price for justice and peace, says he."

"We had heard that all Thirteen Treasures had been gathered," Ziza said in her bell-like voice, "and that there was to be a meeting of the Kingdoms in Tartessos, but I mourn the loss of the Janawar. We will send out messengers tonight to get the word out about his death."

"And the peace that follows it," Mérimée said.

"Have you heard anything from Nyx?" Eluned asked.

"She remained in Hardaigh Forest until it was heard that the three kings were no longer attacking along the borders of their Kingdoms," Ziza explained. "It is dangerous enough for a unicorn to move about. Once things were safe, she began her travels to search for other unicorns."

"It be her intent to stay within the boundaries of the Triquetra Alliance kingdoms until peace be announced," Mérimée added.

"It should be safe now," Eluned said, "and not just for humans but for all magical creatures, as well."

THEY SAID GOODBYE TO MÉRIMÉE, ZIZA, AND RUA that evening, and the following day buckled down and travelled as quickly as possible to Aden.

It was such a relief to be travelling without the fear of being spied on or attacked, Eluned thought the day after camping in the pine forest. They could stay in lodgings, and mostly did, although they would occasionally sleep under the stars or in tents just because they could—a reminder of the many times they'd camped together.

This time when they arrived in Ponike they travelled straight to Castle Bennu, which Eluned had now begun to think of as home. After showing Yona, Njima, and Dev to their rooms, she took them on a quick tour of the castle.

"You've already begun adding your own touches," Yona said when she showed them her office. While their bedroom was a compromise in tones of dove grey and deep purple, Eluned's office, which was on the ground floor, was pink, lavender, sea green, and glittery. Sitting in her office made her happy because the decor reminded her of her room at Castle Mykerinos. The window in front of her desk looked out on a courtyard with a fountain and numerous bird feeders. Watching the birds brought her great joy. Wind chimes and sun catchers also adorned the outdoor space, and she had a bench she could retreat to, if she needed fresh air, just beside the Weeping Willow next to the fountain.

Tired from travelling, they retired early that night following a light dinner of game hens and roasted root vegetables. The following day, Eluned showed off her new education program, taking them to see classrooms both in the castle and where she intended to have classes held in Ponike.

While preparations were being made for their departure to Castle Indalo that afternoon, servants gathering the food and gear they would need to travel, the group gathered in Gwrhyr's private study.

As the orange glow of the setting sun painted the far wall, the five Questers sank gratefully onto the leather couches that straddled a long, low wooden table. A servant entered with spiced wine for the adults and fruit juice for Dev, filled their glasses, and quietly left the room.

For a few moments the only sound was the silvery song of the larks as they soared around the castle walls.

"Jabberwock once said I reminded him of a lark," Eluned said. "It was during our last meeting in the glade before we began what later would become the Quest."

Gwrhyr chuckled. "He told me that, too. He said when he first met you he thought of you as a nightingale, but that you had grown into a lark."

"Am I still a lark?"

"A dove," Yona said. "A mourning dove. You've experienced grief, but you've also helped bring peace to the Thirteen Kingdoms."

"I hate to see you go," Eluned said, hugging Yona, who was sitting next to her. "I'm terrified that this is it. We will now go on with our lives and the Quest will soon become just a memory."

"No!" Yona's voice was stern. "Do you not understand how much all our lives have changed because of this? It boggles my mind to think that I could be married to King Hevel right now. No, Eluned, never. I will never forget you and how you changed my life. And Faolan and Chokhmah would say the same thing."

"As would I," Njima said looking at Yona.

"Me too!" Dev chimed in, looking indignant. "I'm living the life I dreamed of, not the one I dreaded."

"And mine, as well," Gwrhyr said, placing a hand on her shoulder. "Because of your persistence, we can expect to live in peace for a very long time."

"Thank you," Eluned said, "but it's not just because of me. Every single one of us was essential to this Quest." Lifting her mug of wine, she said, "To the Quest and its completion!"

"Here! Here!"

"Now we just need to make sure that the peace continues," Yona said. "I think I should go to Prythew and help Prince Aahil by showing him which of King Arawn's citizens worshipped the Sacred Three with him."

Njima's full lips flattened into a frown. "Absolutely not. We've fulfilled our duties to the Quest and peace has returned. If Aahil needs help, he can demand it from King Hevel."

Eluned nodded. "It's time for us to enjoy what we've worked so hard and sacrificed so much for. By Omni, we deserve the time to lead normal lives again."

Seeing Yona's crestfallen countenance, Njima tried to equivocate. "Perhaps next spring we can travel to Pelf with a battalion of my army to see what's going on there."

"No!" Gwrhyr said, aghast. "Slow down, you two. You know we agreed to take the next five years to reestablish the Thirteen Kingdoms. We will discuss the Kingdom of Pelf and what to do about it at our next meeting in Zion."

"But what am I supposed to do for the next five years?" Yona asked. "You two have your Kingdoms, Eluned has her schools, and Dev doesn't need me anymore."

Dev winced. "I'll always need you."

"I've spent my entire life pouring myself into other people's lives," Yona said. "First Libni, then Hevel, Eluned and the Quest, and now Njima. I'm not even sure I know who I am."

"I know what Brother Columcille would say," Eluned said, taking Yona's hand.

"What's that?" Yona sniffed, blinking back the tears that had begun to form.

"Whenever I began to despair about being stuck in Zion and then Aden forever," Eluned said, "he would send me to the chapel and tell me I needed to spend some quiet time with Omni."

"Did it work?"

"It did," Eluned said, "but I suspect you need more than an hour alone in quiet. You would probably really benefit from the spiritual exercises offered by the Sisters of Holy Supplication. They help you to see who you truly are and what Omni wants for you."

"There is a convent of Sisters in the Hallow Hills," Njima said. "Is that something you would like to do?"

"How far is it from Jazeel?" Yona asked.

"It's located on the eastern bank of the Pegasus River," Njima said, "not more than twenty miles south of Drezzar's farm."

"I might like that," Yona looked thoughtful remembering how peaceful she'd felt as a Sister while sitting with Lady Naomi. Maybe some time alone with the Thirteen Kingdoms finally at peace would do her a world of good.

Eluned and Gwrhyr stood in one of the towers at Castle Bennu watching until Yona, Njima, and Dev were just specks lost among the other specks in the harbor town of Ponike.

"I'm going to miss them," Eluned said. "I hope that we get together as often as possible."

Gwrhyr hugged his wife closer. "Then we'll have to take it upon ourselves to make a concerted effort to see each other every year or so. Our Kingdoms aren't so far distant that it's impossible. After all, Jabberwock went out of his way to visit me every year."

Eluned smiled. Jabberwock had disappeared every Autumn during their eleven years together. Time off, he'd told her, because he had to tutor her the remainder of the year. She had been naïve enough to believe him. Her husband was right, she thought, if Jabberwock could do it, then so could they.

A dove landed on the sill of the window at which they were standing before noticing they were there and taking off with a startled coo.

Eluned smiled. "You know what I want to do?"

Gwrhyr hugged her closer.

"No, not that. I want to write it all down before I forget."

"That's an excellent idea, Fy Drysor," Gwrhyr agreed.

The next morning, Eluned hurried to her office as soon as breakfast was over and pulled out a stack of paper from one of the drawers, and a couple of pens and a bottle of ink from another.

She stared at the blank sheet of paper for a moment before writing "Prologue" at the top of the page. Pausing, she considered for a moment, and then pulled out the journal that held her favorite quotes. Beneath "Prologue", she wrote, "The most difficult path to tread is the way that leads to one's own soul."

It seemed appropriate to start the book with a quote by her favorite author, Geillis Saille. And the quote was from the book she'd read while at Castle Pwyll in Annewven, read before she knew just how dangerous the Quest for the Thirteen Hallowed Treasures would become.

But what should the prologue say? Should the story start the day before she and Jabberwock left Castle Mykerinos? No, she smiled to herself. It should start with the day I met Jabberwock because even though I didn't know it then, that was the day that changed the course of my life.

"Eleven years ago," she wrote, and then paused, trying several sentences in her head. None of them seemed right. She could almost hear Jabberwock's voice calling her his impetuous lark.

"But I am no longer a lark," she murmured. "I'm not that little girl any more, and I don't need to write this in first person." She thought a moment more, smiled, and wrote:

PERCHED ATOP HER GOLDEN BALL, Eluned made a great show out of searching for a four-leafed clover amidst the brilliant green patch that grew profusely in one of the castle's many courtyards. She found herself smiling, her cheeks flushing as she pondered the mischief she might achieve . . .

The Thirteen Kingdoms

The Triquetra Alliance

I. The Kingdom of Zion
Sigil: Golden Gryphon on Black

Ruled by: King Seraphim and Queen Ceridwen

Children:1 daughter—the Princess Eluned

Capitol: Castle Mykerinos is located in Goshen

The River Musk flows southward through Zion and Castle Mykerinos is located on a plateau above the river. Other towns and landmarks include Roodspire and Muskroe, the Mountains of Misericord and the Misrule Pass.

II. The Kingdom of Aden

Sigil:
Scarlet Phoenix on Gold

Ruled by:
King Uriel (son of King Gavreel
and Queen Angharad, both deceased)

Children:
Not married but betrothed to Princess Eluned of Zion

Capitol:
Castle Bennu is located in Ponike,
which is a harbor town on the Gulf of Eudaemon

Other towns and landmarks include Batum.

III. The Kingdom of Sheba

Sigil:
Red Hawk on Green

Ruled by:
King Adeyemi and Queen Yobachi

Children:
Three sons—Daud, Paul, and Uwem;
Two daughters—Nala and Prisce

Capitol: Salama Palace is located in Mwezi-barafu

Sheba is bordered to the east by the River Mab. Other towns and landmarks include the Desert of Serket, and Baharimoto, a port town at the River Mab delta into the Anoon Ocean.

IV. The Kingdom of Favonia

Sigil:
Copper Sea Turtle on Blue

Ruled by:
Queen Miryam (King Rangatira is deceased)

Children:
Prince Mauri. He is married to Princess Elili,
and they have three children—one son, Prince Irirangi,
and twin daughters, Leleua and Talei

Capitol:
Whanga Palace is located in Seemu on the island of Favonia.

The other Favonian Islands include Hakinaipo, Hemamoku, Tapurora and Paliaina. Vailima is the main town on Paliaina, which is the smallest and most remote of the islands.

V. The Kingdom of Dyfed

Sigil:
Silver Unicorn on Purple

Ruled by:
King Cian and Queen Chelli

Children:
Eldest child a daughter, Gittan, and a younger son, Bryan.

Capitol:
Castle Abbert is located in Portuma on the Anoon Ocean

The River Leprican flows out of The Seven Sisters, a mountain range in the west of Dyfed and into Hardaigh Forest. The harbor town of Thírnagall is just west of Adamah's western border. Bogaine is a small village to the northwest of Thírnagall.

The Awen Alliance

VI. The Kingdom of Annewven

Sigil: Crimson Dragon on White

Ruled by:
King Arawn (aka The Crimson King)

Children:
King Arawn is not married although he does
have a number of illegitimate children

Capitol:
Castle Pwyll is located in Prythew; King Arawn winters at
Castle Emrys in Arberth on the Anoon Ocean

The River Mab forms the western border of Annewven, and
the River Duir flows through the Prythew valley. Ruisidho is a
village near the western border of Annewven that is home to
Standing Stones atop a hillock. Avalach Forest, near Arberth,
was once home to the unicorn, Nyx.

VII. The Kingdom of Simoon

Sigil:
Grey Wolf on Forest Green

Ruled by:
King Hamartia and Queen Foehn

Children:
4 sons: Kaiser, Jarvis, Bemot and Raynor

Capitol:
Castle Rodolf is located in Sigwald

The River Duir flows southward through Simoon and into Annewven before reaching the Anoon.

VIII. The Kingdom of Adamah

Sigil:
Gold Lion rampant on Silver

Ruled by:
King Hevel

Children:
King Hevel is betrothed to Yona

Capitol:
Castle Lavieven is in Stonehelm

The mountain range of Panavhadesh runs through the center of the kingdom, north to south. It towers over Adam's Way, a trade route running from Hashirim southward to Markhesh-van. Other towns on Adam's Way include Tobermory and Hagafen. The major port of Seagirt is located on Adamah's eastern border on the Anoon Ocean.

IX. The Kingdom of Kamartha

Sigil:
Black Satyr on Pale Blue

Ruled by:
King Janak and Queen Lakshmi

Children:
3 sons: Amit, Baldev, Chetan;
4 daughters: Amala, Bala, Chandra, Divya;
Amit and Amala are twins

Capitol:
Lamaxana Palace is located in Kaumari

Queen Fuchsia, the Princess Eluned of Zion's great grandmother, is from Kamartha and grew up in the Wilds of Discord near the Kingdom's southern border with the lost Kingdom of Pelf. Later, she returned to Kamartha to become an actress on The Masala, the theater district in Kaumari.

X. The Kingdom of Dziron

Sigil:
Golden Dragon on Crimson

Ruled by:
King Zhang and Queen Ling

Children:
3 sons: Qiang, Chao and Huang.
One daughter: Xiang. Princess Xiang, who is 16, is betrothed
to Prince Aahil of Tarshish who is 22 years her elder.

Capitol:
Tsering Palace is in Jungnay

The Vale Vixen in the Peaks of Vulpecula was once home to the
Janawar. The Peaks of Vulpecula is home to the Yeti.

The Neutral Kingdoms

XI. The Kingdom of Naphtali

Sigil:
White Winged Horse on Red

Ruled by:
Queen Njima

Children:
She is single, having broken her betrothal
to Prince Aahil of Tarshish.

Capitol:
Castle Indalo is located in Jazeel on the
western side of the Pegasus River.

The former capitol—Shamash Palace in Kamea on the Djed Sea—was deserted after the events that caused the Devastation of Pelf and formed the Sea of Blood.

XII. The Kingdom of Tarshish

Sigil:
Black Cobra on Tan

Ruled by:
King Dodi and Queen Chahindra

Children:
2 sons—Boutros (the eldest) and Aahil (the youngest child)
and one daughter, Huda

Capitol:
Iqbal Palace is in Tartessos, a port town
on the western border with the Anoon Ocean.

Tarshish is the southernmost kingdom. Smuggler's Bay is located to the east, and is a favorite hiding place for pirates.

XIII. The Kingdom of Pelf *aka* The Devastation of Pelf

Sigil:
Black Kraken on Red

Ruled by: No current rulers.
King Alborz and Queen Jazmin ruled before the Devastation.

Children:
2 sons—Alborz and Gaspar;
1 daughter—Parisa. Only Alborz survived.

Capitol:
Zhaleh Palace was located in Buta on Pelf's southern border
with the Anoon Ocean.

Currently the Devastation of Pelf is inhabited by what are known as the Aberrations.

Pronunciation Guide

Princess Eluned: E-leen-ed
Gwrhyr: Goor-heer
Chokhmah: (ch as in loch) Hock-mah
King Arawn: Aroun as in around
Queen Foehn: Fern
Captain Bleddyn: Blethin (th as in the)
Lord High Steward Hywel: Hoo-well
Lady Celyn: Kay-lin

Animals

Heiduc: Hi-duke

Other

Prythew: Prith-yew
Dyrnwyn: Doorn-win
Castle Pwyl: Poo-ull

Days of the Week

Monday: Deethyeen
Tuesday: Deethmarth
Wednesday: Deethmerker
Thursday: Deethyai
Friday: Deethgwener
Saturday: Deethsadoorn
Sunday: Deethseel

Months

Beth (December 24 to January 20)
Luees (January 21 to February 17)

Neeon (February 18 to March 17)
Feharn (March 18 to April 14)
Saitheh (April 15 to May 12)
Eeahth (May 13 to June 9)
Deer (June 10 to July 7)
Teeneh (July 8 to August 4)
Colth (August 5 to September 1)
Meen (September 2 to September 29)
Gort (September 30 to October 27)
Hetal (October 28 to November 24)
Rees (November 25 to December 23)

Acknowledgements

A special thanks goes to my writers' group, Gail and Katie, who have made the journey with me. I am also grateful to Frank, Margaret, Melissa, and Belinda who read the first full draft of this book. And finally to Olive, who once again had my back as I completed the edits on this third novel in the trilogy.